I

"From the first sentence, you know you are in the hands of a master storyteller, who is ready to whisk readers off into another captivating novel."

Chris Fabry, author and host of *Chris Fabry Live*, on *Between the Sound and Sea*

"Amanda Cox does it again, delivering an emotionally gripping must-read. Taking readers to the captivating Outer Banks, she reminds us that life is a beautiful gift and that love overcomes all."

Julie Cantrell, *New York Times* and *USA Today* bestselling author, on *Between the Sound and Sea*

"Will draw fans of redemptive family sagas that cross time and space."

Library Journal, starred review of *Between the Sound and Sea*

"I love stories of restoration, and Amanda Cox delivers it twofold through her characters and a mysterious lighthouse."

T. I. Lowe, bestselling author, on *Between the Sound and Sea*

"With an expert hand, Amanda Cox offers a tale that resonates with masterful metaphor, captivating story, and a conclusion that wraps reader and characters alike in a cloak of belonging, hope, and healing."

Amanda Dykes, bestselling and award-winning author, on *He Should Have Told the Bees*

"Cox's hopeful, heartwarming novel touches on complicated relationships, the value of friendship, and the impact of trauma with great heart and kindness."

BookPage on *He Should Have Told the Bees*

"Cox is a brilliant writer, and her characters feel like old friends. With humor and a tenderness for the struggling, the novel explores what happens when people let the light in on their journey to healing."

"Cox is a writer to turn to for emotionally rich and redemptive fiction."

THE
BITTER END
BIRDING
SOCIETY

Books by Amanda Cox

The Edge of Belonging

The Secret Keepers of Old Depot Grocery

He Should Have Told the Bees

Between the Sound and Sea

The Bitter End Birding Society

THE
BITTER END
BIRDING
SOCIETY

AMANDA COX

Revell

a division of Baker Publishing Group
Grand Rapids, Michigan

Published by Revell
a division of Baker Publishing Group
Grand Rapids, Michigan
RevellBooks.com

Printed in the United States of America

Library of Congress Cataloging-in-Publication Data
Names: Cox, Amanda, 1984– author.
Title: The Bitter End Birding Society / Amanda Cox.
Description: Grand Rapids, Michigan : Revell, a division of Baker Publishing Group, 2025.
Identifiers: LCCN 2024057588 | ISBN 9780800746612 (paperback) | ISBN 9780800747053 (casebound) | ISBN 9781493450558 (ebook)
Subjects: LCGFT: Christian fiction. | Novels.
Classification: LCC PS3603.O88948 B58 2025 | DDC 813/.6—dc23/eng/20241209
LC record available at https://lccn.loc.gov/2024057588

Scripture used in this book, whether quoted or paraphrased by the characters, is taken from one of the following:

The King James Version of the Bible.

The Holy Bible, New International Version®, NIV®. Copyright © 1973, 1978, 1984, 2011 by Biblica, Inc.® Used by permission of Zondervan. All rights reserved worldwide. www.zondervan.com. The "NIV" and "New International Version" are trademarks registered in the United States Patent and Trademark Office by Biblica, Inc.®

Cover image: David Lichtneker / Arcangel

Baker Publishing Group publications use paper produced from sustainable forestry practices and postconsumer waste whenever possible.

25 26 27 28 29 30 31   7 6 5 4 3 2 1

Prologue

Viola Chambers had always wondered at what point in the dying process a person understood they weren't long for this world, and now she'd give anything to unlearn it. The newborn nestled in her arms squirmed and stretched. Tiny fingers escaped the swaddle and gripped hers. The strength in that tiny hand exceeded her own.

Though it was a struggle, Viola shifted her body to look into those fathomless newborn eyes. That scrunched, pink face. A tiny auburn curl rested on the baby's forehead. Just like her father's hair.

Viola memorized her daughter's features, hoping for evidence that a piece of herself would outlive the next few days.

Her baby girl yawned.

A shadow loomed over her, and it took everything in her to lift her chin. She blinked, trying to focus her eyes on her husband. When had the head on her shoulders grown to such a weight? Trilby shifted her pillows, helping her into a more comfortable position.

The sorrow and fear in her husband's face confirmed what she already knew but no one had had the guts to tell her.

Trilby leaned forward. "Let me take her, Vi. You need your rest. You've got to get your strength up so you can raise this little spitfire." The lie came out low and graveled.

She attempted a smile, trying to play along, but the corners of her lips drooped like peony blooms after a rainstorm. "Not yet," she croaked.

Illness had reduced her song sparrow voice to that of an old woman.

Poor Trilby had lost his father eight months prior. And now he'd lose his young wife.

She'd stay if she could.

But she couldn't.

She'd seen that truth in her doctor's solemn face. Her nurses' pity. Trilby's trembling hands. Her soul repeated the same refrain. What had once been fierce and full of fight inside her chest was light and wispy, as if it was liable to float away like down feathers on the wind.

But her mind screamed otherwise. That this could not be the end of her story. That she could not, would not, be leaving her fragile, broken husband alone to raise their child.

Who would be left to guide him through the fog of pain? Who would help him remember the vibrant seminary student he'd once been?

With her failing voice, she beseeched the man in front of her—the reticent foundry worker who ceased to speak the name of the God he loved. "Pray for me."

Several aching, empty moments throbbed in her ears.

"I'll have the chaplain come by," he said, unable to meet her eye, as if he believed he no longer possessed the wherewithal to bend God's ear. Not even for his dying wife.

Her tiny, unnamed girl squirmed in her arms and grunted. Needing. Wanting.

But Viola had nothing left to offer.

The grunts turned to whimpers, then wails.

Trilby stared at their daughter as if she was a copperhead poised to strike and not his own flesh and blood. *Lord, help him*. Maybe he had no heart left to pray for her, but she had enough faith for them both.

"I'll call for the nurse," he said, and then he was gone from her sight.

Her daughter's cries rent Viola's heart in two. She'd give anything for the strength to sway by the window and sing a lullaby, letting the light of day kiss their faces. To bring solace to discomfort.

"When peace like a river attendeth my way. When sorrows like sea billows roll," she rasped out the words, inaudible now beneath the baby's hunger cries. Breathless, she paused the deathbed dirge of her favorite hymn and wished for the sweet tones of Trilby's mountain dulcimer to lift her threadbare spirits. It seemed a lifetime since she'd last heard him play.

Images of her mother and then of her little sister, Cora, flashed in her mind. Her mother's visage lonely. Cora's, angry and abandoned. How she wished she could tell them she was sorry. For what, she wasn't entirely sure. It wasn't marrying Trilby she regretted. But she sure wished things could have turned out different.

That her father wouldn't have excommunicated her from the family for marrying the preacher's son.

That her father wouldn't have resorted to taking a life to solve his problems.

If nothing else, she wished she could have kept her promise to her sister.

She had more wishes than she had breath.

She only hoped when Cora got the news of Viola's passing that she wouldn't be flooded with guilt or blame or bitterness. But that she'd remember playing hide-and-seek in the cottonwood trees. Walking to school with her little hand hidden in Viola's. Cora was ten years her junior, but she was her very best friend. Forever and always.

After everything that happened, did Cora still feel the same?

A nurse clad in white appeared. Viola's nameless daughter cried while the nurse puttered to and fro, checking vitals and making indications on her chart. Did the woman not notice her baby's cries? She was the one who needed attention. Not Viola.

The nurse and Trilby made some sort of silent exchange, but only Trilby's face was in her view. The color drained from all but the freckles that dusted his nose and cheeks, making them stand out in stark relief.

The nurse leaned over Viola to scoop up her crying child. With the last ounce of strength, Viola grasped the woman's arm, causing her to pause. Somehow the nurse must have understood.

She lifted the squalling babe closer to Viola's face. Viola inhaled the scent of her daughter and pressed her parched lips to the velvet cheek. "I'll love you forever," she whispered.

The baby turned her head toward the touch, open mouth searching.

The nurse swept out of the room to supply the child with sustenance Viola ached to provide but could not.

Trilby pulled a chair close and held her hand. How she missed the playful curiosity that danced in his eyes when they'd first met. Would this man have what it took to give their daughter the love she needed? Would he ever find it in himself to rise from the pit of grief he'd fallen into after his father's murder?

He had to. There was no other choice. She squeezed his hand, hoping her frail grip said all the words she lacked the strength for.

"Viola, I have to tell you something." His hollowed-out voice made her failing heart constrict. "It wasn't Wayne who killed my father."

She blinked hard, fighting to stay conscious. Fighting to make sense of the words Trilby spoke. Her father had confessed to that crime. Would rot in prison for it.

He took a shuddering breath.

"Who?" she ground out, though in that moment she knew.

The answer lived in a pair of haunted hazel eyes.

SIXTY-SIX YEARS LATER

Ana Leigh Watkins was a hero, at least according to the plaque she buried in the cardboard box full of teaching supplies. The entire time she packed up her kindergarten classroom, she'd let it air out on her desk, wrestling with the discomfort of such a title.

It was the same undeserved designation the news outlets had assigned her eight months ago, but somehow it seemed harder to escape when it was etched in brass.

Was it really heroism when you acted on sheer instinct?

A core memory she'd carried with her from her own elementary days was one of the few things that had kept her sane over the past several months. Those many years ago, the motivational speaker had stood on the stage in the school auditorium, framed by ugly mauve velvet curtains, and told the eager ears of Pearson Elementary that bravery wasn't the absence of fear. It was about being afraid and doing the thing anyway.

Now her community touted her as a hero for a single moment of instinctual action. Self-preservation or self-sacrifice? She was never quite sure. Emotion and thought hadn't had time to register. But later, in her million-and-one mental replays, she'd seen a truth she didn't want to own. She'd escalated a situation that could have been avoided.

A hero? She scoffed. That word fit about as well as young David in King Saul's armor.

She taped the cardboard box closed and stacked it with the others. Her summer away with her aunt Cora would be the prologue to a brand-new chapter in her life. It had to be.

Someone tapped on her open door and her heart froze in her chest. Her fellow kindergarten teacher Lexi stood in the doorway. Ana let out a breath as her heart resumed its normal function.

Lexi offered her a sympathetic smile that was almost Ana's undoing.

"I'm fine," she said before her friend could ask.

A corner of Lexi's mouth twitched. "Of course you are." She looked past her to the stacks of boxes. "Looks like you've made good progress. Can I help?"

Ana stepped to the side. "I'm finished, but I could use a hand carrying these to my car."

Ana had met Lexi seven years ago when they'd both started out as newly minted teachers at Ridgeford Christian Academy. They'd become fast friends. This past year had solidified that friendship. With Lexi, she didn't feel the pressure to pretend. Maybe because Lexi understood that it could have just as easily been her class the intruder walked into that day.

After all the boxes were loaded, Ana gave one last look over the room. Bare without all its charts and artwork. It still had that new carpet smell. After the "incident"—the sanitized word she used to refer to that early fall day—they'd had to replace it. They'd painted too, though she could never figure out why. As if changing the wall color from drab beige to a cheery light blue could make the kids forget.

Many people said God saved their little school the day that troubled nineteen-year-old came looking for violence. Others gave all the credit to Ana. Some said it was a mixture of both, calling Ana God's instrument.

Ana just wished her face had never found its way onto the local

TV stations and was relieved when the news cycle moved on to other people's tragedies.

As soon as the doctor had given her clearance, Ana had hobbled back into her classroom, determined to be an example to her students. To give them a living and breathing example of resilience. Together they could fight back the darkness by showing up every day and learning.

What a fool she'd been, thinking she could help those kids navigate the traumatic beginning to their school careers—a teacher with a bad knee and frail faith who was scarred by just as much trauma as they were. She shut and locked the door behind her, still unsure if she'd ever have the courage to force herself back into that room to face a new crop of beautifully naive and unscathed five-year-olds.

Lexi waited at the car. "You're still planning on staying over tonight, right? Before you embark on your big adventure?"

"Yeah. Thanks for letting me store my stuff in your basement for the summer."

Lexi stared at the school grounds. "But is it really just for the summer?"

"That's what I'm trying to figure out, Lex."

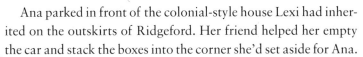

Ana parked in front of the colonial-style house Lexi had inherited on the outskirts of Ridgeford. Her friend helped her empty the car and stack the boxes into the corner she'd set aside for Ana.

Once they emerged from the basement, Lexi trudged to the living room and sank onto the couch. "You're really sure this is what you need?"

Ana sat down beside her. "I probably need decades of therapy, but I can't fit that into one summer. I'm settling for a few months in a place where no one except my aunt knows my name. A restart."

Lexi snickered, then lifted her hand in apology. "I'm sorry I laughed, but you have to admit how funny that sounds. Going to a place called Bitter End for a fresh start?"

Ana scrunched her nose. "No doubt about it, the place has a pretty unfortunate name."

Lexi absently braided her long dark hair. "Seriously, call me if you ever figure out the story behind that. I'm fascinated."

Ana collapsed into the sea of throw pillows lining the back of the couch and wiggled her shoulders until she was fully ensconced. "It will be good for me to be somewhere where I can just be me. Where no one stops me at the supermarket and says, 'Hey, aren't you the teacher who . . .'" Ana massaged her temples. People meant well, but she was just so tired of being recognized by people who knew nothing at all about her.

Her aunt had called two months ago, asking if Ana might be willing to come for the summer to help prep her house to be sold. The timing was positively providential.

Her phone dinged, and Ana shifted to work it free from her pocket. *Mom.* She tucked her bottom lip between her teeth as she read the message.

Come home. Stay with us for the summer. The guest room is all made up.

Guilt stabbed in her gut as she typed her reply.

I wish I could. But I promised.

Her thumb hovered over the send button. She released a sigh and sent the message.

Lexi cleared her throat and raised an eyebrow.

"Mom doesn't understand why I want to spend the summer with Cora instead of with her." Ana grabbed a throw pillow and hugged it to her chest. "She means well, but I can't handle someone hovering and starting endless conversations about what happened. I want to go where no one knows."

Lexi put her hand on Ana's shoulder. "I hear you, but don't

14

stuff this mess down. You spent this entire year taking care of your students. It's past time to put yourself first. Find *you* again."

"That's what I'm trying to do, Lex. I promise." She pulled her gaze away before the ache in her friend's eyes could quite reach Ana's heart. "Aunt Cora will be good company. It will be nice getting to know her better." And to hopefully learn a little more about her family history. All Ana had grown up knowing about her mother's side of the family was that her mother's parents had died when her mother was young, leaving her to be raised by her stepmother. Ana discovered her mother's aunt, Cora, while digging around an ancestry website for a college project. "We've kept in touch for a few years now. I met her in person once."

Lexi raised an eyebrow again. "And now you're off to spend a whole summer together?"

"It will be fun." Ana could tell her friend was just as convinced as Ana sounded.

Lexi slid off her sneakers and pulled one knee up under her chin. "I'm going to miss you, my friend. Who else is going to listen to my saga of trying to date in your thirties in this weird world?"

Ana chuckled. "We'll still have the phone for that. Please continue to keep me posted on the dates your mother sets you up on."

Lexi shuddered in mock horror. "Nobody is going to be worse than the last one. Nose Hair Ned was a new low."

Ana busted out in laughter. "You've got to stop nicknaming them. My heart can't take it."

"Halitosis Hank. BO Bobby. Apron Strings Aaron." Lexi ticked off the list on her fingers.

Ana snorted. "What was the deal with Apron Strings?"

Lexi shook her head, glee still alight in her eyes. "He was the one who couldn't stop talking about his mom and all that she did for him. She'd even picked out the clothes he was wearing that night. I'm surprised she didn't tag along so she could tell him if I was an acceptable option or not."

"Oh, dear." There might be a lot of proverbial fish in the sea, but from Lexi's perspective, most of them had gone belly-up.

Lexi stood suddenly. "It's our last night before you're out of here. That calls for girl dinner."

"Girl dinner?" A slow grin overtook Ana's face.

She couldn't remember the last time they'd raided the cabinets on a Friday night to assemble random food, then kicked back and traded stories of kindergarten antics, administrative woes, and encounters with high-strung parents. Their weekly tradition had been lost over this harrowing year.

"Let me see what I've got in here." Lexi disappeared into the kitchen, and the noise of opening and closing cabinets filled the air.

Moments later, her friend popped back around the corner and held a firestarter log out to her. "You get the fire going, and I'll make up our charcuterie board." When Ana took the log, Lexi pumped her fist into the air. "Girl dinner!"

Ana raised the kindling in salute, catching a spark of her friend's energy. An energy they once shared. Ordinarily this reminder of the person Ana had been before the incident would have caused her to dive inward and grieve the loss. But not tonight. She refused to allow it.

Before long she had a modest blaze going in the firepit and Lexi joined her with a board piled high with a wild assortment—everything from brie and pancetta to goldfish crackers and gummy fruit snacks. Two cups of sweet tea were also precariously balanced on the board. The woman should join the circus.

They snacked and traded celebrity gossip. Something Ana never cared much about, but after the incident had participated in, joining Lexi's obsession. It was nice talking about people whose biggest problem was deciding which publicity stunt would get them the most traction.

"It's summer!" Lexi cupped her hands around her mouth and let out a jarring whoop. Then she grinned. "Ah. That felt good. Your turn."

Ana let out a half-hearted "woohoo."

Lexi nudged her. "Uh-uh. You wouldn't have let one of your students get away with that puny effort. I'm calling the real Ana Leigh Watkins out of hiding."

Ana sighed and gave her friend a weary glare. At one time, she'd had the reputation as the fun teacher. The one who could coax the most reserved class into being engaged through her made-up songs and dances. But she'd lost the capacity for silly.

"Stand up and let's do it together." Lexi cajoled until Ana complied.

"One, two, three!" She and Lexi simultaneously sucked in a breath, but the sound that filled the air was Ana's solitary squawky yelp. She smacked her friend on the shoulder.

"You jerk," she said as both dissolved into hysterical laughter.

About that time, Lexi's neighbor, an elderly woman whose favorite hobby was peering out her window, peeped over the privacy fence, wide-eyed, and then ducked down when her gaze collided with Ana's.

Gasping from laughter, Lexi said, "Miss Busybody is gonna be telling the whole neighborhood that there's something other than sweet tea in our red plastic cups." Then she threw an arm around Ana, squeezing her tight. "You're going to be all right, kid. We both will. New women by summer's end. I'm sure of it."

Ana really wanted to believe her.

"Cora, I'll leave you if you don't hurry up," Viola whispered through the door to her little sister, who was still lingering in their shared bedroom, looking for her aggie shooter.

"I'm comin', Vi. Hold yer horses."

She took a deep breath, trying for patience. After all, Cora was ten years her junior. It only made sense that things like lost marbles should weigh so heavy on her mind. "If we don't get out of here before Daddy's back from the stills, you know he won't let us go."

Neither dared to speak above a whisper even though Momma was out back milking the cow and there was no one to overhear.

They'd never directly disobeyed their father's directive before. The harshness in his tone when Viola had mentioned the new family moving to Old Buck Mountain Road was as fresh on her mind as the milk Momma coaxed from their Jersey cow.

"Stay away from them," he'd said, knuckles white on the edge of the supper table. "I'll not have my daughters mixing with that ilk."

But it was too late for that.

It had been too late the first time Viola caught sight of the family standing outside that dilapidated church. A man and woman with bright, hopeful faces. A girl about Cora's age. And a boy.

18

A tall and lean boy with auburn hair. Dressed in slacks and a crisp white shirt. He was older than her. But he couldn't have been *that* much older. There was something in the way he'd carried himself, so different from the other mountain boys. Different from the men too.

Cora came out of the room, holding up her marble between her thumb and forefinger. "Found it. Let's go."

Viola's gaze shot to her sister's feet. "Not until you put on some shoes to hide those grimy little toes."

Cora shook her head. "No way. I'm not going if I gotta wear shoes."

"Then stay. I'm not taking you into that church barefoot."

Cora rolled her eyes skyward. "You act like we're walking into that Sistine Chapel in Momma's encyclopedia. Ain't nobody gonna notice my toes in that run-down place."

"Fine. Stay here. Maybe someone else will take up with the new girl and play her in marbles."

Cora's cocky attitude faltered. Her scamp of a sister had designs on the newcomer. For some reason, Cora had dreamed up that this girl had a whole cache of beautiful marbles and no idea how to play. She was convinced she'd snooker her out of the lot of them.

Cora scurried back to their room. Thumps and bumps of things being tossed about came through the walls. Viola sighed. So much for being discreet.

Cora stomped out of the room, limping a little. "These dang thangs are too small."

"First of all, don't say dang. Second, nobody is forcing you to come," Viola said as she walked to the front door of their log cabin. Cora clomped behind her. That girl would follow her to the end of the earth, even in too-tight saddle shoes.

Just as they reached the front door, it swung open. Momma stepped inside, a pail of milk gripped in her slim, strong hands.

Her eyes flicked over their pressed dresses and shoes, her lips pursed.

"Momma, please." Viola clasped her hands in front of her chest.

Momma's gaze traveled to the mantel where the family Bible rested.

"Please," she whispered again.

Momma set the full pail on the wood floor, shoulders slumped, looking more tired than Viola had ever seen her. "Go on, then. But be smart about it. I'll not defend you if you're caught, and you won't bring my name into it if you are. Do you understand?"

Viola restrained the joy attempting to light her face and gave a solemn nod. "Yes, ma'am."

Momma leveled a glare at Cora. She cleared her throat. "Lil bit?"

"Yes, ma'am," Cora piped up.

The girls hurried past her, making sure not to let the screen door slap in the frame. They ran down the road, getting out of earshot quick as possible in case Momma thought better of aiding their duplicity. Once they reached the bridge that crossed Mouse Tail Branch, they slowed. Viola paused a minute and straightened her hair and dress and then she helped her sister do the same. They continued down the road at a more sedate pace.

"You reckon this ole preacher will stick around longer than the last 'un?" Cora swiped at her nose. It had started to run a little in the morning chill.

Viola handed her a checkered hankie. "At least pretend to be civilized, Cora Leigh. Surely you can manage the act for an hour or two."

Her sister stuck out her tongue and blew her nose with a loud honk. "Why'd that last preacher man leave again?"

"Idle gossip I ought not be getting into with a little kid." Truth was, Viola was as clueless about the whole ordeal as Cora. But a few of their older cousins who'd quit school to join in on the family business said they'd seen the preacher out with the other men, passing the jug instead of preaching. And she'd once heard Daddy bragging to Momma how he'd converted the preacher instead of the other way 'round. She couldn't understand Momma's reply, but it hadn't been happy.

Momma was a God-fearing woman.

Daddy said that he believed in God but wasn't "skeerd" of nobody.

They rounded the bend and then took a narrow trail that cut across Mr. Beavers's land, which bordered the church.

The dingy clapboard structure in desperate need of a fresh coat of paint came into view. Viola's heart thumped in her chest. This had been a mistake. It was all well and good sneaking out of the house, but how would she ever explain if one of their neighbors mentioned they'd been there?

She tugged her sister to a stop. "We'd better not."

Cora shot her a withering glare. "You stuff me into this ugly dress—and *shoes*," she said it like donning footwear was something blasphemous, "and you're gonna chicken out now? No way."

Cora ran ahead, and Viola had no choice but to follow, because one thing Daddy always said was to stick by her little sister come hell or high water. She'd always thought that was an awful funny thing to say since they lived on a mountaintop where high water was never a concern.

One thing was certain though, he'd consider it a greater sin to lose sight of her sister than to set foot in that church on a Sunday morning.

Cora's hand was on the front door before Viola could stop her. And then they were inside. Light streamed through the freshly washed windows. Gone were the liquor bottles and the stench of stale cigarettes that had littered the floor before. In its place was a fresh lemon scent. The pews had been straightened into a handful of tidy rows.

The place was near-about empty though. The preacher sat on the front row. A few rows back sat old Widow Calloway, the apothecary of the hills. The woman had so many tinctures and concoctions on hand that the children on the mountain told stories about her being a witch instead of a healer. But there she sat in the third row, prim, eyes fixed ahead. The boy sat on the raised platform, his little sister beside him. Each had a mountain dulcimer across their lap. Their mother stood next to the pair in a light-blue shirtdress.

The boy's eyes met hers, and he smiled, a faint blush coloring his freckled cheeks. Viola ducked her chin as he struck the first note, high and clear, filling what had been an empty room.

The mother began to sing, her voice sweet and strong.

The preacher stood and lifted his hands to the heavens as his wife and children sang about flying away someday. Cora was clapping along, thankfully matching the rhythm and not creating her own. Even Viola's toes couldn't resist tapping against the scuffed floor as the spirited song flowed through her heart.

From the joyful notes of "I'll Fly Away," the boy seamlessly transitioned to the slower, more soulful tune of "Amazing Grace."

Viola's heart swelled to bursting. Partly from the beauty of the music. Partly from the feeling in the room. So alive, joyful, full of hope. And if she was honest, a little because of the shy glances the boy kept shooting her way. His eyes were framed by thick lashes that matched the deep auburn hair curling slightly around his ears.

The hymn concluded, and the preacher traded places with his wife and children.

"Good morning. My name is Reverend Quincy Chambers. It is my joy to serve the community of Bitter End and to open God's Word with His people this morning. Let us pray."

Viola ducked her head and tried to pay attention to the preacher's words to the Lord, but her mind wandered to her fidgeting sister. Cora's knee bounced so that the heel of her saddle shoe clacked on the hardwood. Viola elbowed her a little harder than she'd intended, and a yelp squeaked out of her, echoing in the chapel. Viola sank lower in the pew.

When the preacher said amen, Viola lifted her chin, face as hot as lard sizzling in a frying pan. Reverend Chambers looked their direction, mirth creasing the corners of his eyes. "If you have your Bible, open to 1 Peter 5:8."

Empty-handed, they watched the preacher turn his pages until he reached the one he sought. "And the Word of the Lord says, 'Be sober, be vigilant; because your adversary the devil, as a roaring lion, walketh about, seeking whom he may devour.'"

Be sober? Viola sank even lower in the polished pew. Was that an accusation? Did the man realize that before him sat the only children of Wild Wayne Lee Whitt—moonshining monopolist of this mountain?

Ana pushed the accelerator, going as fast as she dared on the winding curves—at least as fast as she dared on a spare tire. She glanced at the car's clock. She'd promised her aunt that she'd be there two hours ago. Then her gaze traveled to the black screen of her waterlogged cell phone as it basked in a ray of sunshine on her passenger seat. Hopefully when the scummy puddle water evaporated from its inner workings, it would function again.

What if her aunt had been counting on her arrival? Dismissed a friend or a caregiver for the day, expecting Ana to help with things beyond her abilities? But when Ana hadn't shown, Cora had decided she was up for cleaning out a closet and went down to the basement for a box, but lost her balance and fell down the stairs . . .

Ana massaged her aching knee, trying to shut down her dooms-day imagination. She didn't even know if Cora *had* a basement. And if she did, surely the woman had enough sense to wait for Ana's arrival before attempting heavy lifting.

For her first and only in-person meetup with Cora, the woman had driven the five hours to Ridgeford to meet Ana shortly after Ana had connected with her over a college genealogy project. The short, curvy woman had been chatty and full of the vim and vigor Ana was accustomed to from their phone conversations. She'd also had this funny habit of looking around her as if seeing everything for the first time. Ana's apartment complex home with its carefully manicured lawn had seemed to give her a particular sense of wonder.

It surprised Ana a little that eight years after that meetup, Cora's health had deteriorated to the point that she needed help preparing her house to sell so that she could move into a retirement home.

Ana pressed the accelerator a little harder. The five-hour drive—or what was supposed to be a five-hour drive before the flat tire and a rescue by a very burly leather-clad stranger—had stretched into seven.

She glanced at her car's built-in screen. She'd lost GPS signal a little way back, so she wasn't entirely sure she was on the right track, but as far as she could remember from glancing over the directions, she just had to continue along Old Buck Mountain Road where her aunt lived.

The road ceased its steady climb and began a steep and winding decline into a gully. She prayed for the spare tire to hold and that the man who'd assisted her was as skilled as he was confident.

She picked up speed going downhill and gently tapped the brakes as she approached another hairpin curve. But when she rounded the bend going faster than she'd intended, she sucked in her breath and slammed on her brakes. Her car skidded toward the herd of sheep crossing the road.

The vehicle rocked to a stop with several feet to spare. The sheep continued along like a speeding silver sedan hadn't almost crashed through their ranks.

In her relief, she let her head fall forward onto the steering wheel, accidentally colliding with the car horn. She jolted back upright, heart pounding even harder. Her gaze raised just in time to see the man. The man whose horse she'd just spooked.

He expertly rode out the horse's sideways leap, reined the horse in a tight circle, and then urged the animal onward. A sheepdog darted ahead of the horse, hot on the heels of the herd. She could have sworn that dog scowled at her as it streaked past. She inched lower in the seat as the man on horseback drew closer.

"Please keep going. Please keep going. Please keep going," she chanted under her breath. If this guy came over and blessed her out, there was no way she was going to be able to conceal the ridiculous tears attempting to well to the surface.

When he passed, his face was shadowed by the brim of his cowboy hat, so she couldn't quite make out his features, but she could somehow still feel the ice in his stare.

Finally, the road was cleared of sheep. Ana continued at a slower pace than before as the road climbed once again. The glare of the setting sun burned her eyes as she tried to make out the faded house numbers on the mailboxes she passed. Five minutes later she turned down the winding gravel drive that led to her aunt's house.

Once she was safely parked, she unfolded from the sedan and did a few quick stretches her physical therapist had taught her, trying to ease the stiffness in her bad knee. Ana straightened and smoothed her hair. Just because the trip had been laced with minor disasters didn't mean the pattern would hold. She opened her back door and hoisted her duffel bag onto her shoulder.

The log cabin in front of her, with its sweeping view of the Appalachian highlands, had raised her grandmother and her great-aunt Cora. Though it still stood strong and steady, there was something about the property that felt . . . She searched for the right word as she surveyed the overgrown lawn and the weeds that were threatening to choke out the purple irises and azalea bushes surrounding the cluttered wraparound porch.

Lonely.

But now that she was here, perhaps Ana could help fill whatever was missing.

She hobbled up the porch steps and wove through pollen-coated lawn furniture that looked like it hadn't seen use in years. She opened the screen door and tapped on the wooden door bedecked with a Christmas wreath.

When no answer came, the mental image of her poor aunt collapsed at the bottom of the basement stairs resurrected itself. Ana slowly turned the knob and stepped inside. "Hello? Aunt Cora?" She blinked, adjusting her eyes to the dim interior. A trio of matching wheeled suitcases waited by the door. Her aunt must have started making her yard sale pile without her. It must be hard, facing the fact that her traveling days were a thing of the past.

Ana took another step inside and set her duffel down beside the suitcases. "Anybody home?"

A clatter came from deeper within the house. "Ana Leigh? Is that you?"

Ana headed down the hall toward the source of the noise. "Yes, ma'am."

"Thank heavens you made it. I thought I was going to have to leave before giving you the rundown."

Leave? Ana passed through an open, rustic dining area into the cozy kitchen. Cora stooped over a pile of Tupperware.

"Are you okay?"

Cora winced as she straightened, one hand propped at her lower back. "Sorry for leaving you waiting at the door. I was trying to get one of my lids off the bottom shelf, and I created an avalanche." She motioned to the mess on the floor. "Would you mind picking that up later?" she asked. "We're short on time, after all."

"What do you—"

But Cora had already speed-waddled into the next room, leaving Ana no choice but to follow her to the den already stacked with boxes. "These here are my personal things." She indicated the right side of the space. "They'll be shipped to my new digs as soon as I get back and get things finalized here. This other side of the room, you can do with it all what you like. Yard sale it. Donate it. Makes no difference to me. The spare room, that's where all the books from my bookmobile are. I've already sorted most of them, and there are names and addresses for you to deliver them to the people I'd like them to go to. And then there's the shed. That's where the vintage treasure is. If you want to mess with selling it, you can keep whatever you make."

A car horn beeped three times, interrupting Cora's rapid stream of chatter. She glanced toward the front door. "Oh, sugar foot. That'll be my ride. I made a list with all this old house's quirks. That water heater gets a little finicky sometimes, but if you just give it a well-placed kick, it will straighten up and behave. I've signed all the papers so you can pay the bills as they come in. Just go on a Tuesday and ask for Harold. He's my personal banker and won't give you any trouble. Said to just bring your identification with you."

Ana realized her mouth had fallen open and she clamped it shut. She followed the woman as she bustled to the door on her short legs. "But . . . um . . ."

Once they reached the hallway, the front door popped open and in came an equally petite, white-haired woman. "Cora, dear! Are you packed and ready to go?" She thumbed over her shoulder to a gangly, solemn young man who looked fresh out of high school. "I brought the muscle and the ride. Point Daniel to your bags, honey, and we'll be on our way. Off to see the world!"

"Mine are by the door there. Let me say goodbye to my niece, and I'll meet you at the car."

"Make it quick," her friend chirped. She glanced at her watch. "We can't miss our flight."

Ana turned to her aunt. "What's going on? I thought . . ."

Cora pressed a hand to her chest. "Did I not mention that I'd be out of town for the summer? That's why I needed you to see to the place."

"Oh."

"You don't mind, do you?"

"I—"

"You'll have the whole house to yourself without me underfoot.

This is mine and Betsy's big hurrah. We planned it a couple years ago. To go on a world cruise and then settle down into a retirement community as neighbors." Cora lowered her voice. "Not that I'm exactly ready for a place like that, but Betsy's started having some health issues and it was time for her, so I decided it was time for me too."

Ana tried to fight the sinking sensation in her gut. Of course this was fine. "That's wonderful. And Daniel?"

"Betsy is paying his way on the cruise. He's our chauffeur and bag boy." Cora chuckled. "Poor kid. I don't know how she managed to rope him into this. He'll be the only one under fifty on that cruise."

Ana inwardly groaned. She could have been spending her summer in exotic locales, sunning on a deck chair as sea breezes blew. Instead, she was stuck with the dusty old house and her bad memories.

Cora stepped to her and wrapped her in a bear hug. "Take care now, honey."

The car horn beeped four times.

Ana sputtered, desperation clawing in her chest. "You barely know me. You can't leave me with all your possessions. What if I'm a thief or something?"

Cora snorted. "A thief would never say that. Besides, it's just stuff."

The horn sounded again.

"Oh, flitter. I wish we'd had a little more time. We were supposed to have had more time."

"I had a flat tire." Ana moved to block the exit.

Concern momentarily erased the excitement on the woman's face. "That's terrible. Everything turned out okay?"

"It did."

"If you run into any trouble, with the house or getting the car fixed, my friend Sam can help you out. His place is just down the way. His contact information is posted inside the pantry door."

The horn beeped again, longer this time. Ana stepped aside, clearing the path for her aunt's exit. "I have everything under control," she said without believing it. "You'd better run before Betsy has a conniption."

"Take care, dear." Cora hugged her again and then turned to go. She paused with her hand on the doorknob and turned back, an odd look on her face. "Steer clear of Marilyn, okay?"

"Who—" But she closed the door between them before Ana could ask for an explanation. Was Marilyn a roaming dog? A feral cat? A hateful neighbor? A faulty toaster she'd decided to name?

Ana sighed and walked to the living room where she had a decent view out the dusty picture window. Cora and Betsy sat in the back seat with oversized sunglasses on. Betsy draped a neon lei over Cora's head that matched the one she wore. Oh, to be in Daniel's place. That kid didn't know it yet, but he was in for an adventure he'd never forget.

Once they were out of sight, Ana placed her damaged cell phone into a bag of rice she'd found in the well-stocked pantry and hoped for the best. Then she sank onto the plush chenille recliner, kicked off her shoes, and leaned the chair back as far as it would go. The events of the day, the hours of travel, the panic over the flat tire, the whirlwind of Cora and Betsy's departure seemed to catch up with her all at once, sweeping her into a deep sleep.

She woke with a start to a room blanketed in darkness.

With shaking hands, Ana wiped the sweat from her forehead, attempting to clear away the nightmare. Her mind always betrayed her in sleep, using her downed defenses as an opportunity to excavate terrifying memories she'd buried in shallow graves.

She heaved herself up from the recliner and stumbled back to the hallway to get her bag so she could change into her pajamas. But the space was devoid of luggage. *Daniel . . .*

She returned to the living room and sat. Lexi's words echoed back to her. *"But you have to admit how funny that sounds. Going to a place called Bitter End for a fresh start?"*

A snort escaped her as she attempted to squelch the hysterical laughter bubbling in her middle. This plan of hers was growing more ridiculous by the second.

She rolled her eyes skyward and sank farther into the recliner. "Welcome to Bitter End, Ana Leigh."

"Wait up." The urgency in the boy's voice tickled Viola's ear as she and her sister hurried down the path away from the church.

Cora stumbled trying to keep up and then shook her arm free of Viola's grip. "What is the matter with you?" She glared at Viola, her silver-blue eyes cut into slits. "We came all this way so we could meet the preacher's kids and then you yank me out of there like I'm a bad tooth."

Viola shook her head. "It was a stupid idea, coming here." She attempted to slow her breaths. "I guess I thought we could blend in with a crowd, maybe say hi, and then disappear. But there wasn't a crowd to disappear into."

Cora propped her hands on her hips. "Which means nobody to tattle."

Viola pursed her lips. "It means the preacher and his wife would have wanted to get to know us, and that means they'd find out who our father is."

Cora sniffed and lifted her chin. "So? I ain't ashamed of my daddy. He's smart and kind and plays the fiddle better than any man on this mountain."

And made the most sought-after moonshine. Viola sighed. "I'm not ashamed of him, Cora." But she was not eager for the handsome preacher's son to figure out whose daughter she was.

The sound of jogging footsteps reached them. Viola groaned. They'd been followed.

"Hey, you left before we could introduce ourselves." The lanky boy jogged up to them, his little sister puffing in his wake, having to sprint to keep up.

Mercy. That smile of his could charm a cat out of its whiskers.

"I'm Trilby Chambers, and this is my little sister, Marilyn." He stuck out his hand, his posture ramrod straight.

Cora approached the younger girl. "My name's Cora. You play marbles?"

Viola didn't hear her reply. A strange buzzing filled her ears when she took Trilby's offered hand. "Viola Whitt," she managed to whisper.

"Thanks for coming this morning. My father sure was hoping for a better turnout." He relaxed his stance and pushed a wavy lock from his forehead, his uncertain expression asking a bucketful of questions.

She offered a sympathetic shrug. "We're a tightknit bunch up on this mountain." *A tightknit bunch of outlaws.* "Pretty wary of newcomers." Because newcomers didn't understand their ways and their whys. And newcomers were known for stirring up things best left alone. "The church sure did look nice this morning. You all must have put in a lot of work."

He stuck his hands into his trouser pockets. "It was pretty rough when we got there."

Good sense told her to hightail it home and forget this boy. But her heart had other plans. "Where are y'all from?"

"A little bit of everywhere, I reckon. But Kentucky most recently, then Virginia before that."

Viola's eyes widened. "That must be exciting. I've lived in Bitter End my whole life." She thought of the hand-me-down suitcase collecting dust beneath her bed, waiting for someday.

A loneliness flickered in his eyes, a wordless life story told in the span of a second. "It's always an adventure with my father. He has a heart to plant churches. Once the church gets established, he's itching to move on to somewhere new that he feels needs him more."

"Well, you'll probably be around a while then." A corner of her mouth lifted. "Seeds don't take too well in the rocky soil up here." Which was how the moonshining business got started in Bitter End—desperate farmers trying to coax food from the less-than-ideal terrain to feed their family during the Depression. Her daddy liked to regale her and Cora with the history every now and then, telling about how his grandfather made such good 'shine that the Whitt children never had to go to bed hungry.

Viola might as well give this boy an honest picture of the place. "Bitter Enders don't take kindly to strangers coming to tell them right from wrong. It might seem backward to most folks, but we live by our own strict code up here."

He seemed to consider her words for several moments. Trilby thumbed to where their two sisters chatted nearby. "Those two are getting on." His sister pulled a frog figurine from her pocket, and Cora drew close, marveling at the little thing.

Cora said, "I kin help you find a real tree frog when spring comes. I find 'em all the time in the woods. These up here are called mossy tree frogs. Real cute."

The girl grinned in response.

"Will we see y'all at school?" Viola asked.

"Marilyn will be there. I graduated Bible college last spring. I'm taking some time off to help my father get things started at the church, but then I'll be off to seminary in the fall." The spark in his eyes when he spoke the last part sent electricity zipping through her.

Bible college? Seminary? Trilby Chambers was at least four years her senior. And smart. Her cheeks grew hot. He probably thought her a silly blushing girl, but she forged onward, pretending to be unfazed by his seniority. "Following in your father's footsteps?"

Viola's father never expected her to follow in his, but he counted on her marrying a good mountain boy to come alongside him and keep the family empire going. She never told anyone, but she'd give anything to spread her wings, soar down from this old mountain, and take a peek at what the rest of the world had to offer.

"The Lord's leading is all I'm looking to follow."

Huh. She'd always thought of God being way up in the sky looking down on His creation, watching them make a right mess of things. But directing people? How did a body know if it was the Lord leading or their own inclination?

Viola glanced at the sun's position in the sky. "Cora, we best be going. Daddy will be back any minute."

"I hope to see you and your family in services next week." Trilby gave her a hopeful smile.

"Maybe," she said, knowing good and well they wouldn't be back. She almost asked him not to mention their names to his parents but didn't want to rouse his curiosity. For now, she was a neat-as-a-pin church girl. And that's all he needed to know.

Cora tore herself away from her new friend and joined Viola on the little cut-through. "She's nice. I reckon I won't trick her out of her marbles, after all."

Viola shot her a stern look. "Keep an eye on her at school. Understand?"

Cora nodded. "I'll stick to her like a tick on a cottontail bunny. Nobody'll bother her."

And nobody would dare lay a hand on Wild Wayne's daughter.

The girls hurried home, Viola's heart thumping in her chest. When they reached their yard, she let out a sigh of relief. The wagon Daddy used for on-the-mountain business was absent from its spot next to the truck he used for off-the-mountain business.

"Quick, change into your regular clothes and let's ask Momma what needs doin'."

Cora groaned, no doubt hankering to disappear to her hidden treehouse to wile the rest of the day away.

Momma put them to work churning butter and darning socks. About an hour later, they heard wagon wheels crunching down the path to the house. Viola hurried outside to help Daddy with the horses.

"There's my beautiful girl," he boomed when he saw her coming. Daddy was an oak tree of a man, over six feet tall, and broadshouldered. He swept her into a hug, his thick beard scratching against her face. "Give the mares a good brush down if you will, darlin'." She nodded and helped unhook them from the wagon. She peered at him over the horses' backs, catching a glimpse of the dark circles under his eyes. By the time she had the horses turned out in their field, he'd likely be rattling the cabin's rafters with his snores.

The people called him Wild Wayne, but the only wildness she had ever seen of him was his hair when he roused from a long nap, the thick dark waves standing every which way.

The man she knew was a gentle giant who'd bring home any injured animal he'd ever found for Viola and Cora to nurse back to health.

And yet her heart trembled at the idea of him finding out she'd been mixing with the "teetotaling preacher and his family"—the kind of people he said threatened the fiber of this community.

But wouldn't a family who knew how to follow God's leading as Trilby claimed be a blessing instead of a threat?

5

The following day, Ana stood in front of a decrepit-looking washer and dryer set wearing one of Cora's floral muumuus. She'd already attempted to dry her single set of clothes three times, but they remained just as damp as when she'd first put them in. Maybe that was one of the house quirks Cora had referred to.

Ana went to the list her aunt had taped inside the door of the pantry and ran her finger down the page full of notes. Yep. Line item 20 read: *"Dryer isn't good for anything other than taking up space. Broken part is on back order. Harley will call when it arrives. Use the line in the backyard."* In the margin, she'd hastily scrawled, *"Most people around here are a good sort, but steer clear of Marilyn"* in red ink. An odd addendum to her neatly numbered instructions. And again, no explanation. She raised her brows. Whoever this Marilyn character was, Cora thought she deserved *two* warnings? Ana chuckled. Now she *had* to meet the woman.

Since the dryer was useless, she went outside to hang her clothes on the line in the middle of the backyard. As she pinned up her shirt and jeans, she glanced doubtfully at the overcast sky. A balmy gust lifted her shoulder-length hair. Maybe the wind would do the work even though the sunshine was playing hooky.

She returned to Cora's well-stocked kitchen to scramble some eggs. As soon as her things dried, she was going into town to get a permanent tire and see what she could purchase to replace the meager wardrobe she'd scrounged from Cora's things.

Over breakfast, she typed a few ideas into her phone notes, prioritizing house projects. Thankfully the rice seemed to have worked its magic, but cell service was very spotty.

She found an online marketplace that locals used to buy, sell, and trade. She figured it could be a great way to winnow down some of the things Cora didn't plan to hang on to.

If she sold enough, she wouldn't even need to dip into Cora's budget to do a few light updates, like changing out the light fixtures, doorknobs, and cabinet hardware. She could even plant some flowers and tidy up the overgrown landscaping.

She added a few sketches on a notepad she'd found by the wall phone, then sat back in her chair, tracing her work with her finger. What would it be like to say goodbye to a place she'd lived her entire life? During her childhood, Ana had moved frequently because of her father's work and had never truly felt rooted to a place. But Cora? She had so much history here. A history Ana had hoped to connect with this summer.

Next, she went into what Cora had called the book room. She wasn't sure what she'd expected. Maybe a quaint library? But this was not that. It was a labyrinth of floor-to-ceiling boxes—each one labeled with a name and an address. Tacked to the wall she found a map that Cora had labeled with names. On closer inspection, what looked like complete chaos became clearer. The stacks were divided based on location. That way Ana could load up her car and make deliveries, area by area. Though Cora's housekeeping style seemed a bit laissez-faire, she'd been painstaking with the book donation project's organization.

When they met eight years ago, Cora had regaled her with countless tales of driving a small bus "up the highest hills and down into the lowest hollers" bringing books to people who lived too far from the library to make regular trips. Now that she'd retired, she wanted to make sure the books landed in the eager hands of her mobile library patrons.

A soft pattering tugged her attention to the window. She groaned. When had the rain started?

She hurried to the clothesline as the wind whipped the oversized muumuu around her ankles. She yanked the hanging clothes free from their pins and raced back to the house, thunder nipping at her heels.

Ana sloshed inside with her dripping clothes. After wringing them out as best she could, she draped the sopping jeans and blouse over the shower curtain rod. She stripped out of the muumuu, draped it alongside her other clothes, wrapped herself in a towel, and headed for Cora's closet in search of a replacement.

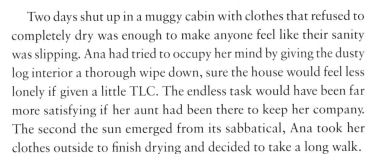

Two days shut up in a muggy cabin with clothes that refused to completely dry was enough to make anyone feel like their sanity was slipping. Ana had tried to occupy her mind by giving the dusty log interior a thorough wipe down, sure the house would feel less lonely if given a little TLC. The endless task would have been far more satisfying if her aunt had been there to keep her company. The second the sun emerged from its sabbatical, Ana took her clothes outside to finish drying and decided to take a long walk.

She certainly wasn't looking her best in Cora's tentlike T-shirt from the 2002 Grandfather Mountain Highland Games, which from her best guess based on the graphic was some sort of Scottish festival in the mountains of North Carolina. She'd paired the shirt with neon yellow gym shorts that she could never in her wildest imagination picture Cora wearing. They had a drawstring waist, so after cinching them as tight as possible and rolling the waistband down a few times, she was no longer in danger of dropping her drawers without notice.

Before leaving the house, she'd swiped on some mascara, as

if that made the whole outfit come together. She laughed at her ridiculous attempt at feeling composed and grabbed her tennis shoes waiting by the door.

As soon as her regular clothes dried and the soggy adventure was over, she was heading down this mountain to buy clothes that fit.

She glanced at the roadmap of scars on her knee as she tied the laces. She hadn't worn shorts since her surgeries, preferring not to draw attention to the ugly reminder of that day. But out in the middle of nowhere, it seemed unlikely she'd bump into someone who'd question the scar's origin story.

Wisps of steam rose from the pothole-riddled road as summer heat sucked the moisture from the pavement. Ana climbed the hills, trying to work off the inner tension that made her want to claw at the too-tight skin she lived in. She shook her head. Too-tight skin, too-loose clothes. When would her life fit again? Would it ever?

Birds swooped overhead, singing heart-piercing songs. Ana translated them to, "The sun has come, the rain has gone, time to fly."

An odd longing thumped in her chest.

She took a misstep on the uneven pavement and winced at the twinge in her bad knee. Forget flying, she'd better focus on walking.

She paused on the narrow concrete bridge. Water rushed by below, the creek having swelled with the recent rain.

A memory replayed in her mind of her fifteen-year-old self. The familiar, indefinable scent of her gymnastics training center. The slight chill hanging in the air on that cool fall morning. Chalk dust on her hands. The four-inch-wide balance beam beneath her feet. Arms overhead, body aligned. Knees a little shaky with anticipation mixed with a healthy awareness of what could happen if she was off by even a fraction.

She took a deep breath.

And then she went for it.

Back handspring connected into a floaty layout step out. Solid landing without a hint of a wobble. There had been nothing like her gymnastics days. The confidence she had from simply being in perfect control of her body.

She eyed the eight-inch-wide concrete guardrail. It wasn't a balance beam by any stretch, but it called to her. Beckoned her to feel free and brave again. Once on top of the wide railing, she walked the length of it. Back and forth. Back and forth. It felt good. Right.

Ana stopped and looked down at her turned-out feet, positioned that way by muscle memory. She could do a beginner skill, like a handstand or a cartwheel. Though her body was a decade and a half out of practice, her mind remembered the feel of performing those simple skills like she'd done them yesterday. She lifted her arms overhead, placed her dominant leg in front, toe pointed, weight on her back leg, poised to do a handstand. A gust of wind caught the tentlike neon shorts, causing them to flap and rustle. And then her gaze snagged on the rushing water beneath her.

What was she thinking? She wasn't a fifteen-year-old on the cusp of college athletic dreams anymore. And even if she was, it was stupid to consider doing something that could completely wreck her already fragile knee. Out here on the backside of nowhere. Alone.

She dropped her arms, turned sideways on the wide rail, and watched the roiling creek beneath her.

Just a moment there, she'd felt that old confidence surge in her chest again. Its sudden absence brought tears to the surface. Tears that welled daily since the incident, but she never allowed them to spill over. Because as sure as she knew that kindergartners licked the purple glue sticks when her back was turned, she knew that if she let herself fall apart, she'd never in a million years be able to pull herself back together again.

But out here, there was no one to witness her weakness. Just this once she'd let all she'd been stuffing down spill out. Maybe then she could finally sort through the mess and decide which parts of herself she was meant to keep and let the creek water wash the rest away.

Those spilled tears morphed into sobs that shook her shoulders. It was like she was having some strange out-of-body experience, watching herself standing on a bridge rail, her emotional fortress crumbling. This was exactly why she never allowed herself to cry.

The rumble of an approaching vehicle reached her ears. She groaned. *Please keep going.* She attempted a shuddering breath, trying to rein it all back in again.

"Ma'am?" The voice was soothing and deep. The kind someone might use to calm the fatally wounded.

Her shoulders crept toward her ears as she thought of the impression she must make. Standing on a bridge rail, hair windblown, wearing oversized mismatched clothes. "Good afternoon," she said without turning to face the voice. She'd attempted to sound bright and carefree, but her words had croaked from her throat like a sick bullfrog. She swiped at her tears. Black mascara streaked her fingertips.

The vehicle door slammed shut behind her. She groaned and turned around.

She winced at the sight of the ruggedly handsome shepherd-cowboy she'd almost run over a few days prior. His dark blue-gray eyes reminded her of storm clouds gathering on the horizon.

She thumbed over her shoulder. "I was just out for a walk and . . ." And what? She'd wanted to hop up there and throw some gymnastics skills on a guardrail real quick? *Because that sounds like a perfectly normal explanation.*

He approached slowly, hands out in front of him, as though she were a spooked horse. "You don't have to explain. Please, just let me help you down."

Before he could reach her, she jumped onto the road. Pain shot through her bad knee as she landed the two-foot drop, and she fought to keep discomfort from registering on her face. She'd pay for that foolishness later. "Really, I'm fine. I was just looking at the way the creek had risen. I'm sorry if I concerned you, but I'm fine. Really." *Well, that was convincing.*

He continued moving closer, eyes narrowed in study of her. "You seem upset. Is there someone I can call for you?" His throat worked like he was trying to swallow a stone. "Or do you need to talk?"

She scrubbed her hand over her face. This was so awkward. How could she explain, in as few words as possible, that all she'd been doing was searching for buried confidence without sounding as desperate as she felt. Or better yet, what was the simplest thing to say to get this guy to go away? She started walking toward Cora's house, looking back over her shoulder. "Like I said, I'm fine. This is all a misunderstanding."

He followed her, leaving his old red truck idling in the road. "What is it that you think I've misunderstood?"

That stopped her. "That you thought that I . . . that I . . . Listen, if I wanted to do what you think I wanted to do, I would find a much more expedient method than jumping off a short bridge into a shallow creek. Not that I . . ." She trailed off. *Just stop talking, Ana.*

"Is that something you've put a lot of thought into? Ways to die . . . um, ma'am . . . I'm sorry, I didn't catch your name." This poor guy thought he was being some kind of hero, but he was just making an embarrassing encounter so much worse than it needed to be.

"That's because I didn't throw it." She attempted a smile that she was pretty sure looked more like a manic grimace. "Look, I'm fine. I said I was fine, and I meant it."

She felt a sense of triumph when he didn't reply.

But a minute later, he pulled his vehicle alongside her, jostling down the uneven road, keeping pace with her. "Let's start over," he said. "My name is Sam. I live over the hills, not too far from here."

This was Cora's friend Sam? She'd pictured a grizzled old

farmer closer to Cora's age. Not this . . . this thirty-something, overly conscientious cowboy.

She straightened her shoulders. *Act normal and he will go away. Act normal?* She was normal. *Ugh.* "I'm Ana. Cora is my great-aunt. Maybe you know her?"

Something passed over his face, and he nodded. "I do. So, you're staying alone?"

She inwardly groaned. "I promise, I'm fine."

He adjusted the brim of his hat and looked ahead as his truck rolled along. "Fine is the biggest lie people tell. You ask someone how they are, and the answer is always fine, but it's rarely the truth. And you've told me you were fine six times in the span of two minutes." He squinted at his dashboard. "Maybe less than two minutes."

He wasn't wrong. Every "fine" she'd uttered was a bold-faced lie. But he had no business spending another moment worrying about her. "You drive around every day looking for people who don't need help?"

His face went slack like he'd been slapped, and he jerked his gaze away.

She winced. What was the matter with her? She'd always managed to handle her own pain without inflicting it on others. This guy didn't deserve her snark.

Before she could apologize, his expression smoothed, and he shrugged. "I was headed over to check on some land where I keep sheep. I moved the flock a few days ago, but it seems I've got a ewe missing."

"I better let you get back to that lost sheep. I know my way home. No need for you to keep burning daylight on my account."

He glanced at the sky. "Fair enough." He grew quiet, still following her. "I know I've no right to ask this, but would you mind giving me a hand? I'm really worried about her."

That night, Sam lay in the dark, staring at the ceiling. The still fan made him think of a giant five-legged bug hovering over the top of him. He scoffed at his imagination's poor attempt at distracting him from *her*.

It's none of my business.

She said she was fine.

His heart pounded in his chest, reliving the tortured look in her eyes when he'd found her on the bridge. It hadn't been Cora's housesitter he'd seen at first glance but his Marcy.

"God—" Sam choked on the rest of the prayer. It felt wrong, asking God to help him forget the woman on the bridge. He'd promised Cora he'd look out for her. But that was supposed to mean fielding a call or two about the ancient appliances Cora was too frugal to replace. He was never supposed to have gotten tangled up in someone else's problems. Not when he couldn't manage his own.

He scrubbed his hands over his face and groaned before kicking off the tangled sheets and springing from the bed.

He paced.

Objectivity. He needed someone to tell him he was overreacting. Worrying where he had no place worrying. Marilyn. She'd know what to do.

He picked up his phone, checking the time. One in the morning.

Forget it. Objectivity didn't exist at this hour. He sighed, grabbed his keys, and strode out of his house.

6

February 1958

"Vi, dear, prop open the window just a smidge. It's getting a little stuffy in here."

Viola gave the cornbread batter one more stir and then did as her mother told. She dabbed at her brow as a cool breeze cut through the house. "Daddy'll be home early if he catches a whiff of that fried chicken on the wind."

Her mother laughed from where she stood at the stove, carefully turning a drumstick sizzling in lard. "You might be right."

Viola poured her batter into the prepared skillet and slipped it into the oven.

"What did you think of the new preacher and his family?"

It had been three days since she and Cora had snuck off to church. Momma hadn't breathed a word about it until this moment and, thankfully, neither had any of the neighbors. "They seem nice enough, I reckon. They sure worked hard on that old church. Had it bright and shiny as a new penny."

"Did many people attend?"

Viola shook her head as she wiped the dots of cornmeal from the table. "Just me and Cora and Widow Calloway."

"Bless their hearts. They'll have a hard row to hoe getting in good with these mountain folk." Momma plated the chicken, her shoulders slumping a fraction as she placed it in the center of the kitchen table, next to the cut flowers from her garden. She let out a long breath. Momma was born and raised in the valley, and even after being the wife of Wild Wayne for the past twenty years, Viola knew she still felt like an outsider at times.

"Do you miss home? Going to church all the time with your folks?" Momma didn't talk about her life before her marriage very much, and Viola would love to know what made a girl from the valley hitch herself to a man like her father. Meeting Trilby had raised a lot of new questions in Viola's mind about what falling in love might look like.

Momma grabbed the pot of green beans and set it on a metal trivet next to the chicken. "Going to church? Yes. My life in the valley? Not so much." A dark look crossed her face, and Viola was desperate to know what was behind it but didn't know how to plumb the depths of her mother's thoughts any more than Reverend Chambers knew how to get in good with the mountain folk.

Her mother bustled around the kitchen, cleaning up. Viola fell into step beside her, searching her mind for the right question to get her foot in the door. She craved to understand what Momma had given up, choosing to live on this mountaintop with people who were more accepting of her daughters who were born and raised here than the woman who birthed them.

"Did you know Daddy was a moonshiner when you met him? Did your parents?"

Her mother's gaze bore into hers. "I did. They didn't."

"You must've really been in love." It was the only scenario Viola could conceive of for a prim, well-mannered girl to trade kith and kin for an outlaw of a man revered by his friends and feared by his enemies.

"I know you must hear all kinds of stories about your father. About the kind of man he is, but let me ask you something. Have you ever gone hungry a single day in your life?"

"No, ma'am."

"Has he ever raised his hand or his voice to you?"

Viola shook her head. "No, ma'am." Now that she thought about it, on the rare occasions she'd gotten a whipping, it had been her momma sending her out the door for a hickory switch, not her daddy.

Her mother seemed to track her thoughts. "He left the discipline to me for a reason, Viola Mae. He knew how my daddy did me as a girl. Knowing just how to land a blow so that no one would ever know that behind his smooth talk lived a monster of a man." Momma paused her distracted tidying, focusing on Viola.

"Stories about Wild Wayne are more rumor than anything. Some choices he's made I surely don't agree with. But he has loved, protected, and adored us. Given the choice between the smiling banker in the front row of the church who beat his wife and children in secret or the mountain man moonshiner steeped in illegal trade, I took the latter. And I would choose Wayne Lee Whitt again and again. Every day of my life." Momma wiped her hands on her apron. "He's a complicated man who lives by morals of his own making, ones I wish he'd submit to the Lord, but I can't change that. I just love him best I know how."

Viola's mind reeled, trying to absorb her every word. Momma never talked about her raising, and this sudden deluge made Viola feel as if she'd been invited over the threshold between being a girl and being a woman.

The front door swung open, and her father's boots thundered on the wood floors. "Sakes alive, something smells good in this house." He wrapped his muscled arm around Momma's waist and pulled her close, smacking a kiss on her cheek.

Though a smile teased at the corners of her mouth, she swatted him away. "Get on with you and go wash up. You're tainting my good-smelling house with your dirt and sweat."

He grumbled good-naturedly and then did as he was told. Momma went out to the front porch and rang the triangle, calling Cora in from wherever she played. That girl was spoiled plumb rotten. When Viola was Cora's age, she was firmly affixed to her mother's side, cooking and cleaning. Cora ran about like a ragamuffin.

Just as they were putting the final touches on setting the table, someone knocked on the front door. Who in the world would come around at suppertime? Daddy always made sure his business dealings were done away from home.

Her mother went to the door and Viola listened from the kitchen.

"Hello, ma'am, my name is Reverend Quincy Chambers."

Viola's heart raced like a fox with its paw caught in a trap.

The reverend continued, "My family and I are new to the area, and I'm just going around to introduce myself and to tell you about Sunday services."

Viola stiffened at the thud of her father's footsteps coming up behind her. "More like he smelled the chicken frying from the church steps," Daddy said loud enough for the preacher to overhear.

"Thank you, Reverend. Do come in and join us. We were just about to sit down for dinner."

What was her mother thinking? The minute the man laid eyes on Viola and Cora, he'd say something about them being there, and despite the conversation she and her mother had just had about the gentleness of her father, she knew their church attendance would be viewed as a betrayal.

And in Bitter End, betrayal was a transgression of the highest order.

The next morning, Ana slid her briar-scratched legs from beneath the bedsheets and winced. Spending an entire afternoon looking for a lost ewe in the company of a stoic shepherd had not been on her Bitter End bingo card.

As taxing as it was to scour those hills with a stranger who'd made a sudden shift from prying to reticent as they'd searched, she had to admit there had been an undeniable thrill finding that ewe with her newborn lamb. Sam had loaded the weary animals in the back of his truck and then dropped Ana off on his way home, leaving her to apply antibiotic cream to her flesh wounds in peace.

She went to the kitchen to brew some coffee. At least her clothes had finally dried, and she could search the town for something decent to wear today. It was enough to make her forget yesterday's embarrassment. *Almost.*

Her eyes widened at the sight that greeted her beyond her kitchen window. Sam's pickup blocked her driveway. She squinted, trying to see past the glare of the sunrise on his windshield. Was he in there? Asleep?

Heat flooded her cheeks. He hadn't asked her to look for that sheep because he needed her. He'd used it as an excuse to keep an eye on her.

She started toward her front door, indignation roaring to life. Words swelled and collided as she pictured herself banging on the driver's side window to wake him by serving up a steaming hot piece of her mind. She slid her feet into a pair of Cora's pink rubber clogs and then stopped herself. Maybe this wasn't the best tactic for convincing this Sam guy that she was a stable and well-functioning adult.

Trading the borrowed floral nightgown and garden clogs for her jeans and blouse would be a good start. She caught sight of her bedhead in the hall mirror. And maybe she would run a brush through her hair.

She took a steadying breath and put a pot of coffee on. Yes. She'd get ready for the day, and then walk out calmly, presenting him with a fresh cup of coffee and a pleasant "good morning," as if waking to find a neighbor sleeping in her driveway was a perfectly normal way to start the week.

As she changed her clothes, she mulled over her response to Sam's behavior. Why did his belief that she needed help make her so angry? Was it pride? Or was it because after eight months of pretending for everyone else, this man had seen right through her in seconds, and it scared her half to death?

Bitter End was supposed to be where she could be an ordinary, boring human being. Which she was.

Her heart softened a fraction. Cora said to call Sam if she needed anything, so he was probably harmless. The poor guy was probably trying to be a good neighbor to his friend's niece. It was still weird, camping out in her driveway. But, for Cora's sake, she'd temper her tone when she asked him to cease and desist his unwanted vigil.

She exited the bathroom in her fresh clothes, with a washed face and her hair pulled back. She poured a cup of coffee for herself and then a second for her neighbor. Should she bring out cream and sugar too or go on gut instinct that the guy took his coffee black?

Just then the truck growled to life, backed out of her drive, and disappeared like it had never been there.

"You slept in her driveway?" Marilyn held the landline tighter against her ear as if her attempt at hearing him better would clear up her confusion.

"Cora asked me to look in on her," Sam said like a chastised child.

Marilyn sat at her kitchen table and nudged aside her doctor's notes. No use looking over those again. They weren't going to change. "I'm pretty sure all Cora intended was for you to swing by and introduce yourself, dear."

"I found her standing on a bridge." His voice shifted to something hollow and achy.

"Oh." She knew better than most the effect something like that might have on Sam. She struggled to picture the scene. "What bridge? Where?"

"The one over by my fields. Mouse Tail Branch."

She clamped a hand over her mouth. No matter how ridiculous the scene, she could not laugh at Sam's anguish. "Honey, I can't imagine why she'd be standing up on that railing, but I seriously doubt she intended to harm herself. That can't be more than a seven-foot drop."

A sigh came through the line. "I overreacted?"

"Safe to say." Bless his heart.

"She'd been crying."

"Yes, well . . ." She'd heard about Cora having a young lady housesit while she was away. Though Marilyn and Cora weren't on speaking terms, they shared the same hairdresser. "People cry. When they are sad. Angry. Happy. Lots of reasons."

"It should have been you there, not me. I don't know how to handle people. Or their pain."

That was a lie. One she hoped he'd someday leave behind. "I'll check in on her if it will put your mind at ease." Cora never had to know.

"Thank you." His words weren't much more than a breath.

"See you on Thursday?"

"Yes, ma'am."

She hung up her phone and made a mental note to invent an excuse to stop by Sam's place while she was over that way. Poor boy was likely worse off than Cora's housesitter from the ordeal.

Marilyn went to her pantry and pulled out a few of her prize-winning jellies. Apple, peach, plum. She tucked each one into a blue gingham-lined basket. She snickered to herself thinking of the "unwelcome basket" Cora had left on the porch when Marilyn had moved back to Bitter End six years ago. It had been filled with expired homemade preserves, rotten eggs, and a note that said, "We'll get along just fine as long as you stay as far from me as you'd like to stay from rotten eggs and botulism." When Marilyn had seen it, she'd laughed and laughed despite the twist in her chest, both devastated and relieved that the eight-year-old version of her ex-best friend still lived on.

Her oven timer went off, and she removed six golden biscuits that had risen sky-high. She tucked five of them into the basket and split the sixth in half and slathered each side with a healthy helping of butter and blackberry jam. She sat back in her seat and bit into the fluffy sweetness with a contented sigh. When life's clock started to run a little fast, it was funny how the smallest things could bring so much comfort.

After she finished her own biscuit, she loaded the gift basket into her car and took the short drive down Old Buck Mountain Road. Cora would be madder than a wet hen if she knew Marilyn deigned to set foot on her property in her absence. But what her stubborn neighbor didn't know wouldn't hurt a thing.

She parked just as a young woman stepped out of Cora's house. Her auburn hair was pulled back in a ponytail. A stranger and yet there was something so, so familiar about her. Marilyn's heart rate picked up as she climbed out of her car.

The young woman gave her a quizzical frown. "Can I help you?"

Face hot, she grabbed the basket and held it out in front of her. "Hello. I'm Cora's neighbor, Marilyn."

An odd look crossed the younger woman's face. Curiosity? Confusion? Suspicion? Maybe she wasn't used to the hospitality in these parts.

Marilyn stepped closer. "I brought you a little something sweet to welcome you to Bitter End."

8

MARCH 1958

Viola sat at the front of the classroom, her desk positioned near Mrs. Lambert. Because she was the oldest student in the small mountain school, Mrs. Lambert had given her the role of class assistant for the final semester of her education. Many children on the mountain left school to help with the family needs before getting a high school diploma. But not Viola. It was Daddy's pride and joy that his daughters never had to make that kind of sacrifice.

Most of the students were bent over their copy work, carefully printing a poem onto their papers. But Cora had scooted her desk close to Marilyn, and their heads were nearly touching as they tittered over whatever was on Cora's sheet.

Viola looked to Mrs. Lambert, who nodded at her. Viola stood from her desk and walked silent as a cat to the two girls, who were oblivious to the rest of the world. She hovered over them and cleared her throat.

Both girls' heads popped up. Cora's startled look transformed into sheer mischief when she realized it was her sister and not the teacher who'd pounced on them. Marilyn's blanched face filled with color as Cora proudly held up the drawing.

A caricature of Viola with oversized eyes, a menacing scowl, and exaggerated hips stared back at her.

Viola sighed and plucked the page from her sister's grasp. "Separate your desks and get back to work. If the two of you cannot behave, I'll permanently move you to opposite sides of the classroom and you'll be sent home with notes to your mothers."

Cora let out half of a snicker before she got herself under control. As much fun as she had mocking her sister's classroom authority, Cora had zero interest in inviting Momma and her hickory switch into the conversation. Viola turned on her heel, skirt swishing about her calves. She wadded up the unflattering drawing and arched it expertly into the trash.

She settled back at her desk, grading math tests from the elementary students. As she checked answers against the teacher's key, her mind wandered to Marilyn's older brother. It had been two days since Reverend Chambers had made his impromptu visit to their home. Two days since that stilted dinner in which she waited every moment for the man to say something to her parents about her and her sister's covert church attendance.

He must have deduced from his less-than-warm welcome by their father that it would be wise to keep that tidbit to himself.

The final hour of school passed in a blur. She rang the dismissal bell, and the schoolroom emptied like an anthill doused with boiling water.

Viola gathered her things at a slower pace. Cora would be long gone by now, off to her secret woodland hideaway.

She bade her teacher goodbye and exited the one-room building. Her heart stutter-stepped at the sight beyond the school's double doors. Trilby Chambers stood beneath the budding oak tree, hands shoved in his pockets, laughing at Cora and Marilyn's antics.

She walked toward the handsome, hazel-eyed boy, drawn like a fly to a picnic. When he saw her coming, his face lit with a wide smile. Of their own volition, her lips did the same.

"Good afternoon, teacher."

Heat rose to her cheeks. "I'm not a teacher. I just help because I'm the oldest in a group of kindergartners."

"I am in third grade, thank you very much," Cora blustered from where she and Marilyn played marbles in the dirt.

Trilby winked over the heads of the younger girls. "Is that what you want to do after you graduate? Teach?"

Her shoulders crept to her ears. "I don't know." Truth was, she never thought much past getting out of Bitter End to see a little more of the world, whatever mode it took. "I mentioned teaching to Daddy once, and he said the mountain already has a teacher and doesn't need another. I'm not sure he'd pay for an education off this mountain." Dare she confess her secret wish? "I . . . I'd like to travel some. See places I've read about in books."

Curiosity gleamed in his gaze as he stepped around the younger girls, drawing nearer to her side. "Like?"

Images of the Eiffel Tower, Buckingham Palace, and the Roman Colosseum flickered in her mind, wispy and so far out of reach. "Oh, I don't know. Anywhere."

He nudged her. "Come on. I know you have somewhere in mind."

She shook her head, schooling her grin. "What about you?"

"Oh, nothing so grand as traveling the world. Lord willing, I'll pastor a church someday and play a small role in bringing hope to weary souls." His words were humble, but his eyes were full of anticipation.

It took everything in her to keep from blurting, "Take me with you." Her travel dreams were a vaporous fantasy, but Trilby spoke with surety and conviction about his future.

The younger girls picked up their marbles and tucked them into little bags. Cora's lip poked out a fraction when she stood. Marilyn must've been a savvier player than Cora originally anticipated. But the loss must have inflicted a superficial wound, because in another minute the girls were giggling as they skipped down the path.

Trilby and Viola followed them down the packed-dirt road.

"Cora was so glad to have a new friend at school. Most of the other kids her age are boys," Viola shared. "She has another friend, but her mother passed away, and she's had to stay home to help tend the younger ones."

"I thought school attendance was required?"

She gave him a sideways glance as they continued toward the fork in the path that loomed in front of them. "You're in outlaw country now, Mr. Chambers. People up here do what they want and expect to be left alone about it."

They slowed to a stop as their paths split. "I can see that. I'm fraternizing with a thief at this very moment."

She opened her mouth to protest. Her daddy might illegally make and distribute moonshine, but he was no thief.

A corner of his mouth quirked upward, and he tapped his chest three times, before taking the path that led to the church, leaving her to float home.

People up here always said that if you breathed your first in Bitter End, that's where you were destined to breathe your last. A foregone conclusion most were content to embrace.

Not her. Not if she could help it. Something about Trilby Chambers, who was not tied to this place like she was, made even her daydreams seem possible.

Later that evening, Viola was helping her mother wash up in the kitchen. Her father sat at the table, reading the paper that one of his runners had brought up the mountain. They'd had an early supper that night because Daddy had said he had some business to attend to that evening. He said it as though it was as normal as a man going to have a shareholder meeting at his office in the big city.

As she was drying the last of their supper dishes, the screen door creaked open and a knock sounded. Before either she or her mother could drop their dishrags, Daddy was at the door.

Viola slowed her task as she strained to hear who it was this time. "Good evening, sir. My name is Trilby Chambers. I believe you've met my father, Reverend Quincy Chambers?"

Viola glanced at her mother and gripped her hand, begging her to intervene. Momma shrugged as if to say there was nothing to be done.

Trilby cleared his throat. "It is such fine, unseasonably warm weather this evening. I wanted to ask your permission to invite Viola for a sunset stroll."

Viola's legs held as much strength as her mother's bone broth gelatin. *Foolish boy.*

"Let's you and me step outside a minute." The edge to her father's tone made her hands shake so hard, she dropped the rag and it plopped onto the wood counter. She was freshly aware of the restrained force that lived beneath the surface of the man. She'd give just about anything for the cabin walls to be a little thinner to find out what became of the first boy who had ever dared climb the front steps and request the privilege of her company.

"We'd best finish up in here," her mother said, jarring Viola from her frozen state.

"Yes, ma'am." She wanted to ask her mother what she thought was happening out on that front porch. Or what she should say when her father returned. But she lacked the wherewithal to form a coherent sentence. Poor Trilby. He'd been so proper when he'd asked. Hopeful and innocent. And he'd wandered straight into the maw of a bear.

She dipped her rag into a bucket of clean water, wrung it nearly dry, and went to wipe the kitchen table she'd already cleaned, putting her closer to the door. The muffled and unintelligible tone of her father was the only sound she could detect.

She blew out a breath. His tone was matter-of-fact. Firm. But not angry. Everything would turn out just fine.

Just then the front door burst open. Cora sailed into the room, fresh from feeding the livestock, hay stuck in her hair.

Their eyes locked. Viola gave a meaningful glance over Cora's shoulder and then raised her eyebrows in question.

Cora shook her head and sucked her teeth, eyes wide, then she closed the door behind her, once again muffling the conversation.

"Cora Leigh, go wash up," their mother called from the kitchen. "I know you got filthy playing with the baby goats."

"Yes, ma'am." Cora sighed and trudged to the washroom.

A few moments later, her father came back inside, looking older and more tired than when he went out. Towering over her, he rested his huge hands on her shoulders.

"How did you meet the Chambers boy?"

Had Trilby told him about her coming to church? She prayed not. "He was at the school to walk his little sister home. We spoke for a few minutes." The truth. Just not the whole truth.

"Those folks aren't mountain people, and they don't understand our ways. You will not see that Chambers boy again. If he walks toward you, you will turn the other way. Are we clear?"

"Yes, sir." And though she lived to please her father, the little fire flickering in her heart would not be easy to tame.

9

With her car safely in the care of Gus's Garage, Ana ventured into the heart of Roan Mountain. She traversed the cracked sidewalk, passing sporadically spaced businesses, none of which were currently open. Some looked like they hadn't flipped their Closed sign in a decade.

On her unfruitful stroll, she puzzled over her brief visit with the mysterious Marilyn. The gentle-spirited older woman with her hospitality basket sure didn't seem to deserve Cora's double warning. Still, she'd refrained from sampling the biscuits. Just in case.

Ana reached the end of the pavement and stopped. What now? She scanned the area, hoping for sanctuary from the caustic smells and greasy chairs waiting for her at Gus's. Then her eyes snagged on a blinking Open sign. *Perfect.*

A bell chimed as she walked through the front door of The Sweet Bean Coffee Shop.

"Hidey-ho, neighbor. I'll be right with you," called a hoarse voice from the back. Ana glanced around the nearly empty establishment that had the feel of an old saloon. In the dim interior, everything was wood. Floor. Ceiling. Counters and tables.

A couple of older men sipped coffee in a corner booth, too engrossed in their conversation to notice her.

A few moments later, a wiry woman with a pixie cut and a weathered face came around the corner. "'Scuse me, darlin'. I was on my way in from a quick smoke break," she wheezed. When she reached the register, she looked up. "I'm Frankie, proud owner of The Sweet Bean. What can I whip up for you?" She flashed an indulgent grin.

Ana returned the smile while studying the extensive chalkboard menu. "I'll have the Bee Sting."

"Excellent choice. The honey comes from this farm in Sweetwater, Tennessee. It's run by these two sisters, and I'm convinced they have the best-tasting honey in the state. My brother lives over that way, and he got me hooked on the stuff. Brings me more every time I run low."

Something about this woman's enthusiasm and her attachment to her honey supplier warmed Ana's center. "It sounds like I made a good choice, then."

"You here to drop off a care package for one of them thru-hikers?"

"Thru-hikers?"

"The Appalachian Trail runs nearby." Frankie started making her drink. "So, if that's not it, what in the world brings you to the area? Wrong season for snow skiers."

"I'm housesitting for Cora Whitt."

Frankie nodded. "Oh, yes. She did mention something 'bout that last time she was down the mountain. Cora's a good woman. The work she did with the bookmobile over these many years sure blessed a lot of people." Frankie bustled about behind the counter, working on her latte. "Lotta folks can't make a thirty-minute drive just to get to a library."

Maybe Frankie was her chance to learn what was behind Cora's strange warnings. "Do you happen to know a lady named Marilyn who lives on Old Buck Mountain Road?"

Frankie paused a moment. "Marilyn? Sure. Gets coffee here once in a blue moon. She and her husband moved here several years ago. He was some kind of bird scientist or something before he passed away." Frankie turned her back to her to get some milk from the fridge, and Ana heard her mutter "A little judgy but nice enough," as she prepared Ana's drink.

Maybe those biscuits and preserves were safe for consumption after all. Good thing. They looked delicious enough to risk being poisoned. But that meant Cora's boycott of Marilyn was personal. *Interesting.*

Ana wandered the room looking at the black-and-white photographs on the walls. Pictures of people posed by wagons and teams of mules, old wanted posters. There were framed news articles about prize pie winners at the county fair from the early 1900s. The Sweet Bean had as much character as its proprietor.

When Frankie called her name, Ana approached the counter, remembering Lexi's request. She settled on one of the counter stools. "Do you know how Bitter End got its name?"

Frankie passed her the coffee and propped her hands on her hips. "Only the old-timers still know it by that name. An uncle of mine used to live up there and he'd tell stories about that place that could make the hair stand up on your neck. Makes sense if you know its history." Frankie lowered her voice and raised her brows. "A long, long time ago a group of outlaws were on the run. They were a wily sort, so they evaded capture for weeks as they traveled through these mountains. But after a while, their supply had run out and half of 'em had some sort of injury or another. Hungry, tired, beat-up, and cold, they huddled around a small fire and made a pot of coffee with the last of their supply. They drank it to the last drop, even chewed the burned grounds as the lawmen closed in. The ringleader looked around to each of his faithful men and said, 'Well, that's it, boys. We've done drunk up this life, all the way to the bitter end.'" Frankie slapped the counter, making Ana jump. "And that's how Bitter End got its name."

Ana studied the woman's deadpan expression, looking for any

signs she was pulling her leg. She took a long sip of her latte, then closed her eyes in pure bliss. Frankie had good reason for bragging on her honey supplier. "This is delicious."

Frankie beamed. "Yes, ma'am, only the best served at The Sweet Bean. Anything else I can help you with?"

Ana surveyed Frankie's oversized cargo pants and western style shirt with a little unease. "Can you recommend a clothing store nearby?"

"There's a huge thrift shop down the way, Second Chances. Elizabethton or Johnson City might have more what you're looking for if you're not a thrifter. Wally World is about half an hour from here."

"Wally World?" Ana asked.

Frankie guffawed. "Oh, sorry. I meant the Walmarts. My family always called it Wally World for some reason or another. I forget why."

Maybe she should advise her new friend to lay off the espresso shots between customers. But then again, Frankie's buzzing energy was a good kind of contagious. Ana lifted her coffee before standing from her spot at the counter. "Thanks again, for the coffee and the story. This has been the highlight of my week."

Frankie glowed with the praise. Ana laughed under her breath as she exited the café. She would refrain from mentioning the fact that said week had been a string of one mishap after another.

Ana headed for Second Chances. Thrifting had never been her thing. Not because she had a problem with secondhand clothes but because the hodgepodge of sizes and styles overwhelmed her. But she might as well give it a try. She wasn't trying to impress anyone. She just needed clothes that weren't in danger of falling around her ankles every time the wind blew.

The bell tinkled as she entered the shop. "Welcome to Second Chances," came a voice from somewhere beyond the overflowing shelves. Her heart rate upticked at the endless array of boxes. How did a person ever find what they were looking for in a place like this? What needed to be kept and what needed to be tossed? She backed toward the exit, ready to escape the scent of mothballs and stale clothing.

"Pardon the mess." A woman with long gray hair appeared around a tower of boxes, expertly guiding her motorized wheelchair. "We just got in several big donations, and I'm in the middle of reorganizing the store. If you need anything in particular, I'm happy to point you in the right direction. Or feel free to browse if you'd rather." She stuck out her hand. "I'm Beatrice, by the way."

Feeling trapped, Ana shook her hand and introduced herself.

"What can I help you find, hon?"

Something about the woman's warm welcome overrode Ana's instinct to flee. "I don't need anything fancy. Maybe some T-shirts and jeans?"

Beatrice's gaze flicked over her form. "Come with me. I'll show you the clothes in your size."

She followed Beatrice through the maze. The woman pointed to a large box marked with a huge black 6. "This one here has some casual duds that might meet your needs. The next row over has some medium and large T-shirts, depending on the fit you prefer. And if you find this to be the wrong size, you'll find smaller to the left and bigger to the right. I'll be in the back sorting some baby things. Come find me when you're ready."

After Beatrice glided away, Ana contemplated making a break for the door. But something about the box of T-shirts called to her. Some were so worn she'd have dropped them in the trash rather than donating them. Others still had their store tags on. So different, and yet all on sale at Second Chances.

She pulled out a Maroon 5 shirt and next to it found a One Direction shirt. She smiled, flashing back to listening to music on the radio, making up dance routines and cringe-worthy lyrics in her friend's bedroom. She hadn't known it then, but that had been the precursor to the songs and dances she'd one day make up for her students to help them learn numbers, colors, vocab words.

She worried her bottom lip between her teeth and typed a text to Lexi.

Hey. Thanks for sticking by me this past year.

Not more than a second passed before her reply came through.

Of course. Don't forget. This summer is about taking care of you.

Ana stuffed her phone back into her pocket. She was trying to follow her friend's advice. The latte had been a good place to start. She eyed the boxes of clothes. She was a little doubtful about the "new" wardrobe she was about to treat herself to. Could the chaos be an opportunity for joy?

She searched through the box, pulling out every band shirt she could find, whether she'd heard of them or not. Something about her selection made her feel a little closer to that carefree girl she'd been. She then grabbed a few pairs of jeans that looked new enough.

Beatrice seemed to sense that Ana had finished shopping and met her on the way to the checkout counter. Ana set her purchases down.

"Are you new to the area or just new to Second Chances?" Beatrice inquired as she rang up the clothes.

Ana smiled. "I'm staying at my aunt's over in Bitter End."

The lady's eyes widened. "Bitter End? Butter my butt and call me a biscuit. I haven't heard somebody call it that since I was a girl."

Ana held in a snicker. "That's what my aunt always called it, but I noticed her address is Roan Mountain."

"As time went on, more and more little hamlets got absorbed by Roan Mountain."

"It surprised me when I first drove up there," Ana said. "I expected a little town square or something, but it's really just one road that loops up and then back down the mountain with a few dead ends along the way."

Beatrice nodded. "It was a tightknit, self-sufficient community once upon a time. Most people grew and raised what they needed and bartered with their neighbors for the rest. They kept to themselves on account of all the moonshining they did, I reckon."

Ana stared at her. *Moonshining? Cora certainly never mentioned that.*

"You know why they called it Bitter End, don't ya?"

"The outlaws drinking the last of their bitter coffee before the law enforcement caught up to them, right?"

Beatrice snorted. "Frankie over at The Bean feed you that yarn?"

Ana admitted she'd fallen for it.

"Well, if you've got a minute, I'll tell ya the actual story. I guarantee it's a far cry better than whatever Frankie's served up."

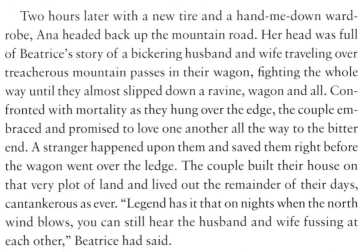

Two hours later with a new tire and a hand-me-down wardrobe, Ana headed back up the mountain road. Her head was full of Beatrice's story of a bickering husband and wife traveling over treacherous mountain passes in their wagon, fighting the whole way until they almost slipped down a ravine, wagon and all. Confronted with mortality as they hung over the edge, the couple embraced and promised to love one another all the way to the bitter end. A stranger happened upon them and saved them right before the wagon went over the ledge. The couple built their house on that very plot of land and lived out the remainder of their days, cantankerous as ever. "Legend has it that on nights when the north wind blows, you can still hear the husband and wife fussing at each other," Beatrice had said.

Ana chuckled, not sure which of Bitter End's backstories to believe. She'd have to call Lexi when she got back to the house. She'd get a kick out of this.

10

Ana lay in bed, heart pounding in her chest, the memory of the assailant's frightened eyes connecting with hers burned into her mind. She vaulted into action, exchanging her pajamas for a T-shirt and jeans and heading outside.

Standing on the wide front porch in the morning light, she took several deep breaths of mountain air. She needed to move. To do something. To do anything but be still.

She descended the steps and set off at a brisk pace. To distract herself, she made a mental checklist of all she wanted to complete that day. Her thoughts drifted to the small stack of boxes in the living room that Cora planned to take with her to the retirement home. How in the world could seventy-some years of living in one house be narrowed down to a few boxes? How did she decide what to leave behind and what to keep? Ana had a sudden desire to go through her aunt's personal things, as if that could help her sort through the mess in her own head. If nothing else, those boxes contained clues to her heritage. And even though Ana couldn't quite grasp who she was anymore, she could at least cling to her roots.

Ignoring the nagging twinge in her knee, Ana pushed herself into a new gear, swinging her arms like a speed walker, reaching a pace that forced her back into focusing on keeping her "in through the nose, out through the mouth" breathing pattern steady.

But when she crested the next hill, she drew to a stop. Standing smack-dab in the middle of the road was an emaciated dog, still as a statue. It had a dark brown head and a white body that was flecked with brown speckles and big brown patches. The poor thing was a skeletal version of the hunting dogs in the painting that hung in her dad's home office.

Her heart went out to the animal, but the eerie way it stared made her wonder if the thing was rabid. She turned in the other direction and pulled out her phone to look up the number for animal services. No signal. Of course.

A weary whine reached her ears, forcing her to look back. The pathetic creature had lain down, its snout resting between its paws. She took one step in its direction, ignoring the internal protest reminding her that she was not an animal person. She'd never shed a single tear at those "arms of the angel" ASPCA commercials.

The dog's short tail wagged at her change of direction, tugging Ana onward despite her better judgment.

"Hey, there, buddy," she said as she approached. She'd recently scrolled past some infographic on social media that warned against holding your hand out to greet a dog, but for the life of her she couldn't remember the right way to do it. She kneeled next to the animal, and it rolled to its side, letting out a long huff.

The poor dog deserved its own heart-tugging commercial. There were scratches and sores all along the animal's legs and protruding ribs. The raw pads of its feet looked like they'd traveled across the country and back.

She tentatively stroked the dog's side. It released another weary sigh. Was the poor thing about to give up the ghost then and there? "Hold on, old boy." She glanced at the dog's undercarriage. "Girl, I guess?"

What in the world was she going to do with this dog? She stood. It was too big for her to carry over these rolling hills to her car, and she had serious doubts it could make it on its own power.

She sighed. "Stay here, okay?" Ana walked a few steps and heard the whine of a dog that knew its last hope had walked away. "I'm coming right back. I have to get my car."

After taking a handful of paces, a heartrending yelp sounded behind her. She turned. The dog hobbled toward her, slightly listing as if the soft morning breeze was enough to topple her.

"Stay," Ana said, attempting to sound gruff, but her voice cracked, ruining the effect. The dog kept following, letting out a pitiful cry every time its left front paw touched the ground. She groaned and went to it. She considered putting aside her squeamishness to pick up the filthy, world-weary creature, but where could she touch it to cause the least amount of pain?

Then she heard a vehicle in the distance. *Please don't be the cowboy.* This time, however, she was more than ready to admit she needed help. He was an animal person who'd likely be eager to take the dog off her hands.

Dum. Dah. Dah. Dum.

The bridal march? She turned. That was *not* cowboy Sam. A minibus with lace curtains showing through the windows slowed as it approached her. The driver's window rolled down revealing a man with a long white beard and a craggy face. If she'd typed *mountain man* in her search bar, this was the precise image she would expect to pop up. Aside from the tuxedo he wore, that is.

"Need a hand?" His voice was kind and earnest.

"Oh, dear. Is that a dog there in the road? Has it been hit?" The woman in the passenger seat, with hair big enough to give Dolly Parton a run for her money, pressed a hand to her cheek. She was definitely the sort whose purse strings came untied every time Sarah McLachlan's voice rang out on TV.

"I don't think so, but she's in really rough shape." Ana turned back to the dog for a second. "I don't know what to do."

The mountain man thumbed behind him. "We could give you a ride down to the vet's office."

The woman nodded, her bouffant never moving.

"It's not my dog," Ana said weakly.

The man must not have heard her, because he opened his door, knelt, and scooped the dog against his chest, paying no mind to the dirt and hair doing so deposited on his formalwear. He smiled at her. "Name's Jacob, by the way. Folks call me Jake. And that's my wife, Inez."

The dog let out a low groan despite how gently Jake cradled it.

"My name's Ana," she replied as she followed him to the back hatch. *Mobile Wedding Chapel* was decaled down the side of the minibus. *So many questions . . .*

"Open the handle there if you don't mind." Jake nodded at the door latch. "I don't want to jostle the poor thing."

She opened the back and stared. The inside was decorated with white tulle and silk flowers. Electric candles glowed in the sconces attached to the walls.

Inez had vacated the passenger seat and was laying a blanket down on the carpet near the door. "Just put the little darling right here."

Her husband complied, cooing gently to the dog as he laid her inside. "There, there. It's going to be all right." He stepped to the side and held out a hand like he intended to help Ana into the minibus.

She stared at his offered hand and backed up a few steps. "Well, thank you for coming to the rescue."

Jake, Inez, and the dog stared at her like she was an intimate associate of Benedict Arnold. The dog attempted to rise and released a whine that could melt an ice cap. *Oh good grief.* Was it too much to ask for one normal day in Bitter End? Ana accepted Jake's hand and climbed into the back of the minibus.

The musky scent of unwashed dog competed for dominance with the smell of roses. She sighed, looking at the pathetic animal. "You need a bath."

The dog gave her a worried whine.

The van lurched into motion and Ana braced herself. They'd

both be lucky to make it to the bottom of the mountain in one piece.

Even though Jake drove down the mountain pass at a snail's pace, the lace curtains swayed. The *Unsolved Mysteries* theme song played in Ana's mind, followed by the hauntingly suave voice of the show host she remembered from her childhood. *"Ana Watkins, beloved kindergarten teacher, kidnapped by an innocent looking middle-aged couple in a mobile wedding chapel. Never seen or heard from again."*

11

MARCH 1958

In the two weeks that had passed since she'd been forbidden to see Trilby Chambers, Viola had burned her cornbread three times, let the cow kick the milk bucket over twice, and gotten scolded by Mrs. Lambert for being absent-minded in class just about every day of the week. Had her father known his edict would triple the territory Trilby Chambers occupied in her heart and mind?

He must have had an inkling, because he'd taken to bringing young men in his employ home for dinner a few nights a week. Something he'd never done in the past. Those lackeys sitting across the table with their sly eyes only made her crave Trilby's earnest, hopeful presence all the more.

The day after the front porch incident, Viola had passed a note to Marilyn at school. A note apologizing for Trilby's reception at their home, assuring him that she did not feel the way her father might have implied.

The day after, Marilyn brought her back an answering note full of questions. Some Viola answered. Others she ignored. How much did Trilby really need to know? Her whole life, she'd been cautioned against discussing the family business outside of Bitter End. Not everyone understood the finer points of life in these highlands. They'd judge. Or report the Whitt's underground live-lihood to authorities who were happy enough to look the other way or even partake of the goods themselves as long as no one made a fuss about it.

But if a report was made, they were duty bound to venture up Old Buck Mountain Road and make an investigation.

The day after she'd sent her reply, she found Trilby waiting after school. Her father's words reverberated in her memory. *"You will not see that Chambers boy again. If he walks toward you, you will turn the other way."* But her feet rooted in place.

He came to her, slowly rotating the hat in his hands. "I'm sorry if my showing up at your house caused problems, Vi."

Butterflies took flight in her belly at his shortened version of her name.

He swallowed hard. "If you want me to leave you alone, just say the word, and I will."

She opened her mouth, but no words would come. She clamped it shut, torn between the words she was supposed to say and the ones she meant.

He worked something from his back pocket. "When I was work-ing in the valley yesterday, I saw something at the secondhand shop that made me think of our conversation the other day. It's outdated and torn in places. I understand if you don't want it . . ." He held out a thin book. *A Pocket Guide to Paris.*

She cradled the gift in her hands. No mountain boy would ever understand her like Trilby Chambers did after only a few conversations. "It's perfect," she said as she hugged it to her chest.

A crooked smile stretched one corner of his mouth, and his cheeks flushed.

"Trilby, don't leave me alone."

From that day onward, little Marilyn became the conduit for Viola and Trilby's forbidden communication. Viola was always very careful about what she put in her notes, seeing as how she was certain Marilyn and Cora snuck behind the school before and after class to read them, though heaven knew why. They kept their letters boring as milk toast. A sketch of a sparrow perched on a clothesline and a word or two about the weather from her. A line about a Scripture from his father's sermon from him. Or a verse from a song he was writing. Lately they'd taken to playing a game in each letter, asking three questions about anything they wanted. The only rule was that the other person had to answer whatever was asked.

Viola had been itching to open Trilby's latest letter ever since Marilyn handed it to her that morning, but she'd forced herself to leave it unopened until school ended. By the time Viola gathered her things that afternoon, Cora was already occupied playing hopscotch with Marilyn. Viola settled on the school steps, ready to savor every word Trilby had written.

Dear Vi,

You asked some tough ones this time. I had to think long and hard, but here goes.

As to question one, my favorite color is golden yellow like wheat when it's ready for harvest. It makes me feel like the world is warm and full of promise.

For question two, my scariest childhood memory was when I was eight and I had taken a trip into the city with my father. I got distracted by a Christmas window display in a bookstore, of all things. When I turned back around, my father was gone. I panicked and started running down the crowded sidewalk when he suddenly called my name. When I turned, I realized he'd been there the whole time but someone had stepped between us, blocking my view. But he'd never lost sight of me.

And question three, how do I know God called me to be a preacher? That's a tough one to nail down. It wasn't like I heard an audible voice or anything. It was more of a consistent nudging in my heart. When I serve in the church

and I see hurting people come to faith, I feel like I am home.
I want to spend my life making the world better for other
people. I know my words probably don't do justice to what
I feel inside, but I don't know how else to say it.

This time, I just have one question for you, and it's a
humdinger. It's one I've been pondering myself. What would
you do if you could erase your worry about what other
people think?

Always,
Trilby

She folded the letter, a plan formulating in her mind as she hurried home with Cora in tow. This time she'd answer him with something more than a letter. She waited as her father packed a suitcase and headed off in his truck. He'd be gone a few weeks. Momma said that the price of sugar had spiked, and he was hoping to rally some new investors.

As soon as dinner was done, she rushed through her evening chores, washing up the kitchen in record time.

She slipped into a clean dress and walked softly toward the front door.

Just as she reached for the knob, her mother's voice rang out, "Viola, wait."

Viola took a deep breath and turned as her mother approached from her bedroom. The knowing in her mother's eyes tore at Viola's heart.

"I know where you are going and why. I understand probably more than you realize, but you're playing a dangerous game sneaking out to see this boy."

"It's not a game. I lo—" She stopped herself before she finished the ridiculous thought that had flown from her heart to her mouth, skipping her brain altogether. She couldn't love Trilby Chambers. She barely knew him.

Her mother pinched her lips tight and sighed. "There comes a point in everyone's life when they must choose their own path, Viola Mae. But if you choose this boy, it will have repercussions I'm not sure you're ready to pay."

With that, she swept back to her bedroom, leaving Viola standing there, trying to piece together her mother's words.

A dangerous game? Surely Momma didn't think Daddy would bring Trilby to harm just because they took a sunset walk together and exchanged friendly letters.

She exited the house, the wings that had felt so ready to lift off and soar now tucked tight against her.

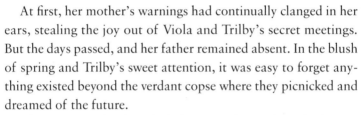

At first, her mother's warnings had continually clanged in her ears, stealing the joy out of Viola and Trilby's secret meetings. But the days passed, and her father remained absent. In the blush of spring and Trilby's sweet attention, it was easy to forget anything existed beyond the verdant copse where they picnicked and dreamed of the future.

They never explicitly included one another in these daydreams about family and home. But Viola couldn't resist inserting an image of herself sitting on the front row of the someday church Trilby would pastor, proud of the goodness he brought to the world.

One day, as they sat on a quilt under the canopy of rhododendron, he threaded his fingers through hers. "By the time I finish up my training, my father might have this church revived and be ready to move on. Then maybe I could take over in his place." He squeezed her hand.

It took a moment for the reality of his declaration to sink in. "Here? In Bitter End?" She pulled away. "Why would you want to do that?"

Confusion clouded Trilby's hazel eyes, and he dropped his chin.

"I thought . . . I thought the reason would be obvious." Meeting her gaze appeared to take concerted effort. "I want to be close to you."

But Trilby didn't realize that being at the helm of Buck Mountain Church under her father's eye put him at more of a distance than moving to Kentucky for seminary school.

She started packing away the remains of their shared lunch, searching for a way to infuse peace and simplicity back into the moment. She shot him a playful glare. "You say that now, but just you wait, Trilby Chambers. You'll be off at your fancy school and forget all about your barefoot mountain girl. You'll be surrounded by young women fawning all over you, hoping to snag a preacher man."

She stood and he followed suit, the discomfiture having dropped away, leaving behind the boyish demeanor she adored. "*My* barefoot mountain girl?" He stooped to pick up the corners of one side of their quilt, and she picked up the other. The patchwork fabric linking them was stretched taut enough to bounce a penny on.

Heat crept into her cheeks and she lifted a shoulder. "Maybe you don't think of me that way, but you sure feel like mine." Her heart thudded hard in her chest. *Good heavens.* What was she thinking? Making brazen declarations to this forbidden older boy who would be entirely out of reach in a few short months.

His face broke into a full grin. "I sure do like the sound of that." He took a step toward her, and she matched his movement. The fabric slackened.

They took another step closer, drawn together like a pair of magnets. But unlike magnets, they had to consider the consequences.

"If you said you'd be mine, Viola Mae, I'd settle down on this mountaintop a happy man and never leave. No matter how hard the moonshiners up here tried to be rid of me." He took another stride toward her, his corners of the quilt extended toward hers.

She stumbled slightly at his words and pinched her lips tight.

What would he say if he realized the moonshiners he referenced included her father? But beneath the cover of their wooded hideaway, it was easy enough to forget whose daughter she was.

"What do you say, Vi? Will you truly be mine?" Their hands, grasping each side of the quilt, were mere inches from touching now. The rest of the world and its myriad complications floated a hundred thousand miles away.

She came the rest of the way to him, the corners of the blanket meeting, their fingers twining together like tree roots. She tipped her chin to catch his gaze, but his attention swooped to her lips. The quilt was sandwiched between them.

The effect of that brief kiss was unlike anything Viola had ever imagined a kiss could be. The only other ones in her life had been pecks on the cheek from her family and the one time she and Johnny Coulter had exchanged an awkward smooch behind the schoolhouse on a dare.

This was none of those things.

They both took a step back. Trilby kept hold of the quilt's corners. He folded it in half again and then draped it over his arm. He looked up at her, the flush in his cheeks hiding his freckles. "So that's how you mountain folk fold blankets up here. You oughta give a boy a warning."

12

Marilyn waited in the Roan Mountain State Park lot for her birding companion. She'd avoided telling Sam that Jake and Inez weren't going to make it today, worried he would've skipped out too. That was how all groups ended. One or two couldn't make it, and then others followed their lead until meetings were sporadic, leaking into nonexistent. She couldn't let that happen to her late husband's birding society. At least not while she was still able-bodied enough to lead it.

Calling it a birding society was a bit of a stretch, considering it had been just her and Obadiah until he passed. This hobby had saved their marriage though. Now that he was gone, it seemed fitting for her to collect a few people that could use a little saving of their own. People who, like her, knew what it was to feel out of place, sometimes even in their own skin.

Sam's tap on the glass of her passenger window interrupted her nostalgia. She exited the car and then grabbed her small backpack from the rear seat.

She slid the bag onto her shoulder and turned in the direction of their favorite trail. "Ready?"

Sam's brows arched. "We're not waiting on Jake and Inez?"

She smiled to herself. Sam had been doubtful when she'd

originally invited the couple to join the group. Admittedly, their bickering tended to scare the birds off at the beginning, but over the past year, they'd learned to quiet themselves and listen to the birds—and maybe to each other in the process.

"They left me a voicemail telling me not to wait. Something about finding a woman on the side of the road and taking her to the vet."

Sam tilted his head. "I think you may have something mixed up there."

She chortled and started walking. "I'm just telling you what the message said. Don't blame me for Inez's communication skills."

He fell into step beside her, a scowl fixed on his face. "Have you talked to Cora's niece? She doin' all right?"

"Brought her some biscuits and had a quick chat." She stopped on the trail as the weight of Sam's words sank in. "Did you say niece? I didn't realize she was related."

Her heart pounded in her chest. If Ana was Cora's niece, that meant—

"I think she said something about Cora being her aunt." He shrugged. "But maybe not. I wasn't myself that day." His cheeks reddened.

She was pretty certain Cora had only had the one sister. Unless her mother had remarried and had more children sometime after ten-year-old Marilyn left Bitter End. "I invited her to come out with us after she got settled in a bit."

Sam's scowl faltered. "I don't know—"

She rolled her eyes. "You say that every time I invite someone new. If they're meant to be a part of the group, they stay. If not, they have a nice walk or two with us and move on."

He gave her an appraising look, the corners of his mouth twitching. "Like Frankie?"

She swatted at his shoulder. "Listen, Frankie and I patched things up. I'm not even banned from The Sweet Bean anymore." Marilyn shook her head. "I wasn't judging her tobacco consumption. But when I'm out in nature I wanna smell the pine, not nicotine."

Sam chuckled under his breath.

"Ana is not going to be another Frankie. I get the feeling she'll fit right in."

He jerked his gaze away.

She'd noticed that his brief encounter with Ana had brought the pain of his past far too close to the surface for his comfort. Hence the overreacting. At least, that was her impression. Sam had never fully shared the details of his life before Bitter End.

She searched for a way to broach the subject. Being just the two of them, it was the perfect opportunity to pry.

He gestured ahead. "Are we taking this trail today?" He hurried onward before she could answer, walking at a pace that was faster than she could maintain for very long.

"Sam?"

He slowed his steps and gave her a forced smile. "Sorry."

She smirked. Did he realize then that he was running away? The one thing he'd never be able to escape was himself. At least, not for very long. The self always had a way of catching up.

They walked down the wide trail side by side, quieter and slower now so that they didn't frighten off their quarry. A bird twittered overhead. Sam closed his eyes for a moment. "Eastern bluebird?"

She nodded. "I think you're right." Lately the group had made a game of identifying birds by their calls and songs before they lifted their binoculars to confirm by sight. Little did they know what this game meant to her.

Soon, sound would be her everything. She pointed to the binoculars hanging around his neck. "Check it out." She unzipped her backpack and pushed aside her safety kit and field guide to retrieve her binoculars, doubtful she'd be able to make out much of anything with the bird so high in the tree.

He inspected the branches overhead. "Sure is. Bright little male bird up in that pine."

The bonny little thing sang its heart out, trying to impress a female somewhere up there, Marilyn was sure.

They both pulled out their journals and made an entry on the page. The Bitter End Birding Society was not exactly what she'd call official. They were the most ragtag bunch of amateurs Marilyn could gather. And she wouldn't have it any other way.

Obadiah had had a degree in ornithology. She'd driven him up a wall with her odd questions and ignorance when they'd first gone out together. But they'd eventually found their rhythm. Bird-watching together had not been a scientific pursuit but, instead, a pursuit of nature's small delights.

She glanced at Sam as they marched on, remembering the day she'd first happened upon him. She'd driven to the park for the first time without Obadiah at her side, her own heart crumbling in her chest. She'd passed the younger man standing on the footbridge while she crossed a stream. He nodded a greeting as she passed, but his tortured eyes beckoned her back to him.

She asked if he'd seen any birds out. He described one to her but didn't know the name of the species, which was just the opportunity she'd been hoping for. She dug out her field guide and flipped through, even though she recognized the pine siskin by his description.

She'd gotten Sam talking about nature. Before the poor chap knew what hit him, they were walking together.

The anguish in Sam's eyes hadn't fully disappeared over the past two years that they'd been birding together, but it had softened. A little.

She often prayed as she walked, hoping that this time in God's gorgeous creation was good medicine for his soul. But she sometimes wondered if she should push harder for him to overcome the pain he carried. Did he truly find those sheep of his to be a sufficient substitute for the pastor's heart the Lord had placed inside of him?

For now, she'd continue to leave well enough alone. It was her job to be there for him, not to fix him. She studied his profile. "Have you stopped by to check on Ana again?"

His scowl returned. "Best if I steer clear, don't you think?"

No, she did not. The man had so much kindness and wisdom to give. "Stopping by for a neighborly 'hello' might make a better impression than camping out in her driveway."

He grunted an unintelligible reply.

"What exactly were you trying to accomplish that night?"

His mouth opened and then clamped shut after a few more strides. He shook his head and continued down the trail. "We'll scare off the birds if we keep on yapping."

"I'd rather miss the birds than miss the point."

He quirked an eyebrow.

"Of why we're out here," she continued after she'd pulled in the necessary oxygen while they crested the small hill. "You ought to know that I don't come out here every Thursday for the birds, Sam."

13

What started as hidden picnics in the grove of rhododendron had transformed into reckless handholding in plain sight as Viola and Trilby took sunset strolls in the fields adjacent to the Chambers's home while her father was away.

Like Momma said, Viola could choose her own path. Just because she had an outlaw for a father didn't mean she couldn't choose the life of a preacher's wife for herself.

She could be the captain of her own destiny.

So that Sunday, with their father still down in the valley, Viola and Cora ventured back to church for the first time since their first clandestine appearance. But this time, they didn't scurry along the hidden paths. They walked the main road. Viola held her chin high, daring any busybody to spread the word that she was brazenly disobeying the infamous Wild Wayne.

When they entered the church, she didn't slink into the back row. She marched all the way down the aisle and sat at the front, Cora following behind.

Reverend Chambers approached them with a wide smile. When he shook their hands, he pumped both their arms like he expected water to come out of their mouths instead of words. "So lovely to have you ladies in service with us today."

His wife came in behind him, just as warm in her greeting but much gentler with her delicate handshake.

Marilyn skipped over and flung her arms around Cora's neck, and both girls giggled. From his place on the platform, Trilby gave Viola a nod and a smile that melted her insides like butter left in the summer sunshine.

A few more women came in, children in tow. Widow Calloway took up the same space she had during the last visit. Viola felt an odd sense of pride in the Chambers family, as if it were her own. Little by little they were making connections with the mountain folks.

It wasn't so much that the people in Bitter End didn't believe in God, Viola mused. More that He was not the center of their existence. Only a part. Left waiting too long on the mantel, like Momma's Bible.

Trilby plucked out a tune on the mountain dulcimer resting across his lap. Viola was certain there was nothing more beautiful than hearing him play an instrument common to her mountain home.

His mother joined him on the platform, but this week Marilyn didn't head up front, opting instead to sidle in beside Cora.

Trilby began playing "Rock of Ages." His mother joined in song, and a little thrill shot through Viola as Trilby lifted his voice, his deeper tones harmonizing with his mother's high, clear lilt.

She tried to focus her mind on the subject of the song instead of the singer. She really did. Though she was just a simple girl who'd never set foot outside of Bitter End, she was smart enough to know it wasn't proper to moon over a boy when she was supposed to be praising the Lord.

She shut her eyes and lifted her voice. Her heart felt so light and free, she was sure she was just about to soar right up to the rafters.

A crash at the back of the church followed by a rush of wind that fluttered the pages of the hymnals silenced the tiny congregation.

Her father's hulking form eclipsed the open door. His hair stood up on his head, and his long beard was mussed.

Viola's heart thudded so hard she looked down, sure the thrashing of her vital organ was visible through the fabric of her best dress. She gripped the pew with one hand. With the other, she reached for her sister. So this was what it was like to stand in his enemies' shoes.

"Viola. Cora. Let's go," her father thundered.

No matter how much she wanted to apologize to Trilby for the scene her father was causing right in the middle of the worship service, she could not bring herself to meet his gaze. A gaze that bore into her back as she and Cora slinked back up an aisle she'd boldly strolled not ten minutes prior.

Passing by her father as she exited the building, she was sure she could feel a literal chill coming from his stalwart figure. She and Cora walked out the door single file, and still Cora gripped her hand so tight that the fingernails that she habitually gnawed to the quick pricked Viola's palm.

"Truck." Her father spoke the word in a low growl and pointed to where the vehicle idled by the roadside.

During the short ride home, with his girls crammed together on the bench seat of his truck, he said not a word.

Viola silently prayed. She wasn't sure what to ask for, other than for God to calm her father's anger. She'd never seen him quite like this, but then again, Viola had never been caught defying her father's commands outright.

Daddy parked beneath the hovering branches of the tall oak in their front yard.

He sat silent for a moment, heaved a breath, and then said, "Cora, go to your mother. Viola and I have something we need to discuss."

Cora shot her a sympathetic look and then wriggled her hand free from Viola's clutch.

After the screen door closed behind Cora, her father opened

the driver's side door. He turned, stooping slightly to catch her gaze. "Viola?"

She obeyed, sliding out of the truck and straightening her dress. She glanced at the house where Cora and Momma peered out the picture window.

Her father walked in the direction of the barn, cresting a small incline, and Viola followed even though everything in her wanted to run into her mother's sheltering arms. When they reached the top of the hill, he spoke again. "Do you see all of this? This beautiful land. The well-fed livestock." He fingered the lace on her dress sleeve, the delicate weave catching slightly on his calloused skin. "The clothes you, your sister, and your momma wear." He gestured toward the house. "The roof over your head that has never leaked, not one day in your life." He crossed his arms over his chest. "Do you think that all the families up on this old mountain could have afforded the medicine that saved your life last winter?"

Her heart clenched, remembering how close to death she'd been.

"Well, do you?" His harsh tone battered her soul.

"I—"

"They could. Every single one of them. Because of *me*, Viola Mae Whitt. Because either I provided the work, or I had the ability to give provisions to those strugglin'." He shook his head, disgust on his face. "And to see you, my own flesh and blood, high and mighty in the pew, playing church with those outsiders who are here to threaten everything I've built."

"They're good people. They're kind. They care about the community too. Just in a different way."

He turned on her, his glare sharp enough to draw blood. "Well then I've failed as a father if the child I've raised eighteen years doesn't understand the delicate balance of life in these hills.

"Before my grandfather, people were nearabout starving to death up here. Rocky soil. Wrecked crops. It wasn't enough to eke out a living on. People were suffering."

"Why didn't they just move somewhere better?"

Her father looked at Viola like he pitied her. "During the Depression, there wasn't anywhere better." He turned to the east, and she followed his gaze, beholding the beauty of the mountaintops that rolled all the way to the horizon. "Regardless, this mountain is more than a place to live. But you, dear one, have lived too privileged a life to see how people are connected to this place—blood, sweat, tears. Heritage is embedded in this old rocky soil."

"Daddy, I'm not trying to deny my heritage by simply going to church."

"You're smarter than you're acting, Viola Mae. You're doing more than going to church. You're courting a boy in secret. A boy whose family has come up on our highlands, inserting themselves in our way of life, hoping to disrupt it. Telling people who they are and how they put food in their families' mouths is a sin."

"Isn't it?"

Her father's face grew red as Momma's pickled beets. "You ever watched a baby die from starvation right in front of your eyes?"

She swallowed hard, and he tore his gaze away from hers. "Until you have, I don't want to hear your judgment. Or that preacher's."

He went quiet. Merry little songbirds filled the silence, oblivious to the roaring in Viola's ears—the tectonic shift between father and daughter. There was a brokenness she'd never seen in her father's eyes. For just a moment, the vulnerability behind his gruff exterior slipped through the cracks forming between them. Momma's words echoed back to her. *It's a dangerous game you're playing, Viola Mae.*

His gaze hardened as he shifted away from her. "Our family saved this mountain."

She blurted out the question that had been burning in her mind since she was old enough to understand what her daddy did for a living. "But moonshining is illegal. And what about all the sinning that people do because they're drunk off the very stuff you make? What about the killing people have done over stills and territory?"

Her father drew himself to his full height. "First off, I don't owe an explanation to you. Second, what killin'? Might be that you've read the papers about things happening on other mountaintops. But not up here. Not in Bitter End. Ever wonder why that is, little girl?" He scoffed. "You want me to shut down? Stop being Wild Wayne Lee Whitt who strikes fear in the heart of any man who even thinks about crossing him? Sure. Then there will be little operations popping up all over these hills. Rough characters taking advantage of the lack of law and order. Feuds and fights. *Killin's.* There will always be people ready to buy white lightning. Question is, who do you want selling it? Me or them?"

He gave her an appraising glance. "I'll leave you with your thoughts, Viola. You've decisions to be made today. Do you want to be the daughter of the wicked ole moonshiner or do you want to be the young preacher's wife? You can't be both."

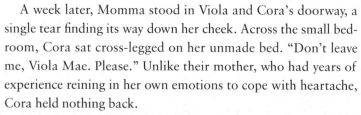

A week later, Momma stood in Viola and Cora's doorway, a single tear finding its way down her cheek. Across the small bedroom, Cora sat cross-legged on her unmade bed. "Don't leave me, Viola Mae. Please." Unlike their mother, who had years of experience reining in her own emotions to cope with heartache, Cora held nothing back.

"I'm only moving in with the Widow Calloway," Viola told her. "Not more than a mile away. You're both acting like I'm going to the moon."

But all three of them knew better. When Viola had chosen to follow her heart to the old clapboard church and into Trilby Chambers's arms, she had chosen a different world. Her father's interruption of that service had been a blessing in disguise, because it had forced her to explain to Trilby who her father was. She thought he'd turn and run the other way, but when she told him about her father's ultimatum, he'd simply held out his arms and said, "Pick me."

The decision had been easier than she'd anticipated. Choosing Trilby was choosing to be truly free from the Bitter End life that had been predestined for her.

Viola packed a few belongings into the suitcase that had never been on a single trip. She closed the lid, and the metallic click of the latches rang out in the bedroom.

The rest of the spring and summer, she would assist the widow in her apothecary. And though there hadn't been an official proposal, there would be a wedding. Then off to Louisville she'd go. A new life. A preacher's wife. A world of clearly defined right and wrong, far from her father's many shades of gray.

The three women huddled in an embrace, clinging to one another so long that Viola's arms started to ache.

From the doorway, her father cleared his throat. "Best you get going before dark falls." His words were like ice slipping down her spine, but she noticed moisture glistening in his eyes. She wanted to scream at him. Tell him that it did not have to be this way. But he had already laid down the law and would not recant, forcing her to choose between her past and her future.

She released her mother and sister and hoisted the suitcase. Her father stepped out of the doorway and let her pass.

It might as well have been a funeral procession, this final walk through the house that had raised her. Deep down, a knowing grew in her gut that once she crossed this threshold, she would never come back. At least, not as the girl she'd once been.

Across the porch, down the stairs, the moonshiner's daughter no longer.

She turned back one final time. Cora, Momma, and her father stood on the porch, watching her walk the long path alone. It was enough to make her want to forget the love thrumming in her heart.

But at the road, Trilby waited. He'd take the heavy load from her arms and carry it for her, off into their new life.

14

Two hours later a vet tech met Ana in the waiting room with a piece of paper in hand. She rattled off a list of the dog's ailments and the corresponding treatments administered, the greatest concerns being dehydration and malnourishment. She passed Ana the bill and told her that the vet would like to go over the finer details of the dog's needed care.

Ana glanced at the bottom of the invoice, and her eyes widened. "This isn't my dog."

The tech tilted her head. "You stayed."

Ana had planned to hightail it out of there as soon as Jake and Inez helped her through the door with the sick animal, but she found herself glued to that plastic chair in the waiting room like it was a family member having a touch-and-go operation instead of a stray. She'd never had a pet in her life. Her parents were both extremely allergic to everything with fur, so she'd always assumed she was too.

"We thought perhaps you'd decided to adopt. Or donate to her care fund?"

What they'd hoped was that some sucker had come along ready to foot the bill. Ana massaged her temples. *She* was that sucker. At what point was someone going to jump out with a hidden camera and confess that her mishaps in Bitter End had all been a part of some elaborate prank?

She sighed and looked again at the total. It would put a hefty dent in her savings account. Maybe this selfless act would help her feel a little more like the hero people claimed she was. If the dog's care was covered, it would help them find a home for it. "Okay."

The tech brightened. "Wonderful, just see the front desk, and I'll let Doc Underwood know."

Ana approached the counter after the tech bounced through the door to the examination area. The receptionist thanked her as she processed the payment, then handed her a receipt. "If you'll wait right here for just a moment, Zoe will take you back."

The vet probably wanted to thank her in person for the donation. She sent a text to Jake to let him know that she was almost ready to go. The couple had kindly offered to give her a ride back home after she was finished at the vet's office. She shook her head and entertained herself imagining what kinds of couples would pay to get married in Jake and Inez's minibus.

Ten minutes later, the vet tech, whom Ana now knew was named Zoe, motioned her through the door. "Follow me!" Her blond bob bounced with her stride.

The odd scent of antiseptic mixed with animal wrinkled Ana's nose. Zoe opened one of the doors, and Ana stepped into an exam room. A woman in a white coat stood next to the table, crooning softly to the dog that stared back at her with bleary eyes.

The vet turned to them as the door shut behind Ana. "She's a real sweetheart, this one." The dog's short tail quivered, and she whined at the sight of Ana. Ana remained rooted to the spot despite the tug on her heart, beckoning her closer. She was not a dog person.

The vet introduced herself as Doc Underwood. "You found her on the road?"

"Standing in the middle of it."

Doc Underwood nodded thoughtfully. "I'm not sure where she's from, but she's had a long, hard journey trying to get somewhere. I was a little surprised she wasn't microchipped. I know she doesn't look like much at the moment, but she appears to be a well-bred German shorthaired pointer. Likely someone's hunting dog. If she's had formal training, they've invested a pretty penny into her."

"Oh?" Ana said to fill the momentary pause in the vet's words.

"They have a high prey drive, so sometimes they start chasing after something and end up separated from their owner. Or with breeds like this, people just turn them outside because they can't deal with their energy level, and they end up lost. She's lucky she found you. I'm not sure how much longer she would have made it on her own."

The dog crawled to the edge of the table like it wanted to jump down.

Affection bloomed in Ana's middle. At least she'd done someone some good today. "Well, she's in your expert care now. I'm glad I could help. I'd be happy to put up some posters or something. Or maybe post in an online group for lost dogs."

"That might turn something up," Doc Underwood said, but she didn't look hopeful. "About her ongoing care . . ." The vet glanced at Zoe, who was rolling her bottom lip between her teeth. "Zoe told me about your generous donation. I know it is a lot to ask, but I was hoping we could ask one more thing of you."

Apprehension tiptoed up Ana's spine.

"We've made some calls, and all of our approved medical fosters are currently full. One might come open next week. We have a rescue that specializes in rehoming sporting breeds that she can go to, but they won't take her until she's adoptable. We could board her here, but we think she'd be happier and heal faster if she could get some one-on-one care in a quieter environment."

Ana swallowed. And they thought she could provide that? They didn't know her from Adam. "I'm not a dog person." *And I barely know how to deal with my own issues.*

On cue the pointer whined and laid her scratched-up head on her paws.

Doc Underwood gently stroked the dog's side. "That may be so, but it sure seems like this pup is an Ana person."

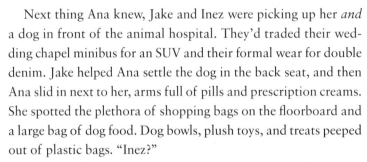

Next thing Ana knew, Jake and Inez were picking up her *and* a dog in front of the animal hospital. They'd traded their wedding chapel minibus for an SUV and their formal wear for double denim. Jake helped Ana settle the dog in the back seat, and then Ana slid in next to her, arms full of pills and prescription creams. She spotted the plethora of shopping bags on the floorboard and a large bag of dog food. Dog bowls, plush toys, and treats peeped out of plastic bags. "Inez?"

Inez turned in her seat. "Seein' as how you probably didn't have any pet supplies on hand, and how we sorta contributed to you being in this situation, it was the least we could do."

Ana smiled weakly. "*You* could take her home."

Inez flipped down the mirrored visor and inspected her vibrant makeup. "We've got an old one-eyed cat. If my Merlyn sets his green eye on a dog, half his hair'll fall out."

It was worth a try. Ana rubbed one of the dog's velvet ears between her fingers. "Looks like we're stuck with each other for a little while then, girl."

Jake cranked the engine. "Got a name picked out?"

Ana wrinkled her nose. "For the dog?"

"No, the freckle on my big toe," he deadpanned. "Of course, the dog."

"Whoever adopts her should have that honor." The animal gazed up at her in adoration. Ana stifled a groan.

Jake glanced in the rearview mirror, catching her eye. "You can't keep calling that poor thing 'the dog.'"

She glanced at the canine's speckled fur and raised an eyebrow. "How about Spot?"

"Well, she does have a lot of spots." Inez giggled. "Jacob, she oughta get to know the dog a little before coming up with a name."

Jake scoffed. "No need to use a sledgehammer to swat flies. It's just a name, Nezzie."

"You know I hate when you call me that."

Ana cut in, attempting to diffuse the slight tension rising in the front seat. "I'm not going to have this dog long enough to get to know it, but if you think of a good name, text it to me."

The dog whined and scooted closer to her on the bench seat, until its wet nose bumped her bare forearm. "Cool it, Spot. This is temporary."

15

The choice to leave her old life behind had made Viola feel brave and reckless. Free.

But two days after she moved out of her parents' home, as she sat in a straight-backed wooden chair, mending the widow's holey underthings beneath a roof that required a handful of pots to catch the rainwater pouring from the sky, her decision didn't feel adventurous. It felt foolish.

What had she really been chasing?

God?

The love of a boy she barely knew?

Freedom from a life that had started to feel stifling?

Had she simply been trying to figure out who she was apart from her father's reputation? If that was the case, had she really needed a declaration of independence to achieve the desired result?

Viola tucked away her mending. She needed to get started on her two-mile trek to school. It would not be pleasant in the pouring rain, but there was no way she'd miss the chance to see Cora. She never thought she'd miss sharing a room with her noisy little sister, but at least Cora didn't rattle the rafters with her snores like Viola's new elderly housemate. She slipped into a borrowed slicker and tied a plastic rain bonnet in place to protect her hair.

Just as she stepped onto the sagging front porch, a car stopped in front of the house.

Trilby exited the vehicle and jogged around to the passenger side. "Hop in. Let me give you a ride."

He looked so handsome with rainwater curling his auburn hair that all the worry from moments before faded. She was not venturing into this new world alone. Trilby would be there.

She slid into the passenger seat.

"Good morning," Marilyn chirped from behind her. "I'm so glad Daddy let Trilby use the car today."

"Me too," Viola replied as Trilby slid into the driver's side. He threaded his fingers with hers, and though both their hands were damp, his were warm and provided the comfort she so desperately craved. She might be a fool, but she was a fool in love. And this love of theirs could conquer anything. Maybe even her father's hardened heart. One of these days he'd come around and invite her back into his life. She just needed to give it a little time.

At the school, Trilby pulled as close to the front steps of the schoolhouse as he dared without earning a scolding from Mrs. Lambert. He planted a kiss on Viola's cheek and then she and Marilyn dashed inside.

Viola took her seat next to the teacher's where a stack of writing assignments from the younger children had already been waiting for her attention. Viola graded papers, ears trained on the door. Anytime it creaked open, she lifted her chin, hungry for the sight of her little sister.

But she never came.

After Mrs. Lambert rang the morning bell, Viola took attendance. A handful of students always stayed home in wet weather. But her father typically drove them to school on days like these.

She set the attendance sheet on the teacher's desk. "I wonder what kept Cora home today."

Mrs. Lambert's brow creased. "Oh, honey, I thought you'd know. Your father stopped by my house Sunday and told me that Cora was being withdrawn from school for the rest of the year. Your mother is going to handle her education from here on out."

Viola couldn't stop the gasp that slipped between her lips from the gut punch of the woman's words.

Was her father that worried Cora would be lured away from the fold by Viola's poisonous influence?

16

Ana gasped awake in the predawn as a cold, damp dog nose slid under her hand. The animal sidled closer and let out a pathetic whine. "Oh, all right. I'm getting up." Ana shucked off her blankets and slid her feet into borrowed slippers, blinking the sleep from her eyes.

At the movement, the dog bounded from the bed, paced to the bedroom door, and bumped it with her nose before returning to Ana.

"Patience, you." Ana slid on a pair of shorts and threw a sweatshirt over the large tee she'd been sleeping in. She stumbled toward the front door, her limbs still dead-certain she should be horizontal in her bed until the sun rose over the mountaintop. After two weeks as a temporary dog parent, Ana would have expected to have adjusted to the animal's insistent wake-up calls.

Doc Underwood had advised her to keep the dog on a leash at all times, especially during her recovery. She was starting to understand why. As the dog began to heal, Ana caught glimpses of the typical activity level of her breed. Hopefully whoever adopted her would have a large fenced-in place for her to play.

While Ana slipped on her shoes, the canine repeatedly circled

Ana and then went to the door as if to say, "Come on. Open it already."

Once her laces were tied, Ana picked up the leash. "Sit, Pippi," she said, trying out a name for her temporary charge. Pippi instantly sat, quivering with potential energy.

Ana clipped the leash, and the dog shot toward the door, practically dragging her. Ana groaned. The forty-five-pound canine was far stronger than she looked, inspiring her temporary name. Ana's favorite childhood character, Pippi Longstocking, was known for possessing strange degrees of strength in her scrawny body.

"Hey. You have to behave. Sit." The dog sat, eyes locked on the doorknob. "Now, wait." Ana cracked the front door open, and Pippi surged forward. As she'd learned from an online instructional video, Ana closed the door quickly and gave a quick tug on the leash. "No. Sit." The dog sat. Ana cracked the door again, and though Pippi's muscles shivered beneath her skin like she'd been caught hairless in an arctic wind, she remained in her sitting position as Ana pulled the door open. Triumph welled within her. In the next instant, Pippi bolted, dragging Ana a few steps before she was able to get her feet under her. "Pippi, no," she ground out through gritted teeth. *Birdbrained dog.*

Pippi circled Ana, wrapping the leash around her legs in the process, and then sat with her ears perked, an adoring gaze locked on Ana. It turned out that training Pippi was an awful lot like teaching kindergartners.

Ana sighed and scratched the dog behind her ear. "I've not had enough coffee to put up with your antics."

The online dog training videos helped. Sort of. Every time she thought they were making progress, Pippi would nearly yank her arm off moments later.

Ana extricated herself from the tangled leash and then followed Pippi, who sniffed in large looping trails before finally doing her business. Like it or not, Pippi had officially wormed her way into Ana's Bitter End summer. The obedience training was for pure practicality purposes, of course. It would be easier for Pippi to be adopted if she was trained, and it might help Ana keep her shoulder in socket until a rescue placement could be found. Had she also found satisfaction in teaching her unwanted companion? She'd never confess it.

As to sleeping in her bed? The first time it happened, the little stinker had snuck up there while Ana was in her comatose stage of sleep. And when she'd woken, sleeping on her side with the warmth of the dog curled in the crook of her knees, she didn't have the heart to make her move. It was also the first morning in eight months that Ana hadn't been startled awake by a nightmare.

Ana walked alongside Pippi, who crept in slow motion, her short tail sticking out like an RC car antenna, as she stalked a bird in the bush. "You look ridiculous with your little creepy walk, you know."

Just then the dog froze on three legs, the front right paw cocked, body in a straight line from nose to tail.

Ana scanned the area. Rustling in the brush ahead snagged her attention. "Oh. I see it. Good girl." At the praise, the dog's tail wagged the barest fraction before stilling in her classic pointer's pose. "Maybe next week we'll try out a hike at the state park. Think your paws are healed enough for that?"

Just then she heard the rumble of an engine and then caught a glimpse of a too-familiar truck coming over the hill. She tugged Pippi inside.

She shut the front door behind her and shook her head. She was being ridiculous. This was probably just part of Sam's normal route home. He wasn't checking up on her.

Yet Sam's daily drive past her aunt's house felt a little too much like Pippi trying to sneak up on the bird in the bush.

Sam had tried to take Marilyn's advice. He truly had. But every time he passed Ana's house, he couldn't quite work up the courage to pull into the drive. He was certain she'd caught him sleeping in her driveway the morning after they'd met. And until he could find a way to explain his behavior, how could he face her?

Sam shook his head, thinking about her following that bird dog around the yard this morning as it walked through the overgrown grass. He had no idea where she'd gotten a dog, but it made him feel better knowing she wasn't completely alone.

He gripped the back of his neck, squeezing tight as he steered one-handed into his driveway. Why had this woman turned him inside out like this? No woman, not since Marcy, had occupied so much of his mind.

He grimaced at the pain that thought carried.

But why? Was it because, like his wife, Ana emanated this odd mixture of strength and fragility? Jaded and yet somehow maintaining an aura of innocence? Or maybe his preoccupation had more to do with him than her.

He put the truck in park and leaned his head against the headrest, eyes shut tight. Him and his stupid pride. No matter how hard he'd tried to bury it, part of him still believed he had the power to help the hurting.

He jumped out of the truck, slamming the door behind him as if it could jar loose the nonsense clouding his mind.

He had sheep to tend. People were not his problem anymore.

A week later, Ana loaded Pippi into the car. Doc Underwood had given them the all-clear to take a trail hike, assuring Ana that Pippi's paws were healing nicely.

Ana plopped behind the wheel and double-checked the supplies she'd piled in the passenger seat.

Leash.

Fanny pack with treats and pet waste bags.

Day pack with water for herself and the dog.

Ana scoffed. Reinvention had been on her to-do list when she'd left Ridgeford, but this dog parent version of herself was not what she'd anticipated.

Pippi's whistling whine grated on her nerves. "Chill. We're going."

When Ana cranked the engine, Pippi pranced back and forth on the back seat.

"Sit." Pippi listened, but not before sneaking a lick to the back of her ear. "Okay. That's crossing a line. Keep your kisses to yourself." She glanced over her shoulder. The bright-eyed dog was completely unabashed.

Pippi was fairly obedient, though her impulse control was lacking, reminiscent of some of the boys Ana had taught. Every year, there was at least one. When reprimanded they quickly obeyed, but in a blink found themselves breaking another class rule. A symptom not of defiance but of abundant energy too-long constrained.

And she and Pippi both had been too-long constrained.

Ana drove along the road, slowing as she passed Marilyn's house. At least, she thought it was Marilyn's house. One time when Ana had driven by, delivering boxes of books from Cora's book room, she'd seen the woman out filling bird feeders in the front yard.

And every time she passed since, she'd slowed, trying to glean what she could about this seemingly innocuous older woman Cora had told her to avoid.

Ana pressed the accelerator, chastising herself. She was as bad as Sam.

After she made it down the winding road, she headed for Roan Mountain State Park. Doc Underwood had recommended a few light hiking trails where Pippi could do a little exploring. She said that exercising Pippi's brain was just as important as exercising her body.

Besides the good news that Pippi was on the mend, the vet reported they had a lead on a potential rescue placement. As Ana parked the car and walked around to the passenger side, she attempted to dissect the ache in her chest at the thought. Saying goodbye was for the best. She was not equipped to steward a dog who required such intense care. If this past year had taught her anything, it was that she needed to accept her limits when caring for others and step aside when necessary.

But would her nightmares return in the dog's absence? A selfish thought, perhaps, but she'd grown to appreciate the comfort Pippi gave.

Ana did a double take as she pulled into the parking area. Jake and Inez's mobile wedding chapel stuck out among the Subarus and Kias like a flamingo in a crowd of penguins. A wedding in the woods, perhaps? That seemed more appealing than being married on a bus.

Ana opened the passenger door. Before she could get a command out, Pippi bolted from the car in a blur of white and brown.

"No. Sit." The one command Pippi reliably obeyed went in one ear and out the other. Those ears flapped with each ground-eating stride as the animal disappeared down the trail.

Ana groaned and jogged after her, ignoring the twinge in her knee. "PIP-EEEEE!" Ana called as loud as she could. She passed a couple hikers coming the opposite direction who looked at her like she had three heads. They scooted to the side to allow her passage.

Breathless, she croaked out, "Have you seen a dog?"

They pointed down the trail.

But how long until the animal traded the prescribed path for the tangle of rhododendron? She continued on, her lungs begging for oxygen and her knee weakening beneath her. The longer she traveled without any sign of her dog, the harder she fought the panic clawing up her throat. *Her dog?* "PIP-EEEEEE! Come, Pippi, come!" Over and over, she called out, knowing full well that the dog was far more invested in chasing down its prey than listening to her.

Side aching, she slowed to a stop. Tears sprang to her eyes that had nothing to do with the throbbing in her knee. She swiped at her face, dreading the call to the vet, letting them know they wouldn't be needing that rescue placement after all. She should have been more prepared. Better yet, she should have refused to take on a job when she knew she wasn't equipped for it in the first place. The past eight months had taught her nothing.

"PIP-EEEE! Come, Pippi!" This last-ditch effort to recall the dog came out as more of a desperate wail than a command. She walked a little longer, heavily limping now, unable to make herself turn back. Occasionally, she'd call out again. Passing hikers gave her the strangest looks, as if they'd never seen a person with a lost dog before.

After about thirty minutes of hopeless searching, she rounded the bend of the trail and saw something that took her a moment to make sense of.

A circle of people stood with binoculars raised to the treetops. In the center was Pippi in a dead point. A bird dog and . . . bird-watchers?

17

One by one the sets of binoculars lowered. Sam. Jake. Inez. And Marilyn. Pippi never moved. She could have been a figurine, if a figurine had the capacity to quiver in coiled anticipation.

"Well, hello there, honey." Marilyn beamed. "I didn't realize that you'd planned to join us, after all. We would have waited for you."

"No, I—"

"You really aren't a dog person, are you?" Jake's cheeks reddened with the effort of holding in laughter.

Indignation roiled in her gut as she approached. "She bolted. I—" Tightness in her throat cut away her words. She snapped a leash on the dog. Ana blinked away tears, all her held-back emotions crashing over her now that the search was over.

Inez drew close and patted her shoulder. "Maybe you should have stuck with Spot, dear. It was a fine name." She glared at her husband, who was now doubled over in laughter. "I shouldn't have pressured you."

Ire rising at Jake's laughing and Inez's patronizing, Ana darted her gaze around the group, hunting for compassion. Sam, the man who she'd thought wore a permanent scowl, attempted to hide his smile under the guise of wiping his face with his hand. Marilyn shrugged and rejoined Pippi in her bird-watching.

Jake straightened, swiping the tears from his cheeks and fighting back his guffaws with little success. "You named the dog PeePee?" He snorted. He doubled over again, lost to his mirth.

She backed away from the group. Somewhere along the way, she must have made a severely wrong turn to land in this moment. Had it been the dog fostering? The hike? The move out here? Something further back? "Her name is Pippi. Like Pippi Longstocking." She managed to push the words past the tightness in her throat, tugging the dog out of her point and urging her back the way they'd come.

She'd laugh about this later, when she wasn't fighting the stupid embarrassed tears welling in her eyes. Ugh. She used to be so much better at laughing at herself. It was practically an official part of a kindergarten teacher's job qualifications. Those little kids had the corner market on brutal but endearing honesty.

"I'm really sorry about her getting loose and running up on you all like that." Ana looked away. "Let's go, girl."

"Wait." She turned back at the sound of Sam's voice, unexpectedly warm, like hot fudge on a scoop of ice cream.

Marilyn looked to Sam, a tender smile curling the corners of her mouth. "Yes. Please stay," she said to Ana. "Your pup there just helped us spy the elusive tufted titmouse. Maybe a bird dog is the perfect addition to our bird-watching group."

Was Marilyn making fun of her too? She'd seen four birds that looked an awful lot like that one at Marilyn's bird feeders when she'd driven by.

Brows raised in a mock-serious expression, Sam said, "Sure, a bird dog would make a great addition. Aside from the small detail that the dog is bred to *hunt* birds."

Marilyn propped her hands on her hips. "She's bred to *spot* them, which is the same activity we're obsessed with. So I think it could work."

"I think I'd better take her home." Ana tightened her hands on the leash, digging her nails into her palm, trying to fight back those confounded, useless emotions welling to the surface.

Jake, who was still trying to calm himself, smoothed his beard. "I'm sorry for laughing at your dog's name. I just got tickled. It's been so long since I've had a good laugh. Whew. I needed that." He braced his hands on his knees.

Inez glared at him and then scratched the dog behind her ears. "Maybe shorten it to Pip? That's real cute."

Despite herself, a corner of her mouth tugged upward imagining what everyone hiking must have heard as she'd called for the dog.

Sam lifted his shoulders. "That would probably avoid it sounding like someone is crashing through the woods, dealing with extreme urinary difficulties."

Jake chortled. "Come, pee pee, come!" He winked. "As a kid I loved Pippi Longstocking too, but it has its drawbacks as a pet name."

Ana fought a war with herself. Half of her laughing, the other half scouting for a cave to crawl into. Again, she edged away, but the dog-who-must-be-renamed resisted the tension on the leash, clearly still excited about the birds overhead.

"Well, it was good to see you all," she lied.

Marilyn stepped closer to Ana. "I do wish you'd join us. I'm now quite curious to see how well a bird dog fits in as a member of a bird-watching society."

"This is a bird-watching *society*?" It seemed a rather stately title for the odd collection of people making an awful lot of noise on this busy trail.

"Sure is. This is the Bitter End Birding Society." Marilyn started walking down the trail like she was a tour guide, and Ana found herself following despite her fractured pride. Pip walked demurely alongside her, as if Ana hadn't just sprinted through the woods to catch her.

"You're limping. Did you hurt yourself?" Marilyn asked, her brow furrowed.

Ana brushed her worry aside with the flick of her hand. "An old injury. It's not too happy with the dog chase. Nothing to worry about though. I'm fine."

Thankfully Marilyn accepted her explanation and continued with her story. "My husband and I founded this little club, and I've attempted to continue it on now that he's passed." Sadness flickered in Marilyn's eyes for a moment before she continued her oral history of the Bitter End Birding Society. "All of us live in or around what was once commonly known as Bitter End, which is smack-dab where Cora lives. As time went on, the unincorporated area was absorbed by the town of Roan Mountain, and the name of the place was lost to history. But it still comes up on the map if you search for it."

Ana smiled. "My best friend from home has me on a mission to find out how this place got its name."

"It's a strange one, for sure." Marilyn hiked onward.

"The name or the story?"

Marilyn took several strides before answering. "Both. It's a bit of a joke around here. You know you are truly a local when you've invented your own version of the story. Nobody knows which one is true."

Ana glanced over her shoulder. Jake, Inez, and Sam all followed. Jake and Inez had their heads bent close, apparently bickering about something judging by Inez's jerky hand motions while Jake scowled. Sam shot them an annoyed look, and after issuing a resigned sigh, lifted his gaze to the trees.

Ana wasn't sure if she was more curious about how Bitter End got its name or how Marilyn had collected this hodgepodge troupe of humanity. A shepherd. The proprietors of a mobile wedding chapel. A widow. And now, it seemed, Marilyn hoped to add a runaway kindergarten teacher and a bird dog to the mix.

The thought gave her pause. Runaway. It was clear enough what the dog-who-must-be-renamed was running after. Birds. Always birds. But what was it that Ana hoped to find this summer away?

"Ana?" The concern tinging Marilyn's tone cued her in to the fact that this was not Marilyn's first attempt at getting her attention.

"I'm sorry?"

"I was just asking how long you thought you'd be staying."

"Oh, until my aunt returns from her world tour. Then I'll be racing back to get ready for my new students."

As Ana spoke, color drained from Marilyn's face. Was the woman unwell? Ana prepared herself to brace Marilyn up, should it come to that. Marilyn was quiet for a few moments and then seemed to regain her composure. "You're a teacher?"

"Kindergarten."

Marilyn chuckled. "God bless you."

"The kids always keep me on my toes."

Marilyn cleared her throat and then stopped on the trail, fidgeting with her aluminum walking stick. "Cora is your . . . your aunt?"

Unsure what to make of Marilyn's unease, she nodded. "My great-aunt, yes. I found Cora through an ancestry website a few years back. We've kept in touch over the past several years."

"How nice," Marilyn said.

This was Ana's chance to get to the bottom of Cora's odd warning. "Do you know her well? Have you been neighbors a long time?"

Marilyn seemed to ponder her questions. "Cora and I met when I moved here as a girl. I was ten and she was eight. But then I ended up having to move away. I returned to Bitter End with my husband for his research work, but Cora was . . . well, we didn't leave on the best of terms all those years ago. Friendship just doesn't seem to be on the menu for us anymore." Marilyn's voice held so much ache, it made Ana's chest tighten.

"You and Cora were childhood friends?"

A corner of Marilyn's mouth lifted. "Of a sort. But friendship is complicated when your daddy is the preacher and your best friend is the moonshiner's daughter."

18

Viola stepped into the bliss of spring sunshine that Friday. She'd stayed after school, finishing up grading the elementary spelling tests. A smile split her face when she spotted Trilby waiting for her by the car. Marilyn had already slid into the back seat.

She hurried over and brushed a quick kiss to Trilby's cheek. "I'm sorry you waited. There's something I need to do, and a car can't take me there."

He shook his head. "I was trying to save you from having mud to your ankles," he said as he walked around to the driver's side.

She laughed over her shoulder as she walked away. "I'm a mountain girl, Trilby Chambers. Mud washes off just fine."

It had rained every day since Viola had left home, as if her exodus had ushered the spring storms. Beneath those gray skies, new life was budding and surging forth all around her. Just like love was blooming in chaste kisses under the dripping eaves of the widow's shed. But Viola sure couldn't deny the gray.

In the distance she glimpsed one of her daddy's stills and sent up a prayer that this wasn't the territory he'd be checking on today. He'd run her off his land if he knew what she was up to.

She rounded the bend, and there stood a sight as welcome as one of Momma's fried apple pies. The little clubhouse her father had helped her build when she was Cora's age. Her foot found a twig in the path. The resounding crack seemed to echo in the quiet woods. Cora's blond head peeked out of the open doorway, her smile brighter than the sunshine. "Vi! I knew you'd come."

She closed the distance between them and wrapped her little sister in a bear hug. "First chance I got."

After a moment, Cora squirmed free from the embrace.

"How's Momma?" Viola asked.

Cora lifted a shoulder. "Missing you, that's for sure." She huffed. "I'm a disaster in the kitchen, making everything harder instead of easier on her. But I guess it feels too empty to her without you in it."

Viola's heart ached at the words, but Momma would have had to learn to get on without her eventually. It had just happened more suddenly than any of them anticipated.

She attempted to steel herself against the conflicting emotions boiling inside of her—the ache of disappointing the man she'd idolized tossed against her anger at his rigidity. "And our father?"

Cora picked at a loose thread on the sleeve of her shirt. "He goes about doing the same old things."

Viola resisted putting her hand to her breastbone to provide counter pressure to the pain her sister's words inflicted.

"But he doesn't hum anymore." Cora's eyes went round and watery. "And he hasn't picked up his fiddle to play a single note since you've been gone."

Viola drew her little sister into her arms. Like erasing the teacher's words from a blackboard, she swiped away the scrawl of pain on her own heart to make room for Cora to write her own.

"I can't believe he pulled you out of school."

Cora cocked her chin as she swiped at her face. "You did me a favor. Having to sit still all day makes me itch all over."

Cora did hate being still, but she loved learning as much as she loved playing class clown. "You should tell Marilyn about the clubhouse."

Cora's face pinched. "What about Daddy?"

No wonder their father cut Viola out of Cora's life. The first time she laid eyes on Cora in a week, she encouraged her to continue a friendship he'd forbidden. "Tell her to keep it quiet. And pay attention to his circuit for checking the stills. If he catches you, he'll just tell you to stop. He won't turn you out like he did me. You're too young for that."

Cora looked up at her with watery eyes. "So are you."

Viola braced her hands on Cora's shoulders. "I've been able to hang onto childhood longer than most in these hills. This summer, Trilby and I will wed and I'll be off this mountain. Free to choose my own life."

Cora swiped her eyes with her sleeve. "You're really going to leave?" Her bottom lip quavered.

She cupped her sister's cheek. "There's no place for me here. Not anymore. Not sure there was ever going to be. You know I've always wanted to come down off this mountain. See the world." Their father might blame Trilby for Viola's restless, wandering spirit, but if she thought back, it all started with those encyclopedias her father had bought as a gift for Momma when Viola was a little girl. A whole world in books.

She took her sister's hands in hers. "You could stay with us in Louisville next summer."

Cora's expression was equal parts hope and doubt. "You actually think he'd let me go? He won't even let me attend school."

Viola's jaw dropped. "He admits it, then? That he took you out of school to keep me away from you?"

She shrugged. "He said Momma was in the family way again, and because her health is delicate, I'm needed at home."

Viola's eyebrows shot high. Momma had lost three babies after Viola was born, ten years passing before she had Cora, followed by more losses. A row of tiny gravestones in the family plot was all there was to show for the siblings that should have been.

Cora continued, "You're not there to help, and he wants me

to help Momma with the house and do my learning while I'm at it." She pushed her hair away from her face. "That's what he said, anyway."

They curled against each other in the small space, gazing out into the forest through the opening in the lean-to.

"If I drop out of school, do you think he'd let you go back?" Viola braced herself for the answer. Could she really sacrifice her diploma to help her sister?

Cora shook her head. "You can't, Vi. I'm only in third grade. Momma can teach me all I need to know."

"Maybe I could go ahead and take the end-of-year exam now. All I do at this point is assist Mrs. Lambert and read the books she brings up from the library. I've done all the learning I'm going to do."

This time Cora gripped Viola's shoulders. "I told you I'm fine. School will be out soon anyway."

Viola searched her sister's face, looking for the anger Viola deserved. But all she found was ever-present adoration.

"I'm proud of you, Vi." There was a grit to her little sister's words. Grit that reminded her of Momma. Grit that told Viola that no matter what happened, Cora would find a way to be all right.

They exchanged hugs and promises to keep in touch using this little haven between their respective worlds to leave a note, steal a hug, and pray their father changed his mind. But Viola knew there would be no mind changing. Hers or her father's. When they'd set their minds to something, the pair of them were as immovable as Buck Mountain.

Over the next month, Viola visited the lean-to as often as she could, always bringing Cora a letter from herself and another from Marilyn.

Cora would leave behind treasures rather than words—a little bit of cheese from her goat or blossoms from Momma's flower beds. These little gifts always gave Viola a fresh douse of guilt.

Her sister made Viola the center of her world, while Viola had been wrapped up in dreaming of her new life with Trilby. Strolling hand in hand along the thicket. Stealing kisses. Making plans for the home that they would one day share. Other days were spent working at the church and visiting the young women Viola had grown up with who now had families of their own. A couple of them had even accepted her invitation to Sunday services. She couldn't explain the feeling she'd found, lifting her voice in song alongside Trilby as he played the dulcimer over a congregation that continued to grow little by little.

It didn't take long in her new life, living with Widow Calloway and taking most meals with the Chambers family, to realize that the majority of folks on this mountain had far less than what she grew up with.

The first dinner together she made the mistake of asking Mrs. Chambers if she needed help bringing out the rest of the food after the woman set the beans and cornbread on the table. The poor woman's face had taken on the blush of a summer peach.

Her words made it abundantly clear to all present at the table that being the daughter of Wild Wayne Lee Whitt provided far more creature comforts than being the child of Reverend Chambers.

Trilby, shifting in his seat, had said that being a pastor's wife wouldn't always be like it was at this mountain church. Someday they'd be in a community that wanted them there. That appreciated what they had to offer.

Reverend Chambers had bristled at his son's assertion. As he scooped a hearty portion of pinto beans onto his plate, he'd said, "Son, Jesus was not welcome in every place he went. That didn't stop him from going. Being a man of God is not about going where you are wanted. It is about going where you're called."

When they'd taken a stroll after dinner that night, Trilby had told Viola that the Chambers family hadn't always lived this way—in a little rundown house with pintos for dinner most nights. They'd once dined at parishioners' homes three out of the seven days in the week. Before Bitter End, there had been a salary that didn't force both him and his father to work a second job. But the comfort in that city church had always rubbed his father the wrong way. Trilby smiled at her then, a hint of pride in his voice when he said, "Even though people warned him not to, Dad came to Bitter End determined to reach this unchurched mountain."

She slid her hand out of his. "The people up here might not behave the way you city folks expect, but we know who Jesus is. There's a Bible on my family's mantel, and even though it doesn't come down as often as it probably ought to, come down it does. You might have noticed my sister and I knew every word to the songs you sang without cracking the hymnal." She crossed her arms over her chest.

"We might be a little rough around the edges and act less sanctified than the city folk you're accustomed to," she said, "but we have church. Occasionally." She shot him a daring look. "Meeting times and places get passed by word of mouth to those in the know, but if you behave yourself, I might sneak you in sometime."

19

Ana sat up straight in bed, startled by the crash in her dream. Panting and heart racing, she hugged her middle and forced her breathing to slow. *Strange.* Her nightmare always ended before the crash, the moment the classroom door opened and she was face-to-face with the terrified eyes of that nineteen-year-old. She always woke up believing there was time to make a different decision.

In the darkness, she reached for the comforting warmth of the renamed Pip. Up until now, the pup's presence had kept the nightmares at bay. But she was absent from her normal post. Pip stood at attention at the end of the queen-size bed.

Another crash rang out. Pip released a sharp bark. Ana stifled the shriek that shot out of her. *It wasn't a dream.*

Icy sweat bloomed across her forehead as she forced herself from the cool sheets and crept through the house, Pip following tightly behind. Her imagination conjured a thousand possible causes for the noise, but she pushed them aside. *It's probably just a nocturnal animal.*

Once they were in the living room, Pip raced ahead, pounced on the couch, and smudged the picture window with noseprints. The motion-activated floodlights threw the shadows of the surrounding maples into stark relief.

Pip emitted a guttural growl.

Ana patted her side. "It's okay, girl."

The dog continued her vigil, as doubtful of the claim as Ana was.

Another crash seemed to come from within the nearby shed. Ana smoothed her sweating palms on the legs of her pajama pants. What now? Call 911? But she couldn't have the police racing up the mountain pass to evict a wandering opossum.

She scanned the room, eyes landing on an ornate fire poker propped near the door. Which was odd, considering the fireplace looked like it hadn't been used for half a century.

Was this conveniently placed weapon an indication that Cora had left possible break-ins off the list of the house's many "quirks"?

"Stay, Pip," she said. Pip remained unresponsive to her owner, locked on the view beyond the window, muscles quivering. Ana picked up the fire poker.

Just as she opened the front door, Pip released another low growl that made the hairs on Ana's arm rise. "It's probably nothing. Do brave things, Ana Leigh Watkins. Brave things." She spoke the words aloud, but it did little to still the churning in her stomach or loosen her vise grip on the fire poker.

"Who's there? I'm calling the police."

Silence met her ears. She cautiously descended the porch stairs, straining to hear any indication of what might be lurking in the shed twenty yards away.

When she took her first step off the sidewalk, something slithered through the overgrown grass. Ana yelped. She slung the fire poker over her shoulder and ran for the house. She was ninety percent sure it wasn't fear convincing her a snake was chasing her back to the porch.

From within the house, Pip barked and pounced against the glass at the sight of Ana fleeing. Ana didn't stop until she had the front door slammed behind her. Pip jumped, cavorted, and wriggled like Ana had been gone a month and had finally returned.

She pushed the forty-five-pound bouncing canine away from her. She ought to let whoever or whatever was out there have what they wanted, snake included.

Once her heart rate slowed to something that didn't warrant emergency services, she weighed her options.

Try to go back to sleep and assume that the noise that had come from the shed wasn't a real threat to person or property.

Make herself check it out once more.

Or call for assistance.

The first two were out. There was no way she could sleep knowing someone or something lurked in the shed, nor did she possess the wherewithal to make another attempt at canvassing the situation. She opted to keep watch from the window and call for help if she had any definitive evidence that someone really was out there.

Pip circled by the door and whined.

"Uh-uh. No walks until the sun is up." She patted the couch beside her. "Lay down." Pip released a hyperbolic huff and then complied. Gaze locked on the view beyond the glass, Ana stroked the dog's short, smooth fur.

After several minutes with no further disturbances, the motion-activated floodlight extinguished. The sliver of a moon did little by way of illuminating the view.

In the dark and now silent night, with a warm, softly snoring dog curled next to her on the couch, Ana's nerves began to settle. It must have been an animal in the shed that she'd frightened off with her ruckus about the snake. If there was someone out there, surely Pip wouldn't have settled into sleep so quickly.

If not for the lingering throb in her bad knee and adrenaline in her veins, she might just follow suit. She sighed and glanced at her smartwatch. Two in the morning.

Just as her eyelids started to flutter closed, another loud crash rang out. The floodlight activated. She jumped to her feet, interrupting Pip's slumber.

Ana stared out the window, breathing hard. There had been a

tall shadow there for a moment. She was sure of it. Beside her, Pip alternated guttural growls and sharp barks.

Ana grabbed her phone, about to call the police when the image of Sam's face flashed in her mind. Not the image from their first meeting, but the Sam in the woods whose welcoming presence beckoned her to stay instead of run away to nurse her embarrassment. And Cora had told her to call him if she needed help. Ana went to the list hanging on the inside of the pantry door.

With shaking hands, she dialed.

"Hello?" Sam answered after only a few rings, his voice clear and alert.

"It's Ana. I . . . I . . . ." She swallowed and willed her voice to steady. "I think there's someone in the shed. I don't know what to do. Should I call the police?"

"Did you see anyone?"

She sank onto one of the kitchen chairs. "No. But I did see a shadow, which I could have imagined. And there was a snake I almost stepped on, but that wasn't what caused all the noise." She related everything that she had seen and heard, as well as Pip's reaction to the excitement. "Do you think someone's out there?"

"Doubt it. I'll run over real quick and check things out."

"Are you sure—"

"I'm two minutes away."

A few minutes later, she heard the low rumble of his truck pulling into the driveway. From the window she watched as Sam exited the vehicle. Ana kept her phone at the ready in case there really was a burglar.

Sam called out, "Hello. Who's there?"

He crept through the yard, picked up the fire poker, and leaned it against the maple tree, shaking his head. She might be mistaken, but the way his shoulders bounced, it looked like he was laughing. She hoped the snake bit him on the ankle. It would serve him right.

He paused and pulled a small flashlight from his back pocket, though the security lighting had the area lit up like it was bathed in noonday sun.

"Lord, protect him," she whispered, even though she'd wished a snake would bite him two breaths ago.

He walked to the shed, nudged the sliding door open, and five hunchbacked, ring-tailed intruders scurried out of the building. Pip's hackles raised, and she growled as the critters disappeared into the gully.

Ana covered her mouth, heat rising in her cheeks. She'd gotten the poor man out of bed for raccoons? Though, he didn't look like somebody recently roused from sleep. Leaving Pip, Ana went out onto the porch.

He met her on the steps. "All clear."

"I'm sorry for dragging you over here for nothing." Part of her wanted to explain her past to validate her fear, but a small voice whispered within her heart, *You don't always have to be the brave one.*

He shrugged. "I was up."

"At this time?"

"Don't sleep much." He thumbed over his shoulder. "Let me show you the shed. I suspect the raccoons decided this would make a good spot to start a family and were fighting over it. There's some damaged glassware, and there will likely be more if you don't make some repairs to the structure. Trust me, you do not want raccoons taking over that shed."

She descended the porch steps but stopped the moment before her feet left the sidewalk. Sam, sensing her hesitation, turned back to her. "The snake is long gone. You probably scared that poor thing into the next county." He had the grace to tame the upward turn at the corners of his mouth.

She followed, cringing at the whisper of their shoes in the dew-damp grass. He stopped in front of the opened door of the shed and shined his flashlight in.

There had to be at least a hundred moonshine jugs filling the room. Some neatly lined, others stacked a little haphazardly.

She stared.

"I take it you didn't know what was in here?" She could hear the smile in his voice.

"Cora mentioned that there were things of value in the shed, but I never imagined . . ."

"People will pay a pretty penny for antique moonshine crockery. At least the ones in good condition." He focused the flashlight beam on amber glass littering the ground. "The crockery is pretty tough, but they managed to knock down several of the more fragile glass stored on those upper shelves."

There was something else on the ground covered by shards. Rolled paper? "Marilyn said something about my great-grandfather being mixed up in moonshining." She glanced at him.

He nodded. "Most people who lived up here back then had a hand or two in that business. Or so I hear. My family kept sheep and maybe partook of said moonshine but didn't brew it. That I know of, anyway. Now Cora's family, your family, they were legendary." His face darkened, seemingly lost in thought before he added, "I'm a little surprised you don't know about Way—"

She bristled. "My mother's parents both died fairly young, so when my mom married into my dad's huge family, she never felt the need to go looking for her roots. I found Cora in college. Moonshining never came up." Ana clamped her mouth shut. She needed to get to bed. There was no reason to defend her scant knowledge of her family history to the man who had selflessly rescued her from territorial raccoons in the middle of the night. And it wasn't his fault that Cora had skipped town instead of spending the summer sharing their heritage with her.

"I didn't mean—" He dragged a hand over his mouth. "Never mind. But if you have questions, Marilyn might know the answers." He pointed his light toward some rotted boards near the base of the shed. "I'd get that fixed sooner than later. I doubt resident raccoons would make a great selling point."

"Thanks," she said. Her waning adrenaline had left her exhausted and cranky. She feigned a yawn. "Oh boy. The night's catching up with me."

"Yeah. I'll let you get your rest." He studied her face. "Want me to stay a little while until you get settled in?"

If only he knew what memories the night had electrified. She didn't dare sleep. Nightmares of the incident were sure to be closer to the surface tonight, even with sweet Pip at her side. "I'm fine." She gave him a half smile, remembering how much he'd hated that word when they first met. "But for real this time." As much as she wanted him gone so that she could process everything in private, the good manners her mother ingrained in her spoke out of turn. "Do you want to come in, though? I could make you some decaf or some herbal tea or something. I kinda owe you one."

He looked like he was going to say yes for about half a second before he declined. "I'll at least wait until you get inside and get settled. Good night, Ana."

She said good night to his retreating form.

The two of them were a real pair.

One moment, he felt as warm and welcoming as a well-worn flannel shirt. And the next, there was this force repelling them, like they were two magnets with the same poles pushed together. But why?

20

Between helping Mrs. Lambert prepare for the end of the school year and assisting Widow Calloway, who had been under the weather, Viola hadn't been able to make it to the lean-to in three weeks. Would Cora be waiting, or had her little sister given up on her making a reappearance?

Viola dodged the sludgy low spots in the path that cut through Mr. Beavers's back field.

The silence surrounding the lean-to made it evident Cora was absent from their little nest.

But there was a note.

Viola worked the scroll free from where it poked out of the knot hole.

Dear Viola,

Momma lost the baby. I think she always knew she would. Was she sad and tired when she carried me too? I wish you were here. You'd know how to tend to her.

Love,
Cora

The note fluttered from Viola's hands. *Dear, sweet Momma.* She ran from the lean-to to Widow Calloway's. The elderly woman sat at her workstation, binding herbs she'd collected into tidy bundles for drying in the shed.

"My mother has lost her baby. Do you have anything I can bring to her?"

The widow stood and shuffled over to where she stored all her prepared herbs and tinctures. Remedies at the ready whenever the infirm came knocking. She muttered to herself, placing things in a basket without saying a word to Viola.

When she finished, she held out the basket. "Take these. Your mother'll know how to prepare the teas and things. She's taken them all before, for the other times." The woman patted Viola's hand when she took the basket. "I'll say a prayer for her."

Viola expressed her thanks and raced for the house as fast as she dared without jostling the tiny amber bottles nestled in the straw. If she hurried, there was a good chance she'd make it home before her father returned from the day's business.

A few precious moments could be stolen. A little love and care could be infused before she disappeared back to the other side of the great divide she'd chosen.

She walked in the front door without knocking. "Cora? Momma?"

"In here," came her sister's voice, sounding decades older than it had when Viola left home two months ago.

Viola proceeded through the house, following the well-worn path. Her mother sat in bed, covers drawn across her lap. Cora nestled beside her, darning Father's socks under Momma's watchful eye.

They both looked up at her entry. Tears instantly sprang to her mother's eyes. "It sure does a body good to set my sights on you, Viola Mae." Her voice was little more than a whisper.

"It's good to see you too, Momma. I brought some herbs and

126

things from Widow Calloway. She said you'd know what to do with them."

Momma swiped the moisture from her cheeks. "Thank you, dear. Just place them in the kitchen if you will. And do you mind bringing me a slice of bread while you are in there? I suddenly feel as though I could take a bite to eat."

Cora smiled at Viola, relief washing over the girl's face like drinking a dipper full of spring water on a parched August day.

Viola recognized the emotion. It was one she'd felt many times when someone with more experience stepped into a situation she felt ill-equipped to handle. Like the time she was helping one of the goats with their birthing. Viola and that little she-goat had struggled and struggled, nearabout losing hope, until her father had strolled into the barn. Suddenly life and death no longer rested solely upon Viola's shoulders. There was someone bigger and better prepared to carry the burden.

Viola went to the kitchen and placed the herbs on the counter. She located the small misshapen loaf she assumed her sister had made. *Bless her heart.* She sawed through the dense bread, feeling sorry that this was all she had to present her ailing mother.

But Cora had to start somewhere. Viola's sourdough once resisted raising too. Love might cover a multitude of sins, but butter would have to do in this case. She spread a thick layer over the bread and then returned to her mother's bedside.

"I can make you some soup." Such a paltry salve for the heartbreak on her mother's pallid face.

Momma patted the bed beside her. "I'd rather you just sit with me a little while. Cora can make tonight's dinner."

"I'm a disaster in the kitchen," Cora muttered.

Momma shook her head. "You're not a disaster. Just a bit impatient. And you dash out of doors any time you think one of the animals might need you, as if the meal can cook itself." Her words were dry, but there was a slight twinkle in her eyes.

Indoor chores had primarily been Viola's domain until she'd upset the delicate balance of things.

What had she been thinking chasing after Trilby Chambers and the life he'd promised? She was needed *here*.

"I'm proud of you." Her mother's quavering voice broke through Viola's downward spiral.

Viola lifted her gaze to meet her mother's. How did Momma always know the very words she needed to hear?

"I'm not saying I agree with the choice you've made, but there comes a point when we each must make our own decisions. And you've made a bold one, my darling girl. I just hope he'll treat you as good as your father has always treated me."

For just a moment, her father ceased to be the villain he'd become the day he'd asked her to leave home. Instead, he was the man who had saved Momma from an abusive father, who would do anything to make sure his family was safe and provided for.

Viola might have some serious doubts about the methods he employed to ensure those things, but one thing no one could argue was that he took great pride in providing for his people, and he would let no one get in the way of that. Not even his eldest daughter. "Does he really think that my association with the Chambers family will have an effect on his business?"

Her mother sighed. "I'm not sure if it's fear, wounded pride, or maybe a little conviction that made him draw such a hard line."

"Conviction?"

"Conviction from knowing that moonshining was a necessity to keep food on the table for years, but now it's an excuse to keep on doing something he's found he's quite good at."

"He said that if he stopped, smaller operations would move in. That there would be feuding and trespassing. Killings."

"I'm sure he knows what he's talking about, Vi. I just hope you'll never forget that Bitter End raised you. I hope you don't forget the good lessons it taught you too. And that your father, though he is a flawed man, loved you in the best way he knew how."

Viola spent a few more precious moments with her mother and sister before she stole out the back door to the familiar wooded trails. When she traded these old deer paths for Louisville's streets, would these byways remain as clear to her as the lines on her palm, or would time and distance erase them?

21

Unwilling to face the nightmares that would surely come, Ana had spent the remainder of her harrowing night fixed at the kitchen table in the glow of her laptop screen, scanning listings for moonshine crockery.

Sam had been right. If she managed to sell the cache in the shed at the prices others were asking, Cora would have a nice chunk of change to use for minor updates on the house.

From there, her caffeine-propelled curiosity took her on a tour of the history of the Tennessee moonshine trade. Try as she might, she found no evidence of the Whitt name being linked to moonshine. But then again, secrecy had to be key to any illicit operation.

She riffled through the memories of her conversations with Cora. Her aunt had regaled her with tales of the mischief she was always getting into as a child, to her serious and much-older sister's chagrin. She'd talked about the music her father played on his fiddle and the way her mother could coax any flowering thing to grow. But she'd never once brought up how their family had made its living.

Was it because she was ashamed? Did she think Ana would think less of her?

When the sun finally made its appearance over the horizon and the first bird sang, Ana stood with a wince and dumped the cooled remnants of her coffee in the sink. Her charge would be begging for her morning walk any minute. On cue, the tip-tap of Pip's nails clicked on the hardwood as she made her way from the bedroom to the kitchen.

Ana smirked at her bleary-eyed companion. "You sure didn't have any trouble sleeping."

As if in answer, Pip stretched and yawned before strolling to the dog bed to resume her slumber.

It was oddly comforting that the hyperactive pup seemed as worn-out as Ana after the terrible night. Since Pip didn't seem to have any urgent needs, Ana headed for the shed in the comfort of daylight to catalog the contents and assess the needed repairs to keep nocturnal visitors at bay.

After tugging open the sliding door, Ana surveyed the scene. Drawn into the maze of jugs, she followed the narrow path, just wide enough to put one foot in front of the other. She stopped in front of the pile of shattered, amber-colored glass. Furled paper was lying among the shards. Ana bent and retrieved the pages, carefully shaking out the glass bits. They must have been inside one of the bottles lining the higher shelves.

She carefully unrolled them. *Letters?* Some held lovely writing on floral stationery, faded with time. Others were written with coarse, blocky print scratched on letterhead of the Roan Mountain State Penitentiary. Ana swallowed hard and scanned the signature at the bottom.

Wayne Lee Whitt.

"Ana?"

She started. The letters fell from her hands, fluttering to the ground like drunken butterflies. "Yeah, Sam?" she said as she stooped to gather them.

His broad form shadowed the doorway. "I had some lumber left over from my last project on the farm and thought you could use it." He pointed to the damaged boards on the east-facing wall, where light spilled into the darkened space. "I'm no carpenter, but I can make a decent patch that will hold up against your little masked friends."

She smirked. "You mean fiends?" She almost declined the offer, sure that this was another attempt at keeping an eye on Cora's erratic housesitter. But then, she'd invited him into the mess this time. Might as well go all in. She summoned courage knowing this was probably a bigger ask than leaving the man to handle it outright. "Would you mind teaching me how to fix it?"

Maybe she'd never fully heal from what happened in her classroom—or help the kids who had been there that day truly heal— but surely it would bring her some level of comfort to know how to fix *something*. And maybe, just maybe, some applicable truth could be found amid the sawdust and nails.

"Uh. Sure." He glanced back to his red pickup. "We might need to run to the hardware store over in Elk Park." He shifted his feet. "And like I said, carpentry isn't my first skill set, but I make do. You sure you don't want to call in a professional?"

She shook her head. "For all I know, the new owner will want it torn down. As long as the repairs we make are sturdy, they don't have to be HGTV curb appeal worthy."

He nodded once. "Ready to get started?"

"Now?" She glanced at the letters in her hands, begging to be read. Had her great-grandfather served time in prison for the moonshining business? Or something else?

"I've got somewhere I have to be this evening. But I've got the time this morning. Are you free?"

Was she free? The innocuous question collided with her heart at an odd angle. She hadn't felt free in months. But she had plenty of time on her hands. "Give me just a minute to grab my purse and change my shoes."

Sam stepped aside so that she could exit. "Take your time. I'll unload what I brought over and see what else we might need."

Once inside the house, she stowed the letters in her room and slipped her purse strap over her shoulder. Pip bounced around her, begging.

She stuck her head out of the front door. "How do you feel about having a dog for a passenger?"

He set down a load of lumber and gave her a thumbs-up.

She closed the door and turned back to Pip. "Looks like it's your lucky day." She grabbed the leash. Pip lay down and squirmed like a worm on hot pavement before hopping up, racing three tiny circles around Ana, and finally sitting in front of her. Ana laughed. "Good girl."

Ana loaded Pip into the truck's small back seat, then slid into the passenger side at the same time Sam got behind the wheel, his gaze colliding with hers. The truck cab seemed to shrink around them. This was a mistake. What had she been thinking, volunteering to spend the day with someone who made all her weaknesses feel exposed with a single, searching look?

Just as she was about to bail, he put the truck in reverse and backed out of the driveway. Pip draped her head over Ana's shoulder, panting hot air on her cheek. "You need a breath mint."

"Sorry 'bout that," Sam said, eyes twinkling.

Her face heated. "Not you. The dog."

He laughed quietly.

For the life of her, she could not figure out the man. One minute he was distant and guarded. Quiet. Like he lived in another world that no one was privy to. The next, he had this unexplainable draw to him. Not necessarily a physical attraction, though he was definitely nice to look at, but something inviting. When she'd walked with the bird-watchers last week, she could tell that the others seemed to feel that same comfort in his presence. "Thanks again for helping me with this."

"Cora is a good woman, and I'm glad to help out." He dropped his gaze from her face and drummed the steering wheel with his index finger.

Sam might be able to fill in some of the blanks in her family history. "Have you always lived here?"

His jaw flexed, and he leaned away from her, resting his elbow on the armrest on the driver's side door. Storm clouds gathered in his expression, reminding her of the day they'd met. "I took over my grandfather's place a few years back," he said.

That touched a nerve. She considered digging deeper but thought better of it. She had plenty of her own tender spots and wouldn't appreciate someone poking them. She reached for a safer conversational route. "You like keeping sheep?"

He pushed out a breath and gave her a tight smile. "Like is a strong word. But I find purpose in it, if that counts."

"Purpose definitely counts." She thought of the shining little faces in her typical kindergarten classes, peering up at her, expecting her to hold the answers to the questions of the universe, like "Why is the sky blue?" which she happily answered. And "Where do babies come from?" which she told them to ask their parents when they got home.

Last year's class, however, had been confronted with far bigger questions than little shoulders should ever have to bear. They wanted to know why bad things happened to good people and how to feel safe in an uncertain world.

The day she'd limped back into the classroom, she thought she'd not only teach reading, writing, and arithmetic but that she could also model how to move forward. How to feel safe and whole again, proving by example. But she'd been a fool thinking she could teach something she hadn't learned for herself.

"Ana?"

His voice interrupted her musing. "Yeah?"

"You were deep in thought."

Her shoulders crept toward her ears. How many times had he tried to get her attention? Frequently getting lost in thought was a trauma response, according to the crisis therapist she saw for a few months after the incident. "Just thinking about my students. I'm a kindergarten teacher," she volunteered.

He kept his focus on the curves ahead. "That's impressive."

She gave him an appraising glance. Most people assumed the job simply entailed wiping noses and teaching kids to tie their shoes.

"Being in charge of little people like that, any people at all, really . . . it's not a responsibility anyone should take lightly." His Adam's apple bobbed, face contorting like he'd just forced down a bitter pill.

She nodded. "I always think about the memories I have of things my teachers did and said growing up, and I worry that I'll say the wrong thing or react in a way that hurts. That I'll inadvertently mishandle some fragile part of their psyche, unaware of the impact I've made." Would last year's kids remember any of the good she'd tried to infuse in them? Or just that awful day?

She stared at Sam's profile, heart throbbing faster and faster in her chest, silently begging him to say something. Anything.

Pip whined and leaned her head around the truck's headrest. She snuffled the crook of Ana's neck. Ana reached back, scratching Pip behind the ears, taking a solid breath. "Good girl," she whispered.

Sam remained quiet for what seemed like a day and a half in awkward car ride years. Then he said, "Do you have bad memories from your school days?"

It wasn't her own childhood memories that concerned her. It was memories of little Kaitlin who had taken to doing her math underneath the table. And Mason, a bright-eyed, energetic boy, who'd become sullen and angry, sent home multiple times for hitting his classmates. Sarah who dissolved into tears without warning and refused to walk to the lunchroom unless she was holding Ana's hand.

She pushed back those tormenting thoughts. Instead of answering his question, she pivoted. "I want to plant seeds in the lives of my students that blossom into flowers, not thorns." You reap what you sow. That was the way it was supposed to work.

Ana had sown good things into her students, but she was afraid the soil had been so razed by trauma that nothing she planted could grow. She prayed their first-grade teacher would help them navigate life better than she had.

Sam parked in front of the vintage-looking hardware shop, and before he could formulate a follow-up question, she sprang from the truck cab and strode for the front door.

Sam growled under his breath as Ana entered the hardware store without looking back to see if he followed. The slight limp she sometimes tried to disguise more apparent than usual.

He'd always prided himself on being able to read people—to somehow know the emotions that lay hidden beneath spoken words. In the past three years he'd asked God on more than one occasion if this "gift" he'd been given had a return policy.

He'd once failed to understand the depth of what had been going on with the one person he'd vowed to cherish and protect above all others. And now . . . The entire drive here, though Ana looked the picture of calm, he could feel the tension, the anger, the despair, coursing through this stranger as if the emotions were his own. His abilities once again mocked his pain.

Pip whined from the back seat, gazing with mournful amber eyes at the door Ana had passed through. Sam rubbed the dog's velvety ears between his fingers. "Sometimes the people you love go off where you can't follow." He picked up the leash and Pip's hindquarters shimmied. "But you're in luck today, girl. Harley loves dogs."

Pip walked obediently beside him toward the front door of Harley's Hardware. Ears perked, short tail pointed skyward, head swiveling side to side searching for birds, coiled energy coursing through her body.

This was a quality hunting dog. *"Just because something is lost doesn't change its worth."* That familiar still, small voice nudged at him. Sometimes he wished he could turn that off too. Not the type of thing a pastor ought to be thinking, but then again, that wasn't a title he carried anymore.

He shook off his unhelpful thoughts and pulled the door open.

Ana stood in the entryway, phone to her ear, a stricken look on her face. Heart thudding in his chest, he strode to her. Pip wriggled like she hadn't seen her in a month instead of two minutes. Ana lowered the phone, the tension bracketing her mouth dissolving.

"Something wrong?" Sam passed her the leash.

She shook her head. "No," she croaked before clearing her throat. "That was the vet's office. They've found a rescue placement for Pip."

"You decided not to keep her?" The connection between the two of them was so evident, he'd thought for sure she'd changed her mind.

Ana averted her gaze. "It wouldn't be fair. There's someone out there who's better for her. Maybe someone who loves hunting as much as she does." She smiled weakly. "And besides, I'm not a dog person."

"She's put on weight. She listens to you." He patted Pip's side. "And it's clear she likes you."

Ana shrugged. "No matter how much she likes me, I'll end up doing her more harm than good if I step in where I don't belong." There was a weight to Ana's words that had nothing to do with the dog staring up at her like she deserved the sole credit for inventing bacon.

Awareness roiled in his middle, making him want to breach the walls she put forth, to push her to be transparent. He stepped closer to her, a protest pressing against his lips.

But then the truth rocked him back on his heels. No matter how much he felt drawn to alleviate whatever pain lived beneath her words, he had no business challenging someone else when he was still content to half-live his own life. "I can run you by the vet's office on the way back up to your place so that you don't have to make a separate trip down." Whatever this act cost her, he could ensure she didn't face it alone. That much he trusted himself to manage.

"I appreciate it," she said and then gestured to the hodgepodge aisles, a wobbling smile on her face. "Lead the way. Show me what we need."

Sam shrugged. "We'll have to speak with Harley. He's the only one who knows where anything is in this place."

Ana mopped the sweat from her brow and straightened. Sam stood nearby, watching her progress. She patted the board she'd nailed in place. "That look all right?"

He nodded. "Yep. How's the injury?"

She held her hand up, showing off the gnarly blood blister on the pad of her thumb. "Looking lovely."

He winced. "You sure took that lick in stride."

A little of her archived confidence sparked to life. "I was a gymnast for twelve years. Most of the old callouses have softened, but this is nothing compared to what these hands were once accustomed to."

"So you were a pretty tough kid, then?"

"I guess. It was just normal life to me." She stood and stretched out the tightness in her back before carrying another board over from the stack they'd precut.

Sam helped her hold the board in place as she lightly tapped the nail a few times to get it started. "Did you have Olympic dreams?"

"College scholarship dreams, but that didn't pan out." She swung the hammer and missed the nail altogether. She growled under her breath.

"What happened?"

She paused and adjusted her grip on the handle. "Injury I couldn't quite come back from." That was the simple way to explain it, anyway.

"You miss it?"

She was about to shrug off the question, but something about the earnest way he studied her made her feel like he'd understand. "Most people don't get what it's like to lose a sport that raised you. It was how I defined myself." Ana shook her head. "Without it, I lost my compass. My confidence."

Emotion clouded Sam's expression, and he swallowed hard and averted his gaze to the lay of Cora's land. He nodded as though agreeing with something she'd said.

"I still dream I'm doing bar routines." Her shoulders crept toward her ears. "The day we met, I was actually standing up on the rail, remembering how it felt on the balance beam. Silly, I know."

"Oh." He refocused his gaze on her. The tips of his ears turned red. "I thought . . ."

"I know. But you weren't wrong about me being really . . . upset." Upset seemed a safe, vague word. She thumbed over her shoulder. "It's getting late. I can go throw some food together. If you're willing to finish this up?"

"Happy to."

She passed him the hammer and went inside. No Pip raced to greet her. She sighed and glanced at the empty dog bed. She'd been so distraught about saying goodbye to Pip, she hadn't even considered how all her things were waiting at home. Maybe she could drop them off at the rescue and get one more chance to say goodbye.

Ana warmed up yesterday's chili and made a couple grilled cheese sandwiches to go along with it. The entire time, she tried to forget the forlorn look on Pip's face when she'd handed over the leash and walked away. How had she gotten so attached so quickly?

Ana found a tray sticking out of a box slated for donation. She rinsed away the slight film of dust and loaded it with the bowls of chili and a small stack of grilled cheeses. A meal more suited for a cool fall evening than the swelter of mid-June, but it would have to do.

She brought out the tray and set it down on the patio table. She'd cleaned up it and the matching chairs yesterday afternoon after a man in town who refinished furniture bought the surplus Cora had collected over the years. The wraparound porch wasn't quite photo ready, but it was certainly more inviting than the piles of rusty furniture had been.

She found Sam loading tools into his truck.

"Finished already?" she asked.

He closed the tailgate. "There wasn't much left to do."

Her "help" had likely drawn out a project he could have knocked out on his own in a few hours instead of six. "Thanks again for taking the time to teach me a little bit. I enjoyed the work."

"No trouble. You're a natural."

She lifted her injured thumb and wiggled it in his direction as they walked back to the porch. "Don't lie to spare my feelings."

He chuckled under his breath and shook his head. "Mind if I say grace?" he asked after they'd taken their seats.

She wondered at the strain in his voice. "Not at all." Had he thought her likely to refuse a request to bless the meal?

"Heavenly Father, thank You for Your provision. Your . . ." Sam cleared his throat. "Your kindness. Your mercy. Bless the meal before us and the hands that prepared it. In Jesus's name."

When she lifted her chin, the tension had smoothed from his features. The only way she could describe the change was by comparing it to the strange sense of accomplishment and relief she'd felt when she forced herself to call the dentist to set up an appointment she'd guiltily avoided for months.

"Thank you. I've gotten a little out of the habit of saying grace recently. Or sitting down to meals in the first place," she said, hoping her transparency put him at ease.

"Oh?" He had this habit, she'd noticed, of expressing interest and then leaving other people to fill the silence. Was it a result of being a man of few words, a defense mechanism, or a habit?

She wasn't taking the bait. Ana took a huge bite of her grilled cheese, an involuntary sigh slipping out of her at the taste of gooey cheese. "Jesus and grilled cheese. Soul food that's been missing from my life lately."

Sam chuckled. "I reckon you can't go wrong with either one of those, especially not in combination."

"What soul food have you been missing?"

He considered for a moment and then put on a wistful smile. "As for literal food, my mom's fried chicken and mashed potatoes." He took a long drink of water and seemed to be wrestling his thoughts. "I was a pastor before I came here. But now . . . my relationship with God . . . I guess it's best described as 'it's complicated.'"

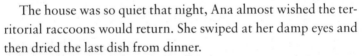

The house was so quiet that night, Ana almost wished the territorial raccoons would return. She swiped at her damp eyes and then dried the last dish from dinner.

Never in a million years would she have guessed she'd be standing at the kitchen sink crying over a dog.

But she couldn't erase the mental image of Pip straining against the leash when she'd left the vet's office. Everything within her had begged to turn around—to bring Pip home for keeps. But she would not allow herself to repeat the mistakes of this past year.

As she returned the dishes and utensils to their rightful places, she thought more about Sam's quiet revelation and the way he requested to pray yet seemed so uncomfortable. And he was supposed to have been a pastor at one point in his life? "It's complicated" sounded about right.

She certainly had more questions, but his sudden vulnerability wasn't something she took for granted. She knew what it was like to carry a title that made you uneasy. One you'd rather hide than confess.

Maybe they had far more in common than she'd realized.

With cleanup complete, she walked into her bedroom and retrieved the letters from the shed that had been waiting all day for her.

My Dearest Ruby,

If she'll hear it, please tell Vi I'm sorry.

There are so many more things I wanna explain that I can't. You understand why.

I used to be so angry that she'd run off with that boy. He'd made my beautiful girl, who once peered up at me with shining eyes, look down her nose, acting holier than thou. But being in here has given me thinking time. It wasn't fair to ask you to lose a daughter and Cora to lose a sister just cause Viola chose a different life.

I thought she rejected me and all I'd done to make sure y'all were cared for. But now I see that the only thing her choice wounded was my stubborn pride. Real sacrifice don't happen cause you wanna be appreciated. It's done cause it's what's best for somebody else.

A lesson I'm finally learning.

I'll rest easy now, knowing you've found all I've put away for you in case something like this should ever happen. At least I've succeeded in that. All the rest of the world might judge, but Bitter End folk won't turn away from you.

I sure wish I could stand on that bald one more time and see the view from our back porch. I'd hold you and pretend that everything our eyes landed on was ours.

Always,
Wayne

Ana set the letter aside and went out to the porch, just as dusk fell. Her heart weighed heavy in her chest from the somber, regretful tone in Wayne's letter. Remnants of the sunset gave her just enough light to bask in the beauty of the mountaintops that rolled out before her in endless waves. This was the view Wayne Lee Whitt missed. Maybe he didn't deserve to enjoy it because of whatever it was he did, but she hoped that he'd been able to draw up this picture in his mind as a comfort, a bird's-eye of the mountains he called home.

23

"Come on." Viola tugged Trilby's arm as they wound through a thicket. "We're going to be late."

"Vi, I'm going to have holes in my clothes and skin too if you don't quit dragging me through these briars."

She giggled. "Just trying to keep you holey, preacher man." There was something about the mountain air and the prospect of sharing one of her favorite Bitter End traditions with Trilby that had her feeling as mischievous as Cora. They slowed as they drew closer to the farm of the newly wedded Mr. and Mrs. Duke.

The bride, Hattie, had come up in school just ahead of Viola. A thought struck Viola square in the chest as she and Trilby crouched in the underbrush.

This could have been her.

The blushing newlyweds shook hands and welcomed everybody onto their land. Men and women gathered round the hay bales that formed a neat semicircle.

Such joy. Laughter.

The Bitter End marriage blessing was a tradition that had been going on for a century.

She whispered to Trilby, "Two weeks after the wedding, everyone gathers on the newlyweds' land for singing and prayer. The women keep the food coming all day long. The men and older boys build the barn or help with some other big project that needs done. The little ones play and are kept out of the way by the elderly women and a couple of the older girls who prefer to avoid the kitchen." She squeezed his hand. "And tonight . . . a party."

The way she spoke of the tradition must have carried more emotion and attachment than she'd realized. The corners of Trilby's mouth turned down, and his hazel eyes gained a sudden gloss. He opened his mouth like he was about to say something but then closed it.

"Do you want to go over?" she asked. "I could introduce you to some folks." They'd probably look at him a little sideways, but they'd be polite.

Trilby leaned close, his whispered words stirring the air and tickling her ear. "Go on over if you'd like, but I'll stay put. I know everyone will be more at ease without an outsider horning in on their celebration."

He wasn't wrong. As much as she longed to join the others, she wouldn't leave him standing there alone.

On one side of the gathering, tables had been constructed out of planks and sawhorses. Her mother placed mason jars bursting with flowers from her garden on each one. She spoke politely to the other women, yet as always, her mother seemed to live on the outskirts of conversations.

Being born in Bitter End was the only way to ever truly belong in such a place.

Her father's booming voice cut through the gentle swell of chitchat. "Congratulations, Mr. and Mrs. Duke." He slapped the man on the back and took the young woman's hand. Did her father see his eldest daughter in the face of that new bride?

Her sister's voice drew Viola's eyes to the spot Cora played marbles with a group of children beneath a leggy pine. The sight of her little sister laughing and ribbing her friends over missed shots almost tugged Viola from Trilby's side.

Widow Calloway walked to the front of the scattered assembly. Without a word, everyone ceased their chatting and game playing and found one of the bales to sit upon. The woman, who Viola secretly believed was as old as the mountain itself, bowed her head and began to pray. "Lord, we thank Thee for this day. For this gathering of hearts to support these young folks. These 'uns are Yours as this mountain is Yours. We ask, Lord, for a blessing over this man and wife—that their crops would grow, that their children would be healthy and have hearts that love You, that their livestock would be hearty and their hooves find nary a gopher hole, and that their house and barn would stand strong and steady for generations to come. Now, Heavenly Father, we lift our voice in song for Your glory and honor. Amen."

A hushed chorus of amens echoed throughout the gathering. As soon as the widow took her seat, a ragtag choir lifted their voices as one, singing "Amazing Grace." The familiar tones swelled in Viola's chest and flowed through her veins.

She stole a glance at Trilby, whose eyes had gone round as a hoot owl's. Did this music connect with his spirit in the same way it did hers, or was he simply in a state of shock that these people who wouldn't darken the doors of his daddy's church, who produced half the county's illegal moonshine, could sing with such soul-stirring ardor about the grace of God?

These were her people.

This mountain was in her blood.

A fact she could never escape.

Sweat bloomed on her brow as that knowledge tightened around her gut like a noose.

Viola grabbed Trilby's arm and pulled him back the way they'd come, mincing through the brush until they were out of earshot. And then she released his hand and broke into a run. She could hear her own pulse, a rhythmic whooshing in her ear canals.

On and on they went. Trilby asked her to stop a few times, but her feet refused to obey. She had to get out of there. To break free from the music—the voices, the timbre, the passion. An unending chant that cried out to her over and over again, *You belong to us.*

Flashbacks played in her mind, barn raising after barn raising. Some were literal barns. Others, gifts of provisions instead. A vigil for the critically injured. Funerals. Newlywed celebrations. The entire range of the human condition. If someone needed help, if someone needed care, the people of Bitter End gathered and provided.

And she was going to leave that behind.

Why?

She stopped short and spun on her heel. Trilby barely avoided a collision in the abrupt end to their breakneck sprint through the thicket. She gripped the front of his shirt, pressed her lips to his. Her fervent embrace bore no resemblance to the chaste kisses they'd shared before, but she had to know. Could this man fill the space that would be carved out of her when she left this mountain behind?

He pulled back a fraction in shock. She grasped him tighter, refusing to let his questions form, drowning them both with her wordless interrogation. He melted into the kiss with a groan of capitulation.

Each caress of her lips asked if it was possible to be sown into his life in the way she was sown into this mountain. If she plucked herself from that rocky, seemingly inhabitable soil, would she thrive or wither up when transplanted into his world?

They broke apart, breathless. Trilby stared wide-eyed at the girl who blushed at even the lightest of kisses. His fair, freckled cheeks had gone ruddy, his ears scarlet. "Vi?"

She covered her mouth with her hand. "I'm sorry."

Trilby rubbed the back of his neck, and a corner of his mouth twitched upward. "Don't be sorry. But would you care to explain what in tarnation that was?"

She shook her head, tears welling in her eyes. His arms were around her in an instant, holding her together while her shoulders shook with sobs.

Was she losing her mind? Kissing the boy senseless and then falling apart in his arms the next moment?

When she'd worn herself out crying, Trilby loosened his hold, his eyes searching hers. "I'm the one who's sorry."

"For what?" she croaked.

"I didn't understand what I was asking when I asked you to start a life with me. What I was taking from you." He swallowed hard. "I never belonged to a place, Vi. I've never had roots. Not once in my life." He laced his fingers with hers and squeezed tight. "I understand if you've changed your mind about us. It'll break my heart in half. But I do understand."

They headed down the narrow path in silence until it widened enough for them to walk side-by-side, hand in hand.

"When I moved up here, I thought I understood what it was to be a minister," Trilby continued. "Sitting in a classroom, reading textbooks about theology, I thought I could fit everything into tidy boxes and sort right from wrong. But now I see that sometimes a saint acts like a sinner, and sometimes a sinner acts like a saint. And I confess, I'm not always sure what to make of it." He tugged her to a stop, his gaze boring into hers. "When your father stands before God someday, will God see the man who sang His praise and helped his neighbor, or the moonshiner who made his living in an illegal trade? Will God know me, who spoke beautiful words about His holiness with no one to hear because I thought I needed to convert people to my way of thinking before they could approach the throne of God? I don't know what to think anymore." Trilby shook his head. "But I do know it's wrong to ask you to leave your family behind to come with me. I thought at first . . ." He grimaced. "I thought I was rescuing you, giving you a better life. I was a fool."

The tender humility glistening in his eyes chased all the questions from her mind.

She turned to face him, grasping both his hands and squeezing tight. "I don't want to be the daughter who justifies her father's lawlessness because it puts food on the table of the innocent. I want to be the wife who goes to sleep at night knowing her husband served his people and stayed obedient to God's Word, all the gray washed out of the situation. I crave those tidy boxes you're talking about."

Trilby's mouth worked like he was wanting to form words but lacked them. His brow wrinkled with worry. But then she kissed him again, hoping to banish all doubt. Scared as she was to lose the girl she'd always been, she was ready to become someone new. Somehow she'd find a way to become the wife he'd need in their beautiful, uncomplicated, unsullied life.

24

The next afternoon, several people stopped by to purchase items Ana had listed on the Roan Mountain Marketplace. Apparently the online classified ad service Google had suggested got quite a bit of traffic. She'd rid herself of a few sets of pots and pans, two antique sewing machines, and a boxful of holiday-themed table linens. After her last customer had driven away, Ana loaded several boxes of books in her back seat to make deliveries on the route to her destination.

Cora would be pleased with the progress made so far.

But what would she think about her new side quest? Guilt pricked at her as she pulled out of the drive, feeling like a trespasser venturing into forbidden terrain. Surely she had some right to the information she chased.

Half an hour later, she parked in front of the library in the quaint town of Elizabethton. After she finished up at the library, she planned to snag a latte from a coffee shop in the town square and check out the covered bridge before she made her book deliveries.

She consulted with the librarian about the best way to view the local newspapers from the period her great-grandfather had been convicted. The woman gave her a quick tutorial on using the microfilm machine and then left her to her research.

Ana was swept back to the late 1950s. She skimmed years of local interest articles about the opening of Roan Mountain State Park, various barn dances where the apparently well-known Gospel Players were said to have provided the music, the long-standing Rhododendron Festival, and the construction of State Route 143 that took people to the top of Roan Mountain.

Finally, she found the headline she was looking for.

"Manhunt Continues for the Moonshine Magnate Wayne Whitt: Wanted for the Murder of Reverend Quincy Chambers."

A reverend? Her heart thudded in her chest. Hadn't Marilyn said her father had been a preacher and Cora's a moonshiner? She'd failed to mention, however, that Cora's father had gone to prison for murdering hers.

The short article stated that the well-known moonshiner was on the run after the reverend was found shot dead in the woods in Bitter End. Ana sat back for a second. *This* was her family history? She rewound time to the day she'd left for Bitter End, naively hoping that connecting to her heritage could help her trace her way back to who she'd been before that ugly fall day.

"Ana?"

She turned at the familiar voice. Marilyn stood across the room. Ana bolted from the chair and walked over to her. She wasn't entirely sure why she felt compelled to conceal the topic of her research from Marilyn, aside from the fact she felt like an interloper digging into Marilyn's life like a dentist drilling a cavity without Novocain.

As she approached, Marilyn maneuvered a stack of books. Ana caught the words *Coping with* on the spine of the thickest tome before it was shifted out of view.

"I didn't expect to see you here," Marilyn said, her gaze darting over Ana's shoulder. "Your aunt's house is practically a library in itself."

"I was out and about, doing some book deliveries, and thought I'd stop in to make sure I'm not missing out on any important information regarding next school term. The internet and cell service works well enough on the mountain, but it's a little spotty at times." Ana internally cringed. Could she not have come up with a more realistic excuse?

Marilyn quirked an eyebrow. "Your emails are on microfilm?"

"Oh, that . . . um . . ." Ana swallowed and forced a smile. "Some things you said got me curious about Cora and my grandmother, Viola. So . . ."

"So you thought you'd look into things?" Marilyn sighed. "I'm sorry to say that it isn't a very happy story." The older woman glanced toward the door. "I best be off. I don't want to miss my hair appointment. Have a good one." She took a few hurried steps toward the exit, then turned. "Be careful not to pass judgment reading headlines, my dear. You can learn things from those old news stories, but they rarely give you the full picture of a person."

A reality Ana had become well acquainted with over the past year. "I'll be sure to keep that in mind."

"You'll join us tomorrow, won't you? For bird-watching?"

"Oh, I wasn't—" The look of disappointment clouding Marilyn's features made her pause. "Maybe. What time?"

They went over the particulars together.

"Be sure to bring that dog of yours," Marilyn added as she walked to the checkout counter. Ana didn't have the heart to correct her.

Marilyn climbed the steps of the clapboard building, trailing her father, mother, and brother like an afterthought. Being twelve years younger than her brother often left her feeling that way. Not that she felt unloved. Just unexpected. Sometimes she'd see an almost surprised look light in her mother's expression when she'd sit at the kitchen table. It would last only a fraction of a second, but it was there, nonetheless.

Inside the building, she stared. Pews sat at odd angles instead of tidy rows. Old cigarette butts disintegrated beneath their feet. The building had been used as an ashtray instead of a place of worship.

Her big brother went to the front and sat on an orphaned piano bench that wobbled a bit under his wiry frame. She turned to her mother and father, who attempted to converse quietly in the echoing cavern as they strolled the center aisle.

Her mother wrung her hands, her yellow shirtdress swishing about her calves as she walked. Her father loosened his tie and determinedly rolled up his sleeves. Swathed in sunlight from the one unbroken windowpane, dust motes swirled around them. Her parents were beautiful. Even here.

"Quincy, are you sure?"

Marilyn understood the question. This was a far cry from the beautiful brick building they'd left behind with its white, pillared veranda and carpeted center aisle. The scent of furniture polish was always heavy in the air. People in shiny shoes and fine suits and dresses lined up to shake her daddy's hand after service. She had a feeling this building wouldn't draw quite the same crowd come Sunday morning.

"I'm sure, honey. I'm sure as I am of the sun rising each morning. The Lord called me here."

"Marilyn?" The sound of her name cut through the rushing wind of the domed hair dryer she sat beneath.

Marilyn blinked, clearing away the memory that had had her tangled somewhere between asleep and awake. "Am I done?"

"Yes, ma'am. Let's get you in my chair and styled."

As sweet Deanna removed the curlers from her gray hair, her mind drifted back to that first memory of Bitter End. Her mother's question again echoed in her mind. *"Quincy, are you sure?"* Even after all this time, the query plucked a discordant twang in Marilyn's heartstrings.

For many years she'd concluded that if God had indeed called her father up to that old mountain, He was a being with a cruel bent.

It was a mite easier believing her dear father had heard wrong.

But when Obie had gotten the research assignment whose benefits included housing on Old Buck Mountain Road, she couldn't deny that something inexplicable had returned her to the place of her greatest pain. She'd never know if God truly called her father to Bitter End, but she couldn't deny that God had called her back.

Deanna ceased fussing over her hair and then turned her chair to face the mirror and removed the cape. "How's that look, Marilyn?"

She squinted and tilted her head. The view before her was blurrier than the last time she'd been in. "A lovely job, dear. Thank you." She'd just have to trust in the woman's expertise.

Marilyn paid and left a generous tip, then sat in her car. The books from the library waited, their exposed spines declaring her fate to the world. *My Vision Is Failing, Now What?*, *Hope in the Darkness*, *Thriving with Vision Loss*. The irony was not lost on her. The printed word would cease to be useful before long.

I once was blind, but now I see. She scoffed. *And now I see, but I'll soon be blind.* She cranked her car. How much longer could she retain the independence she'd taught herself to cherish after Obie's passing?

Marilyn pulled out of the parking lot and headed back to Bitter End. Her thoughts floated to Ana and the stories that she might find displayed in those old articles. She prayed that what the girl found wouldn't cause her to disappear behind the stone wall Cora had built.

Ana delivered the final box of books to an elderly woman who was unable to drive. She hugged Ana and repeatedly told her how grateful she was for Cora's visits and how much she would miss seeing the bookmobile pull into her drive.

For the life of her, Ana could not figure out why Cora had not wanted to be here to pass out these final gifts herself. People truly adored her.

Simmering beneath the joy Ana found during the book dropoffs was the discomfort she felt about what she'd uncovered at the library. Had her great-grandfather really killed Marilyn's father?

Yet it had been Cora who told Ana to avoid Marilyn instead of the other way around. Was she concerned Marilyn would uncover this ugly family secret? An ugly secret Ana might want to distance herself from.

Back home again, she set her shopping bags on the kitchen table and then went to the blinking answering machine. She pressed the button.

"Hello, dear, it's Cora. It seems I've missed you yet again. I can't keep the time zones straight. I'm sorry I haven't kept in better touch. I didn't realize that these international internet and phone packages were going to be so steep. Anyhoo, I'm off to my waltz class."

The second message was from the vet's office. She'd called that morning, asking how Pip was settling in, and they'd promised to call back with an update.

"Hello, Miss Watkins." Doc Underwood's voice filled the living room. "We called to check in at the rescue at your request. I hate to be the bearer of bad news, but it seems Pip escaped their yard this morning. They assumed she'd be secure, considering the property is surrounded by a six-foot fence. However, Pip was able to climb the enclosure. They haven't been able to locate her yet."

Ana's heart sank as her eyes drifted to the dog bed and food bowl she'd gathered but never made herself drop off at the rescue. Pip was going to end up in the same condition Ana had found her in. Or worse. Those people were supposed to be able to give her the experienced care Ana couldn't. Yet still, they'd lost her.

Or maybe Pip was simply prone to wander. To leave the ones who tried to care for her. To end up on her own.

Ana went on about her day, putting away groceries, penning plans for the house, and listing items on the Roan Mountain Marketplace. But her mind was haunted with images of Pip trotting down the road alone, looking for a safe place to rest her head. Looking for Ana.

She shook off the ridiculous thought. Pip had run off because she'd sighted a bird or a squirrel beyond the fence. Not because she craved Ana's company.

To distract herself, Ana cozied in bed with Ruby's and Wayne's prison letters. When she'd read through them all, she picked up her phone and dialed her mother's number. She owed her more than the occasional "I'm great, how are you?" messages she'd been sending in response to her mother's check-ins, and Ana had questions she needed someone to answer.

"Ana? Is everything okay?"

"Yeah, Mom." Ana pulled her blanket up under her chin. "Just thought we were overdue for catching up." She filled her mother in on her many mishaps, including the run-in with the raccoons.

"I still can't believe that woman left you alone all summer. She's taking advantage of your generosity."

Ana suppressed a sigh. She couldn't argue with the fact that she'd had far different expectations about how the summer would go. "It was a miscommunication. Probably my fault. I'd been so distracted with work."

"Which is why I wanted you to come home. You deserve to be pampered, not left to take care of other people's problems."

Ana scrunched her face and chose to ignore her mother's last statement. "Cora has always been so sweet and eager to get to know me. And she always asks about you. I've never understood why you haven't been open to meeting her." Ana waited, the silence echoing against her eardrum.

Her mother's sigh came through the line.

"Mom? Why?" Did she know the truth about their family history?

Her mother sighed again. "When I was about fourteen, I started asking my stepmom about my biological parents. I pestered her until I must have worn her ragged. She said that my father's dying wish was that she take me to her people to raise me. He wanted her family to become my family."

The line went quiet, and Ana held the phone tighter to her ear, straining for the words her mother hadn't yet said. "Mom?"

"Still here." She paused for another excruciating moment. "Momma M said . . . said my dad called our family tree broken and asked her to graft me into a lineage that wasn't so damaged."

Ana shut her eyes tight at the ache in her mother's words. She couldn't imagine hearing something like that at fourteen, especially about the people who had given her life. "And getting to know Cora felt dangerous in some way?" Ana asked. "A betrayal of your father's last wishes? A betrayal of your stepmom?"

"I don't know. Something like that. Whether my biological daddy and my stepmom's choice was for the best, I can't say, but I can tell you my childhood was full of warmth and kindness. Her people truly became my people."

She knew her mother's words to be true. Every holiday spent with her mother's side of the family had been full of love. She hadn't realized that she and her mother didn't have a biological connection with the rest of the family until her mother mentioned it during a family tree project. It had been a shock at first, but it had pushed her to dig deep enough to find Cora.

Ana spent some time telling her about the newspaper articles she'd found. About moonshine and murder. "Do you think your father was right to ask that of your stepmom? Is it really better to forget the past and pretend it never happened?"

25

AUGUST 1958

"Almost ready, Viola, dear? Your mother and sister are just out-side," the widow cajoled from the other side of the curtain.

Viola parted the fabric. "Yes, ma'am."

She passed Viola a bouquet of rhododendron and mountain laurel tied together with twine. The woody stems were rough against her palms. "This is beautiful."

"A little bit of your heritage woven into your wedding day so that no matter how far you go, you never forget where you came from."

Viola studied the woman's wrinkled face, searching for traces of judgment. Though the old mountain woman had readily taken her in, Viola often wondered what she truly thought about Viola leaving behind her kin to cleave to a family of outsiders. But the widow was different from most. She'd been the first to befriend Viola's mother those many years ago.

As if detecting Viola's train of thought, she said, "It will be tough, learning a new way of life. But your young man is a good sort." Trilby had sealed his place in Widow Calloway's heart the June day he'd brought home scrapped building supplies from the general store to shore up the sagging porch and patch her roof.

Viola craved the sight of him. He'd been off in Louisville the past two weeks, making sure their housing arrangements at the seminary were squared away. She'd spent more than a few sleepless nights trying and failing to imagine her new life in a city. Shops within walking distance. Neighbors separated only by walls instead of miles.

Doubt about her choice crept so readily into the empty space Trilby had left behind. But she took comfort knowing that when she saw him at the other end of the aisle of Buck Mountain Church, all reservations would fade.

Widow Calloway patted her hand. "Your father will come around one of these days. Perhaps this goodbye to Bitter End won't be forever."

Perhaps. But it was difficult to believe considering they'd carefully planned the ceremony around one of her father's business trips down the mountain so that her mother and sister could attend the simple church wedding.

Viola stepped into the bright morning light, blinking a few times before she could focus on her mother and Cora, who were waiting beneath the mimosa tree. They rushed to her, fawning over the way the widow had woven her hair and pinned it high on her head.

Momma tugged at the flutter sleeve of Viola's blush pink dress. "It fits you like a glove. I'm so glad." Momma's graduation gift was a simple frock, appropriate for any given Sunday, but it was brand-new, just like the life Viola was about to embark on.

Cora gave her a wobbly smile. "You really gonna get hitched to that preacher boy and leave me high and dry up on this mountaintop?"

Viola pulled her into a bear hug. "Next summer, you are coming to stay with us. Every spare cent I can scrounge will be put toward saving up for your bus ticket."

"Promise?"

"Of course."

Today was a day for hope and joy. Worries about reality would keep.

With Momma on one elbow and Cora on the other, the Whitt ladies took the short path from Widow Calloway's to the chapel. Birdsong swelled in the trees, and summer sunlight filtered through the leaves, the warmth chasing away Viola's lingering concerns.

She could almost forget that this wedding was not a joining of two families but a permanent separation from her own.

Outside the church, Marilyn waited patiently beside her mother. Cora broke away from Viola's side and ran to her friend. "Mari!"

Marilyn shrieked and dashed to Cora, and the two collided in a haphazard bear hug that ended with them both in a heap on the ground in a fit of giggles.

Momma sighed but smiled. "So much for keeping this quiet. Now half of Carter County knows something is going on down at the church."

Viola tugged her mother to a stop. "Don't let Daddy keep her shut away at home. I know you need help around the house, and she needs to grow up a little, but there is time enough for that. Cora needs outdoors and laughter and friendship. Don't let her spirit wither."

Something apologetic passed over her mother's face, and Viola wished she could call the words back. It wasn't Momma's fault that Cora had been called upon to take Viola's place.

"If I can scrounge up the money for that bus ticket, promise me you'll find a way to get her to us," Viola pleaded. "She needs to see that there is more to the world than life on this mountain." She spoke with unfounded conviction.

Her mother patted her arm. "Today is your big day. Don't spend it worrying about Cora. I'm well again. We'll find our way." The steel lacing her mother's lilting voice served as the reminder she needed that her mother was a far stronger woman than Viola often gave her credit for. She, too, had had the strength to leave all she knew and carve out a home where she did not belong. "But we will miss you more than you'll ever know, Viola Mae."

Mrs. Chambers approached and embraced Viola and her mother. Trilby's father poked his head out the church doors, likely in response to the ruckus the two younger girls had stirred up in the churchyard. He descended the steps and greeted Viola and her mother with gentle handshakes.

He then smoothed the front of his worn suit coat and straightened the sprig of mountain laurel stuck in his buttonhole. "Are you ready, my dear? Your groom awaits."

After giving everyone time to take their places inside, Viola entered the clapboard church. She stood at the end of the aisle, the gentle, dulcet tones of Marilyn's instrument urging her to the front of the church where four women sat witness. Her mother, Mrs. Chambers, Widow Calloway, and young Cora.

And then her eyes found the one her soul loved. As she took that first step forward, she exhaled the breath she'd held too long and remembered all over again that this journey would not be one she'd face alone.

Trilby's smile was tremulous and dear. Did the same doubts weigh the corners of his mouth as they did hers? Doubts that said they were too young and formed from such different material that they might combust should they attempt a single, unified life.

But then his hands were covering hers, their warmth a reminder of the love that could fill all the cracks whenever the differences in their upbringing could not be reconciled.

It would be enough.

Still, when the reverend read the Scripture about a man leaving his parents and cleaving unto his wife, becoming one flesh, she couldn't help but wonder what kind of creature that would be— the moonshiner's daughter and the preacher's son, joined into one.

By the time the bus delivered Viola and Trilby to Louisville, she was ready to scurry into any old hole in the wall and call it home.

People milled in the streets beneath bright lights and shadows of tall buildings. And the *noise*. Even at ten o'clock at night car horns blared and people rushed about, in a hurry to get goodness knew where at such an hour.

Beside her in the taxicab, her husband gripped her hand, running his thumb over the gold band on her ring finger.

Her *husband*.

She angled her head to see the tops of buildings. Lights backlit people going about their business. Some dancing to music she couldn't hear. Some turning off lights and closing drapes. One woman stood at the window, gazing out, a glass in her hand.

Could a mountain girl survive this wilderness of asphalt, concrete, brick, and artificial light? She shut her eyes and saw again the back porch view she'd grown up with.

Some desperate, craven creature clawed to life inside her chest, making her want to grab the door handle and fling it open. To flee back to her Tennessee highland home.

"Vi? Are you all right?"

She forced her breathing to slow and turned to him. "There's hardly any trees."

He smiled softly. "Have you ever been to a city before?"

She shook her head. "Not like this one." *What have I done?* It had seemed like such a grand adventure. But she'd forgotten a simple truth. Though an adventure might take you uncomfortable places, a body could always come home. But she'd made this foreign land her home.

He pulled her closer, tucking her under his arm. "It's not all like this. You'll see."

She snuggled against his warmth and shut her eyes. She was fatigued and overreacting. Everything would look different after a good night of sleep.

The vibrations of the car lulled her, and Trilby's solid warmth calmed her nerves. In what seemed the span of a second, Trilby jostled her awake. "Honey, we're home."

Home.

The image of home painted on her heart and the view she awoke to were jarringly incongruent. But at least there were trees.

Trilby exited the car, then held out his hand to her. After he'd helped her out of the taxi, he assisted the driver in removing the pair of suitcases from the trunk.

While she waited, she gazed into the canopy of beech trees overhead. There were buildings and pavement and light here too. But she'd woken to a gentler place. Graceful lines had taken the place of the harsh edges. Whoever had been in charge of creating this manicured oasis had loved nature too, allowing space for trees and flowers to grow.

After Trilby paid the driver, she followed behind him, down the short sidewalk to the married student housing. He stopped in front of the door with a brass number 6. He fit the key in the lock and then swung the door open. He set the suitcases just inside.

Then he scooped her into his arms, and she let out a giggling shriek as he carried her across the threshold. "Home sweet home," he said before returning her to solid ground.

Listing slightly, she grasped the rumpled lapels of the suit coat he still wore from their wedding that morning and leaned into him, pressing her lips to his.

Losing herself in the kiss.

In the darkness.

In his arms.

When they broke apart, Trilby led her down the hallway to the bedroom, to a bed he'd made with linens her mother had sewn as a wedding gift.

This was home.

It did not matter that home was a sparsely furnished student apartment in a city that left her feeling like a frightened country mouse. It didn't matter that the pair of them didn't know a thing about what it was to be husband and wife.

Just as their hands now fumbled over buttons, zippers, and snaps, they would fumble their way through this new life.

Together.

26

Ana's dreams that night were riddled with lost dogs and prison bars, a strange reprieve from the nightly replays of the incident. She rose, put on a pot of coffee, and found herself walking the property, eyes hungry for a brown-and-white dog streaking through the brush on the hunt for a bird.

Which was ridiculous. But hope was like that sometimes.

As Ana washed her face and readied for the day, her thoughts swiveled to the letters she'd read the night before. Simple. Homespun. And surprisingly tender. Ruby always ended her letters with a quotation from 1 Corinthians 13:13: *"And now abideth faith, hope, and charity, these three; but the greatest of these is charity."*

Ruby seemed a devout woman and yet the papers claimed her husband had been the ringleader of a lucrative illegal operation that kept half the county supplied in moonshine. And he'd killed a reverend. But her love had *still* endured?

As Ana tamed her long hair, she wrestled with the conflicting attributes she'd collected of her great-grandfather. Wayne Lee Whitt was a murderer, a fact as black-and-white as the newsprint she'd read the day before. And yet the tender way that Wayne talked of his children to his beloved wife painted a picture far different than the press. How in the world did those two things align?

And then there was her own mother who'd been raised to believe that the past could be buried and forgotten. But Cora had been here all this time, alive and well in this same lonely house. It wasn't right that Cora's existence had been kept hidden from Ana and her mother because of other people's choices.

Ana finished her coffee and took a long walk along the roadway, mentally cataloging her day. She needed to distribute more of the books. After having to drive all the way to Elizabethton to access a library, Ana better understood what a gift Cora's bookmobile must have been to the Roan Mountain community. Especially during the pre-internet age.

She puffed a little as she tackled a steep incline in the road. Her knee protested, but Ana pushed onward. Working through pain had become second nature during her years as a gymnast. But this past year had taken things to an entirely new level when she'd forced herself back into that classroom. Maybe strengths could be taken too far. Becoming weaknesses instead.

The engine rumbling behind her made her turn. Sam's pickup drew into view. He pulled up beside her and rolled down the window. "Need a lift?" His storm-cloud eyes were brighter than they'd been when they'd talked over chili and grilled cheese.

She gestured to the road ahead. "Just out enjoying the walk."

"All the way down the mountain? You'll never make it in time." The corner of his mouth twitched upward, letting her know he was joking. But somehow she'd missed the punchline.

"That wasn't the plan . . ."

He tugged at the brim of his ball cap and gave a full grin. She might need to recant yesterday's assertion that physical attraction played no role in his draw. Ana banished the wayward thought as soon as it crossed her mind.

"You'll break Marilyn's heart if you skip the hike," he said. "She was talking to me last night about you being there."

Ana groaned. She hadn't fully processed how *she* felt about her connection to Wayne Whitt, and she certainly wasn't ready to discuss it with one of the victims of his crimes. "I never told her for sure I'd—"

"Hop in." He patted the side of the truck. "You can't possibly have something so pressing up here in Bitter End that can't wait an hour or two."

She gripped the back of her neck. A conversation needed to happen with Marilyn at some point, and Sam seemed close to her. Maybe he would know what Ana should say. "We'll have to stop by the house. I'll need to bring the stuff she gave me last time."

A few minutes later, she had collected the borrowed binoculars, field guide, and journal and was seated beside Sam, heading down the mountain.

"I've been doing a little digging into my family history," Ana said, breaking the silence. Her heartbeat thumped in her chest. Why did revealing this fact make her feel like she'd been the one to wield the rifle and level it at Marilyn's father? "It seems that my family and hers . . ." Ana swallowed. "My great-grandfather went to prison for killing her father."

Sam took another curve. "That is the gist of it."

Ana braced herself on the dash though he navigated the bend in the road with finesse. "You knew?"

Sam shrugged. "My grandfather was a boy when all of that happened. I grew up hearing tales about Wild Wayne like he was some sort of morally gray Robin Hood."

She stared at him. "He was revered even though he murdered a man?"

Sam scrunched his face in concentration. "I don't think most folks up here believed he did it. They figured it was some rival who had come to challenge Wayne, and the reverend got caught in the cross fire. No one could ever figure what the reverend was doing out there in the first place. Or why Wayne confessed."

Ana tried to absorb the information. "And still Marilyn reached out to me, knowing my connection to Cora and her family?"

Sam glanced her way. "She didn't realize you were related to Cora at first. Not until the hike you and Pip—sorry, PeePee—uh . . . joined." He smirked at the last bit, and she rolled her eyes.

"She brought up that she and Cora had some sort of falling-out back when they were girls, but I had no idea . . . she never said . . ."

Sam's forehead grew as lined as a freshly plowed field. "Maybe she was trying to see what you knew?"

"Which was nothing then. But we bumped into each other at the library, and I told her I was researching family history. She hurried off, making excuses about getting to an appointment."

And now Marilyn knew what Ana knew. She glanced behind her, out the back window of the truck. "How late will I make you if I ask you to drive me back home?"

Sam was quiet for a few moments. "Take this walk with her. Soak in the beauty. Feel the rhythms of nature. A lot of things can be resolved without a word."

"I have to apologize or express condolences. Something." Ana scraped her bottom lip with her teeth. "Where do I begin?"

"Don't force the conversation. Get to know her first. Listen." He gripped the steering wheel. "We miss out on so much when we don't listen first." The last bit came out thick and graveled. Had she not been staving off her own panic, she might have questioned him on it.

Ten minutes later, Sam parked near the trailhead, where Marilyn, Jake, and Inez waited. Ana's nerve endings tingled. What could she possibly say? Did the rest of them know?

Everyone offered a wordless nod of greeting, and then Marilyn set off down a narrow trail. Sam brought up the rear, hemming her in. Not that she could've made an escape as the caboose. He was her ride home.

This walk was nothing like the bird-watching session she and Pip had crashed. That had been jovial and conversational. At the time, Ana had wondered how they ever managed to hear anything above their chatter.

169

Today, birdsong and the crunch of last year's leaves were the only things filling her ears.

She shot Sam a questioning look as they walked.

A spark of mischief glinted in his eyes. He drew closer and spoke over her shoulder, his breath ruffling the wisps of hair that had slipped from her ponytail. "The third Thursday of the month is our silent stroll." His voice barely rose above the whisper of their tread, yet Jake and Inez simultaneously glared and shushed them. Ana quashed the nervous laugh attempting to spring out of her.

It was unsettling, walking in silence with a group of people she barely knew. Ana's thoughts thrummed at high volume. About Pip. About what to do next at the house. About her great-grandfather and his sins. About the trail of hurt and destruction the taking of a life must beget for generations—for both the family of the victim and the family of the perpetrator.

Little by little her internal monologue quieted, and other noises filled the vacancy. The distant trickling of a brook. Wind rustling leaves. What sounded like a thousand-bird chorus, trilling, chirping, and singing in the trees.

They reached a clearing surrounded by brush and were able to abandon their single file formation. In the center, logs had been arranged in an oval. Marilyn, Jake, Inez, and Sam stopped their progression down the trail and chose a log to sit on.

Uncertain of the protocol, Ana observed from the periphery. Inez wrote in her journal. Jake scanned the trees. Marilyn sketched. Sam lay back on his log, eyes shut. Listening? The absolute serenity of his features made her realize how much tension normally resided on his face.

Ana sat, unsure of what to do with herself.

A round-bodied brown bird with a striking white strip by its eye alighted on a nearby twig. It let out a whistling song with shocking volume for its size. She'd seen one on the clothesline outside her aunt's house, but she had no idea what kind of bird it was. She flipped through the tattered field guide. A Carolina wren.

She dutifully wrote the name down on her life list, as Marilyn had encouraged her to do the last time she'd hiked with them. Then she turned another page and began sketching, attempting to accurately render the bird's shape and coloring.

It was odd, the connection she was beginning to feel with this plucky bird. Before it would have come and gone with little notice on Ana's part. But now, it inspired wonder. Wonder at the intricate way the creature moved among the branches and the raucous song reverberating from its tiny frame. Wonder at the keen way it studied her from its perch. Sunrays filtering through the trees illuminated the individual vanes of its feathers, transforming what at first glance was a monochromatic brown into a kaleidoscope.

In a flash the little sprite flitted away.

As she sketched, her thoughts drifted back to her great-grandfather. If only understanding who a person was could be as straightforward as knowing a wren. Parsing together the newspapers, prison letters, and Cora's sparse stories about a kind father was like trying to identify a bird that half fit the description of both a dove and a sharp-shinned hawk.

Ana finished her sketch, tucked her things into her bag, and lay back on the log, mirroring Sam's position.

There she remained for some indeterminate stretch, refusing the temptation to check her watch. As songbirds twittered in the canopy, she floated in a somnific state in which fear and worry had no place.

Time passed, noticed only because of the changing angle of the sun.

Something indefinable shifted in the atmosphere, and Ana slowly sat up, as did everyone else in their party. Though it wasn't a chapel, the place had felt holy. The thump of her ailing heart had kept time with the jubilant, hopeful song of God's creation, reminding her even in a broken world, there was still wonder and delight to be found.

One by one they filed onto the trail, heading back in the

direction of the parking lot. Maybe she was imagining it, but she was certain that it wasn't just her who walked out of these woods different than they'd gone in. This change was evident in the set of their shoulders, the lightness of their tread, and the softness in their faces that hadn't been there before. It had been such a long time since she'd felt this way, she had to search for a word to describe it.

Peace. This is what peace felt like.

After a couple of hours in the woods without a single word between them, this motley group of strangers had become something more to Ana than they had been before. Like a flock of Carolina wrens, she would have looked right past them before. But not now.

If only she could have found a way to do *this* for her students. An idea began niggling in her mind. Was it possible to bottle an experience and bring it back home with her?

Her thoughts were interrupted by a cell phone chime. Jake wrangled his phone from his pocket, and his eyes went wide. He waved it toward Inez who snatched it from his hand. "*Oh.* Emergency wedding! Emergency wedding! Make way. We have got to go. We have got to *go!*"

The tall broad man and his petite wife skirted around the group and hurried down the trail before anyone had the chance to question it.

Emergency wedding?

Ana shot a questioning look at Sam, who snorted and shook his head.

Surely Inez had meant a wedding emergency, not an emergency wedding.

At the trailhead, Marilyn gave them a nod and a wave as a goodbye. Ana felt certain that somehow things were okay between them. A conversation would surely come later, but for now, this was enough.

She and Sam walked shoulder to shoulder to his truck.

Once she was seated in the passenger seat, she whispered, "You didn't mention it was a silent meeting." Even her soft-spoken words seemed to boom in the truck cab after the long quiet. She cringed. "Sorry. Are we allowed to talk now or was this supposed to go on for the rest of the day?"

He chuckled, low and deep. "Speaking is permitted."

She cut him a playful glare. "I was all worked up, trying to figure out what to say to Marilyn, and you—"

"Told you not to force conversation." He winked and cranked the engine.

"Fair enough, I guess." She crossed her arms over her chest. She was always on the wrong foot with this man, but somehow it didn't matter. Not today.

"You did good, by the way."

She scoffed. "Because I kept my mouth shut?"

He chuckled again. "There's a difference between silent lips and a quiet spirit. The first is easy enough if you have a thimbleful of self-control. A quiet spirit is another matter."

Maybe so. But how could Sam know whether she had achieved the second?

Before the question had a chance to form on her lips, he said, "Spend enough time with the Bitter End Birding Society and you learn the difference. First in yourself, and then you sense it in others."

27

Sam grimaced as he drove past Ana's house. He had to stop doing this.

When Cora first asked him to look out for her housesitter, he'd politely agreed, but he never intended to let his walls fall.

Ana's ponytail and freckles gave her a look of innocence that, when paired with that haunted, broken look that too often darkened her hazel eyes, told him that she somehow understood what it was to have your world irreparably fractured. And it drew him to her, against all reason.

Yesterday in the woods, she'd temporarily shed the burden constantly affixed to her shoulders, and he'd seen the person beneath. She'd become so light. Free. *Alive.*

A tender ache gripped his chest. How he wanted to feel the peace he'd read in her face.

Today he'd longed for one glimpse of her to know if she'd managed to achieve the thing that still eluded him—how to continue walking in peace after leaving the sanctuary of those woods behind. He needed evidence that someone brought to the brink could make their way back and learn to feel whole again.

He scrubbed a hand over his face and blinked eyelids that felt like they had sand behind them as he headed to the address Jake had supplied. Apparently, the chapel had blown a tire on its way to a wedding. As much as he craved sleep, his friend was in need.

Sam had spent a long night with a laboring ewe. Poor girl had a long struggle before she'd brought forth her stillborn lamb. It tore at his heart, watching innocent things mourn.

When he'd moved back here—fled back here more like—he'd thought sheep would be easier to shepherd than people. He should have taken up working with cars or some other repair work. Metal parts instead of flesh-and-blood creation. At least he'd been wise enough to leave the shepherding of people's eternal souls in more capable hands.

But there was a reason that God often referred to his people as sheep. Scriptures about shepherds constantly rose to the surface unbidden as he worked with the animals in his care. Parallels between his old and new profession were painful reminders of his failure.

Memories flashed in his mind. Memories he spent every waking moment trying to forget. Finding her. Understanding the vital information he'd missed. His failure had cost a life. *I'm sorry, Marcy.*

He swerved to the side of the road, braking hard, his tires skidding on the rocky soil before finding purchase and lurching to a stop. His heart drummed against his rib cage. Was this how it ended for him? A busted-up heart could only take so much pounding before it burst. He gripped the steering wheel, trying to find some way not to drown. *Drown.*

Cold sweat broke out across his forehead.

His breath seized in his chest. He wanted to scream. Let loose the beast that took up residence there, twisting him into knots so tight that he couldn't remember the comforting Scripture verses he'd once woven into sermons like it was second nature.

Instead, Jesus's words on the cross thundered in his mind. *Eli Eli Lama Sabachthani?*

Forsaken. That single word began throbbing in his mind,

keeping time with his heart. An accusation. Not against God. But himself.

He should have been there for her that night. Not out caring for other people.

At the tap on his window, he nearly leapt from his skin.

"Sam?" He turned toward Ana's tentative voice and gave his best attempt at forcing air back into his panic-constricted lungs.

Her eyes were round with worry on the other side of the glass. "Everything okay?"

"No," he rasped, refusing the temptation to lie. There was no hiding that he was in a bad way. "But it's nothing you can help with." His clenched jaw laced his words with an unintended bite.

Her face hardened for a moment, but then her expression smoothed. "You have no idea what I'm capable of." Her blithe tone was incongruent with the determination in her gaze.

She walked around to the passenger seat and climbed in, then she placed a hand over his where it had locked onto the steering wheel.

Ana sat in silence while he relearned to breathe. Though a million questions must have been firing in her mind, she didn't voice a single one.

Finally, the joints in his hands released the wheel. He untied the bandanna from his neck and mopped away the tears that had leaked without his permission. He glanced in the rearview mirror. Her compact car was parked behind him, flashers on.

He cleared his throat, trying to rid it of the vestiges of the vise grip that had choked the life out of him moments before.

"Your first panic attack?"

He shook his head. Not by a long shot.

"You okay to drive?"

He nodded though he wasn't and then made himself meet her eye, hoping there was something reassuring to be found in his expression. "I just need a minute. You don't need to stay." His voice was hard and hoarse.

"If you're sure. You know where I live if you need to talk." The corner of her mouth teased upward. "Or I can come camp out in your driveway if you'd prefer." In the next instant, she'd hopped out of his truck and had pulled out of sight.

The mobile chapel wasn't hard to spot, not with the precise directions Jake had given him. Sam grabbed the tool bag, hand still shaky as he fumbled with the handles. He might as well be Atlas, bracing up the world on his back.

Jake came around the corner, cheeks rosy above his long beard, forehead glistening. "You found us."

Sam nodded. "Looks like you're pretty much finished. Sorry about the delay."

"Not to worry, Sam."

"Where's Inez?"

Jake thumbed over his shoulder. "Over that-a-way." He shrugged. "She won't talk to me. That's one reason I asked you to come. You're good at talking to people."

Sam's pulse upticked, and his attempted protest came out an unintelligible sputter. His nerves, like a frayed rope, unraveled a little more.

Jake chuckled. "I know Inez is a force to be reckoned with sometimes, but, Rev, you know she'll listen to you. She always does."

Sam's soul slithered beneath the nickname.

It had startled the socks off him the first time Jake called him that. He'd confronted Marilyn, sure she'd betrayed his trust—shared what little he'd let slip to her. But she'd denied it. "I didn't breathe a word about your past," she'd said. "No matter what happened, and no matter how hard you run from it, you can't escape the heart in your own chest. It's a pastor's heart. And you don't have to be standing behind a pulpit for people to sense that caring quality in you. Especially us bird-watchers.

We're well-versed in being attentive to things that other people don't see."

Whatever she wanted to call it, it felt like a prison at the moment.

Jake huffed. "She's upset. Doesn't want to go to the wedding I'm officiating this afternoon. When we finish up here, will you take her home while I run the chapel to Gus's for a new tire?"

"Sure." That much he could manage.

They made quick work of getting the spare on. Then Jake was on his way to get the replacement on before racing to the wedding location. He sure hoped the man had a spare tuxedo packed in that bus.

Inez stood by the roadside in a ruffled pink dress, her back to Sam.

Whatever calling or gifting Marilyn claimed still lived inside of him, the aftermath of the panic attack left Sam as useful as a dried-up wishing well.

He thought about the way Ana had climbed into his truck and sat, hardly saying a word, and how something about her presence had cracked the prison door, freeing him. Maybe it was okay if he didn't have the right words today.

He approached Inez, clearing his throat to announce his presence. She jumped like a startled rabbit.

"Let me give you a ride home."

She nodded and turned. Her eyes were red-rimmed. Coal-colored rivulets marred her cheeks. He placed a tentative hand on her shoulder and guided her to his truck before opening the passenger side door for her.

Had the busted tire spooked the woman, or had she and Jake had a blowout of another variety? He shut the door after her and then went around to the driver's side. He passed her a crumpled box of tissues that had bounced around the back seat of his truck since last winter's bad cold.

She flipped down the visor as he drove, using the reflection in the mirror to dab away the smudges as best she could. Her movements were punctuated by shuddering hiccups.

He pulled into the gas station and told her he'd be right back, then he jogged in and grabbed a honeybun and a diet soda, a treat he'd seen her with on a couple of occasions. He got a bottle of water for himself.

Her eyes welled when he passed her the drink and sweet a few minutes later. She swatted him on the shoulder. "Oh, you. You've got my waterworks going again."

He grinned. "Sorry." He took a long swig of his water, bracing himself. "Did the tire busting shake you up?"

Somehow he didn't think so, because he had a feeling Jake would have been more sensitive to her state instead of dumping his wife on the side of the road and driving off.

Inez took a big bite of her honeybun and laid her head back against the headrest, sighing like she'd just gotten a taste of heaven. When he'd determined she had chosen to stay mum on the subject, he put the truck in gear and turned toward her house.

"Morgan called a little before we left the house," she said a moment later.

"Oh?" He would have thought that would have been a joyous occasion, seeing as Jake and Inez had spent months asking the group to pray for their estranged daughter to reunite with them.

Inez sniffled. "Without even a 'Hi, mom, I miss you,' she tells me she's about to be evicted and asked if I could send her some money.

"Jake told me to refuse. But all I could see was my baby on the street, homeless. He took the phone from me and told her that we just didn't have anything to spare right now. It's true, I guess. Starting up this business has drained our surplus. But Morgan is our baby." Inez dropped her chin. "But then our baby shouted a few choice words at us and hung up."

Inez swiped at her eyes. "I lit into Jake like a mockingbird mobbing a hawk. Our baby, reaching out after all these months, and he has the nerve to turn her away. Helping her out would have made things tight, but she's our responsibility. Jesus left the ninety-nine to go after the one." She huffed. "Jake said I was looking at the wrong parable. That she knew the way home and she just had to choose it. He said prodigals needed tough love. That if we bailed her out, she'd never learn."

Inez clutched the honeybun so tight, crumbs spilled from the wrapper and landed on her lap. "I don't know if Jake is right or wrong, but from the moment I knew that baby was in my womb, I had one mission in life—to protect that child, to make sure she had whatever she needed to thrive, even if it meant I did without." Inez took a drink of her diet soda, the bottle trembling in her hand. "I can't tell you how much her rejection hurt. Rejecting the love we want to give. Rejecting the God we raised her to follow. But to turn her away when she's in need is against everything I am. I'm abandoning my child when she needs me most."

A sob shuddered her shoulders. Sam removed one hand from the wheel and gently rested it on her shoulder for a moment before he placed it back on the wheel to safely navigate a hairpin curve in the road.

He remained quiet until he pulled into her driveway, heart throbbing in his chest. He'd never been a parent, but he sure did know what it felt like to attempt to love people back to life. And to realize that sometimes, no matter how hard he tried, it would never be enough.

Inez turned her watery gaze on him. "How do you know the difference between a lost sheep and a prodigal, Rev? What if refusing to help her only makes things worse?"

He pried the crushed pastry from her hand, dropped it in the plastic bag, and then took her sticky hands in his, choosing to own the nickname she bestowed on him.

He still felt like a fraud acting like he held an ounce of wisdom. But his friend was hurting.

He pushed out a breath. "Those lines can seem pretty blurry sometimes. One can look just like the other from the outside. I'd say that the difference comes down to the heart. A lost sheep wants to come home but can't for some reason. Something is getting in their way. But a prodigal is running in the opposite direction on purpose. You can't make someone come home if they don't want to."

Sam pushed onward. "I don't know all the particulars of your situation, but it doesn't seem like Morgan called because she wanted anything restored. She called because she wanted assistance staying on the path she's already on. I think it's important to keep that in mind."

Inez's lips formed a line. "But what if something terrible happens? How will I be able to live with myself?"

I don't know. I can't help you. I'm hiding, not living. His mind screamed the words so loudly, he had to resist the urge to cover his ears. Instead, he said, "Even when you can't be there, care for her, remember God loves your girl even more than you do. You can't force love on people who don't want it. They'll see it as a curse instead of the gift you intend it to be."

Inez thanked him and climbed out of the truck. He took a few more shaky breaths before pulling away.

What an imposter he was—speaking words of comfort he could not personally embrace. His head insisted they were true. But his battered heart was another matter. No matter how much faith he'd had, no matter how much he'd pled before the Lord on behalf of people in his care, bad things had still happened.

28

NOVEMBER 1958

Viola took her sketchbook and wandered to her favorite bench beneath the beeches. Every day before lunch she came out and sketched the little birds that flitted among the leaves. The foliage that had been lush and green when they'd moved in was now yellowed and beginning to drop.

She shut her eyes for the briefest instant, appreciating a sudden lull in the noises surrounding her. Listening to nature's song, she was transported back to her mountains.

But then a car backfired, cutting off the symphony mid-crescendo.

Trilby strode over to her an hour later, fresh from a lecture. Seminary life seemed to be food not just for his bones but his body and soul too. He was made for this. "Are you ready for lunch?"

"I am." She tucked her sketching things into her bag and then crossed the campus with her hand tucked into the crook of his elbow.

He chattered about the lively debate the class had just concluded involving some theological minutiae beyond Viola's interest.

Before they entered the cafeteria, he tugged her to a stop. "Are you happy, Vi?"

She nodded. "Of course."

The crease between his brows smoothed away. "I want you to be happy. More than anything. And I know all of this has been a lot of change. Change is what I'm used to. But you . . ."

"This is what I wanted, Tril. What I chose." She patted his shoulder with the hand not tucked in his.

"I know. You just seem . . ."

She laughed to herself. It was oddly comforting knowing he struggled to put a name on her mood as much as she did. "I'm fine. Let's get lunch." It was probably like this for all new wives. Being thought of as someone's daughter was familiar. Being someone's wife was as foreign to her as Louisville. She was adjusting to both. The happiness that now came in fits and bursts would become lasting. With time.

One thing she could not figure out was how living in an automated world with a laundromat, electric appliances, goods easily bought from the market down the street, and food served on neat trays in the cafeteria was more taxing than the one she'd left behind. No matter how much she rested, she couldn't shake the lingering fatigue.

He rubbed his thumb over hers. "Did you find any new books?"

She grinned. "A huge stack of them." She loved having such an extensive library a short walk away. "I'll have read every book in circulation by the time you graduate, Trilby Chambers."

He gazed at her, tenderness in his eyes. "I bet you will. You sure you don't want to try for a teaching degree? I bet we could find a way to make it work."

She shook her head and laid it on his shoulder. "I have everything I need right here, Tril."

Inside the cafeteria, they waved at Evelyn and Nathan, a married couple that they'd befriended who sat at a table nearby. Viola made sure to don her "city manners," as she and Cora once called the etiquette their mother had instilled in them. Before, she and her sister had chafed at their mother's instruction, but now those lessons in civility served her well. Whether citizen of the hidden mountain or the city streets, she could blend in like a chameleon.

Did the lizard's insides change with his surroundings? Or was it just the outsides?

She shook off the intruding thought. *Pull it together, Viola.* She was sitting next to her handsome, well-liked husband, eating a meal prepared by someone else's hands, surrounded by bright minds and hungry souls. *Lord, help me to love where I am as much as where I came from.* A comfort filled her center, unfurling the little tangle in her chest. If anyone knew what it was to walk around in a place that you loved but still wasn't your home, it was Jesus.

A few days later, Viola suppressed a squeal as Trilby took a curve a little too fast. "You'd better be careful, Trilby Chambers. Don't you go wrecking your professor's car."

He shot her a devil-may-care grin. The wind racing through the open windows tossed and twisted his auburn curls. "Don't you worry, my dear. I've got it all under control." He winked and took another curve, this time slinging her into him on the bench seat.

She laughed. "You'll get yourself kicked clean out of that seminary if you're caught driving us around like Bonnie and Clyde on the run."

They felt a little bit like jailbirds set free. Trilby had just passed his exams with flying colors. To celebrate, a professor who was dear friends with Trilby's father had loaned them his car in exchange for Trilby washing and detailing the vehicle when they returned.

"Where in the world are you taking me, anyway?" Viola asked.

They'd shed the bustle of the city hours ago and now hadn't passed another car for miles.

"It's a surprise. I told you that."

She wedged her arm between the leather seat back and his body and then reached the other across his middle, hugging him tight.

"Woman, stop trying to squeeze the truth from me. You'll see in a few minutes. I promise," he said as he poked her in the ribs, making her loosen her grip.

They passed a "Welcome to Indiana" sign.

She beamed. "Indiana is officially the third state I've ever been to."

He chuckled. "A regular world traveler you're becoming." He took his eyes from the road for a moment and smoothed wild hairs from her face. "I hope you still have that Paris travel guide I gave you. On my life, I'm taking you someday."

She locked her gaze on his. "I don't need Paris if I've got you."

A little while later he turned by a sign declaring that they were entering Brown County State Park.

She drank in the sights as the car wound through the park. The mountains rose up around them decked out in autumn splendor.

Not her mountains. But they called to her just the same. She sighed in delight, warmth swelling in her chest.

Trilby parked at a trailhead. "Are you up for a hike?"

She gave him a mock glare. "Have you forgotten who you're talking to?" She took up their picnic basket and started marching up the trail, Trilby in her wake.

Despite her bravado, she ended up needing to pass the basket to her husband within a few minutes. Try as she might, even in that clean mountain air, she found that she could not quite catch her breath.

The trail that should have taken an hour took two with the stops her shortness of breath forced them into.

When they finally reached the vista, Viola propped herself against the trunk of a tree while Trilby laid out their blanket and picnic.

As she ate the lunch she'd prepared, she relished the colors cascading like waterfalls over the rolling slopes. Birdsong filled her ears, and she smiled at her husband. "Thank you."

Worry clouded his features. "I thought maybe you were just homesick. That maybe that was why you seemed pale and tired this past month."

She reached for his hand. "I'm happy, Tril. I'm glad to be your wife."

He squeezed her fingers. "That doesn't change the fact that you haven't been yourself. I thought bringing you up here might help. It did in a way." He blinked away the moisture gathering in his eyes. "It helped me see that this is more than missing home. I think when we get back, you ought to see a doctor."

She wanted to argue. To explain away the lack of energy she'd felt. Weeks had gone by without relief, and she, too, had wondered if it was melancholy that had sapped her strength. Her mother sometimes suffered bouts of sadness too. But they'd always passed.

This shortness of breath and dizziness—they were something more.

So instead of protesting as she normally did, she scooted closer to him and laid her head on his shoulder, letting her fear leak from her eyes onto her husband's shoulder. "I'll make an appointment when I get back."

"Good."

For better or worse, they'd promised.

In sickness and in health.

They lay on the blanket on that solitary mountaintop, finding balm for their worries in each other's arms.

29

Throughout her entire book delivery trip, Ana couldn't stop thinking of Sam—the stalwart shepherd-cowboy, frozen by panic on the side of the road. That image twisted her insides in a way she didn't quite understand.

As always, her automatic response was to do something to help.

Somehow that impulse led her down a few aisles in the grocery store so she could attempt to make fried chicken, mashed potatoes, sliced tomatoes, and cornbread. Comfort food Sam had told her he missed. She'd never fried chicken in her life. But surely the plastic box of index card recipes on Cora's counter had some instructions she could follow.

With ingredients bagged in the back of her sedan, she rounded the last bend and pulled into Cora's driveway. She pressed the brake and stared, trying to make sense of the image in front of her eyes.

A dog with a white-and-brown ticked coat with big brown patches was curled tight as a cinnamon bun in her driveway. The dog's head had popped up as she neared, ears perked. It jumped to its feet and cavorted in circles around her sedan.

Ana's face split into a wide grin.

She opened her car door, and forty-five pounds of dirt-streaked animal squished between Ana and the steering wheel. Pip's hindquarters bumped the car horn, interrupting their reunion. Pip froze, and Ana giggled at her look of canine concern. She took the furry face in her hands. "How in the world did you find me?"

Those soulful eyes stared into hers, then her pink tongue darted out, quick as a frog after a fly, swiping Ana's cheek.

"Blech. Gross." She pushed the dog's snout away from her face and then nuzzled behind her velvety ear. "I'm sorry I left you. I thought it was for the best," she murmured against Pip's fur.

After Ana extricated herself out from under the dog and dusted off her clothes, she called Pip inside. Her stubby tail wagged so hard it sent her entire body into motion—until Ana led her to the bathtub.

She pointed to the basin. "Load."

Pip obeyed, but her ears drooped and her eyes were so sorrowful Ana had to laugh. "Wait," Ana said and then went to retrieve her groceries from the car.

Pip was right where Ana left her, still as a statue, when Ana returned. "Good girl." She dutifully submitted to Ana's ministrations, obeying every request, but not without complaint. Whines, grunts, and other conversational dog noises made Ana feel like she was bathing a grumpy toddler.

"Even ignoring the drawbacks Jake pointed out about Pippi, the name didn't exactly fit you. And your personality is way too big for a diminutive name like Pip. But Piper—you fussy thing—that might be perfect." The dog let out a soulful "ahroo" as Ana sluiced warm water over her back. "Piper it is."

After being dried by her old companion, Piper curled up on the dog bed that Ana had dragged into the kitchen. Played out from her adventures, the canine slept.

Ana picked up the phone and dialed the vet's office.

"Roan Mountain Veterinary Clinic. How can I help you?"

"Oh, hi, Doc Underwood. This is Ana Watkins. Sorry, I planned to leave a message. I didn't expect anyone to be in the office after hours."

"I'm here with a sick kitten that needs a little TLC. It's going to be a long night. I'm sorry, but I don't have any updates about the pointer you brought to us."

Ana sat on the floor next to the sleeping dog. "I do. She's snoozing in my kitchen as we speak." She then told her about Piper's return.

"That's incredible. The rescue will be so glad that you located her. I'll call and let them know. Hopefully they still have space and can come pick her up."

Ana pushed out a breath and sat tall. "Actually, I'd like to keep her. If there's forms or paperwork or training I need or—"

"She's already yours."

A smile stretched Ana's cheeks to the point of aching.

Doc Underwood cleared her throat. "You found her. You cared for her. No one else has a claim on her. But I will let the rescue know she's safe. They felt so bad about what happened."

"I'll do my best to give her everything she needs."

"I have no doubt you two will be just fine, Ana."

How she wanted to believe that.

After she ended the call, she watched Piper sleep for a few moments. Something about seeing that wandering pup at home and at complete ease put Ana's heart at rest.

She picked up her aunt's plastic recipe box and went to the kitchen table. Cora had left a sticky note on top that read "In case you need a little inspiration in the kitchen." With more than a little trepidation, Ana thumbed through the tattered cards until she found the one she was searching for. Though Ana was comfortable cooking, she'd never fried anything. Her mother's gluten allergy didn't lend itself well to breaded foods, so they'd always been avoided in the household Ana grew up in.

As she carefully followed the instructions on the card, she caught herself humming a little tune that she made up.

An hour later she packed a picnic basket she'd found in Cora's things with the piping hot fried chicken and sides. Before she left, she sampled one of the pieces she kept out for her own dinner.

A happy sigh slipped out of her. She'd done a lip-smacking good job, if she did say so herself. She fired off a quick text to Lexi, updating her on the Piper situation.

Her friend responded with a string of confetti emojis. A few seconds later another text came through.

"I went on another one of my mother's blind dates last night."

Ana snickered. "What did you nickname this one?"

Three undulating dots appeared, leaving her in suspense. Finally Lexi's answer came through. "Just Brian. No nickname."

Ana's eyebrows raised. *Interesting.* She sent a matching string of confetti emojis, then stashed her phone into her purse and gathered the basket.

Piper didn't even lift an eyelid as Ana exited the house, still tuckered from her journey home.

Ana took the two-minute drive to Sam's farm. While she'd cruised by his place on her way down the mountain on several occasions, this was the first time she dared to venture beneath the metal archway of Selah Meadows. The immaculate fields were verdant and dotted with snow-white sheep. The place looked like B-roll footage of the Scottish Highlands.

She stopped in front of a sweeping farmhouse. Her hands shook a little as she retrieved the basket from where she'd buckled it into the passenger seat, heat rising to her cheeks. Would he think she'd lost her senses, showing up on his porch with a basket of food? As if fried chicken could somehow heal whatever it was that haunted him.

Just when she considered jumping back in her car, the screen door of the house creaked open. Sam stepped onto the wrap-around porch with a sheepdog following in his wake. Too late to retreat now.

She lifted the basket and offered a wave. "Brought you some comfort food."

He descended the steps and strode toward her. "That was kind of you."

"I had to eat." She shrugged. "No trouble at all to make a little extra." The sheepdog circled Ana, sniffing her warily.

"Lie down, Max." The dog instantly obeyed Sam's command. "Is that fried chicken I smell?"

She nodded. "And mashed potatoes and cornbread. Sliced tomatoes."

"You remembered." The words were not much more than a whisper.

She passed him the basket, searching for a way to answer the question in his eyes. "The way to my heart has always been through my stomach, so I have an excellent memory when it comes to my friends' favorite foods," she said, hoping to lighten the moment. "My friend Lexi loves Funfetti cake when she's feeling low." She tipped her head to the side. "Actually, Funfetti cake with a single Swedish fish on top."

His eyebrows raised. "That's very specific."

She laughed. "She's that kind of girl." She gestured to the basket. "I knew you'd had a rough day, and I just wanted to do something to make it a little brighter." She shifted her feet. "I should run."

"Did you want to join me?" He thumbed over his shoulder.

She looked to the farmhouse behind him. What would those walls reveal about the reserved shepherd? Anything? She was about to take him up on his offer when the image of Piper unsupervised flashed in her mind. "I better get back. But thanks."

"Hot date?" he teased.

"Kinda." She clasped her hands. "My dog's back."

His eyes widened. "Pip?"

"Yep. Showed up in my driveway a filthy mess. Although, I've changed her name. *Again.* It's Piper now." She shrugged. "I think this one will stick."

"You're going to keep her?"

"Yeah." Ana laughed under her breath. "I suppose this means I'm a Piper person."

December 1958

Viola lay in her bed, the darkened bedroom closing in around her. Her breath came short and fast, unwilling to feed her lungs. The warmth of her sleeping husband powerless to ease the fear crawling up her throat.

She placed her hand on the tiniest swell in her abdomen, replaying the doctor's prognosis.

The pregnancy had put a greater strain on her weak heart. A weakness that likely sprang from the illness that had almost killed her two winters prior.

Viola struggled up from the bed and went to the window, trying to escape the stale apartment atmosphere. She pushed up the sash. The night was dark and deep, beckoning her to fall into its embrace.

If only she could be transported back to where she belonged. Home, where December breezes were as sharp as a razor. Home, where birdsong choruses could soothe a breaking heart. If not that, she'd at least like to feel at home in her own skin instead of at war with her failing body.

"Help," she whispered. She needed a sign to know that God was still there. That he had not forsaken her like her earthly father had.

But the world remained a silent, inky nothingness.

She stayed by the window, gripping the sill so tight her fingers ached. Refusing to accept the silence for an answer. Her shoulders shook and tears dripped down her face.

By now the living room in Bitter End would have a tree decorated with little glass ornaments her father had bought her mother their first Christmas together. He would have begun his nightly Christmas concerts on his father's fiddle, the one that had belonged to his father's father before that. She could almost taste the cinnamon and vanilla of the cookies she and Cora baked throughout the season.

Viola was supposed to have been able to dive headlong into being Trilby's wife, shucking all vestiges of the moonshiner's daughter. But on nights like these, when fear overshadowed her faith, she ached for the part of herself that she'd cut away.

Over dinner she'd told Trilby that she wanted to go back to the mountain for Christmas. If what the doctor said was true, this one could be her last. Would that knowledge be enough to soften her father's hardened heart?

"You must take care of yourself," Trilby had said, refusing her request and dismissing her worries that this could be her last chance to visit home. Long bus rides through the mountains did not align with the rest her doctor had prescribed.

The sky on the horizon lightened a fraction, pushing back the night. "I feel so alone," she prayed, feeling foolish for uttering those words when her husband slept in the bed on the other side of the small room.

Somewhere beyond her view, a single song sparrow trilled, a winged missionary who spoke a language her frail heart could understand.

She went to the desk in the living room where Trilby always did his work and pulled out a sheet of paper. She wrote to her mother and Cora, telling them about the baby, omitting the details of her delicate condition. With flowery words, she painted a merry picture of Christmas in Louisville. Told them about all the storefronts decorated with lights and Christmas scenes. About Trilby acing all his exams. All the good and lovely things she felt they'd enjoy. She folded the pages and addressed the letter to Marilyn Chambers.

Her young sister-in-law knew the drill—she'd place the letters in the old lean-to for Cora to retrieve.

Viola didn't know if their father's anger had cooled like Momma hoped it would. But Momma must have at least been a little worried he'd intercept the communication between them, because she'd gone along with Viola's scheme to use Marilyn as messenger.

"Viola, darling?"

She shifted in the chair.

Trilby stood in the doorway, hair tousled, arms wrapped around his middle. "Are you all right?"

"I'm fine."

"The window's wide open, and it's freezing in here."

"I'm sorry. I was feeling warm."

Tenderness softened the concern etched on his face. "I'd freeze to death to keep you happy."

She trapped her bottom lip between her teeth. Her faith in many things might be frail at the moment, but she never doubted his love for her. No matter how scary the doctor's prognosis, she could count on Trilby to be her rock. "Go to Bitter End for Christmas. Please."

He crossed the room and scooped her hands into his. "And leave you here alone on our first Christmas? Why in the world would I do such a thing? Why would you want me to?" Hurt and confusion crumpled his expression.

She forced strength and resolve into her voice. "Because *I* can't be there. And if you were there, if you could lay eyes on my family and yours, then it would feel like a part of me was there too." She squeezed his hands. "I wouldn't be alone. We've got friends living on all sides of us. And I know for certain that Evelyn and Nathan said their families were coming to them since they couldn't afford the travel expenses."

He sighed, eyes searching hers. "I'll talk to my boss and see if I can have off the week before Christmas. I'll bring them a few little gifts and notes and then be back in your arms before Saint Nick's sleigh leaves the North Pole." He studied her, a pair of vertical lines forming between his brows. "I'll do this for you, if it's what you really want."

Viola went to the tin can in the back of one of the kitchen cabinets where she'd kept her savings for Cora's summer bus fare. She handed it to Trilby. "For your ticket. Consider this trip your Christmas gift to me." Since Trilby had started classes in the fall, she'd taken in laundry from professors to make extra money and pass the day. She'd had to give that up after her diagnosis. But maybe somehow, she could replenish it in time and pay Cora's way for her summer visit.

He took the can with a knowing smile, then went to the little filing cabinet the school had discarded that now served as his nightstand. He pulled out what had once been a box of rice. "I've been saving too. So Cora could come. Or for a ticket to Paris if you'd rather." He winked.

Then and now, the man sought the things that made her heart sing. "Thank you, Tril."

Viola paced the floor. The cheery Christmas music scraping out of the speakers of her new radio grated her nerves. She switched it off but found the space too solemn without it. Trilby was supposed to have been home on the twenty-third, but now it was midnight on Christmas Eve.

They'd chosen to forgo decorations this year, saving their money for their growing family. She switched the radio back on, so there would be something festive about the room when he came through the door.

She sank into the chair, overcome by the tightness in her chest. Her mind riffled through imaginary scenarios. Snow up in the mountains that kept him from coming. A bus accident. Trouble at home. She should have gone with him.

She could have managed it.

Then, almost as if summoned by her worry, Trilby came through the front door. His eyes were vacant and his face pale and haggard. Stubble lined his jaw. His mother and little sister wandered through the door after him like lost lambs, a small suitcase in each of their hands.

Bobby Helms's jaunty voice belted out over the radio waves. She reached for the knob, cutting off the voice.

"Tril?"

He stared at the floor. "My father is dead."

31

Marilyn opened the little suitcase she kept in the back corner of her attic. Things from that long-ago past had followed her out of Bitter End and then made the journey back when Obie had gotten the research position. It was a silly thought, but she sometimes imagined the suitcase had played some part in her return to Bitter End, the memories inside begging to be reunited with their birthplace—memories woven into the history of this mountain and into the fabric of her being.

She brought out a quilt her mother had made. One of her father's favorite neckties. An essay her brother Trilby had written on the sovereignty of God before he stopped believing in such things.

And then she pulled out the little corn husk doll. What would Cora think if she knew Marilyn had cherished that handmade Christmas gift all these years?

She thought of Ana, cleaning out all the things Cora had collected over her life on these mountains. Was the carved soapstone heart still numbered among Cora's possessions? And if so, had it landed in the discard or the keeper pile?

It was a mystery how some trinkets and knickknacks were alive with meaning and memory while others were soulless souvenirs.

Marilyn placed all the memories of her Bitter End childhood back into the trunk.

She descended the attic stairs and stopped in the doorway of Obie's office. Her husband's library of ornithology texts filled the built-in bookshelves. The framed sketches decorated the wall space not occupied by shelves. She was the last remaining witness to his genius.

That's what a marriage was—a determined witness to someone else's life. To decide that out of the eight billion people on the planet, that person was counted most important. But now that Obie was gone and her eyesight failing, she'd wondered what would become of the beautiful things his hands had made with no one to pass them to at her death. Would they collect dust in the corner of a thrift store? Or be discarded in a landfill?

She and Obie had never had children. A decision that they'd been happy with for years, but a few regrets had crept in in their later years. But she supposed that was the way with most things. If you took one path, it was tempting at times to wonder how life would have turned out if you'd taken another.

A soft knock at her front door freed her from her heavy thoughts. She wasn't blind or dead yet. Surely she'd find a home for Obie's things with his colleagues. No need for despair. Not yet.

Marilyn opened the door to reveal Ana standing on her welcome mat holding a purple Pyrex dish. The slight young woman shifted her feet. It was a little shocking knowing that this was the same heroic woman from the articles she'd read last night.

A woman who also happened to favor Marilyn's own brother—with that auburn hair, those freckles, and fair cheeks that blushed with ease.

"I brought brownies. Can we talk?" Ana ran the two statements together as if payment was required for the request to be granted.

Marilyn smiled. "Fried chicken for Sam last night and now brownies for me. Do you always feed your friends, or is it just a way to get your foot in the door?" She laughed and swatted the air. "Either way is fine by me, those brownies smell amazing."

"Word gets around fast, I guess." Ana's cheeks pinked.

Marilyn stepped aside and motioned her in, heart fluttering in her chest. Cora would not like Ana in her house. Not one bit.

But Cora wasn't here.

"Let's go to the kitchen." She headed down the hall.

Ana's gentle tread ceased. Marilyn turned.

Ana was looking over Obie's study. "You really do love birds, don't you?"

Marilyn lifted a shoulder. "An acquired appetite. That was my husband Obadiah's study. We moved here several years back because he'd gotten a research grant involving the study of migratory birds in the Appalachian Mountains." She continued to the kitchen and Ana followed. "When we moved back here, I'd just retired from teaching, and adjusting to retirement was more difficult than I anticipated. Add to it the fact that I was returning to a place that had some awful memories attached to it."

Ana's gaze jerked away. Evidence of the headlines she'd likely discovered on the microfilm was tattooed in her guilt-ridden expression.

"I never imagined I'd set foot on this rocky soil again, but Obie had this gleam in his eyes that had been missing for years, and I couldn't say no." Marilyn poured two glasses of milk and brought them to the table, then retrieved two saucers. "I started going out with him on the trails. It was a little uncomfortable at first. But something about being in nature as a couple knit us back together. So even after his research was completed, we stayed."

Marilyn traced her finger around the rim of her cup. "We started this bucket list of birds we wanted to find in these mountains. We made it a good way through the list before he passed away." She swiped away the moisture that had collected in her eyes. *Goodness.* Those flash floods still snuck up on her at times. For whatever reason, her heart was extra tender today.

Ana cut two generous squares from the brownie dish and placed them on saucers. "Are you still working on it?"

Her no was so weighted that it barely made it past her lips.

"But . . ." But lately she'd been tempted, knowing her time to view those species they'd listed was limited. Was she really going to make this confession now, to this girl whose ancestry intertwined with hers in such a painful way?

Ana's questioning eyes probed at the walls Marilyn had built around the secret she kept from the Bitter End Birding Society.

Marilyn shook her head to clear it. "Never mind that. You didn't come here today to hear an old woman go on about an old pet project." She pinched a piece of the brownie and rolled it between her thumb and finger until it formed a fudgie ball. "You're here because of what happened to my father."

Ana sucked air between her teeth as if she'd accidentally put her hand on a hot stove. "I never knew . . ." She shook her head. "My grandmother died young, and my grandfather remarried. It was like life and family before his second marriage never happened. And when my mom married into Dad's huge family, she lost all connection with distant relatives. So, I had no idea when we met that . . ."

"That your great-grandfather murdered my father?"

Ana nodded, wide-eyed.

Marilyn sat back in her chair with a sigh. "So, you came here for what? The real story or . . ."

"To say I'm sorry."

Marilyn blinked. "Whatever for? You didn't hold the gun that fired the shot."

"I know but . . ."

"You feel responsible somehow?"

Ana nodded again.

"Funny, that. The guilt felt for something that you had nothing to do with, because of the blood that flows through your veins." Marilyn took a bite of her brownie, allowing the pain to sit heavy in her chest. "Cora was my best friend when I moved here. Secret best friends, because Wayne didn't want the teetotaling preacher putting ideas in his daughters' heads."

"He sounds like a horrible man."

One corner of Marilyn's mouth curled upward. "That's not how Cora described him. Granted, there was no way she was going to tell him that we snuck around to play together. He was a man you didn't cross, and he was unfair at times. Mostly because he was scared to lose his daughters' respect, I think. But he loved his girls according to Cora.

"When my father was killed, I moved away from here. I went to live with Vi and my brother Trilby—that was another upset that rocked Cora's world. Your grandmother marrying my brother."

The bite of brownie in Ana's hand fell to the saucer. "Your brother? Then you're my . . . you're—"

Marilyn watched the changes in Ana's expression as she connected the dots. "I'm your great-aunt, as is Cora. And my great-niece is something of a hero it turns out."

Ana's face blanched. "N-no. I'm not. Really."

"You're not the only one who can do research, my dear. I thought Google might turn up a social media page. Imagine my surprise when—"

"Please . . . don't. I'm here to leave all that behind me. At least for a while."

Ana's expression was so tortured that Marilyn instantly regretted bringing it up. "I'll not breathe another word about it unless you do." She cleared her throat. "So back to the reason for your visit today."

"Cora never told me . . ."

Marilyn gave a knowing shrug and continued her story. "Old Wayne Lee Whitt's world really unraveled when Viola chose Trilby over her family. My mother always believed that was why he shot my father—for having stolen away one of his daughters from this old mountain. Nobody could figure out what my daddy was doing out at Wayne's still that night in the first place."

They were quiet for several moments as Ana seemed to absorb

her words. Eventually she cocked her head. "Did you say you lived with my grandmother Viola?"

Marilyn sighed. "For about six months. Cora felt like I stole her sister." She took another bite of her brownie. "You see, the plan had always been for Cora to spend that summer with Viola and Trilby. Despite the age gap, Viola and Cora grew up tight-knit as denim, and as you can imagine, they hadn't had a whole lot of contact since Viola's marriage. But after the murder and manhunt, Vi and Trilby offered to take me on for the summer while my mother made arrangements for our future. Cora was stuck dealing with the fallout in Bitter End instead of escaping to her sister. All because of me."

"Did she come later?"

Marilyn shook her head. "Viola passed away. A heart condition her pregnancy exacerbated."

"My mother," Ana whispered.

"Yes."

Ana dropped her gaze. Marilyn could only imagine what the young woman must be feeling. Sadness was understandable. But feeling as though she was somehow to blame? There had been more than enough misplaced blame in this rotten situation.

"Ana, dear, there's so much hurt wrapped up in that old story. Mine. Cora's. My brother's. Your grandmother Viola's." Marilyn shook her head. "If you're wondering if I hold a grudge against you because of who you're related to, honey, put yourself at ease. Your lineage is as tangled with mine as it is Cora's. And even if it wasn't, this broken part of our shared history doesn't define us. We're just a couple of women trying to make sense of this thing called life. I just wish Cora could see it the same way."

32

In the days following Trilby's return, Viola tiptoed around the mourning family. They huddled in the small apartment as if in a daze—lost in a world Viola wasn't privy to. She was hungry to understand what had happened to her father-in-law, yet afraid her questions would somehow shatter them in their fragile state.

Young Marilyn wasn't speaking, and Mrs. Chambers said little more than her daughter. Finally, one night after she and Trilby had lain down in bed, Viola prodded him. "Trilby, what happened?"

They lay there in the dark without touching, seconds ticking by like years. His voice came low and harsh. "He was shot."

Shot? How could that warm, kind man have such a violent end?

When she'd tried to inquire further, he'd refused, insisting she wasn't well enough to hear such upsetting things.

A week later, a letter came from Cora.

Viola made sure no one saw her pluck the message from the mail stack and slip it into the pocket of her dress. She escaped the oppressive grief weighing the apartment and went out among the beech trees, choosing her favorite bench.

She slid her finger beneath the envelope's seal and slid out the lined paper. When she unfolded the letter, a gust of wind blew, scattering newspaper clippings that had been tucked inside. Viola scrambled after them, snatching up one and then stepping on the other before the wind could sweep it away. She bent to retrieve the one beneath her shoe. The headline glared back.

The Manhunt for Wild Wayne Lee Whitt Continues

The shaking started in her knees and rattled all the way through her. Viola stumbled back to the bench and sank into it. She stared at Cora's short letter.

> *They say Daddy's done gone and killed the reverend. Momma's in a real state. Says it can't be true. I wish you were here.*

Viola scoured the newspaper clippings, which held dramatic re-tellings of how the reverend had been found dead at one of her father's stills. And how he had cut town.

She knew better though. He hadn't cut town. He didn't need to. The hills and hollows provided all the hiding spots he'd ever need.

Her stomach twisted as her mind scrambled to make sense of it all.

She gathered the papers before returning to the apartment. She held the clippings in her trembling hands as she approached her husband.

Her legs gave way beneath her. He rushed forward to brace her up.

The newsprint fell to the ground, soon trampled beneath their feet.

"I'm sorry. I'm so sorry." How could he love her now?

He pulled back from her, something tortured in his eyes. "Please stop. Please don't apologize."

He helped her into the closest chair and fled the apartment.

Mrs. Chambers stayed through the rest of Christmas break but had her suitcase packed the morning before spring classes resumed.

"You can stay too," Viola pleaded.

Mrs. Chambers, looking small and gray, shook her head. "I need to see about starting a life for Marilyn and myself. Thank you for seeing to her in the meantime."

She kissed her son on the cheek and then her daughter, and then she was gone. Marilyn collapsed on the secondhand sofa, sobbing—the first tears the shell-shocked child had shed. Trilby again disappeared out the front door.

Viola was left standing in the middle of her apartment, wondering how in the world she'd help any of them navigate this pain.

Over the spring, Mrs. Chambers boarded with a friend, getting work at a rayon factory, and saved money for a place for her and Marilyn.

Viola dutifully kept her mother-in-law posted on Marilyn's progress at school. Though the girl was quieter than when Viola had first met her, she seemed to be coping. Her grades were good. She made new friends. She assisted Viola with household upkeep. A welcome help since Viola lacked the stamina for even the simplest tasks most days.

She sometimes heard the girl crying in the night, but that was to be expected.

Trilby's grief was another matter. He'd turned inward, existing in some unreachable place. And though he still worked, still passed his exams, the light had gone out of his eyes, and Viola was beginning to doubt it would ever come back.

Cora kept her abreast of the news in Bitter End, sending articles Viola didn't want to read yet couldn't resist. Articles about the manhunt. Articles about how her father had eventually turned himself in and confessed. About the trial. The sentencing. Justice had been swift and triumphant in locking him away.

In the middle of it all, Viola was like a woodland creature robbed of its den. Nothing could bring back Trilby's father and nothing could erase the fact that she was Wild Wayne's daughter.

One afternoon, when Trilby was in class and Marilyn was off at grammar school, she pulled the various clippings out and arranged them on the kitchen table—a black-and-white patchwork of ugly, angry words she did not want to believe about the man who'd raised her.

She glanced to Trilby's Bible on the end table. She stood and wiped off a fine sheen of dust with the hem of her dress. This Bible that Trilby once opened every morning over his cup of coffee had remained untouched since his return from Bitter End. He'd become a student of God's Word who scoured all the textbooks but left the original text unopened.

The front door flung open. Viola stood, startled by the sudden interruption in the middle of the day. Trilby squinted at her, as if trying to make sense of her presence.

She swept the articles into a pile and hid them beneath the Bible's leather cover.

"Tril? Are you okay?" She stepped closer to him, but the sour scent on his breath caused her to draw up short. His eyes were unfocused. His step toward her unsteady.

Never in her life had she smelled spirits on her moonshiner father's breath. Yet here stood her seminary student husband smelling like he'd tipped headfirst into a barrel of whiskey.

She was not naive enough to believe that her father never partook of the product he created. But the men of Bitter End had lived by a strict code. Drinking in front of women and children was not done. Instead, they'd go off into the woods together and pass a jug whenever they were keen to sand off the hard edges of life.

But who was she to judge Trilby? Her father had killed a man. Sometimes men violated the codes they vowed to live by and she was left not knowing how to respond.

She supported her husband under the elbow, guiding him to their bedroom. "Go on to bed, Trilby. Just go on to bed."

Did he know that what he needed for his pain was healing, not an anesthetic? The numbness he felt was not a cure.

Anesthesia was not the sort of thing a body could live on. Pain had a purpose. Pain let you know something was wrong inside so that you could address it.

But numbness let you forget. And in that neglect, things would fester.

In the kitchen Viola stared at the Bible and then she removed all her father's misdeeds from beneath its cover. She held the Bible in one hand and the newsprint in the other, praying without words.

She wasn't quite sure if she should pray the school would catch Trilby in his violation of their rules or pray they wouldn't. But she trusted the Lord knew what was best for the tormented man who had replaced the boy she'd married.

33

The next Thursday, Ana met the bird-watchers at the Forest Road Trail. The sun had started its descent toward the horizon, casting everything in a pink glow. The area was populated with old growth and dead trees, which made it a great place to study woodpeckers, according to Marilyn.

When she approached, everyone greeted Piper first. The dog scampered and twisted as she received a quick pat from each of the members. Inez clasped her hands together. "I knew it would work out in the end. I just knew it."

Ana asked Piper to sit, giving her leash arm a break. "Working out may be overstating it. This poor thing needs more exercise than she gets. I wish Cora's yard was fenced so I could let her really cut loose." She scratched Piper behind the ear, and she flopped her head skyward, blissfully gazing back at Ana. "Then again, I'm also afraid to let her go even if I had a fence. She's prone to getting lost."

Sam nudged her shoulder. "The last time Piper split, she wasn't lost. She was making her way back home."

"True." Why did the thought of a floppy-eared nightmare vanquisher racing back to her make pinpricks fire off behind her eyes?

Ana dabbed away the gathering moisture with the collar of her shirt, pretending it was sweat from the late-day humidity.

She turned to Jake and Inez. "Did your wedding emergency end up alright?" She had been dying to find out what that had been all about.

"Oh, honey, let me tell you. It. Was. A. Mess." Inez patted Ana's shoulder for emphasis and kept talking with her hands waving about. "A pipe had broke over at the Baptist church just an hour before this gal's ceremony, so the church called us and asked if we could throw an emergency wedding." She slapped a hand over her heart. "The momma was all in a tizzy."

Jake put his hands on his hips with his chest puffed out. "But the Mobile Wedding Chapel came to the rescue. We pulled up just in time and threw together a little shindig in the park next to the church."

Marilyn cleared her throat. "Alright, folks. We're burning away our daylight chattering. Lead us on the hike, Sam. You know this path well."

As Ana turned to follow, a young man standing on the fringe of the parking area caught her eye. He gazed into the dense forest, a lit cigarette in his hand. Something about the way he stood there—that adolescent stance that tried to prove that he was adult enough to handle life on his own—tugged Ana to him.

For a split second she envisioned a younger version of the nineteen-year-old who frequented her nightmares standing in the woods contemplating his first cigarette, lost and confused, needing someone to rescue him from the dark musings tempting his mind. Somehow it was compassion not fear that swept over her.

The kid took a long drag and then doubled over, choking. Ana stifled a chuckle as she and Piper approached. "Hey."

The kid straightened. He threw the cigarette on the ground and stomped it, then shoved his hands in his pockets.

"We're looking for a certain kind of bird and I wondered if you'd seen it." She flipped her field guide open to a random page and showed it to him. A cardinal? Couldn't she have landed on something a little more obscure?

His brow creased. "There were about twenty redbirds in my backyard this morning. They're literally everywhere around here." He glanced at Piper, who looked longingly at him, begging for attention. "Cool dog. Is it some sort of brown Dalmatian?"

She shook her head. "German shorthaired pointer. At least, that's what the vet said. She was lost, and I adopted her."

"Sweet. Can I pet her?"

"Sure." There was something magical watching this sullen teenager morph back into a bright-eyed kid as he scratched Piper's side. She leaned against his legs, eating up the adoration.

"I'm Ana. This is Piper."

Gaze still on Piper, he said, "I'm Trent."

Ana glanced behind her. Her friends were already disappearing down the trail. "I'd better get back to my group. There's supposed to be a lot of cool woodpecker varieties in these woods. You can join if you want." She hoped the invitation came off as welcoming and not weird. "I mean, it might seem a little lame, but I'm pretty sure it's better than hanging out around a parking lot, choking on cigarettes."

Trent's face colored, and he shrugged. "I'll come."

They hurried down the trail to catch up.

As they approached the group, Ana called out, "Hey, everyone. This is Trent."

Marilyn gave a nod of approval, and Sam grumbled under his breath, something that sounded like "as bad as Marilyn."

"Hey, Trent," Jake and Inez chorused.

The kid lifted one hand in an awkward wave.

Marilyn opened her backpack and pulled out binoculars and a field guide. Did she always have spares at the ready?

They walked noisily through the woods for the first section of the trail, chatting amiably about all the different types of wedding emergencies Jake and Inez had averted and emergency weddings they'd thrown. Apparently they were emergency on-call with all the churches and event venues within a twenty-mile radius. Ana's side almost split laughing at their anecdote about an impromptu raccoon removal Jake had done for a church fellowship hall minutes before a reception. She congratulated Jake on his courage. She knew just how troublesome raccoons could be.

She glanced toward Sam, who grinned knowingly back at her. For some reason, the humor in his often-pensive gaze made warmth bloom in her middle.

When she turned her attention back to Inez, the woman lifted her eyebrows and wiggled her index finger like she was drawing little lines between Ana and Sam.

Ana's eyes shot wide. "Oh. No. Raccoons. We—I mean, I—Cora's shed had raccoons, and Sam came over to help."

Inez nudged Ana's shoulder. "He came over? Well, now. Wasn't that neighborly of him?" Ana did not dare look to see if Sam had overheard Inez's insinuations.

Trent thankfully switched the subject, pointing out Piper's slow-motion "creeper walk" as she stalked, scanning the trees for birds with her short tail sticking out like an antenna. Every now and then, she'd shoot her walking companions a confused look, as if she couldn't understand why they'd make so much noise while on the hunt.

Ana passed the leash into Trent's eager hands, intending to maneuver herself closer to Marilyn so she could ask her more about her brother, Trilby. When he'd requested his new wife whisk Ana's mother Quinn away, he'd effectively done the same to his own young sister as he had to Cora. Had that severing from the troubled Whitt family been a relief? Or had Marilyn felt abandoned in the same way she was sure Cora felt?

But the trail took a steep incline, forcing them all into silence. After the trail evened out, no one spoke above a whisper, and everyone walked more softly.

A shrill call echoed. Sam held out a hand and everyone stopped. Marilyn grinned at Ana. "Downy woodpecker."

"How do you know?" Ana whispered.

"If you pay attention long enough, you learn that every species has its own unique call," Marilyn said. "And different types of woodpeckers even have their own drumming pattern."

It was Inez who spotted their quarry first. Ana watched the little bird zip to another tree and then drill the bark with its sharp beak. Piper sat at Trent's feet, head swiveling as she followed the movement of various birds twittering overhead. Trent absently patted her side while he looked at the trees.

Ana took a deep breath of the mountain air. What was it about watching these creatures going about their business without a worry in the world that made her own cares fade, if only for a moment? She sat on a downed log, slipped off her hiking boots and socks, then stood, feeling the slim shafts of pine needles and cool earth beneath her feet. The tightness in her chest eased. She sketched the woodpecker clinging to the side of a towering pine. Beside it, she recorded the details of the day and things she observed about the little bird. It wasn't scientific and perfect like the drawings Marilyn's husband had displayed on his home office walls. But they made her slow down and notice details she normally would have missed, allowing her to get out of her head and be fully present.

Piper went into a point, laser focused on rustling in the underbrush. Trent motioned Ana over. "What kind of bird is that?"

He pointed to a bird larger than the downy. It was a soft tan with black speckles on its breast. Its most striking features were a bold black bib on its chest and a vibrant patch of red on its head.

"I don't know, but it's stunning. Let's ask the expert." She called Marilyn over. "What kind of bird is that? It's beautiful."

Marilyn's face lit up. "A northern flicker. Great find."

A shy smile bloomed on Trent's face at the praise. And in that instant the unvarnished joy and wonder of a child broke through the teenage mask—like tender green things unfolding in spring.

How had this become her life? Dog owner. Nature enthusiast. Birding society recruiter.

On the way back to the parking lot, she shared all the new species she'd added to her life list with Marilyn. Northern flicker, downy woodpecker, white-breasted nuthatch, pileated woodpecker, Carolina chickadee. Marilyn smiled at her. "Told you this would be a great spot. Obie took me here on one of the first birding outings we shared."

"Did you love it then like you do now?"

"Those first few times out together were a little rough," Marilyn said. "We'd forgotten how to connect, to communicate in the rush of life. Being outside together slowly brought us back to life."

Ana peered at her. "Your bucket list helped?"

Marilyn nodded. "It gave us something to work toward together without it being about his research," she said. "I think it gave him a chance to fall back in love with birding too. Nobody talks about how hard it can be to get paid to do something you love. That's supposed to be the dream, but when a paycheck comes, expectations get attached. And when you're doing something for your livelihood and not just for the fun of it, joy can get a little slippery. Over the years Obie had lost a little of his boyish wonder of his beloved birds. And our marriage had lost joy and delight in the small things. Our list helped us rediscover life."

Ana fidgeted with the binoculars hanging around her neck. "Have you ever thought about finishing it?"

Marilyn sighed. "For a while there, I couldn't bear to think about working on it without him. It was just too painful. And now, I'm not sure I need to."

Ana pushed a little harder. "We could help you finish it."

Sadness swelled in Marilyn's voice. "I don't think so." She motioned ahead. "There's something I need to ask Sam."

Worried she'd offended Marilyn, Ana dropped back to check on Piper who was still in Trent's capable hands.

When they reached the trailhead, he passed Piper's leash back to Ana. "Thanks for inviting me. It was actually kind of fun."

Ana smiled. "Surprised?"

He shrugged. "My mom would love this."

"Bring her next time." Ana gave him the location and time of the next meeting. As she drove home, she felt an odd sense of accomplishment, like she'd had the chance to share a little of the peace and wonder she felt out in God's creation with another searching soul like her own.

34

Dusk began to settle over Bitter End, and Piper's typical last burst of restlessness drove her and Ana outdoors. "Come on, girl. Let's get your walk in." Ana grabbed the leash off the hook and led Piper down the walkway and out to the road.

Piper stopped suddenly, pointing. A mourning dove was silhouetted on a branch. Piper tensed as the bird took flight, watched it for a moment, then continued her walk, looking to the path ahead.

Ana loved how Piper was always so focused, attentive to the smallest details, reminding Ana to do the same.

There was something so grounding about considering the small things. It reminded her of the mindfulness exercise the therapist she'd seen after the incident had taught her.

"Name five things you can see. Four things you can hear. Three things you can smell. Two things you can touch. One thing you can taste." That awareness of her senses forced the chaotic spiraling inside her head into an orderly cadence.

With birds, you listened for the individual birdsongs. You looked to where the sought-after species could be found—whether on the ground, in the brush, or in the higher canopy. And when you saw the bird, you had to look very carefully for the subtle field markings that confirmed the species before you.

It was a practice in directing thoughts and attention. A skill she wished she would have known how to teach the children in her class.

As she passed Marilyn's house with Piper, Ana noticed the older woman stooped beside her birdhouse. "Hello. What are you up to?"

Marilyn straightened and dusted off her gloved hands. "Sad business, I'm afraid."

Ana and Piper drew closer.

"I've been watching a mated pair of bluebirds for the past few weeks, building this nest, laying a little clutch of eggs, zooming in and out to keep their young fed." Marilyn looked to the ground and sighed. "But yesterday some sort of predator got in, killed the babies, and destroyed the nest."

Ana winced. "That's terrible."

Marilyn nodded. "It happens sometimes, despite my best efforts to put protective measures in place. It broke my heart seeing the parents fly about, confused and disoriented, when they discovered the destruction. They're such bright, lovely creatures." She pulled the gloves from her hands and stuffed them in her overalls pockets. "All I can do is clean out the box and make space for them to start fresh."

Marilyn's words pinged against Ana's heart. "They'll build a new nest here, even after losing their brood?"

Her aunt placed a hand on the sloped roof of the birdhouse. "That's one of the things that inspires me most about nature. Like all of life, it is both beautiful and severe. But those bluebirds will return to start again. Their irrevocable expectancy and hope for new life makes me want to have the faith of a bird. They do what they're created to do without question or regard for the outcome."

Ana wrapped her arms around her middle. "Sometimes I wish we were a little more like animals. They don't seem to be plagued by worry in the same way we humans are."

Marilyn chuckled. "Life is certainly simpler for the birds. But the Bible tells us that we are loved by God even more than the sparrows. If they don't worry, that means we don't have to worry either." She shrugged. "Not that I ever fully succeed in abandoning worry. But the birds at least remind me that I don't *have* to."

Ana and Marilyn said goodbye before Ana turned back toward Cora's house. She walked on, making good time as Piper trotted merrily beside her. But then an uneven clip-clop met her ears just before she reached the driveway. Piper stopped and sat, expectant.

Curious as she was about the noise and Piper's reaction, it was getting late. "Come on, let's go home." She tugged on the leash, but her companion remained oblivious to her existence.

The figure of a man leading a horse crested the rise in the road behind them.

Piper stood, tail wagging. Ana lifted her hand to her brow to cut the glare of the setting sun. "Sam?" she called out.

He waved in greeting as the horse limped toward them along the edge of the road.

"Everything okay?" she asked when he reached a conversational distance.

He tugged on the brim of his cowboy hat. "Yeah, Tupelo here just threw one of her shoes while we were out on the trail. It's less risky to walk her home than to ride," he said. "And this is a straighter shot home than the last part of the trail."

"Want some company?" Piper certainly wouldn't mind extending their walk.

"Sure." He scratched Piper behind the ears. "Whatever her past life, your pup is used to horses."

She shrugged. "Yeah. Just squirrels and raccoons get her hackles raised."

He chuckled under his breath.

They walked on together, enjoying the symphony of birds singing good night songs to their lovers, with crickets and bullfrogs adding in background notes.

From the corner of her eye she studied the kind, warm man

beside her and the unseen heaviness that seemed to perpetually rest on his shoulders with few exceptions. "Sam, what happened the other day? When I found you on the side of the road?"

He gripped the back of his neck with his free hand. "I can't have this conversation. Not . . . not right now."

"Marilyn said—"

"Marilyn needs to mind her own business." He shot her a wry smile in a clear attempt to soften the way he'd derailed her mid-sentence. "Marilyn is an amazing woman who knows more of my story than most. But it's not something I talk about."

"I can understand that." She was struck with the desire to confess what had brought her to Bitter End. She chose to believe it was because it was a story he needed to hear and she was ready to tell it. "I'm running away from my real life. At least for the summer." She shared the version of history that everyone in her hometown knew, and then said, "And they called me a hero. But the truth is, so much of what happened that day was my fault."

His brow furrowed, glancing down to her knee and back up again. "How could you think that?"

She took a few steadying breaths and then forced the words past the tightness in her throat. "I didn't know it at the time, but the nineteen-year-old had planned on confronting a new teacher at our school who had taught him many years ago. He said she'd contributed to him being bullied. But that's not why he came in *my* classroom."

Sam walked on beside her in silence, as if waiting for her to have the strength to continue.

"My classroom is a portable building separate from the rest of the school. I believe he thought it was an empty storage area, and he wanted a place to hide because he realized he couldn't go through with whatever his plan was. But when I charged at him, it scared him and he accidentally discharged his weapon, hitting me."

They walked along in silence for a few paces.

"You can't take the blame for that." His voice was little more than a ragged whisper.

"But if I had tried to talk him down, my class probably wouldn't have witnessed a gun going off in their kindergarten class. And that one action will now define that kid for the rest of his life. He testified that it was an accident, but everyone just believed it was a convenient excuse."

Sam pulled his horse to a stop, and she and Piper followed suit. "He might have been telling the truth or, just as likely, trying to save himself. For all you know he came to hide in there to plan his next move, not to change his mind. And instead of a wounded knee, it could have been worse." Somehow his declaration that it could have been worse did not grate against her like it did when other people said it.

"You didn't see the fear in his eyes, Sam." She reached down, rubbing Piper's ear between her fingers. "Until Piper, I relived those moments every night, waking up right before I charged with that tiny chair as my shield and sword. That kid's scared face is branded on the insides of my eyelids. And each night I'd flounder in the sheets, believing for a split second I still had the chance to choose differently."

There was anguish in his eyes when he responded. "You need to forgive yourself for being human. You did the best you could with the knowledge you had." He gave his head a slight shake. "With *valor*."

She studied his warm, brown eyes. "I just wish people would stop calling me a hero."

Sam nodded, a knowing in his gaze that twisted her heart. "It's heavy, carrying a title you feel you don't deserve. "

And maybe that was why she'd needed to confide in Sam. Because he *knew* what it was she felt.

Ana sauntered up the sidewalk leading to Cora's house, Piper prancing beside her just as energetic as when they'd left the house.

When she opened the front door, Piper froze, sniffing the air. Ana glanced around the small entryway. A suitcase and Ana's duffel sat by the door.

"Cora?" she called out.

"In here, dear." The weary voice filtered to her from the living room.

Keeping Piper on the leash, she rounded the corner.

Cora's eyes widened. "Tell me I wasn't in so much of a hurry leaving that I didn't notice a dog."

Piper bounced beside her at Cora's tender singsong voice.

Ana gave her aunt a sheepish smile. "She's a new addition. I would have asked if it was okay, but . . ."

"I've been a little hard to reach?"

She nodded.

"I like dogs." She extended the back of her hand toward Piper. "Let her come say hi."

Ana almost told her about the infographic that said not to extend your hand to a dog, but she still couldn't remember whatever the right way was. She walked Piper closer. *Please don't jump. Please don't jump.*

Piper trotted over and sat sideways in front of Cora, leaning slightly into the woman's legs.

Cora scratched the dog's side. "What a good pup. How did you end up with her?"

Ana sank onto a kitchen chair. "That story can wait. I thought you weren't supposed to be home for another month." There was so much she'd hoped to accomplish with the house before her aunt's return.

Cora dropped her chin. "Betsy's health issues worsened. We had to take a flight home from Greece." She continued stroking Piper's side. "We should have taken this trip sooner. I thought we'd have more time."

Ana's heart constricted. "She . . . she's not . . ."

Cora's eyes widened. "Oh no. She's okay, relatively speaking. She's stable and under care at the hospital in her hometown in Georgia. Her family's with her. We were supposed to be moving to that retirement village, but—" Cora's hands trembled. "But now her health isn't stable enough for independent living. In fact, the doctors aren't sure it ever will be." She stopped petting Piper and wrung her wrinkled hands. "We were going to live like . . . like . . . sisters . . ."

That last word held an ache that might be as old as the day Viola moved away. Ana kept her lips clamped tight, holding back all the questions that had built up over the past month.

"Will you still move now that Betsy won't be there?"

Cora's mouth opened and then closed. She traced a finger around the circular brown patch on Piper's back. She looked around the room, at the pile of boxes that had dwindled considerably in her absence. "I haven't gotten quite that far."

35

MAY 1959

Ice had melted from the branches of her beloved beeches, buds formed, and leaves burst forth. Their branches housed little avian families singing with the joy of new life.

Meanwhile, Viola's dresses grew tighter by the day. She ached for her mother's surety and wisdom—for impending motherhood and even more so, for how to be the wife of a complicated and troubled man.

Today, she rested on a bench beneath her favorite tree, newly delivered mail in hand.

Viola held two envelopes. One from the seminary's alumni office. The other from Cora. She tucked the first into her pocketbook and opened the second.

> *Dear Vi,*
>
> *When I prayed and asked God to make a way for me to come to you no matter what it took, I had no idea it would have meant Daddy in jail and the reverend gone. Maybe next time I'll be a little more careful 'bout what I ask for.*

Viola paused her reading and shut her eyes tight. Oh, that she could run to her sister now and assuage her fears. Remind her that

222

she had nothing to do with their father's choices. She continued the short letter.

My suitcase is packed and ready, waiting for you to send for me. Momma gave me money for my ticket from one of Daddy's buried jars.

You asked how Momma was doing, and she's holding up. The people of Bitter End have been kind. Bringing food and sitting with her. She says this is their way of honoring every-thing Daddy's family has done for Bitter End all these years.

When the lawmen came and took him away, people lined the road and gave him a nod of respect. Maybe they don't believe he'd done it. I know I don't.

Momma tries not to let me hear the talk, but there's been unrest up here. Men trying to horn in on our area. Not moonshine but some sort of plant they're trying to grow. Must be something awful poisonous to be illegal. All I know is the women have been whispering about how those were bad men and it was more likely they'd shot the reverend in the back than our father.

I know he is not a law-abiding man, but I've looked in his eyes and seen too much love to believe he'd rob some-body else their daddy. No matter how much he disliked the reverend.

Send for me soon as you can. I promise I'll be a big help and not get underfoot. I've learned a lot while you've been away.

I can't wait to see your big ole belly and tell you that you are as big as a house.

Love,
Cora Leigh Whitt

Viola refolded the letter, mind whirring. Drug growers in Bit-ter End? She sure hoped it wasn't true. Her father's talk of how his presence, his business, kept more-violent men from taking his place replayed in her mind. She'd scoffed at his assertion, claiming he was only justifying his choices.

Guilt stabbed at her. For what she wasn't sure. Maybe for judging without listening. For neglecting to try on the shoes he wore or heft the responsibility strapped to his broad shoulders.

How she wished she had the same faith in his innocence as Cora did.

Hand supporting her lower back, she stood from the bench and started for the apartment.

When she walked in the front door, she could smell something delicious already cooking in the kitchen. Marilyn sang "It is well with my soul," her sweet tones muffled by the wall between them.

Viola gasped when Trilby walked around the corner.

He pasted on a smile. "Sorry to startle you."

She shook her head. "I wasn't expecting you home already."

"The bookstore closed early today." He drew her to him, squeezing her a fraction too tight, and then he pressed a kiss to her forehead—a picture of what their marriage had become. A desperate clutch laced with tenderness.

And somewhere between the tenderness and the clutching, some unspoken thing seemed to grow between them. She wanted to talk about it, but how could she ask her husband if he saw the man who killed his father every time he looked at her?

The night after he came home intoxicated, he prayed and repented for his actions, promising her it would never happen again. And it hadn't. Sometimes she wished it would. It would prove he was lying when he said he was fine. But Trilby still passed his classes, went to work, and slept each night. All she knew was that something she did not understand was slowly killing him.

She passed him the letter. "From the alumni office."

He sank onto the sofa and read it. His face tightened for the briefest of seconds before his expression smoothed again. He refolded the letter and dropped it into the wastepaper basket by his desk.

"Is everything okay?" Their budget was tighter now that he was sending anything extra to his mother. He'd taken a second part-time job at the foundry to try to make up for it.

"Just a notice about tuition for next year. Nothing for you to worry about."

She sat beside him on the couch. "I had a letter from Cora. She has her bus ticket money. She says she wants to come as soon as we send word."

Trilby yanked his gaze from hers. "I'm so sorry. But Cora can't come."

It felt like her spine had been replaced by a metal rod. "I . . . I promised her. The day we married, I promised her."

"Mother called. She needs more time. Her friend doesn't have space for Marilyn, and Mother doesn't have quite enough saved to get her own place. I told her we could keep her the rest of the summer."

"I don't see why that matters."

Trilby lowered his voice to a ragged whisper. "Making Marilyn share a cot with a constant reminder of all she's lost? I can't do that to her."

Viola reeled at his tortured words, her frail heart battering about in her chest. "I guess you'd know better than anyone how painful that is for a person." She stood. "I'd better see if Marilyn needs any help in the kitchen."

"Viola . . ."

She fled the room, feeling like a thorn in the paw of a black bear. Every contact that she had with Trilby and Marilyn must bring so much pain. But they were all stuck in this small space together.

"How can I help?"

Marilyn turned from where she stirred a pot of soup, a sweet expression on her face. "I have everything in hand. Have a seat at the table and I'll bring you a glass of water."

Over dinner, Marilyn chattered. Trilby brooded. And Viola stewed.

She wanted to scream at her husband. Find some way to push the things that festered under the skin of their marriage to the surface.

But before she had the chance, Trilby had risen from the table, changed clothes, and walked out the door to get in a few hours' work at the foundry.

While Marilyn was in the bathroom readying for bed, Viola noticed the corn husk doll laying on Marilyn's cot. She picked it up and hugged it tight before returning the doll that had graced Cora's bed for as long as Viola could remember.

It was Trilby who couldn't bear the thought of being in Cora's presence, not Marilyn. Otherwise she wouldn't keep this memento of their friendship by her side.

Viola went to the wastepaper basket and removed the letter from the alumni office. She sat in the swivel chair as she smoothed it on the desktop and read.

Dear Trilby Chambers,

It is our great joy and honor to inform you that your tuition for the duration of your education has been paid in full. This scholarship, raised by the alumni association, is bestowed in honor of your late father, Reverend Quincy Chambers, who was esteemed and loved by his colleagues. We are pleased to be able to assist you as you carry on his rich legacy. Visit the bursar's office at your convenience to finalize the details.

> *In Christ,*
> *President Benjamin Wilson*
> *Southern Theological Seminary*

This was so incredible. So kind and generous. Why would he have thrown away a letter that honored his father's legacy?

36

The next morning Ana was stirred from sleep by the scent of bacon and freshly brewed coffee, leaving her deliciously disoriented for about a half a second. She snapped fully awake.

Cora was back.

Ana swung out of bed and went to her now-returned duffel. She sifted through the blouses and jeans she had packed at the start of summer, and though they were familiar, they felt simultaneously foreign. Emblems from a previous life that she wasn't quite ready to don. She changed out of her oversized nightshirt and slipped into a pair of jeans and a Dave Matthews Band tee from the thrift store. Once her hair was up, she ventured into the land of savory Southern breakfast.

Piper, who typically would have been nudging her awake for her morning walk, sat at attention, her nose following Cora's every move.

"And here I thought Piper had declared her undying love for me. But all along she would have traded me for a slice of bacon."

Cora turned, a wide smile on her face. "Good morning, dear." She motioned to the table already laden with platters of hash browns, eggs, pancakes, and a decanter of orange juice. Enough to feed six or seven people, not two. "Have a seat, everything's almost done."

"I can't stay too long. Sam will be here in a little bit to pick me up." She took her place at the table and started fixing a plate.

Cora put a final platter on the table then sat, looking pleased with herself. "I thought the two of you might hit it off."

She chose to ignore her aunt's insinuation. Piper rested her chin on Ana's knee, quietly pleading.

Ana sampled her crisp and buttery hash browns. "We're meeting up with the Bitter End Birding Society."

Cora's grin dissolved. "Marilyn's group?"

Ana pretended not to hear the edge in Cora's voice. "I'm pretty sure there's only one Bitter End Birding Society."

"I specifically asked her to leave you alone." Cora stood and grabbed a rag to wipe the flour dotting the counter though she hadn't eaten a bite.

"She's been very kind to me."

"Oh, yes. I'm sure she was." Cora turned to face her. The way she twisted the washrag in her hands didn't escape Ana's notice. "You can't believe everything that woman says."

Ana loaded her fork with scrambled eggs. "No? What about old newspaper articles? Can those be trusted?"

Cora's face blanched. She went back to tidying the kitchen.

Ana finished her eggs and then stood and walked to her aunt's side, setting a hand on her shoulder. "All that time we chatted over the phone about my genealogy project back in college, you never thought to bring up that I had another great-aunt living just down the street from you? That our family made its money in moonshine? That my great-grandfather went to prison for killing my other great-grandfather?"

Cora flinched beneath Ana's touch.

Ana thought of the cut-and-dry flowchart she'd turned in to her professor. At the time she'd been solely focused on getting the grade, and Cora had helped her achieve that goal, tracing her family lines all the way back to Ireland. But the stories behind those people were so much more than a list of names and dates. "Those are some pretty big things to leave out."

Cora turned to her, lip trembling. "I was so happy to get to meet Viola's granddaughter, and I wanted you to want to know me, not the spectacle that is our family history. I was afraid if I told you about all that stuff, you wouldn't want to be connected . . . with me." She crossed her arms over her chest. "Mountain people. Moonshiners. People hear those terms and think they have a picture of who you are without ever taking the time to really *know* you."

Did Cora actually believe Ana would think less of her because of the pain and destruction Wayne Whitt caused all those years ago? Ana swallowed back the argument she'd been forming. Cora had already experienced the loss of her family once when Ana's grandfather made the decision to keep Quinn from her biological family. It wasn't much of a stretch to believe it could happen all over again.

"And now Marilyn has swooped in, just like she always does."

"I don't know much about what happened between the two of you. But I'm not taking sides. And Marilyn never asked me to."

Cora resumed her place at the table and loaded her plate with pancakes. She used her fork to saw them into bite-size pieces. "She asked you to choose sides the moment she brought up what happened to her father."

Ana shook her head. "I brought it up to *her*. Marilyn didn't seem at all inclined to talk about the past. The only detail she supplied was that Grandpa Trilby was her brother."

Cora stabbed her cut-up pancakes, never raising them to her lips. "Then what blabbermouth unearthed all this ancient history?"

"I found letters your parents sent each other after your father was in prison. I couldn't find any information online, so I went to the library and looked at old newspapers."

The fork fell from Cora's hand, clattering against the plate. "Letters? Where?" Her gaze darted around the room as if they had been sitting in plain sight all these years.

"There was a break-in—of the furry bandit variety—in your shed. One of the glass bottles on the top shelf was broken, and the letters were inside."

Hunger bloomed in Cora's expression that could not be relieved by the smorgasbord of breakfast foods. "Where are they?"

Ana retrieved them from the bedroom and laid the scrolled papers in her aunt's trembling hands.

"Does he say he was innocent? He was, you know. I know all convicts say they're innocent, but my daddy really was." Cora carefully unfurled the rolled paper.

Ana shrugged. "It's a conversation between a husband and a wife, passing news about their children."

From the research Ana had done, Wayne Lee Whitt had never claimed innocence. He'd willingly confessed to his crime the moment he was caught.

Just then, a knock sounded at the front door. "That'll be Sam." Ana looked at her aunt, unsure.

Cora waved her off, her expression cool. "I'll see you in a few hours."

Ana pushed back from the table, full of regret for leaving the conversation unfinished. But maybe leaving Cora to read her parents' letters in privacy was the kindest choice. "Okay. See you soon."

Cora muttered a reply, her focus locked on the words before her, hearing from voices that hadn't echoed through this old house in decades.

Ana gathered her water bottle, attached Piper's leash, and headed for the door.

Sam trained his binoculars on a ruby-crowned kinglet, a tiny olive bird who constantly flicked its wings. Marilyn always loved the curious birds who moved about like they'd sucked down a little too much coffee that morning.

He called for her, but when she didn't come over, he lowered his binoculars. Ana, Jake, Inez, Trent, and his mother Lottie were gathered, flipping through their field guides, attempting to figure out what variety of flycatcher perched overhead. Meanwhile their bird dog sidekick stared longingly at a brown thrasher that scratched the dirt, looking for insects beneath a rhododendron.

Marilyn sat alone on a downed tree, staring into her open hands. Sam glanced again at the rest of the group, hoping that someone else would notice Marilyn was not herself. Why did he constantly find himself in the role of confidant and comforter? It was as though his previous occupation clung to him like woodsmoke in clothes after sitting next to a bonfire.

He approached and sat beside her. "There's a kinglet over in the brush."

She gave him a tight smile in reply. "Cutest little things."

"I can point him out," he said, as if she needed any help.

"I just want to sit and listen for a little while. To nature's music—and to God, if He wants to offer some wisdom. I sure could use some."

Sam remained at her side.

After a few moments she bumped him with her shoulder. "What are you doing?"

He studied her, searching for the right words. "Listening to nature. Listening for God's voice. Or my friend's voice, if she has something she'd like to get off her chest."

He glanced over to Ana, who was looking their way, concern etched in her features. On the drive up Ana had mentioned that Cora was not pleased about the connection she'd made with Marilyn. He sighed. "I suppose you heard that Cora is back in town?"

Marilyn nodded. "Would you consider taking over the birding society?"

His mouth dropped open at her non sequitur. "What . . . what's going on?"

"This birding thing started out as a way to rebuild connection with my husband, but it's come to mean so much more to me. My father moved us to Bitter End all those years ago to try and bridge a divide between himself and a community. To transform Bitter End from a place suspicious of outsiders into one that welcomed them." She pinched her lips tight for a moment and then continued.

"When my husband and I ended up back here sixty years later, I didn't realize that there was a bigger purpose at play until I started adding new members to the birding society. I think it was God giving me the chance to take up my father's mantle—bringing together people who might have ordinarily remained strangers and making them into friends. And now it seems my time is about to be cut short, and it is breaking me, thinking that this is where my father's legacy ends."

Sam's heart thudded in his chest. "Marilyn, what's going on? Are you unwell?"

She shut her eyes tight. Tears leaked out of their corners. "I've been trying for months to figure out how to say the words out loud. It's just three words, but I can't seem to make myself form them."

He reached for her hand and gave it a gentle squeeze. "No matter what you are facing, I'm not going anywhere. You can count on that."

She looked at him then and swiped the moisture from her cheeks. "I'm going blind." She took a shuddering breath. "I don't know how much longer I'll have enough sight to navigate the trails, but it's already getting near impossible to identify a bird on anything but sound. Pretty soon, I'll have to be satisfied with sitting in a lounge chair in my backyard, listening." She locked her gaze on him. "Will you at least think about taking the lead?"

37

The next week Marilyn stood before her beloved group in the parking area for the Appalachian Trail. It was supposed to be a silent walk day, but there was no way Marilyn could quiet her spirit until she spoke the words pressing against her heart and mind ever since she'd found the courage to confess to Sam.

But Ana was missing. She'd wondered how long it would take for Cora to convince her to give up the group.

She walked close to Sam, whispering, "Is she coming? Do you know?"

"I went over for dinner at Cora's last night. Ana said she'd be here."

"I'm sure Cora was real pleased about that." Marilyn scoffed.

"She wasn't happy, but she didn't say a word against you. At least not in my presence."

Jake, Inez, Trent, and Lottie watched their whispered conversation bounce between them like spectators at a tennis match.

"I'm sorry," Marilyn apologized. "I know today is supposed to be one of silent reflection, but I have something important I need to share. I should have done it sooner, and now I find I cannot bear to wait any longer. But I was hoping Ana would be here." She pushed out a heavy breath. "You see, I've been seeing some specialists over the past year, trying to get to the bottom of some issues I've been having—"

"I hear a car," Inez said.

Sure enough, there came the crunch of tires on gravel and the soft engine purr of Ana's small sedan. *Praise the Lord.*

Marilyn didn't know if her heart could have borne it if Ana had stopped coming when they were just getting to know one another. Even though Cora might forever shun her, knowing Ana had been like a bridge to that severed childhood friendship—a rebuild with the tensile strength of spider silk.

Ana lifted a hand and gave a repentant smile as she approached. Piper pranced at her side.

"You don't have to play mime," Inez piped up. "Apparently, we're talking today."

Marilyn shook her head. "We'll take our silent walk as usual. I just wanted to share something before we begin." She looked at each of them in turn, drawing strength from the kindness in each of their faces. "I'm going blind."

Inez gasped. Sam bowed his head. Jake kept her gaze, compassion softening his bearded face. Ana's mouth dropped open. They all waited for her to fill in more details, but now that she'd released the confession that had taken up so much space in her mind, she was left empty as a cicada shell.

After a few moments, their questions rose around her, tripping over one another. Questions asking for details in the timeline. About potential treatment. They drew close around her. A ring of compassion and strength. Gentle hands landed on her shoulders. Trent and Lottie joined in offering their support, though they were brand-new to the group. Even Piper snuck into the ring of comfort and grief and gave Marilyn's hand a delicate lick.

"I've been having treatment to slow down the progress, but it has recently seemed to have lost effectiveness, which was expected. I have no idea how I'll cope with this change in life, but it's safe to say I'll have to hang up both my driver's license and my binoculars and leave the hiking to the rest of you folks sooner than later."

Maybe it was selfish, but her heart was a little warmed by the distress on their faces. "I'm hoping one of you is willing to take up the helm." She shot a pointed look at Sam, who averted his gaze. "For now, let's take our hike as planned, and do our best to quiet our hearts and minds in light of all of this. But if that is not possible, let us reflect on the changes coming our way and how we'd like to move forward as a group."

Though their lips were silent, their unspoken thoughts were loud enough to send every bird they passed into flight.

Before they climbed into their cars to go home, Ana stopped her. "I know we're not supposed to talk," she said, "but I couldn't stop thinking about your birding bucket list. The one you started with Obadiah. What if we tried to finish it? Or maybe, is there a place you'd like to travel to? Sights you want to experience? The seven wonders of the world? We could make it happen if we all worked together. I know we could."

Marilyn patted her hand. "That's a lovely idea, but I'm not sure it's practical." She understood the impulse to try to do something, anything, to fight back against her fate. But she'd had the opportunity to sit with her news long enough to recognize there was no action that could soften the oncoming darkness.

Ana shrugged. "Maybe not. But it would be fun. Promise me you'll think about it."

Ana walked into the house. Piper flopped onto her dog bed with a dramatic huff and sigh. All the sights, sounds, and smells had given Piper a sufficient brain workout to sap some of her endless energy, at least for an hour or two.

"Ana, dear, is that you?" Cora's voice came wrapped in the scent of something sweet and cinnamony.

"Yes, ma'am."

The creak and thump of the oven door met Ana's ears.

In the kitchen, Cora slid a piping hot coffee cake onto her butcher block countertop. "Did you have a nice time?" Though her tone was light and airy, tension was evident in her profile.

Ana was tempted to prod that tender place and see what might come of it but then chose another conversational route. "Have you given any more thought about putting your house on the market?"

Cora sank onto one of the kitchen chairs. "I don't know. The plan was to move with my friend to that retirement village. I could still go. I could make new friends?"

Ana smiled to herself, understanding the uncertainty in those words. There was something in the human heart that never grew out of those elementary school nerves. Showing up on the first day of class, wondering who would choose you. Wondering where you would fit. "Sure you could. But this house has an awful lot of memories. Memories I'd love to hear more about."

Cora massaged her hands. "It's getting lonely on this old mountain. More and more people moving away. Fewer familiar faces."

"There's Sam and Jake and Inez. And . . ." Ana stopped herself before she said Marilyn's name. Did Cora feel that Marilyn had some measure of claim on them, and on Ana, somehow placing them all slightly out of reach in her mind?

"Sam will eventually tire of those sheep of his and move on. Jake and Inez are fine people, but if things get straightened out with their daughter, I bet they'll move to wherever she is. I just . . . I don't . . ." Cora sighed. "You want some of this cake? I oughta let it cool longer so it won't fall apart when I cut it, but I'm never patient enough." She stood and went to the counter and picked up a silver server.

Ana's heart ached at the mingling of longing and resignation in her aunt's voice. "Marilyn said that the two of you were friends when you were young."

The cake server fell from Cora's hand, clattering against the butcher block. Cora remained facing away from Ana, spine rigid. "Oh? Did she also mention how she stole my very own sister from me? And how that brother of hers took Viola's sweet baby from me and Momma. Did Marilyn tell you how her family coming to this mountain ruined my life?"

"That was—" Ana bit down on her lip, knowing it was a mistake to voice the thought that reverberated in her brain. But then she continued, despite her better judgment. "It was so long ago."

Cora turned. Her eyes were red-rimmed, but her face was set. "Was it, now?" She shook her head.

And in that moment Ana understood why she'd known better than to finish that statement. Because when a wound remained unhealed and untended, it had a way of warping time, keeping painful memories close to the surface. The only thing time had done was transform an angry and scared young girl into a seventy-something woman who was still bitter about the hand she'd been dealt.

Ana wrestled with what to say next. What could be said to turn the conversation toward healing instead of more harm? "Will you tell me your story, Aunt Cora?"

38

The summer was flying by fast and hot. And now that Marilyn was reunited with her mother, Viola was lonely. Trilby had taken only one class over the summer term, telling her that he needed to put more hours in at the foundry to build up savings for their little one, who, as evidenced by Viola's burgeoning middle, was well on the way to making his or her grand entry.

There had been little for Viola to do besides lay on the couch, knitting tiny booties and hats. She hated how much time she'd spent with her feet up, but the doctor was concerned about her doing anything that would put additional strain on her heart.

Trilby came through the door that evening, his clothes soaked with sweat and his face flushed. Without a word he trudged to the bathroom to wash away the evidence of his hard labor. She hoisted herself up and waddled to the kitchen to make each of them a sandwich.

He sat across from her at the table and tore into his cold dinner without so much as a word of greeting to her or to God. She bowed her head and prayed over her own meal in silence.

Breaking the quiet, she said, "I bet you are ready for the fall term to start. Put the foundry work behind you."

He froze, a bite of sandwich making his jaw poke out. He lifted his gaze to hers and chewed a few times before swallowing hard. "I'm not going back."

Viola returned her sandwich to the plate and wiped her hands with her napkin. "To the foundry?"

"To seminary."

She stared at him. "But you love it here. It's your dream—"

"Higher education is a luxury. One that we can no longer afford," he said around another bite.

She shook her head. "You had last year's tuition and half of this one saved up for before your first day."

He lowered the sandwich to his plate, not meeting her eye. "Money I sent Momma so she could buy that house for her and Marilyn."

"Tril . . ."

"And our baby's going to be here any day now. The boss has offered me full-time pay. I found a vacant apartment. A friend of mine will help us move and fix the place up so that you don't have to lift a finger."

It was as though the bright boy she'd married looked at her through a long, dark tunnel, pleading for mercy.

She had none left for him. "I saw the letter."

The lines around his mouth tightened. "What letter?"

"The one from the alumni association. The one that said everything was paid for. Tuition and housing. I won't let you give up on life. I won't let you hide behind excuses about money. Tell me what's going on."

He stood and walked past her, muttering under his breath. The only words she caught—"*I can't.*"

She flinched when the front door slammed shut behind him. The baby growing inside of her pressed hard against the flesh shielding it from the outside world.

For better or worse.

In sickness and in health.

A girl had made the promise.

A woman faced its consequences.

"Vi, it's time."

She shifted to standing and patted the trunk of the nearest beech, her towering, comforting friends. The bark was cool beneath her hand. A breeze rustled through the leaves and swept through her hair, lifting the sticky tendrils from her neck.

After her final farewell to the stalwart sentries, she settled into the borrowed car and Trilby drove them away from the tranquil campus and into the belly of the city. Even with the windows down, sweat trickled from her temples.

Fifteen minutes later he parked in front of Jacob's Distillery, a neglected three-story building with iron bars over the windows. Trilby exited the car and came around to open her door.

"Trilby? What are we doing here?"

He jerked his gaze from hers. His face flushed a deeper shade of red, even deeper than the one brought on by the oppressive heat radiating from the pavement. "There's an apartment upstairs. The man who owns the building gave us a great deal, and there are two whole bedrooms." He shifted his feet on the pavement, and her heart went to him, wishing she could ease the tortured apology in his eyes.

But this was not the life she'd signed up for when she left her precious mountain behind.

He led her to the backside of the building and steadied her hand as they slowly climbed the endless metal stairs. Once she got up there, she'd be like Rapunzel in her lonely tower. Trapped. Lacking the energy to come down again.

He struggled with the rusty lock. Once inside, her eyes roved over the bare walls. They must have been white once, but with time and neglect they'd gone dingy gray. Dust rose with her footfalls as she navigated the haphazard stacks of cardboard boxes. She toured the remainder of the unfurnished apartment as though in a dream.

If she could only wake up, she'd still be able to smell the loamy green of Bitter End wafting through her bedroom window as Cora snored softly in the bed on the other side of their room. From the kitchen, her father's voice, low but merry, would tease her mother. And if she listened close enough, Viola would be able to hear the rhythmic scrape of the biscuit cutter on the butcher block as her mother cut dough into perfect discs.

Viola placed a hand on her round belly as if to comfort her unborn child as she walked into the second of the two bedrooms. A mattress centered the room. The sad, lumpy thing wore the beautiful linens her mother had given them as a wedding gift. At least this room had been swept first.

Trilby came up behind her, placing his hands on her shoulders. "We'll get furniture. I'll paint the walls. It will be nice. You'll see."

She turned to him, ready to tell him that she was going back to Bitter End until after the baby was born, even knowing she could go into labor midway there.

But the look in her husband's eyes begged her to relieve his suffering. "Trilby, I don't understand why we're here. I don't know why you've cut us off from the life we dreamed of. Maybe you're angry at God. Or maybe you're hurting too bad to even know why you're choosing this. All I know is that I promised you for better or for worse. And I can't lie. This is worse." She cupped his face in her hands, desperate for her next words to reach his heart. "But I still love you."

She even loved him enough to leave behind the gray world of mountain moonshine only to end up living over the top of a distillery.

39

Sam ended his call with Ana. She was so excited about her plan, but he was not so sure Marilyn would feel the same way. He understood the compulsion to do something for Marilyn, but he'd become well acquainted with the fact that some things couldn't be fixed.

He dialed Marilyn's number. She answered with a soft and weary, "Hello," as though her vim and vigor had drained out along with her long-held confession.

"I have a question for you. An admission. A betrayal of confidence."

A chuckle came through the line. "Are you sure you should be saying, then?"

He sighed. "Ana wants to do something big for you. To plan a trip to some exotic locale that you've always wanted to see, or she wants to help you finish the birding bucket list you and your husband started. But I've never known you to update that list and I've never heard you talk about places you'd like to experience beyond this mountain."

She sighed. "I haven't worked on that list since Obadiah passed."

"Is there a reason?"

"I guess because our story felt unfinished, and it seemed right to leave it like it was waiting for him."

"Do you want to finish it? Or plan a group trip somewhere special?"

The line was silent for several moments. "No." The word was like a stone dropped in an empty pail.

Sam sank into his favorite chair, and Max curled up at his feet. He'd walk barefoot over a briar patch if it meant bringing Marilyn comfort. He might even take over the birding society, forever enduring Jake and Inez's marital sniping. Marilyn had altered the course of his life when she'd approached him that day in Roan Mountain State Park and invited him to join her birding hike. "For once, forget about taking care of everyone else. What do you want?"

Marilyn sighed. "I don't need to finish Obie's list or try to stuff in as many experiences as possible in the time I have left with my sight. I'm nearly eighty years old, and I've lived a full life."

She went quiet again for several moments. "But I rather like the idea of working on a shared project with the birding society."

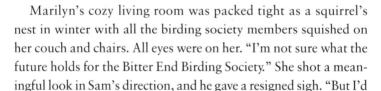

Marilyn's cozy living room was packed tight as a squirrel's nest in winter with all the birding society members squished on her couch and chairs. All eyes were on her. "I'm not sure what the future holds for the Bitter End Birding Society." She shot a meaningful look in Sam's direction, and he gave a resigned sigh. "But I'd like to celebrate this group with a shared venture," she continued.

Ana leaned forward in her seat.

"Some of you who've been birding for a while may have heard of 'Big Days' in the birding community. For those who don't know, birders set aside an entire day and list as many bird species as they can see and/or hear in a given day."

She placed a legal pad and a small stack of index cards on the coffee table between her and the group.

"As our final hurrah with the group as we know it, I propose having a Big Month. Over the next month, our goal will be to locate as many different bird species in our area as we can. Ideally, the birds that count toward the Big Month list should be sighted by everyone in the group, though the species doesn't have to be sighted at the same time. In addition, I would like each of you to write down one bird you would like to see this month. It can be a new bird to add to your life list or one of your favorites. The only rule is that it needs to be a bird that is either native to East Tennessee or that migrates through this area around this time of year. Once the list is established, Sam here has volunteered to do searches on the East Tennessee Birding page and he will plan our trips according to bird sightings that pop up on the site."

Ana's hand shot up like she was the teacher's pet.

"Yes?"

"Does this mean we'll go out together daily? Or at least more often than once per week?"

Marilyn nodded and smiled. "I'll get to those details, I promise." She picked up the index cards. "On the card, write down one thing in your personal life that you would like to focus on while we're working on our list together. Feel free to be as public or private as you'd like with your personal goal. Whatever you decide, I hope you'll make it a matter of prayer and intention." She gestured to Ana. "To answer your question, Jake and Inez have generously offered to let us use their bus so that we can travel together on the weekends. In between that, we can each look for birds around our own homes and add them to our list. Sam has put together an online spreadsheet that we all can edit." She glanced at Ana, who studied her every move.

One by one each person came up to add a bird to the list. Jake wrote down a northern saw-whet owl. Inez, an olive-sided flycatcher. Sam picked the blue-winged teal. Marilyn shook her head at that. Of course, he'd put down something near impossible to find this time of year. After flipping through a field guide,

Lottie wrote down a black-throated blue warbler and Trent added a summer tanager.

Ana came up last. "Are you sure this is what—"

"I'm sure. I'm happy to explain. Later."

Ana thought for a minute and then went back to her purse and flipped through her field guide before coming back to the list.

Marilyn watched her write *belted kingfisher* on the list. "Nice choice." It was a striking bird that was a lot of fun to watch.

After everyone had gone back to their places, Marilyn began, "Now we'll plan on going out each Thursday and Saturday— unless, of course, Sam gets word that there has been a rare sighting that we'll not want to miss."

Ana raised her hand again.

Marilyn grinned. Apparently, you could take the teacher out of the kindergarten but not the kindergarten out of the teacher. "Yes?"

"What about you, Marilyn?"

"I'll be along, every step of the way."

Ana pointed to the list. "What's your bird going to be?"

Marilyn thought for a minute before she picked up the pen resting on the yellow paper. There were plenty of birds she'd never seen and now never would. But none of those mattered. She wrote *Northern Parula*, her spark bird, next to her name.

The first time she'd spotted one, she'd been irritated and mosquito-bitten and weary of wandering through the woods following after Obie, even though it had been her idea to venture out with him. But when she'd spotted a small group of those tiny blue-gray warblers with bright yellow patches on their chests, she'd been utterly enchanted. For the first time, she was the one pointing out the birds to him. That had been the beginning of their shared adventure.

It was the perfect species to endcap her birding journey while soaking in the joy of her fellow bird-watchers making their own new discoveries that would hopefully serve as a gateway to deeper truths.

After the plans were set for the coming weekend, the other members of the Bitter End Birding Society filtered out of the house and went their separate ways. All except Ana.

"You stole my plan," she said as she approached the table and picked up the legal pad.

"I just made a slight alteration, my dear."

She studied the page for another moment and then looked up. "You don't want to finish your list?"

Marilyn shook her head. "Not really. Something about the unfinished nature comforts me a bit."

Ana furrowed her brow and placed the clipboard back on the coffee table.

Marilyn chuckled at her confusion. "I don't know what heaven is like, but sometimes I imagine Obie and me wandering through forests of golden trees, working on this list of ours. Only we never complete it, because there is always more to be discovered. I imagine us forever together, enjoying heaven's birds."

A fine sheen of moisture glistened in Ana's eyes. "I'm sorry if I was pushing you into something that you didn't need or want. I should have listened first."

Marilyn reached across to squeeze her hand. "It was a lovely and kind thought." She peered at the younger woman, hoping her next words would nestle into her heart. "Sometimes things don't come to a tidy conclusion. Words are left unsaid. Things are left undone. But this life is not the end." Marilyn drew another breath. "Our present circumstances, our perceived failures, they are not final."

"The way I left those kids at the end of the year feels pretty final."

Marilyn blinked. Was Ana finally going to open up about her experiences?

Ana swiped at her cheeks. "I'm scared I won't be able to lead a group of hopeful, beautifully naive five-year-olds through their first year of school. I'm too broken. Too aware that anything could happen at any time. What if I transfer that anxiety to them?"

"Too broken? I don't think many people could have managed what you did this past year."

"Sometimes what looks like a strength is actually weakness." Ana paced a moment before settling on the sofa. "My entire childhood, I was a competitive gymnast," she said. "I'd early committed to the University of Georgia as a high school junior with a dream sports scholarship in the works, the whole deal." Ana lifted her chin. "I was really good." There was a fire in her eyes that had not been there before, but then she frowned. "And then one day in practice, doing a skill I'd done a hundred times, I landed wrong and tore half the ligaments in my knee. I had to have surgery. Ironically, the same knee that required surgery eight months ago."

Marilyn sat beside her and scooped Ana's hand into hers.

"After I physically recovered, I tried to get back in the gym." Her shoulders sagged. "But even though I was physically capable, I'd lost my nerve."

Ana stared at her lap. "I wasn't one of those fearless kids who lived for the thrill of doing dangerous skills. I was always half-scared-to-death and had to challenge myself to be brave. But I'd lost trust in myself. In my own body."

She turned to Marilyn, eyes watery. "I quit. Said goodbye to it all. I was so lost. Seventeen years old with no idea who I was outside of my dead dream.

"After the gunman came to our school . . . after I was shot . . . I forced myself back into that classroom as soon as my doctors cleared me. I was so scared that history would repeat itself. That I'd lose my nerve to go back into the classroom. But it was a mistake. I should have taken the rest of the year to heal and let someone else teach in my place."

Marilyn placed a hand on Ana's shoulder.

"I wanted you to complete your list, because I have this fear of not being able to finish what I start, and I don't want anyone else to ever feel that way."

Marilyn pulled her into a hug. "You've been trying to prove something to yourself every single day of this past school year, doing the best you could for those kids, and you still don't give yourself an ounce of credit."

Ana laughed under her breath. "You're not wrong."

"First of all, you don't have anything to prove. And based on what I've seen so far, I'm pretty sure you can do whatever you set your mind to. Even walking back into the classroom again with a new group of students who don't understand what you've been through and starting again if that's what you feel the Lord leading you to do."

Ana loosened her hold and looked into her aunt's eyes. "Anything I set my mind to?"

Marilyn thumbed the tears from Ana's cheeks and nodded.

Then Ana gave her a sly smile. "Like help you and Cora make peace?"

"Sweetie, if you're wanting to build up your confidence with an early win, I'd not start there."

A few days later, Ana walked Piper alongside Cora. Her aunt had lived on this same road throughout every high and low of her life.

Had she been waiting all this time? Believing that if she stayed put, all she'd lost would eventually find their way back to her?

She thought through the stories Cora had shared about Ana's grandparents and their ill-fated romance. Despite brokenness and pain, Ana found herself searching for a thread of hope. There had to be parts of Cora's stories that could still be redeemed.

"After your father was in prison, what did you do?"

Cora glanced her way. "Oh, Momma and I made do. We lived life in Bitter End, with me stuck to her side like glue. She finally taught me how to cook decent. As years went on, we eventually broke most of our land into parcels and sold them off. Not that we hurt for money or anything. Momma and I just didn't need the land, and it was less upkeep."

"I can't imagine how hard this must have been for Great-Grandma Ruby."

Cora nodded. "She was a quiet woman of surprising strength. She went to be with the Lord when she was the age I am now." She shook her head as if reckoning with the shock of the numerical fact. "I started up my bookmobile not long after that as a tribute of sorts to Viola. She loved books and got so excited when the teacher would bring up a new batch from the valley. I knew bringing books to people who couldn't drive the long distance to the library would make her proud of me."

They walked on in silence for several minutes.

"I heard about that bird thing you're doing," Cora said as they drew close to Marilyn's house.

Ana slanted her gaze in her aunt's direction.

"My hairdresser told me. Did you know when Marilyn moved back here, she had the nerve to try and steal Deanna to spy on me."

Ana nudged her. "It sounds like it's you doing the spying."

Cora snorted and swatted the air like she could banish Ana's words. "I don't care a lick about what that woman is up to. Until it starts involving you, that is. I thought you came to help me with this old house. Those books. And now she's after more of your time."

Ana gave her a playful glare. "You weren't even supposed to be back yet, so all our time together is a bonus. Most of the books are already taken care of. I probably got rid of more stuff than you're happy with since you seem to be sticking around. If you're concerned about losing time with me, join in. There's plenty of space in Jake and Inez's bus."

Cora's eyes widened. "Y'all are traipsing about in that mobile wedding chapel?" She sniffed. "That'll be a sight."

"It'll be hilarious. Come with us."

Cora crossed her arms. "No, thank you. I don't want anything to do with that Marilyn woman's schemes."

"*That Marilyn woman?* She was your best friend once upon a time."

Cora stopped cold on the road. It took a second to convince Piper to cease her forward movement, and Ana had to backtrack to where Cora still stood. "Are you okay?"

"Our friendship was a blip in history a lifetime ago. She doesn't mean any more to me than the man in the moon."

Ana snorted. "Do you really believe that lie, or is that your sad attempt at getting me to drop this?" She stood in front of Cora, having a few inches advantage on her aunt. "Y'all were both, what? Eight?"

Cora lifted her chin. "I was eight. She was ten."

"*Kids*, Cora. Kids caught up in a topsy-turvy situation you had no control over. Do you know what I think?"

Her aunt pursed her lips. "I don't recollect asking your opinion, Ana Leigh."

"I have a special deal going and you get a piece of my mind free of charge, *Cora Leigh*," Ana said, matching her aunt's sass. Ana then softened her tone, attempting to cushion the edges of her coming declaration. "Viola and Trilby are gone. His parents are gone. So are yours. And then Marilyn shows up all these years later reminding you that you haven't actually dealt with any of your feelings about what happened back then. I think you resent Marilyn because she's the only one left to be mad at."

Cora's gaze shifted into something vacant and exposed. Ana's wrecking ball had hit its mark. She stepped closer to pull her aunt into her arms.

Practiced wall builder that she was, Cora straightened her shoulders and dodged Ana to keep walking. "There's things you don't understand."

"I'm listening," Ana said as she and Piper hurried after her.

The older woman patted Piper's back when they caught up. "I'm not upset that you're going birding. I just hope you know she does this sort of thing all the time."

Ana resisted rolling her eyes. "What sort of thing?"

"Steal people."

"She's a kidnapper?" She shot her stubborn aunt a withering look.

"Might as well be. Tried to steal my hairdresser. Sam. My own sister. You."

Ana placed a hand on Cora's forearm and tugged her to a stop. "Sam and I are still here, and we still care about you. I know it might have felt like Marilyn stole Viola when you were little, but surely you can see that nothing could have changed the way your sister felt about you."

She raised her brows. "Psh. I never said Marilyn was *good* at stealing people away from me. But it sure hasn't stopped her from trying."

You are being a child. Ana bit back the words before they could spring free. Maybe there was a tender eight-year-old Cora Leigh Whitt living on inside this older woman. And because that part of her childhood hadn't healed, she still stomped about like that feisty, stubborn girl when cornered.

Ana abandoned the conversation, hoping that at least something she'd said had stuck with her aunt, even if she refused to show it.

They walked past Marilyn's house, which sat a fair distance back from the road. A bluebird swooped into the nest box with twigs clamped in its beak, beginning again. Oh, to have that kind of hope and determination to rebuild, knowing it could all be upended.

Ana lifted her hand and waved to Marilyn, rocking on her front porch with a glass in her hand. Piper tried to pull her down the path and huffed when Ana tugged her back on course.

The only thing Cora offered Marilyn was a glare.

Marilyn took a long drink of her sweet tea as the pair of women and the dog passed. Even though her failing vision obscured their identities, the snatches of the voices she'd caught on the wind belonged to her great-niece and her ex-best friend. In the humid air, condensation beaded on her glass and rolled over her fingertips.

She sighed.

Cora had never been her enemy.

There had been some conflicting feelings to adjust to regarding Cora after her father's death. But those feelings had been a forgettable affliction compared to the gaping wound of trying to make sense of a world without the man who'd been her compass.

When Marilyn had left the mountain, she'd tucked that fleeting, tender friendship into her suitcase of mountain memories and pushed it into the attic space of her mind.

That was the first of her three sins against the woman.

A sin that must have been compounded by every loss Cora faced.

When her sister had chosen Trilby and left Bitter End.

When her father was imprisoned.

When Marilyn took Cora's place that awful summer, stealing one of Cora's last chances to spend time with her sister.

Still, Cora's misdirected anger was so unfair.

The two of them had been but a pair of songbirds, their migration through childhood blown off course by other people's storms. If Marilyn could have kept her father and given Cora that Louisville summer, surely the woman knew she would have done it in a heartbeat.

But perhaps not.

Because when Marilyn had moved back to Bitter End, the pain between them had been so fresh it was like no time had passed at all.

And so, Marilyn's second sin was having the gall to return, a living remnant of the year that wrecked Cora's young life. And Cora seemed prepared to punish her for it until one of them breathed their last.

Unfortunately for Cora, Marilyn didn't even have the decency to be afflicted with a terminal illness. Just one that would rob her of her sight.

Marilyn's third unforgivable sin was the hospital conversation she wasn't supposed to have overheard. She could only imagine how Cora would react knowing that if Marilyn had told the truth over sixty years ago, Cora's father might have walked free.

She didn't deserve Cora's wrath on the first two counts of betrayal. But Marilyn's guilt on this third offense made up for it all.

41

August 1959

The guard wheeled Viola to the vacant spot across from the man who'd raised her. The presence of the guards and the restraints on her father's hands a constant reminder that what appeared a small divide between them was wider than the distance between Bitter End and downtown Louisville.

His head was downcast, giving her a few moments to study him. His forearms, where they rested on the table, were still muscled and thick. As a girl, she'd jump to grasp them and then she'd dangle like they were tree branches. The thick chocolate waves that had once adorned his head like a wild crown had been shorn to the scalp and his long beard was now closely shaved. In that moment, the oak of a man somehow reminded her of a motherless lamb.

She blinked back the moisture gathering in her eyes. "Hey, Daddy."

When he finally lifted his head, his bloodshot eyes widened a fraction at the sight of her. He'd been warned she was coming to say goodbye. But surely nothing had quite prepared him to see his eldest daughter wasting away.

Wasting, but still here, praise the Lord. After Trilby had confessed, she'd pleaded with God for one last chance to speak to her father. In a feat of mercy that astounded her doctors, He'd supplied the strength her heart lacked. Though as she'd been discharged into her mother's care, her caregivers warned that her condition remained. Her body would fail.

"Vi." Daddy whispered the word. His hands twitched, and her empty arms ached. How much restraint had it taken to keep from reaching out to her?

"You're a grandpa." She attempted to clear the thickness in her throat that marred her words. She wanted him to hear this next part loud and clear. "A granddaughter. Quinn *Leigh* Chambers."

She drew a photograph from her pocketbook and slid it to him. She tensed, wondering if the guards would stop her. Mercifully, they were preoccupied by a dispute on the other side of the room.

Her father fumbled the slick photograph into his fettered hands. He stared in wonder. "She's your spitting image, Vi." By the tender look in the mountain man's eyes, she knew he was peeling back time to a younger version of himself cradling a tiny babe. A longing without a name welled in her chest, desperate to see this man hold her child the same way he had held her.

"You gave her my middle name?" His chin quivered.

Viola straightened her thin shoulders. "I did." Then, more quietly, she added, "Trilby told me the truth."

He sucked in a breath at her whispered declaration. "The truth is dead, buried, and moldering in the earth. Don't you dare raise it." His tone fearful. Harsh. Wild Wayne Lee Whitt resurrected.

Viola gripped the table's edge. "I won't undo the choice you made, Daddy. I just wanted to tell you I'm sorry."

"Ain't nothing in the world to be sorry for. What I did that night, I did for you." Ferocity still laced his voice, but this was of a softer ilk.

"But why? Why, after sending me away, did you choose me above everyone and everything?"

A tear found its way down his weathered cheek. "I made a

mistake, casting you out. Living afraid I might lose control of that mountain. Lose control of my ability to keep it safe. My power over that place was an illusion. I was never the one in control." He used his shoulder to wipe away the tear. The metal on his wrists clanked with the movement.

"I did it because Quincy Chambers, despite my best efforts, became my friend. So in his death, I protected his son. I protected my daughter. Besides"—a corner of his mouth lifted—"I was raised an outlaw. Is this not where I belong?"

She wanted to scream at him but kept her tone even. "Still meting out justice, are you? Serving as your own judge and jury. Even at your own expense. Cora's. Momma's."

"They're taken care of. I made sure of that."

It was true. The buried cash, gold, and silver their father had hidden all over those mountains was safe from the banks. Money to keep them fed and to pay the cousins to keep an eye on her father's properties.

"I'm not sure Trilby will be. He's locked up in his grief." Thickness welled in her throat and escaped out her tear ducts. "It's worse than this prison, the one he's put himself in. It might've been better if he'd faced the consequences." If only she'd never urged Trilby to go home for Christmas.

Her father's shoulders drooped. "I'll be praying he finds the peace he needs."

The words reverberated through her soul. It must have shown on her face.

"Quincy taught me how, believe it or not. Or at least convinced me that God would hear me. And I know now it wasn't my job to shoulder the load of protector and provider. That was the Lord's place."

She smiled despite her sorrow, wishing she had more time to hear the story of how Reverend Quincy Chambers had loved his way into her father's rigid heart. A story she'd be asking Quincy about when she met him up in heaven sooner than later.

For now, she was in need of another story. "What really happened that night, Daddy? Trilby won't tell me. Or can't."

He glanced at the guards and sighed. "Long story short. I was out at one of my stills. Quincy had taken up the habit of coming to sit out there some nights when I was working or keeping watch, and we'd talk about heaven. About hell." He shrugged. "But most times he'd get me to talking about being raised up on that mountain. He'd just sit back and listen." Pain crumpled her father's face, and it was another moment before he could speak again. "That night I heard a sound behind Quincy, so I stood and pointed my gun over his shoulder. In that same moment, Quincy shifted, trying to move out of my way. A shot came from another direction. A bullet from Trilby's hunting rifle to protect his father . . . from me." Her father dropped his chin. "But his aim wasn't true. I can't tell you how many times I've asked God to rewrite it. To shift Trilby's barrel the fraction it needed to take my life in his father's stead."

She stared at the life-worn man in front of her. They weren't that different, she and her father. Not at the core of it. She'd left the mountain to choose love. He'd left it for the same reason, wrapped in a different package. This man whose way of life she'd disdained had given everything attempting to save her pain. Misguided as he was, he really did love her.

"When you go back to your man"—his voice came hoarse and thick—"tell him that the prison doors are open, Vi. No use in both of us serving time."

———— ❧ ————

Outside the prison, Viola inhaled the clear, sweet air.

Her mother waited beside the car, swaying with Quinn Leigh cradled in her arms. The guard helped Viola into the passenger seat.

She had wanted to keep her heart condition a secret, but when she'd miraculously made it on the other side of birth, she made a call from the hospital, begging Momma to find a way to bring her back home.

Momma borrowed a car from one of Daddy's investors and drove to Louisville that very day.

The penitentiary was the first place Viola requested to visit. And now her heart called for home like a newly weaned calf for its mother.

With the windows down as they drove, she drank everything in.

"How was he?" her mother asked.

"He seemed well. You didn't want to come in?"

Her mother shook her head. "Today was your day. I wanted you to have all the time you could with him."

Viola pushed out a breath. "There's something I want to tell you. I talked to Daddy about it already, and he wants to keep this quiet. I don't know if it is wrong or right, what he's asking."

Her mother stared straight ahead, hands white-knuckled on the steering wheel, as they had been the entire trip from Louisville. "About your husband?"

"Yes." The word came out a choked whisper.

"Viola, *my* husband is a stubborn man. A difficult man to understand at times. But he loves hard. Right or wrong, he took Trilby's place for you. You need to respect that even if you don't understand it."

Viola dared a look at her mother's profile, etched in concentration, not anger. She should be angry. Angry that Trilby's actions robbed her of a husband so that Viola could keep hers. What was left of him, anyway.

"Trilby is a tortured soul, Momma. He's gone to some unreachable place, and I don't know how to help him."

Her mother stayed quiet, driving onward. A scent caught Viola's attention. Something wild and floral. She couldn't quite put her finger on the individual notes, but it was the sweet yet loamy fragrance of Bitter End. She stuck her hand out the window and let the rushing wind roll through her fingers like a caress.

Finally, her mother parked in front of their log house. They both sat staring over the landscape. Memories replayed in Viola's mind. The puppy their father had brought home and the great big belly laughs rolling out of him when that little scamp playfully nipped at her heels and tugged the hem of her dress. The way he'd return from a long trip, pockets full of candy and new seeds for Momma's flower garden. The tones of her father's fiddle. Sometimes strident and mournful. Sometimes joyful and jaunty.

Momma sighed. "You'll never be able to fix your husband. But you can love him the best you can."

Cora emerged with the creak of the screen door. Her younger sister crossed her arms over her chest, as if shielding herself from Viola's approach.

Over the next several days, Viola sat outside in the sun, soaking in the beauty. She tried her best to break down the stone wall that pain had built between her and her sister.

But Cora was furious at her for dying.

Viola supposed it was an easier emotion for Cora to tussle with than sorrow.

She woke one morning two weeks later, her heart full of the mountains yet aching for another home. She might be the ole moonshiner's daughter, but she was also Trilby's wife.

Momma packed her bags and bundled her baby into the car. Viola hugged her sister tight. The walls separating them seemed to crumble just a fraction before Cora edged away.

"I've always loved you best, Cora Leigh."

And then her mother helped her into the car and drove away, Bitter End growing smaller and smaller in the rearview.

42

Ana woke to the chirp of her cell phone. TBEBS alert. That was the name Sam had given to the group text he'd created to keep everyone informed on the Big Month project, and she'd assigned it its own ringtone.

She rubbed the sleep from her eyes to read the text.

> Northern Parulas have been spotted at Seven
> Islands State Birding Park. A great place to work
> on our Big Month. Meet at Marilyn's. 5 a.m.
> Tomorrow.

Ana groaned. Apparently the early bird did get the worm.

Her phone raucously chirruped as every member replied with okays and thumbs-ups. Trent replied with a GIF of a man hunkered in the bushes with binoculars.

Piper, who had been curled in the crook of Ana's knees, lifted her head and stared at the phone, head tilted, probably confused by all the bird tweets with no scent to accompany them.

She laughed under her breath. The bird ringtone was overkill. Especially for a group text.

Ana exchanged her pajamas for leggings and an oversized T-shirt. "Ready to walk?"

Piper trotted after her.

She found Cora stirring batter in the kitchen. "I thought for certain a bird had gotten in the house."

"Sorry. It's my ringtone for the birding group text."

Cora's expression soured.

"We're officially kicking off our birding project tomorrow."

Cora harrumphed as she poured the batter into a pan. "Want some coffee? I've got another loaf of banana bread cooling and ready for you."

Ana nodded. "After I take Piper out."

The morning was warm. A cardinal feasted at the bird feeder that Cora must have recently filled. It was a wonder she hadn't taken it down to spite the birds because of Marilyn's love for them.

Ana walked barefoot in the dewy grass. The trimmings that stuck to her feet unlocked carefree childhood memories playing in her backyard. She followed Piper as she tracked the nocturnal creatures that had traversed the lawn the night before. Moisture lingered in the air and the mountain breeze coursed over the bare skin of her arms and tugged at the ends of her hair. She released a contented sigh.

When Piper froze in a pointer position, Ana attempted to identify the birds singing a chorus in the tangle of brush and in the towering oaks. *Carolina chickadee. Cardinal. And a house finch?* Birds she'd already added to the running list on their online Big Month document.

When she'd first arrived in Bitter End, she never would have noticed that at least a dozen different species of birds lived in and around her aunt's backyard.

After wiping her feet on the welcome mat, she led Piper back inside. Cora sat at the table, perusing yesterday's newspaper.

Ana poured herself a cup of coffee and settled across from her. "Come with us tomorrow. You wouldn't even have to talk to her." If anyone was in need of the precious gift of the birding society, it was Cora.

Decades different in age, she and her aunt were both all too familiar with what it was to have your life wrecked by something outside your control. Cora's interrupted retirement plan must have been a painful reflection of her childhood. Even the sweetest memories Cora had recounted were laced with the losses she'd experienced.

And now the only thing Ana could think about in these final weeks in Bitter End was how to help the woman who sat across the table from her, picking out the walnuts she'd baked into her banana nut bread.

Despite the early hour, the birding society piled onto the minibus like kids on their first field trip and sat in the seats that Jake had reinstalled. He sounded the "here comes the bride" horn as he pulled out of Marilyn's drive, headed for Seven Islands State Birding Park. Inez, Marilyn, Lottie, and Trent cheered, and Ana laughingly joined in. Piper jumped up at the commotion. Sam simply shook his head.

"Settle, Piper." The dog resumed her place in the aisle next to Ana.

Three minutes into the two-hour commute Inez whipped a CD out of the glove compartment. "It's time for a game. This CD is filled with birdsong. Whoever gets the most correct gets this chocolate bar." In her other hand Inez lifted a hazelnut Lindt bar.

The drive was silent except for Inez's CD and the occasional shouts of things like

"Northern cardinal!"

"Downy woodpecker!"

"Whippoorwill!"

"Robin!"

Marilyn, of course, blew them all out of the water, getting almost every single one correct. Some of them had such subtle differences, Ana had no idea how the woman could differentiate much less remember which song went with which bird.

True to form, Marilyn split her chocolate prize seven ways with an apologetic pat for Piper for not having something to offer her.

Did Marilyn ever tire of traipsing about in the woods with people who confused a nuthatch and a wren half the time? Ana smiled as she watched her aunt chatter with Inez. Maybe not. Like Ana, Marilyn had a teacher's heart. And though Ana's trauma made her wonder if it was best to seek a new profession, she knew in her gut that nothing would ever give her deeper joy than witnessing her students learning something new.

When Jake parked the chapel, Sam stood, trail map in hand. "The last sighting was yesterday, on Seven Islands Loop Trail, along the creek side." He disembarked, and the bird-watchers and their bird dog filed behind him in a tidy line.

"Oh my goodness. Who's getting married?"

Ana turned in the direction of the giddy voice. A blond woman with her hair tied back with a bandanna walked toward them. She tugged along a rugged man. The couple looked like they ought to be models for an outdoor sporting catalog.

Jake stepped forward. "No one today, ma'am. We're just a group of bird-watchers out for a hike. But when it's not commissioned as a birding-mobile, my wife"—he tugged Inez to his side—"and I handle weddings. Sometimes we use the bus as a literal chapel, other times we meet couples on location. It's an all-inclusive package, providing everything a couple could want for their big day." From his day pack Jake pulled out a rumpled brochure and offered it to the couple.

Ana stuffed down the laughter bubbling in her chest at the bearded man overselling his services.

The woman glanced at the man beside her. "Kyle? What do you think?"

His expression was equal parts hopeful and doubtful. "Now? Dressed like this? Are you sure?"

The woman nodded and stepped closer to Jake. "This is probably a complete imposition, but would you marry us? Today."

"Now," the groom added.

"Now?" Jake echoed while his brows shot high. "Well, I'd have to consult with the group. We're here on official birding business and you'll need a marriage license, folks."

"We have one," the woman said. "Our wedding is in two months. We just picked it up yesterday, and I forgot to bring it in from the car."

Kyle gazed adoringly at his bride-to-be. "We'll still have a ceremony with family, but we'd love to share this moment out in one of our favorite places without all the stress."

"Well?" Jake turned to the group.

Marilyn clapped her hands together in glee. "Let's do it."

Inez and Lottie looked ready to swoon with the romance of it all. Trent wore a teenage brand of indifference about the whole affair and asked if he could be in charge of walking Piper. Ana passed him the leash.

The bride went to her car and grabbed the paperwork and a short veil from her trunk. Inez helped her arrange her hair. Sam plucked several leggy dandelions from the grass and handed them to the woman. "I know we're not supposed to pick the flowers in a state park, but I figured we could get away with weeds."

She smiled her thanks and then looked at Jake. "We'd like to do the ceremony on the bridge, if that's all right?"

"Lead the way," he said.

They all filed behind the couple, who walked hand in hand, arms swinging. The breeze lifted the wrinkled veil from the bride's shoulders. The groom mopped sweat from his brow with a tie-dyed bandanna. The Bitter End Birding Society contrived the oddest wedding party Ana had ever seen in her life. She leaned toward Sam as he walked beside her. "Is this legal?" she whispered. "Don't we need a park permit or something?"

Sam shook his head. "I have no idea. That's Jake's problem."

The couple in front of her was about to make a decision that would alter the course of their lives. And yet they seemed to go into it with such abandon. "I'd be terrified if I were them."

"Yeah," Sam said, and then pushed out a breath. "It takes a certain kind of courage to tie yourself to someone for life." He smirked. "Or foolishness."

She laughed quietly and swatted a gnat away from her face. "I've never seen myself as the cynical type, but after the year I've had, it's like this subconscious defense mechanism is always running beneath the surface, expecting things to go wrong. Planning my life whether alone or with someone else feels senseless." She shrugged. "I hope that part of who I became will eventually fade. I want to feel as hopeful as that couple looks when I think about the future."

He walked a few more paces, seemingly lost in thought. He released a heavy breath. "I'm trying to come to terms that life, marriage included, doesn't ever come with guarantees." He scrubbed a hand over his face. "I've been hiding a good while, licking my wounds and searching for answers that can't be known this side of heaven." He gave her a crooked smile. "At some point I need to step outside the walls I've built and remember who God created me to be."

"And that is?" She nudged his shoulder, hoping that keeping the moment light would encourage him to remain open with her.

He shrugged. "Still figuring that out, I reckon. Asking myself if I keep those sheep because it's what I'm meant for or because it's safe."

The wedding at the entrance to the bridge was short, sweet, and simple. And the couple's joy was contagious. Ana thought of Marilyn's bluebirds. Little winged emblems of reckless, enduring hope.

After the couple said "I do," the Bitter End Birding Society cheered and congratulated the happy couple before continuing across the bridge to walk along the creek. They scanned the trees in low wet areas for the Northern Parulas. A buzzy, rising trill broke through the other birdsong.

A wide smile stretched Marilyn's face. "That's my bird." Ana followed the sound and raised her binoculars to her eyes, scouting the limbs for the diminutive blue-gray and yellow bird described in her field guide.

"There." Sam pointed a little to her left.

The tiny warbler sang with its head thrown back, the strong grip of its delicate feet keeping it fixed to the branch. Its entire body trembled with the vigor of the song.

A verse from long-ago Sunday school lessons whispered in Ana's mind. "Because you are my helper, I sing for joy in the shadow of your wings. I cling to you; your strong right hand holds me securely."

Marilyn came to stand beside her. "Isn't the volume a tiny bird can produce amazing?" She closed her eyes, listening for a moment. "Birds have several ways to defend themselves in this unforgiving world. Camouflage. Flight. Beaks and talons. But do you know a songbird's greatest defense?"

Ana waited for the answer.

"Singing. Singing at the top of their lungs."

Ana smiled at the answer and the pair of them continued hiking along the shoreline.

"Birds sing to defend their territory," Marilyn said. "They sing to call for help, to warn, and to let others know they're safe. A male with a large repertoire uses his singing skills to prove himself a worthy mate. And if I had to wager, I think birds sing for the joy of it." She put an arm around Ana's shoulder and pulled her to her side. "Because joy is an important survival skill too."

They spent the rest of the day wandering the park that was populated with a wonderful array of birds. They were able to add a few different swifts, swallows, flycatchers, wood ducks, and three different types of warblers to her life list. Sitting by the banks for lunch, they'd been entertained by a great blue heron spearing fish in the shallows.

Now she walked alongside what was once an old stone wall. A remnant perhaps of an ancient boundary line between one man's land and another's.

Moss grew over the stones, infiltrating every crack. Tree roots had burrowed beneath its foundations, causing the once-straight line to bend and buckle. Nature had a way of breaking down walls built by human hands. Gently, gradually. Not with wrecking balls but by infusing life.

Maybe that was why this group was drawn to nature. It was a living example of what they all craved. Little by little, tenaciously reclaiming life.

Ana arrived back at Cora's house just as the sun was setting, pleasantly exhausted. The scent of whatever feast Cora had prepared wafted on the air. Piper collapsed onto the dog bed in the living room with a weary huff.

"I'm home," Ana called out.

Cora walked around the corner with her cheeks flushed, a blue-checked apron tied tight around her waist. "I hope you came hungry. I've got pot roast, mashed taters, green beans, rolls. The works."

After Ana took a quick shower and changed into fresh clothes, she sat across from Cora, the food-laden table between them.

She thought of the treats she'd made for Sam and Marilyn. Perhaps it was a family trait, using food as a gateway toward relationship. This smorgasbord was an obvious overcompensation.

She reached across the table and took Cora's hand. "I feel like this needs to be said, and I need you to listen all the way to the end."

Cora's mouth opened and closed. She sat in her chair like a boxer bracing for a blow they didn't have time to dodge. "Okay."

"I know your history with Marilyn seems like a divide that no one could possibly traverse. But all I see are two incredible women I'm so glad that I get to know. I didn't live through the past you share, so I get the fact that it doesn't make sense that I have enough room in my heart for you both."

Her aunt's eyes watered. "I want to believe that."

Ana shook her head. "If you were this anxious about me meeting Marilyn, why did you ask me to come in the first place? Especially with you gone?"

Cora swiped at her face with the hem of her apron. "I don't know. I had this fear ever since we found each other that Marilyn would ruin it. Logical or not, it seemed inevitable. If I invited you here, I felt a little bit in control of the situation. And being out of town, I didn't have to watch it happen."

Cora straightened in her chair. "I'm not ashamed to be Wild Wayne's daughter. Maybe I ought to be. He did a lot of wrong things, but deep down I've always believed he did 'em for noble reasons."

"It's complicated, caring about people who do bad things." Ana's mind flashed to the image of that nineteen-year-old as he'd come into her classroom. Fear, not malice, in his eyes. The compassion and sorrow she felt for that young man was something she'd never confess. Even thinking about it felt like a betrayal of the trauma she and her school had experienced.

Ana scooped mashed potatoes from the bowl and then ladled a generous helping of tender pot roast over them. "You know what I think? Deep down you want to be friends with Marilyn, but it feels like a violation of your father's wishes."

Cora had pursed her lips and crossed her arms over her chest as Ana spoke, but now her posture softened. "I think I blamed myself for what happened for a while. I believed if I hadn't been sneaking around, hanging out with his daughter, then the reverend wouldn't have shown up at the still that night."

"Even though it was Viola who chose Trilby when your father handed out the ultimatum?"

Cora added green beans to the plate wobbling in her hand. "The day before Marilyn's daddy was killed, my daddy had found us playing in that fort in the woods. Something he'd forbidden."

"He was angry?"

"That's the funny thing. He stared for a moment, this strange expression coming over his face, and then he never said a word." She set the plate down. "I figured that was the last straw. Another daughter choosing the Chambers family over him."

Then Ana could see it clearly, how deeply ingrained it was in Cora that there was a choice between her kin and the rest of the world. Cora didn't know how to love both.

43

The next weekend, Jake led the charge. This time the ragtag bird-watchers tramped through the Cherokee National Forest in the near dark, searching for the northern saw-whet owl. The head-lamps cast their faces in eerie shadows, reminding Ana of a long-ago campout in her backyard where she and her friends had held flashlights up to their chins telling spooky stories.

Sam walked just in front of Ana, with Marilyn's arm tucked in his to make sure she kept steady footing.

Ana was hemmed in by Inez, Trent, and Lottie. Trent was a little miffed she hadn't brought his favorite member of the birding society, but Ana figured she'd have enough of a challenge hiking in the dark without trying to keep up with her quick-footed canine.

Throughout the twilight hike, they'd teased Jake for choosing the diminutive owl with a catlike face that looked like it should be a plushie on a child's bed instead of a wild creature. But the ruling mountain man took their ribbing in stride, winking at his petite wife and saying, "What can I say? I like cute little things."

Along the way they'd heard a distant whippoorwill and a screech owl, but they hadn't been able to sight them. The low rumble of thunder met their ears.

Jake turned back to them, the creases in his brow in sharp relief from the headlamp. "Don't worry. We're almost there. We'll get in and out before the bad weather comes. I double-checked the radar before we started out." He smoothed his beard.

Inez harrumphed. "My armchair meteorologist strikes again. Last week we had a wedding that was supposed to be out at the state park. Jake told 'em the weather would be fine." Inez laughed so hard, she snorted. "It rained cats and dogs, and we ended up with a ceremony *inside* the chapel with half the guests crammed in with the bride and groom and the rest huddled around the bus, fending off sideways rain with their umbrellas."

"That was one time, Nezzie."

She scowled at the nickname.

Jake upped the pace. "I'm sorry, y'all. They probably won't even call if the weather turns bad."

A few moments later Marilyn hissed, "Stop."

They all instantly froze.

"Listen."

A soft "too-too-too" whispered in the quiet evening.

"That's it. That's the saw-whet," Marilyn said. "Now let's see if those of you with better eyes than mine can spot him."

They continued down the trail, walking softly.

The owl called once again, and another answered, even closer than the first bird. Now that they'd ceased hiking, they switched their headlamps to a soft red light to hopefully be less frightening to the nocturnal creature.

"Over there." Jake pointed and Ana noticed the silent flutter of wings. The owl wasn't any bigger than a robin. When it settled overhead, Jake brought out his flashlight, illuminating the bird.

The tiny thing stared back, its curious yellow eyes deep set in its round head.

Lottie said, "I think that little guy might be the cutest thing I've ever seen."

Inez stepped close to Jake, and he put his arm around her, tucking her tight against him.

"This is a first for me." Marilyn's face seemed to glow, even in the low light. "I've heard them from far off before but never come upon one up close."

Distant thunder rumbled again, reminding them that it was time to give up basking in the moment and hightail it to the mobile chapel.

Sam switched his headlamp back to white light and studied the trail map. A fat droplet splatted on the page. He folded it and stuck it in his back pocket. "I think that's our cue."

Everyone filed behind Sam. Ana gave a parting glance to the little saw-whet whose luminous eyes studied the strange beings who'd invaded his domain. He launched from his perch and swept off into the night. Ana lifted a silent prayer of thanks.

With the storm thundering at their heels, the group was subdued, all their focus on getting out of the woods as quickly and safely as possible.

Ten minutes later, that silence was rent by a crash in the brush and a gruff expletive.

The group collectively gasped and hurried ahead. Jake was crumpled on the ground, gripping his ankle. Sam knelt at his side. Through clenched teeth, Jake said, "Pardon my language, folks. A leftover from my unsanctified youth slipped out."

Sam gave a wry chuckle. "I think we're all more concerned about you than the word you let fly. What happened?"

He winced. "There was a stick on the trail, and I rolled my ankle when I stepped on it. I tried to catch myself, but I just made it worse."

Inez wrung her hands. "Is it broken?"

"Don't think so," Jake grunted. "I'll be all right." He struggled to stand, using Sam to brace him on one side and a tree on the other. When he attempted to put weight on the ankle, the color drained from his face, giving him a ghostly pallor beneath the headlamp.

The heavy droplets increased in number, plopping on the dry ground and splattering Ana's head and shoulders.

Lottie shivered. "It's so cold!" Her son passed her his ballcap.

The sky went bright with lightning, and seconds later the thunder crashed, making them all jump.

"Oh, dear," Marilyn cried.

Ana checked her phone. No service.

"You all go on without me," Jake said, grimacing in pain. "It's my fault we're out in this."

Sam took charge. "We're not doing that. When I researched area trails near here, there was mention of an overhang. It's not a cave but enough of a shelter to keep us safe until the storm passes over. Trent, if you'll help me, I think the two of us can provide Jake the support he needs. Ana, can you give Marilyn a hand? Inez and Lottie, stick close. Stay calm, take your time, watch your step as you go, and we'll be all right."

By the time they reached the overhang, their clothes were so saturated, the shelter seemed useless. Even Inez's teased and shellacked bouffant had succumbed to the storm. But when lightning struck a tree far too close for comfort, they flocked beneath the meager shelter in a tight huddle. Ana thought of the birds in the forest all around them. Though it felt like she and her birding companions were alone out here, they weren't the only ones enduring this storm.

"Marilyn, what do birds do in weather like this?" she asked.

The woman's gray hair was plastered to her head, and fatigue had made her face droop, but at Ana's question, she smiled. "They make do as best they can. Cavity nesters like bluebirds like to find places to hunker down, but most birds seek out dense shrubs or perch close to tree trunks to brace themselves against the wind." Her shoulders relaxed. "And if these birds can make it through, so can we." She found a stone to sit upon and began to sing, her voice a little raspy with cold.

The winds and the waves shall obey thy will.
Peace be still.

Singing softly, Sam lent his deeper voice to the hymn.

> Whether the wrath of the storm-tossed sea
> Or demons or men or whatever it be,
> No waters can swallow the ship where lies
> The Master of ocean and earth and skies
> They all shall sweetly obey thy will:
> Peace, be still; peace, be still.

Marilyn's voice faded and Sam continued, singing the last line on his own.

> Peace, peace be still.

The storm raged on, the wind catching hold of the rain and tossing it their direction. Chilled and tired and aching as they all were, peace found them beneath that crowded overhang, wrapping them in the knowledge that storms end and mornings come.

Near dawn they made it back to the trailhead. All of them looked worse for the wear, but most troubling was the way gregarious Jake had gone silent.

Breaking his silence when they reached the bus, he said, "I've hurt my driving foot."

Ana looked at the group. "Anyone else have a commercial driver's license? Inez?"

She shook her head. "Only one other person I know of that has a CDL, and she's the one we bought it from. Your aunt Cora."

Ana studied her phone. One solitary signal bar. Surely Cora wouldn't let her grudge against Marilyn stop her from coming to their rescue.

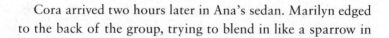

Cora arrived two hours later in Ana's sedan. Marilyn edged to the back of the group, trying to blend in like a sparrow in the brush. Cora looked at all of them in turn, her gaze skipping over Marilyn. "Y'all look like a pack of drowned rats, not bird-watchers."

She then walked a slow circle around the minibus, patted the white hood, and let out a low whistle. "Big Bertha, what have they done to you?"

She turned to Ana. "When she was a bookmobile, she was candy apple red. The kids would come running when they saw her." Cora clucked. "I can't imagine how many coats of paint it took to turn this thing white."

"It's a wrap, not paint. It peels right off," Jake croaked from the bench. Compassion softened the haughty look that Cora wore like armor. "We'd better get you seen to, Jake. And get the rest of you home to dry clothes before you catch your death." She passed the car keys to Ana. "I'll see you at home."

Ana looked like she wanted to say something, but she kept her lips buttoned tight.

Marilyn resisted the urge to ride home with Ana. Maybe the Lord had provided the opportunity for a little forced proximity to help thaw the ice between old friends.

Cora leveled a hawklike stare at her.

Or maybe it was a lost cause better avoided altogether. Only one way to find out.

Trent and Sam helped Jake onto the bus, grunts and groans coming from all three.

As Marilyn boarded, she dared a glance at Cora, who sat in the driver's seat, fussing with the seat adjustments and mirrors, reacquainting herself with the vehicle.

"Thank you." She forced the words out, sure they wouldn't be well received.

"I did it for Ana," Cora replied without meeting her eyes. "I was worried sick when she didn't make it home last night."

"Of course." Marilyn walked the short aisle and found a seat, a smile tugging at the corners of her mouth despite her exhaustion.

A few hours later the screen door slapped in the frame as Cora bustled in. Piper hopped up from Ana's feet to greet her. "I smell coffee. Bless you, child."

Ana handed her a fresh cup when she entered the room. "It was the least I could do after dragging you out of bed at the crack of dawn to come to our rescue."

Cora narrowed her eyes. "Sam coulda driven y'all back. I'm sure he coulda handled it. As long as he didn't get pulled over, that is." She crossed her arms over her chest. "You didn't need me."

"I'm glad you came."

"Of course I came." She settled into her chair and took a drink of the strong brew. The hard lines in her face softened. "I'd do anything for you."

Mischief and hope danced in Ana's chest at her aunt's admission. "Anything?"

Cora's eyes fell shut, and she groaned. "Me and my big mouth."

"Jake isn't going to be able to drive with his injured ankle. Please, be our driver."

Cora pushed wisps of hair out of her face. "Y'all can carpool."

"It wouldn't be the same if we had to split up." Ana was well aware she sounded like a petulant middle schooler who'd been asked to move seats away from a friend.

Cora shook her head. "You barely know these people. Why the fuss?"

Ana clasped her hands in front of her, begging. "I know your feelings about Marilyn are complicated, but she's been good to me, and this group was exactly what I needed this summer."

An idea that had been bumping about in Ana's mind, abstract and unformed, began to take shape. Warmth filled her middle. Maybe she *could* find a way to bring the peace she found here back to her old students. She pressed on. "I only have a few weeks left until I have to go back home and face the life I left behind. I need this. I need this group to finish well." Ana gave her a pleading look.

Cora grumbled under her breath. "Fine."

"You'll do it?"

She gave a single nod.

Ana's phone dinged. A message from Inez. She scanned it and relayed its message to Cora. "Jake is okay. It was just a bad sprain. He has to wear a walking cast for the next several weeks." She hugged her neck. "Thanks for volunteering to take over as driver. Can I tell the others?"

Cora grumbled under her breath. "Might as well get it over with."

Ana updated the group, then spent the rest of the day researching outdoor-based education. What if there was a way to go back and get a redo with her students, one in which she really could provide the emotional support and guidance they needed?

Sam read Ana's text and smiled. She was the only person in the world who could have sweet-talked Cora into that scheme.

He had a feeling he knew what she'd written down as her secret hope for their final days together as a birding society. If anyone could nudge those two aunts of hers toward reconciliation, it was Ana. She might be the most determined person he'd ever met.

His phone dinged again.

Hey, I also wanted to tell you that you did an amazing job handling everything when Jake got hurt. You were calm and assertive. Exactly what we all needed.

He read over Ana's text four times, taking the words to heart and storing them in his memory as a reminder for bad days—the days that obliterated everything except the ways he'd failed.

Ana was so gifted at remaining honest while encouraging others in just the ways they needed. It was probably what made her a good kindergarten teacher. Or maybe it was because she spent so much time with children who were both brutally honest and good at noticing things that other people didn't.

It made him crave more time in her presence than he was afforded.

Taking a page out of Ana's book, he sent Marilyn a few articles he'd read about birding with visual impairments. Just because her abilities were changing didn't mean she needed to surrender her post, unless it was what she truly wanted. Birding was for everyone.

Sam then pulled the slip of paper that had taken up residence in his pocket. He read the words he'd written with a shaky hand. *To forgive myself for Marcy's death.* It was odd, the mix of feelings he had when he read those words. He was hungry for self-forgiveness yet nauseated by the selfishness of craving something he didn't deserve.

But a still, small voice had thrummed in his chest, urging him to write it down. And he'd listened.

Having the capacity to forgive himself was as likely as sighting a blue-winged teal within the next few weeks. He hadn't missed Marilyn's pointed glare after he'd chosen a bird that was not exactly impossible to find but improbable this time of year.

However unwise, he'd laid down a test before the Almighty—if he found the unlikely bird then he'd truly believe it was time to begin the hike toward self-forgiveness. And if not? He was free to persist in self-loathing a little longer.

He opened his laptop and typed each of the group members' birds into the sighting search bar. Inez's olive-sided flycatcher was a little too far off for a day trip. Same with Trent's summer tanager. Though they might be able to find both in one trip if everyone was up for spending a couple days camping in the Great Smoky Mountains National Park.

With shaky hands, he typed the name of his bird in the search bar. He'd never made it this far down the list. He let out a slow breath of release when no recent entries came up in their local area.

Ana's kingfisher should be fairly simple to find. He knew of a nesting area in a cove of Watauga Lake that he and Marilyn had stumbled upon last year. A short, easy trip was what they all needed to recover from their last adventure.

He sent out a text to the group with plans for the following weekend.

44

The following Saturday, the minibus was loaded with bird-watchers, including Jake, who limped down the aisle with his clunky walking cast, determined to accompany them even if the terrain might limit his participation. As always, Trent commandeered Piper the moment he saw her.

Once everyone was on board, Cora took the captain's seat. Ana sat at the front, trying to detect her mood. Angry? Apprehensive? Annoyed?

Cora and Marilyn had exchanged solemn nods as Marilyn boarded the bus and sat in the row behind Ana. She had to give Marilyn credit—had she been in a similar situation, Ana might have headed for the back to put a little distance between herself and the source of her discomfort.

At least the birding spot that Sam found wasn't far.

Ana opened her day pack and pulled out the original birding list and a pencil. "Cora, what's your bird?"

Without taking her eyes from the road, she shook her head. "I'm just the chauffeur."

"Come on," Ana wheedled, "you might as well participate. It'll be more fun than sitting on the bus."

Cora caught her gaze in the rearview mirror, and then it flicked to Marilyn. Both women eyed each other in the reflection. "A cuckoo bird, then."

Marilyn's lips formed a tight line. Ana pulled out her field guide and flipped through the pages. Had Cora chosen a bird outside their parameters?

Or was she implying that they were all a little birdbrained for this endeavor?

"Yellow-billed or black-billed?" Marilyn asked.

"Doesn't make a difference, does it? They all do the same thing. An egg gets laid in a nest it doesn't belong in and then the bigger cuckoo takes up all the resources, pushing the smaller hatchling out of its rightful nest."

Ana watched the hurt ping-pong between the two women. Marilyn dropped her chin. Cora's face hardened, and she refocused on the road in front of her.

Ana scanned the field guide, reading about the harsh way a cuckoo bird ensured its survival. "It might not be pretty, but a cuckoo hatchling has no say on where it's laid. They are just trying to survive." Why did Cora still hold Marilyn accountable for the childhood she'd endured? It seemed so petty. Yet her pain hovered over them like a rain cloud.

A little while later, Cora pulled into the parking area as Sam directed her.

As everyone filed off the bus, Ana waited. Cora remained in the driver's seat.

Ana tugged at her arm. "Come on. They're all waiting."

"No, ma'am. I told you. I'm just the driver."

"One hike and, I promise, if you don't like it, you never have to go again. And since it's my bird we're looking for, it can be a silent stroll. Those are my favorite, anyway."

"A silent stroll?"

"Where we stay silent and focus on the music of nature and what God might want to speak. The things we can only hear if we grow quiet."

"That means giving old Marilyn the silent treatment is fair game, then." Cora smirked. She really was stuck being her eight-year-old self when it came to Marilyn.

"It's not really the point, but—"

"All right, then." Cora disembarked and Ana followed.

She didn't miss the note of surprise on Marilyn's face.

As they took the short hike to the secluded cove, Ana thought about the difference between her two aunts. Marilyn, though she certainly had painful memories of the past, had moved on with her life. Cora was still living in the house she grew up in. And while she had consistently reached out to others through her mobile library, venturing into their worlds, she never seemed to allow them into hers. Was ten-year-old Marilyn one of the last people Cora had admitted into her inner circle before her world fell apart?

Maybe Cora inviting Ana to care for her home this summer had been a bigger statement of faith than Ana realized at the time. She'd allowed Ana into her home because she hadn't yet known how to let her into her heart.

These thoughts cluttered Ana's mind as she walked the forest trail. Jake was so loud with his walking cast that it would be a miracle if they didn't frighten off every bird in a ten-mile radius. She had to hand it to the guy, though. He managed the uneven terrain better than she would have. Inez stuck close to his side, though Ana had a hard time believing the small woman would be any help at all if he stumbled.

Trent, Piper, and Lottie were just behind her on the trail. From the snatches of chatter she could hear, it sounded like Trent had made up a silly rap about a bird dog bird-watcher. Lottie kept jumping in with increasingly ridiculous lines.

Ana laughed to herself. Maybe the kid had a future in early education too. Her students would have gotten a kick out of the goofiness going on behind her. Ana hugged her arms around her middle. Today was a good, good day.

They reached a clearing along the creek. The rest of the group, other than Cora, spread out along the bank while Ana found large rocks for them to sit on. Cora watched everyone from a distance. Ana offered up a prayer for reconciliation and healing to occur between Cora and Marilyn and then did her best to let her mind settle. She pulled the index card from her pocket and read the words she'd written in Marilyn's living room.

To release the guilt I carry.

She was supposed to be looking for her kingfisher. And she would. But right now she had seven sets of eyes on the lookout for her. Eight if Piper was included.

Only she could tend to the thing written on her paper.

She couldn't go back and undo that awful day. She couldn't undo her misguided attempts at shepherding the children in her class through the trauma.

Was hoping for Marilyn and Cora's reconciliation just a stand-in for all the things she'd failed to do for her kindergartners?

Maybe.

But maybe it was a window into who she was.

What if the problem wasn't her desire to mend and comfort but the motives behind her actions?

Nurturing others and helping them find healing and wholeness was a reflection of her Creator. Serving others as a bandage to cover her own shortcomings and feelings of guilt was not.

"Ana." Sam's urgent whisper dissolved the silence, pulling her back to the moment. He motioned her over. She stuffed the index card into her pocket. Maybe she hadn't yet "accomplished the goal" on the card, but healing was an ongoing journey without a fixed destination. Now to learn how to embrace the process.

She drew close to Sam.

"Aim your binoculars that direction." He pointed. "You're going to love this."

She focused her attention across the cove.

"Do you see the burrow in the bank?" Sam moved behind her shoulder, pointing over the water.

Just as she found it, a blue-gray bird with a shaggy crest exited the burrow and perched on a nearby branch.

"I see one. I see my bird!" She started to turn to face him, but Sam placed his hands on her shoulders. "Wait and watch."

Without intending to, she leaned into his touch. He didn't pull away, so she stayed.

Everyone gathered around, looking in the same direction.

The stocky, shrewd-looking bird dove headfirst into the water. Moments later it came to the surface with a small fish. "So cool," she said over her shoulder to Sam.

He laughed. "Keep watching."

When the bird flew back to the perch, it whacked the fish on the branch and dropped it back in the water.

"What—"

"Watch," Sam nudged her. "Or you'll miss it."

A smaller, scrawnier kingfisher, who had been hidden in the foliage, dove into the water and retrieved the fish.

"Not only did you find your list bird, you got to witness how it teaches its nestlings to feed themselves. That's pretty special."

She lowered her binoculars and turned to Sam. She threw her arms around him with the abandon of an excited child. "Thank you. It was so cool."

He cleared his throat. "You're welcome."

She released her grip on him. "Sorry." She laughed under her breath. "Who knew birding could be such an emotionally intense endeavor."

The discomfiture on his face dissolved, and he let out a bark of a laugh. "If you told someone on the street that, they'd never believe you." He squeezed her shoulder. When his hand lingered there, her gaze shot to his. For just a moment the worry that seemed to live in his expression had faded and a warmth took its place. But then something behind her snagged his attention and he dropped his hand.

She turned to look. Cora sat alone on a log while everyone

else watched the kingfishers. There was something wistful in her expression that belied Cora's aloof facade.

She motioned her aunt over. "Come see. You wouldn't believe the way they dive and come up with a tiny fish in a split second."

Cora hesitated a moment and then pushed to her feet. Ana pointed out where to aim her binoculars. In her peripherals, a larger bird swooped in, landing on the water with a delicate splash. She tapped Sam on the shoulder. "What kind of duck is that?"

He lifted his binoculars and studied the bird for a few moments. The duck flapped its wings, causing its body to raise slightly without fully lifting out of the water. A flash of green and powder blue showed on the avian wing.

Sam lowered his binoculars, looking a little pale. "It's a blue-winged teal."

Two list birds in one trip, not to mention the two species of herons, the cormorant, the osprey, and the ibis they'd added to their running total. It had been an exciting day, but Ana noticed Sam looked overwrought rather than exhilarated when he sank onto the bus seat.

Marilyn slid in beside him, and they engaged in quiet conversation, both of their heads bent close. Ana watched them in the reflection of the bus's rearview mirror, feeling like an eavesdropper though she couldn't hear a word of what was being said.

Marilyn patted him on the back and then stood, bracing herself on the chairs as she moved closer to the front of the bus. Once she was abreast of Ana, Marilyn jerked her chin back in Sam's direction. "Will you go sit with him? He could use a friend. Plus, there's something I need to say to Cora."

Ana stood slowly, glancing at Cora.

"We'll be okay. Promise." Marilyn gave her an encouraging nod.

Ana made her way to the back where Sam sat, pensively staring out the window. She sat beside him, wordless, making space for him to speak if he'd like.

After a few moments he turned to her, something warring in

his eyes. "I wasn't supposed to be able to find that bird. They've been spotted in this area before, years ago. But rarely seen since."

"Is there a reason you picked a bird you didn't think you could find?"

He gave her a sad smile and then gazed out the window for a few moments. When he shifted back toward her, his eyes were bright with unshed tears. "I made a deal with God. Shoulda known better than that."

She arched a brow.

"I told God that if I happened upon my bird this month, I would commit to the thing I wrote on my card."

"Which was?" she asked without expecting an answer.

"Something impossible. Something I don't want to do." He clenched his hands into fists. "I told Him I would take it as a sign that it was time to forgive myself for my part in my wife's death. That it was time to start moving forward."

Shock rolled over her. He'd alluded to past mistakes but never that he'd been married, much less that he'd lost his wife. She placed a hand on his tensed forearm. "You *want* to forgive yourself."

He dropped his gaze to his lap. "I really don't."

"If that were true, you never would have made the bargain." She blew out a breath and pulled the card from her pocket. "Our cards have a common theme. My goal is to release the guilt I carry."

His eyebrows raised. "I thought you'd made it your goal to reunite your aunts."

Ana glanced toward the front of the bus. She observed Cora's face in the mirror. It was set like granite, obviously displeased with whatever Marilyn was saying. "I can't fix other people. No matter how much I want to," she told Sam. "But if I happen to create an environment that nudges them in the right direction—I figure there's no harm in that."

"Can I tell you about Marcy?" His voice was low and hoarse.

She barely stopped her jaw from dropping. "I'd be honored to listen."

He nodded as if cajoling himself into talking. "Marcy and I married shortly after I graduated from Bible college. She was funny and smart and full of life. She brought the silly and playful to my too-serious nature. She was always really supportive of my role at the church but told me on a regular basis that I was too focused on serving and not enough on living the life I'd been given. I ignored her. I mean, I was a pastor. That's the gig, right? Putting others before yourself. Their family's needs above your own. That's what I'd always been taught." He sucked in a breath through his nose.

"Life changed when Marcy got into a car accident about four years into our marriage. It was a miracle she survived the traumatic brain injury. I took a three-month sabbatical to be there for her around the clock. Her body healed, but she was never the same.

"She became prone to angry outbursts and was often depressed and withdrawn. She had almost-constant headaches. There was nothing I could do to relieve her suffering, so I eventually dove back into my work, spending more time at the church than ever before, providing care to people I believed I had the capacity to help.

"One night, she was acting more quiet than usual. I asked if she was okay, and of course, she told me that she was fine other than a headache. And headaches were something we'd both come to accept as her normal. Still, gut instinct, or maybe the Holy Spirit, told me something was different that night. But then I got a call from a parishioner whose grandfather was in the hospital dying and I left her to comfort someone else."

Sam grew quiet. He wrung his hands as if trying to massage out the shaking. He took several slow breaths.

"When I got back home, I found . . ." He shut his eyes tight. "I found her in the bathtub. Already gone. Pills all over the floor. I thought . . . I thought for sure she'd done this to herself." He shook his head. "But when I got the autopsy report weeks later, it listed a ruptured aneurysm as the cause of death. Something that must have developed after her accident because of weakened vessels from the TBI." He clamped his mouth shut, and a muscle ticked in his jaw. Ana rested a hand on his forearm, hoping to somehow lend him strength.

She focused on the scenery racing past the bus window, waiting.

Just when Ana had determined that Sam had shared all he could, he said, "She must have taken some meds and gotten into the bath to relieve her pain and—" His voice cracked, cutting away his words. He looked up at her. His anguish was so raw, so transparent, that her own eyes filled.

"If I had been there," he continued, "I could have gotten her help in time. She might still be here. But I focused on people that made me feel good instead of helping the one person who needed it the most. And I can't forgive myself for failing to truly love my wife above myself. Above my own ego."

He grimaced as though a physical pain rocked him. "But maybe you're right. Maybe there's a small part of me that wants something I know I don't deserve. Some days—the better days—I can almost imagine Marcy, whole and healed, looking down from heaven saying, 'There you go again, Sammy. Too serious and still working instead of living life.'"

He buried his face in his hands, taking slow, ragged breaths.

After a few moments, Ana put her arm around him and held him tight. "It's so hard when we want more than anything to have done better for people we promised to love and protect."

He offered her a sad smile. "Maybe you can keep reminding me of the truth about grace and I'll keep reminding you. Between the two of us, maybe we will figure out this self-forgiveness thing."

45

Marilyn glanced into the rearview mirror, smiling slightly at Sam and Ana, who were deep in conversation. They were good for each other.

"Did you need something other than to jaw my ear off about this birding nonsense?"

The coldness in Cora's voice pushed Marilyn to drop the small talk and get to the real reason she'd swapped seats with Ana. "I need to talk to you."

"You've got a captive audience until I pull into your driveway." Cora's knuckles whitened on the steering wheel.

"Not here," Marilyn said. "In private. When we get back."

"When we get to your place, I'll give you ten minutes to have your say. For Ana. That girl has designs on fixing things too broken to be mended."

Marilyn stopped herself from saying, *Are they though?* Because once she told Cora the secret she'd been sitting on all these years, Cora might be right.

After several abrasive moments of silence, Cora added, "I'd like to change my bird."

"Pardon?"

"I don't want the cuckoo to be my bird. I'd like to put mine as a song sparrow . . . for Vi."

Marilyn's mouth went dry.

"I know it's not some fancy bird. Sparrows are common as squirrels. But when we were girls, Viola would drive me up the wall trying to whistle along with the song sparrows outside our bedroom window at the crack of dawn. They were her favorites."

Marilyn absorbed the sudden tenderness in her old friend's voice, and then said, "My husband Obie spent five years studying European starlings, which might be even more common than squirrels. Birding isn't about rare birds. It's about rediscovering wonder and meaning and purpose in the little things of the world." Maybe she imagined it, but it felt like the wall between them buckled, if only a fraction. "The song sparrow is the perfect addition to the list," Marilyn added, hoping that pliability between them would remain after she told Cora the truth.

For the rest of the drive Marilyn rehearsed the one-sided conversation she'd orchestrated in her head thousands of times. Sixty-plus years of wondering how to tell her best friend about the eavesdropped conversation ten-year-old Marilyn was never meant to hear.

Once they disembarked from the bus in her driveway, Marilyn approached Sam and Ana. "Could you give Ana and Piper a ride home?" she asked Sam. "Cora is going to stay to have a little chat about some long overdue things." If her nerves weren't so frazzled, she would have laughed aloud at the startled look the pair gave her.

"It will be fine," she said, impressed with how real her false confidence sounded. *Dear Lord, help this truly be fine.*

After she'd said her farewells to the rest of the society, she motioned Cora over. "Take a seat on the porch. I'll bring out some sweet tea. Unless you'd rather come inside?"

"I don't need refreshments. Just spit out whatever it is you want to tell me, and let's get on with it." Marilyn was not fooled by the growl in Cora's voice, not with the way her chin quivered.

"Well, I need a little fortification to make it through this, so you'll have to hold your horses." She went inside and fixed two glasses in case Cora changed her mind. The woman sure could do with some sugar to sweeten her disposition. Though that wasn't entirely true. She was beloved by the entire Roan Mountain community. She reserved her gruffness for Marilyn alone.

When she returned to the porch, she motioned to the rocking chairs. "Sit a spell."

Cora eyed her warily, then she scooted her rocker farther from Marilyn's.

"Why do you hate me?"

Cora faltered as she sat, almost toppling herself. "Hate you?"

"I've been back here a good six years, and you've been about as hospitable as a porcupine with its quills up."

Cora swallowed hard, shifting in her seat. "Porcupines don't put their quills up because of hate."

"Fair enough. So, before I say what I have to say, will you please put the quills down and tell me why you think you need to defend yourself against me? Because you don't."

Cora blinked rapidly and swiped at her face. "I did hate you for a long time. It felt like your arrival in Bitter End stole my family away. First my sister. And then, and I know it wasn't your fault, but my father ended up in prison." Cora set the chair to rocking, its runners creaking against the porch. "Then at the same time I felt so guilty for blaming your family for something my father was convicted of. But then Viola—"

Marilyn shook her head. "Wayne didn't kill my father."

Cora stilled her agitated rocking. "What did you just say?"

"Your father did not shoot my father." Marilyn wiped her damp palms against her hiking pants. "I-i-it was Trilby."

Cora's face hardened. "You've known for over sixty years that my father wasn't guilty of murder and you never said a word?" The anger in Cora's voice wasn't a defense this time.

Marilyn forced out the rest of her story. "My momma and I were at the hospital to visit Viola after the baby was born. I'd run ahead. Trilby was talking to Vi and, being the nosey ten-year-old

I was, I snuck up trying to listen in. Part of me was sure I heard wrong. But the other part of me . . ." The growing tightness in Marilyn's throat cut away her words. She sipped her tea trying to loosen the knot. She pushed onward. "Right before Trilby passed, he confirmed it. He asked me to take it to my grave."

"He had no right to ask such a thing. You should have told me the second you moved back to Bitter End, if not before," Cora spat out.

"And ignore the unwelcome basket you left on my front porch the day Obadiah and I moved in?" It was too serious a moment to bring it up, but Marilyn couldn't resist. Thankfully she'd never truly lost the girl who'd tried to hustle her at marbles a lifetime ago.

A corner of Cora's mouth twitched a fraction at the reminder, but she swatted the air. "I don't care a rat's hind leg about Trilby Chambers's wishes. He doesn't have a right to wishes."

"It wasn't Trilby's request I was honoring. It was your father's."

Cora looked like she'd been slapped. "Excuse me?"

"He and Trilby kept in touch over the years. Wrote letters and such. More frequently after Viola passed. Trilby begged your father to let him tell the truth. But your daddy refused. He said that Trilby needed to focus on raising his daughter."

"What are you saying?"

"My father was at your father's stills that fateful night, but it was Trilby who pulled the trigger. It was an accident."

"I know all that. But why did my father take the blame for him?"

Marilyn almost dropped her tea. "You knew?"

Cora ducked her chin. "Viola came back for one last visit before she died. Her idea had been to come say goodbye and return home. But she and Momma didn't make it far before deciding to turn around and send for Trilby to come to her. Before she passed, she sent away everyone, including Trilby, and she told me the truth. I think she thought it was important that I know our father, though he'd done many things, had not killed an innocent man in cold blood."

Marilyn set her glass on the small side table. "Let me get this straight. You're sour at me for not telling you something you already knew?"

Cora shrugged. "I'm mad because I've been keeping this secret from *you* about *your* brother all these years for no good reason."

"Why? Seems like the perfect way to twist the knife in my back."

Cora pinched the bridge of her nose. "I never wanted to hurt you, not really. I just didn't know what to do with all these old ugly feelin's. Forgetting you like you forgot me seemed to work there for a good while. And then you showed up here again."

Marilyn reached for Cora's hand and was more than a little shocked when the woman didn't pull away. "I never forgot you."

With her other hand, Cora pulled something from her pocket and rolled it over and over in her hand. The soapstone heart Marilyn had hidden in the lean-to for Cora's Christmas gift. Not only did she still have it, she carried it with her? Moisture sprang to Marilyn's eyes.

"I just wish I knew why my daddy chose to protect Trilby like that."

"I know your father once told Trilby he was an old outlaw who'd done things that deserved prison and everyone would readily believe a moonshiner did the deed. Young and scared with a pregnant young wife at home, Trilby obeyed. He did his best to take his father's place, caring for me and my momma."

Cora huffed. "What about me and my mother? Why didn't my father worry about us?"

"I think he trusted the mountain folk to care for y'all like he'd always cared for them."

"And they did." Cora's voice went soft and thoughtful. "It's just so unfair that my father was locked up. And Trilby went free. Surely it would have been ruled an accident if he'd just faced justice instead of running."

Marilyn braced her hands on her knees. "It would have likely turned out better for them all if he had. Trilby put himself in his own sort of prison. He went from working with people to charring his hands fabricating the same prison bars he thought he belonged behind. Work that eventually killed him."

"At least he had choices. My father was caged."

"Trilby said your father was one of the freest men he'd ever met. He said Wayne had found freedom through the seeds of faith my father planted in his heart during their moonshine still conversations."

Cora's eyes shot wide. "Their what?"

"Sometime after Viola and Trilby moved away, my father started meeting your father out at one of his stills. They became friends of sorts. Neither necessarily agreeing with the other's way of thinking. But they had an understanding. Respect."

Cora shook her head. "When everything happened I thought . . ." She took a long, shaky drink of her sweet tea, the ice rattling against the glass. "I thought it was my fault your father was out there that night."

Marilyn scrunched her face. "Why in the world?"

"You remember the day before the . . . the accident. My father happened on us in our hideout. The way he looked at us both and never said a word scared me more than him flying off the handle at my disobedience. I went to your father and told him that I was scared of how my father would handle it. I'd seen him kick my sister right out of our family. Until Viola told me the truth, I thought your father went out that night to talk to Daddy because of me."

"That's an awful lot for an eight-year-old kid to take responsibility for."

"Yeah." Cora massaged her temple for a few moments and then looked at Marilyn. "Why are you telling me this?" She shook her head. "After all this time—"

"Ana." Marilyn set her rocking chair into motion. And like a mother comforting a child, Marilyn rocked the ten-year-old girl who still lived on in her heart. A girl who still craved the friend Cora Leigh Whitt had been. "I'd resigned to let you be angry at me for the rest of your days, figuring I deserved it. But Ana wanted so much for us to find a way to reconcile. I didn't know if knowing the truth would make it easier or harder for you to stop hating me, but I hoped it would help you make peace with the past. And if you could make peace with the past, you could put it to rest. And if you put the past to rest, you'd remember that you and I were never enemies."

Cora stared into her open palms resting on her thighs. "Did Trilby ever find peace?" Her words carried a hungry ache that took Marilyn by surprise.

"In this life?" She shook her head. "I don't believe he ever stopped punishing himself, not completely anyway. He did take a lot of joy in little Quinn Leigh." Marilyn brushed away the tear that spilled over. "I was there when he breathed his last, at just twenty-eight years old. Right before he went, this smile stretched his face, making him look like a boy again, and he said, 'He came, even for the likes of me.' And then peace washed over my brother's face, and I knew his spirit was at rest."

"I'm glad for that." Cora met her gaze and took a deep breath. "I thought I was over all that stuff. But when you came back, those old, rotten feelings rose up out of the grave I'd buried them in. Can you ever forgive me for acting like a mule?"

Marilyn smiled. "I think it is high time we both forgive those two little girls and let them be what they were—children thrown into a situation neither of them asked for."

"For Ana?"

"For Ana," she agreed. "And for us. We don't have to wait until we're on the other side of eternity to find that peace that passes all understanding, my friend."

46

Ana crawled from beneath her tent's exit flap and stretched. No nightmares, even though Piper had slept in the guys' tent as requested by Trent. Cora and Lottie were already huddled around a grill, fixing breakfast. They'd spent the last three days camping in the Great Smoky Mountains as a finale for their Big Month.

Over the past four weeks, every member had found their hoped-for bird, and they'd identified one hundred and fifty species. Not bad for a ragtag group of amateurs.

Cora waved Ana over. "Give us a hand."

She wasn't entirely sure what all had transpired during Marilyn and Cora's conversation last week, but whatever truce they'd formed had been enough to convince Cora to become a full-fledged member of the Bitter End Birding Society.

Ana helped them plate the food and set it on the picnic tables.

"Have you heard from your school principal yet?" Lottie asked.

"Not yet." Ana had spent the past two weeks cobbling together an outdoor education plan and a request to move to the first grade with her class from last year.

"Well, I'm praying for favor, honey. I know it would mean a lot to you."

"It sure would."

Movement down by the creek caught her eye. Marilyn sat solo. "I'm going to go check on Marilyn."

Lottie grabbed her hand before she walked away, pulling her aside. "I can't tell you how grateful I am that you invited Trent to join you. You didn't know this, but before he met you, he'd really been strugglin'." She wrinkled her nose. "Honestly, we still butt heads five days outta seven. And he still makes a lot of choices I wish he wouldn't." She looked up at the trees, her features softening. "But getting outside together, spending time with other people, it lets us be friends for a few hours instead of a worried momma hovering over a teenager who wants more freedom than he's ready for. Thank you."

Ana pulled her into a hug. "You have no idea how much I needed to hear that."

She left the two women behind and approached Marilyn. She sat beside her on the large rock.

Marilyn pointed. "There's a green heron on the opposite bank. At least, I think there is."

A bird with stilt legs and deep green plumage waded, eyeing them warily. "He's pretty."

Marilyn smiled at her. "It's been such a good summer. I'm so glad I had the chance to meet Trilby's granddaughter. He'd be so proud of you. Not just because of the things you've done, but because of who you are. He'd be forced to recognize that something good and beautiful can come from a broken family tree."

Ana absorbed the kind words instead of letting them ricochet.

"You might have his freckles and auburn hair, but you've got your grandmother Viola's tenacity. Through everything, she remained so calm and steady, even though she must have been so scared and uncertain. Heartbroken for the people she loved. You have that same character living on in you."

Emotion welled in Ana's chest, and she draped her arm around her aunt's shoulder. "Thank you for that."

A splashing tread reached her ears, and both women turned to see Sam walking Piper along the banks as the heron took flight.

Ana lifted a hand in greeting. "I thought that was supposed to be Trent's job."

Sam raised a hand to his brow to cut the glare of the sun breaking through the trees. "I take it you've never tried waking a teenage boy before he was ready."

Marilyn chuckled beside her. "Well, go on. You two walk that dog. I'm going to sit a little while longer."

Ana rose from her spot and joined Sam. He hadn't talked about his past again with her since that day on the bus, but something had shifted after that conversation. Grace was beginning to win in the battle he fought with himself.

And in that shift, something had changed between them. Whatever it was, she found herself looking for excuses to be in his presence to try to figure it out.

"Have you heard back from your school yet?" he asked, anticipation lighting his eyes.

He'd given such great input as she formulated teaching plans that incorporated daily nature exploration.

"Not yet. But it should be any day now. The board had their meeting on Thursday."

He nodded. "They'll go for it."

"I hope so."

They paused their forward movement and watched as Piper stopped to sniff at a small hole in the bank.

"I'm going to miss you." Sam's words were soft. Tentative.

She looked up in surprise.

One side of his mouth quirked upward. "I do actually like people, you know. I'm just in the habit of avoiding situations where I might let them down." He shrugged. "But I'm working on that." He took a steadying breath and squared his shoulders. "So. I'll miss you. A lot. But I am so glad that you may have an opportunity to start new with your students. Not everyone gets that chance."

"If the board agrees, I won't take a single moment for granted."

Sam took her hand. "I know you won't."

Her heart thudded in her chest at his unexpected touch. She would miss this shepherd-cowboy who was slowly coming back to life, learning to take the risk of loving others. "Maybe I could get the Bitter End Birding Society to come as a special guest."

He gave her a full grin. "That would be something."

"I really am hoping to have Marilyn come to guest teach. She can bring Obadiah's drawings and field notes and show them off."

Sam looked back to his friend still sitting along the banks. "She would love that."

"And you? What do you think this next year will bring? Do you think that you'll ever lead a church again?"

He stared into the distance. "I don't think I'm to a place to make that kind of decision yet. When Marcy passed, not only was I grieving but I had this crisis of faith. I wanted to believe in the goodness and kindness of God, but I couldn't see it."

Ana pinched her lips tight and then rushed out the words. "It's hard to feel the nearness of God when you're convinced you don't deserve it." That was the conclusion she'd come to on her own journey, anyway.

He nodded, considering her words. "I wasn't Horatio Spafford, singing 'It is well with my soul' over the watery grave of his loved ones. I was a man on the run from God and from my undeserved title.

"I was supposed to be the strong one, a living example to the people in my care on how to walk through crisis. But when I couldn't manage to keep my faith and stand strong, I began to believe that I was never called to be a pastor in the first place. That it had just been something I made up in my head."

"Do you still feel that way?"

"I . . ." He took a breath. "My head and heart are healing, but I'm not ready to know the answer to that question yet. And I'm okay with that. For now. But I am curious about what the future might hold." He gave her a crooked smile. "Which is new for me—looking ahead with interest instead of dread. Right now, I'm not focused on a role or position, but rather on having the courage to exercise the gifts God gave me with the people close to me. And I trust Him with whatever comes next."

Ana's heart soared. "I think that's incredible, Sam."

"It's been a long journey, but I wouldn't be where I am without Marilyn. Birding with her, I felt no pressure to spiritualize my pain or to be what anyone expected. I could just be. Birds were this gateway to recognizing beauty and goodness in the world again. And even though my thought life still lacked faith, my heart began to fight back, whispering that the beauty found in His creation was evidence of God's goodness and kindness. Even when I was full of doubt, the beauty still remained." There was a quietness and surety in his gaze that had not been there when she first met him.

"Little by little the whisper is getting louder, and I'm working on keeping up my end of the deal I made with God," Sam continued. "Part of that is accepting the grace I feel when I watch a bird in flight or feel a cool breeze on a blistering summer day. Those are gifts I'm ready to see and accept. It's only the starting point to healing those deeply buried things. But it is a start."

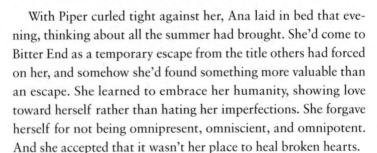

With Piper curled tight against her, Ana laid in bed that evening, thinking about all the summer had brought. She'd come to Bitter End as a temporary escape from the title others had forced on her, and somehow she'd found something more valuable than an escape. She learned to embrace her humanity, showing love toward herself rather than hating her imperfections. She forgave herself for not being omnipresent, omniscient, and omnipotent. And she accepted that it wasn't her place to heal broken hearts.

"Ana?" Cora called from the other side of the bedroom door.

"Come in."

Cora entered and sat on the edge of her bed. She was quiet for several moments before she spoke. "I never thanked you for working on my house this summer. I know I didn't end up going anywhere, but it helped me more than you know." She took a shaky breath. "This house was full of stuff I didn't need or want, but I couldn't make myself get rid of it." She grabbed Ana's hand. "I think so much was taken from me over the years that I hung on to everything I could, whether it served me well or not."

Ana sat up and put her arms around her aunt. "Well, maybe now we've made space for some new things in your life that you *do* want."

Her aunt patted her cheek. "I hope so. And I hope you won't be a stranger." Her eyes were pleading.

"I won't. I promise."

If she picked up a field guide and looked for the field marks of Ana Leigh Watkins, she would be described as frightened. And bold. Healing, but not whole. She was full of faith. But she doubted sometimes too. She had a listening ear yet often spoke too quickly.

Before Bitter End, those conflicting descriptions had overwhelmed her heart with shame. But now the spaces between who she was and who she'd like to be looked like opportunities for growth and grace instead of evidence of failure.

She sent a text to Lexi.

> Heading to Ridgeford tomorrow. Still up for adding a housemate this year? A housemate with a dog?

> Definitely. Have you heard back from the school?

> Not yet. I'm hoping they don't make me wait much longer. How's Beautiful Brian?

Lexi sent her an eyeroll emoji.

> Bodacious Brian? Beguiling Brian? Breezy Brian?

Ana . . .

She snickered and fired off another try.

> Brilliant Brian?

You are too much. This one is just Brian. And I
think he might even be a keeper. Now I've gotta
run. He's cooking for me tonight.

Piper pawed at Ana's arm, nearly knocking the phone out of her
hand. "Okay, okay," she said. "I get it. It's time for belly scritches."
Piper rolled to her back as if she understood.

A few minutes later, her phone dinged again.

A banner on the screen notified her of a new email.

She picked it up and scanned the contents.

Dear Ana,

*I have received your request to move up to the first grade
with your students from the previous year. I also looked
over your proposed education plan and evidence-based research materials regarding nature-based education. While
your proposed plan is unorthodox, we also recognize that
this previous school year was far from expected. I, as well as
our school's board, acknowledge that this next year together
could be cathartic for not only your students but for yourself.*

*We have decided to grant your requests on a trial basis
that includes bimonthly reports on the progress you are seeing within your outdoor-focused classroom. If you are willing to agree to these terms, we will finalize details when you
return from your trip.*

I, along with the board of Ridgeford Christian Academy,

wish to thank you for your commitment not only to academic excellence but also to the well-being of the students in your care.

> *Regards,*
> *Miranda Smith,*
> *principal*

Ana snuggled Piper with a happy sigh. She'd actually convinced them. Though there was no way to erase that awful day, she had a second chance for a better ending.

She thought back to the beginning of all things.

She quite liked the idea that God's voice, when he spoke the world into existence, continued to echo in every bird's song, in every buzz of a bee, and in the trickle of water reshaping the rocks in the creek. It was a language that the human heart could comprehend, even if their ears were not yet tuned to it.

She looked to her nightstand. The Bible Marilyn had given her lay there. *Trilby Chambers* was written in worn gold foil across the front. Her grandfather. She flipped through the pages, turning to Matthew 10:29.

He *knew* every sparrow. He *saw* every heartache. In this broken, aching world, this traumatic event would likely not be the only one her students faced in their lifetimes. But perhaps this next school year would help them all remember that they did not have to be defined by their most bitter moments or their most heroic. And even the most trying of circumstances could provide a doorway to new life.

Full of hope.

Epilogue

Ten Months Later

Ana packed the last box from her classroom. What a bittersweet day, saying farewell to this school. She'd said her goodbyes to her students the week prior. There had been tears on all accounts, but they were ready to move on to second grade without her.

She picked up the binder that had been resting on her desk. The title page read, "*A Field Guide to the Birds of Ridgeford Christian Academy* by Ms. Watkins's First Grade Class."

She sat in her desk chair and flipped through the pages. Each held a sketch of a bird and angled sentences in first grade penmanship describing the bird's identifying features.

A sense of fulfillment swelled in her chest as she relived the days of this past school year. She had loved witnessing her students' wonder and delight as they sighted birds and added them to their field guides. Memories replayed of children relearning to laugh with ease. Of walking on overcast days to hear the birds sing in the rain. Of children loving to learn again. Their daily nature walks brought them beautiful reminders that though the world was sometimes ugly, it held beauty too.

Not that she took credit for it all. Ana, the school counselor,

parents, pastors, and individual therapists had all played supporting roles in each child's journey to varying degrees. But her outdoor classroom had been a sanctuary each child could depend on.
She'd never been more proud of anything she'd done in her life.

She stopped on a page depicting the killdeer they'd stumbled
upon in April. They learned how the birds would feign an injury
to lead predators away from their young. Landon had piped up
that day, saying, "Ms. Watkins, that's like you. You would do
anything to protect us. Even if it put you in danger." His words
had meant more to her than any plaque. Ana went to the media
room to make a copy of the field guide. After she bound the pages
together, she wrote a note inside the front cover.

Dear Christopher,
We are finding peace. We hope you find it too.

She thought of her great-grandfather Wayne and the stories
she'd learned about the incarcerated man. She continued writing,

Freedom can be found even when surrounded by iron
bars. Consider the birds.

Ana Watkins

She slipped the class-made booklet into the bubble mailer addressed to Ridgeford Penitentiary.

Lexi poked her head in the copy room. "I thought you left
without saying goodbye there for a second."

Ana threw her arms around her friend. "Never."

"One question before you go. Did you ever learn how Bitter
End got its name?"

Ana laughed. "I heard a different tale from every person I asked.
But I think Cora's is likely the most accurate. She said it was
kind of like a Greenland-Iceland situation. That way back before

her father's time, an old moonshiner had claimed the land and told people that the water at that end of the mountain was bitter to taste. Nobody wanted bitter water, so those who might have wanted to contest his claim stayed away. But it was actually pristine, sweet spring water. The best on Buck Mountain."

"That's hilarious. Please keep in touch and keep your Bitter End stories coming."

"Of course. You can tell 'Just Brian' I'll miss him too. And I'll be expecting a save the date in the mail before too long." Watching the relationship unfold between the two of them had been so fun. She'd never seen her friend this happy.

Lexi shrugged. "I've been dropping him a few hints about my favorite ring styles. So, we'll see." She caught sight of the package in Ana's hand and the address on the mailer. "You're really going to send him that?"

She nodded. "Yes. His copy has all names and identifiers removed, of course."

"What are you hoping it will say to him?"

"I guess I wanted to give him proof that we might have been struck down for a time, but we were not destroyed. We're still looking for beauty in a broken world. And . . . and I guess I want him to know that he can still find it too."

***

Hours later, Ana took the winding roads to a place called Bitter End, a name only those who grew up there would recognize. But it was what Ana would always call it, for this community with its unlikely name had helped her find a new beginning she never would have dreamed up for herself.

It might not be the tight-knit community it had been seventy years ago, but Ana was thankful that it now welcomed outsiders like herself who planned to make Bitter End their home. If she worked at it, maybe she could find ways to nurture that deeper sense of community young Cora and Viola once enjoyed up on that old mountain.

She'd taken the drive several times to visit her Bitter End friends over the months, and somehow this trip went by quicker than any of the previous jaunts. Perhaps because this time, she was coming home. And this time, her mother sat in the passenger seat.

For the first time since infancy, Quinn Leigh was returning to the mountains. Her mother had been concerned about Ana's decision to move, but the offer to help Ana set up her new home had pushed her to finally make the trip and meet her long-lost aunts.

In what felt like minutes instead of hours they'd parked in Cora and Marilyn's driveway next to Sam's truck and the mobile wedding chapel.

Ana still couldn't believe Cora had invited Marilyn to move in with her, but the two older ladies were excellent company. Aside from the occasional shenanigans Cora attempted to drag Marilyn into. For the time being Cora was able to supply Marilyn with the little assistance she needed, sharing rides and even willingly sharing the same hairdresser.

When Ana had gotten the news that plans for Roan Mountain Outdoor School had been finalized, she had asked if she could rent Marilyn's old house, and Marilyn happily agreed. Her aunt had even thrown in all of Obie's framed ornithology sketches to share with the new school to sweeten the deal.

The lights were off when she guided her mother through Cora and Marilyn's front door. She heard Piper's familiar whistle-whine and Inez's "Shh."

"Hello?" Ana stifled her laugh at their obvious plan.

The lights flicked on with a jumbled chorus of "Welcome to Bitter End!" Piper came bounding forward, jumping and cavorting in front of Ana and her mother.

Ana scratched the wriggling dog behind the ears when she'd finally calmed enough to sit. "I know. I missed you too." Trent and

Lottie had graciously cared for Piper over the past month while Ana prepared for her big move.

Cora threw her arms around her and hugged so tight, Ana had to fight for air. "You're *home*." Cora released her and looked shyly at Ana's mother. "Hello, Quinn. It's so nice to finally meet you in person." Cora sniffled and swiped at her teary face. "You have Viola's eyes."

Quinn smiled at Cora as Marilyn approached them.

Ana was distracted from the reunion when Sam came forward and handed her the leash. "I'm happy to officially relinquish that pestilence back to you."

She knelt to plant a kiss on top of Piper's head and cut him a playful glare. "How dare you say that about this angel? You've only had her three days. Trent had no complaints."

Sam snickered and shook his head. "Love covers a multitude of sins, I guess. Max liked her well enough."

She stood and gave him a hug. "I'm so thankful y'all could help me out with her. I've been so busy, and she would have been miserable."

"The dog was miserable without *you*." The catch in his throat made her pull back from the embrace. She studied the look in his eyes and found emotion she hadn't expected.

"I don't think he's talking about the dog anymore," Inez said as she sidled between them and wrapped her arms around Ana. Into her ear, Inez whispered, "I'll be sure to give you two lovebirds a copy of our newest brochure."

"Inez . . ." Ana hissed in warning as the woman pulled back.

As far as the Bitter End Birding Society was concerned, she and Sam were friends. Ana and Sam may have also gone to dinner a few times when he'd come to Ridgeford for visits. But that was something they'd chosen to keep to themselves. For now.

Inez winked and patted her shoulder. "Just joshing you, honey. But you know if anything changes, Jake and I will give you the family discount."

Sam's eyebrows shot up in question when he overheard Inez. Ana rolled her eyes and shrugged.

Jake blocked him from view with his huge frame and nearly squished the air out of her. As he released her, he said, "Trent and Lottie said to send their love."

"I hate that I couldn't make his graduation. They got off on their cruise okay, though?"

"Sure did. Promised to be on the lookout for some Caribbean birds. Did Lottie tell you Trent is thinking of majoring in biology with a focus in ornithology?"

"Really? I bet Marilyn's tickled pink," she said. "And things with your daughter? How's that going?"

He shrugged. "Okay. Always two steps forward and one step back, it seems. But we had a nice conversation last Sunday. Made it all the way through without anybody hanging up on anybody."

Inez harrumphed. "That's only 'cause this big lug kept his mouth shut."

Ana laughed and stole a peek of the three women gathered in a huddle, smiles on their faces as they mopped their eyes. "When Trent and Lottie get back, let's pack out the birding-mobile and go on an adventure. I'll see if I can convince my mom to join in."

"Ha." Jake chortled. "You think she's ready for the likes of us?"

"Attention, everyone," Marilyn said to quiet the chaos. "First, let's eat cake. Then we'll plot this summer's birding escapades."

They had to select the trails more carefully with Marilyn's declining vision, but they'd managed to convince her that there was no need to give up the helm of the Bitter End Birding Society.

Her entire mission had been to show them that you didn't need fancy credentials, equipment, or a life list that was a mile long to be a birder. You just needed to be willing to slow down and consider the birds—whether it be a little brown sparrow at your feeder or an exotic bird on a remote island. If Marilyn could count a bird dog as a viable member of a birding society, she'd be foolish to count herself out.

Ana was convinced that the restored friendship with Cora more than anything had helped Marilyn remember that her diagnosis was simply the beginning of a new chapter. A challenging chapter. But a beautiful one, all the same.

Gathered around the kitchen table eating cake that was so sweet it almost made her teeth hurt, she thought back to the day she told her students the name of the place she was moving to. Of course, they asked why it was called Bitter End.

Working up into full storyteller mode, she'd said, "Once a long, long, long time ago there was a group of people who found themselves on top of a lonely mountain, a little lost and turned around. All of them were convinced that this was just an awful place to end up, so they called it Bitter End. But as they got to know each other and shared their stories and walked through nature like we have all year, they discovered that what had seemed a bleak and lonely place was actually beautiful once you got past first impressions. And even though they no longer found it a bitter place to be, they kept the name to remember that whenever they felt despair and fear, they just had to look for the beauty and the hope. Because hope and beauty were there somewhere, someway. But only if they slowed down and had the patience to watch for it."

Read on for an excerpt from Amanda Cox's next novel.

Available August 2026 wherever books are sold.

1

People always used the phrase "can't see the forest for the trees" like it was a bad thing, but Tess Holcomb had learned to survive by letting the big picture fade into a meaningless blur. Solace was found in the intricate.

After a last look over the antique stopwatch's now gleaming gears and springs, Tess removed the watchmaker's loupe from her eye. She carefully placed the mechanism back into its casing and turned it over, testing the start button. The second hand swept along, smooth and unhindered, history resurrected. Tess sat back in her chair, a satisfied smile stretching across her face. This same stopwatch had once timed the famous Triple Crown–winning horse Citation back in the 1940s.

At least that was how the story went.

A teenage boy, obsessed with stories of the horse's speed, had snuck to the track with his grandfather's stopwatch early one morning to watch the training exercise before the Kentucky Derby. He'd left his job as a grocery clerk that very day to become a lowly groom at a nearby farm, determined to work his way up the ranks and someday train a Derby contender of his own.

Tess placed the stopwatch in a velvet-cushioned box and set it on her outgoing shelf for tomorrow's pickup. The cleaned and restored instrument was to be the man's ninety-fifth birthday present. She'd give anything to be a fly on the wall during the celebration of his life, surrounded by the children, grandchildren, great-grandchildren, and generations of champion horses he'd raised on his prominent Kentucky farm.

A knock sounded on the frame of her open doorway. "Hey."

Tess turned at the sound of Diane's voice.

"Sorry to interrupt, boss, but a new client is in for consultation. Your favorite part."

"You know it." Tess hopped up from her chair. "Is this the lady all the way from Delaware?"

Diane nodded. "It's wild how far people are starting to travel to get to us. That's gotta be at least a twenty-hour drive."

She and Diane made their way through the old barn they'd converted into a workshop where the Timeless Restoration team restored priceless heirlooms in their given fields of expertise.

"You think this one's genuine?" Tess asked. She had no patience for the fame seekers. Thankfully she'd only had to chase off a few.

Diane shrugged. "Only one way to find out."

A few months ago, while restoring an antique jewelry box, the team had discovered contact information that had ended a birthmother's two-decade search for her daughter. Their office manager, Becky, had seized the opportunity to garner free publicity by spilling the info to her friend at *The Fairhope Courier*. To Tess's horror, the article in the Alabama newspaper had snowballed until it was covered on all the major networks.

Great for business.

Not so great for a person living in hiding.

Diane chatted amiably beside her, updating her on the progress she and her daughter Adreonna had made cleaning an oil portrait that had been passed through a family since the beginning of the Civil War.

As they entered the consultation salon, a woman stood from one of the wingback chairs and walked to the polished farmhouse table where something bigger than a bread box was shrouded beneath a sheet.

Tess's upholstery expert, Joanna, had designed the shabby chic receiving area. Though it was a little refined for an old barn, she had to admit the furnishings and decor lent the space a cozy yet professional vibe.

"Hello, I'm Tess," she addressed the woman, "and this is my associate Diane. She tells me you've got a project you'd like us to take a look at."

The woman reached across the table and shook each of their hands. "I'm Karen." She fidgeted with the hem of her shirtsleeve and nodded at the shrouded object. "I hope you can help."

"May I?" Tess grasped the edge of the worn sheet covering the proposed project.

"Please."

Together, Tess and Diane lifted the sheet away, revealing a Victorian dollhouse that had certainly seen better days. Though old toys, particularly those without mechanical components, weren't her area of expertise, Tess recognized quality when she saw it. She glanced at Diane.

"Lovely," Diane said as she studied the structure, taking it in from all angles.

This house had chipped paint, missing shingles, and broken railings. The interior was yellowed with age, and the wallpaper peeled in several places. But Diane, like every expert who worked at Timeless, had the ability to see beyond all the spots and wrinkles that came with life-worn heirlooms.

Tess braced her hands on the table. "Karen, what can you tell us about this piece?"

As she began to speak, a fine sheen glossed the woman's eyes. "My grandpa was a young father during the Great Depression. He was doing everything he could to find work, even traveling to neighboring cities. Though life was doing its best to beat the joy and wonder out of him, he didn't want his child to face disappointment come Christmas morning." Karen swiped her cheeks.

"He barely had enough money for his train ticket home, much less a present. On his walk to the train station, he passed this grand mansion bedecked in holly and evergreen, with a candle glowing in every window. While he stopped and stared, he caught sight of someone tossing a dollhouse onto a rubbish heap. After they'd gone back inside, my grandfather picked it up. It was a replica of that same beautiful home, but with a broken porch railing, a few scuffs, and no furniture. He traveled with that discarded house on his lap the whole trip." Karen's soft smile stretched into a full grin. "It became a centerpiece in my grandparents' home, and every time I visited, he and I would play with this old house, inventing all sorts of stories about the tiny people who lived there."

Tess studied a broken shingle, and when she looked up, Karen suddenly seemed a decade younger. It took little effort to imagine the little girl Karen had been.

Tess stepped closer. "What has this dollhouse come to mean to you?"

Karen wrapped her arms around her middle as if giving herself a hug. "It reminds me of the simple joy and hopefulness my grandfather brought to every room he walked into, no matter how bad the day was. Not many people can make a child feel as important as he made me feel." Her smile faltered. "He passed away shortly after my own daughter was born, and this dollhouse became a conversation piece that helped my mother and I share the story of the man he was." She shrugged and looked at her hands. "Seeing this restored will let me remember what it feels like to be a granddaughter again."

Tess allowed herself to be swept up in the affection in Karen's voice, and the story settled over her like a weighted blanket.

As the woman continued with the history of the dollhouse, Tess peered inside and traced a fingertip over a red crayon mark and a purple stain. In her mind's eye, she could see a set of weathered hands and a child's pudgy fingers posing dolls and rearranging furniture. Tess's insides bubbled with imagined laughter in a beautiful, light-filled room. For just a moment she pretended the deeper accompanying laugh was someone taking delight in *her*.

Then Tess set the borrowed memory aside, once again giving her full attention to her client. "And what made you decide to bring your dollhouse to us?"

Karen peered through one of the windows. "As you can see, it's had a long and well-loved life. It's the victim of generations of clumsy childhood play. After my daughter left childhood behind, I put it in the attic for safekeeping. But some sort of vermin chewed one of the balcony railings. A squirrel, I suspect." She laughed lightly. "One of the rooms was stuffed with acorns." She touched the peak of the roof. "But now my daughter is pregnant with her first, and when my grandchild comes to visit, I need this old house to be sturdy enough to make memories for generations to come."

Tess gave her an encouraging smile. "And how do you envision the dollhouse after our work is complete?"

Karen studied the structure. "I imagine the old layers of paint sanded away and repainted crisp white, with black shutters. The dingy and peeling wallpaper restored or replaced however you see fit. The chewed balcony railing and wooden shingles replaced, and the overall structure fortified if there are any weak spots." She ran a fingertip along the mismatched porch railing. "But please don't replace the original repair my grandfather made. It's clumsy, I know. But to me, it's the most beautiful part."

"I agree," Tess said, and then she looked to Diane. "What do you think?"

Diane nodded. "We can definitely restore the paintwork. Adreonna and I may even be able to do some hand-stamped wallpaper that would match the design of the original."

"Bert for repairs to the woodwork?" Tess asked. Bert was amazing with carpentry, no matter how large or minute the project.

"Definitely."

Tess took Karen's hand and gave it a squeeze. "I'm honored you've entrusted your grandfather's dollhouse to us."

After they finalized the details and paperwork, Tess carried the dollhouse back to Diane and Adreonna's workstation, her heart light.

Timeless Restoration allowed Tess to borrow other people's sweet memories and hold them close. And when it was time, she gently placed them back in the hands of their rightful owners.

She took a slow turn through the quietly bustling repair shop, relishing the sound of gentle work all around her. There was never a temptation to cling to things that didn't belong to her, because there were always more precious stories coming through her doors.

"Tess?" Becky said, interrupting her reverie.

Tess turned around, wondering at the tinge of confusion in the young woman's voice. "What's up?"

Becky closed the distance between them in a couple of strides, a box in her hands. "A package was shipped here by mistake, I think. And there's no return address."

"Oh?" Tess took the small package from the younger woman and then almost dropped it. Her heart thudded in her chest as she read the name on the address line again and again.

Becky frowned. "I wonder who Teresa Baker is? No one by that name has ever worked here."

"I'll get this sorted," Tess managed to choke out before she hurried to her office.

Tess set the box on her desk and stared at it while absently tracing the series of faded scars seared into the inner side of her left forearm.

Deep down she'd known the life she'd fled eighteen years ago would catch up with her one day.

She stuck the box on the highest shelf.

Just because her past found her didn't mean she had to face it. Not yet.

2

Tess waved goodbye as the school bus pulled out of the Timeless parking lot. Field trips were another one of Becky's grand ideas for increasing revenue at the shop. But Tess was actually on board with this one.

Every field trip Tess led was her own little war against society's draw to the new, shiny, and disposable. On a Timeless field trip, kids marveled as antiques were restored by true craftspeople. Her greatest hope was that one of them would even be inspired to join the next generation of restoration experts.

She waited as the bus full of energetic fourth graders disappeared from the graveled parking lot in a cloud of gray dust, and then she slipped back through the rear entrance.

She stopped by Bert's workbench where the dollhouse waited, sanded down and looking bare, yet fresh and full of promise.

"Hiya, Miss Tess."

"Hey, Bert. How's it coming along?"

The wiry older gentleman grinned. "Swimmingly. I've already replaced the chewed balcony railing, and I just finished up the wooden shingles I made to replace the broken and missing ones." He held out his hand to show her the tiny, intricately carved pieces. "After that's done, I'll be passing it back to Diane and Adreonna for the paintwork and wallpapering. Joanna and I are going to work together to make a few historically accurate furniture pieces as an extra surprise for the family."

Tess took a big satisfying breath, fully expanding her lungs. She could always count on her team to go the extra mile to show clients how much they cared.

Though several timepieces waited in her office to be cleaned, polished, and refitted with new parts, she sat and chatted with Bert as he fixed the new shingles into place.

In the week since the mystery package arrived, she found herself avoiding her office and lingering on the workshop floor. But if she didn't get back to her normal routine, she'd never be able to catch up.

She stood from the stool, again thanking Bert for his attention to detail, and headed back to her office to see to a wristwatch that, though it had little monetary value, had been passed through the family to the firstborn boy on their eighteenth birthday for six generations.

Eighteen. That had certainly been a landmark year in her own life.

Inside her office, her gaze found the Gulf Shores, Alabama, magnet that lived on her filing cabinet. When she was eleven, she'd swiped it from the olive green fridge in Granny's kitchen the day before the dear woman's funeral and held on to it like a promise.

Tess sighed, turned on her lamp, and donned her watchmaker's loupe. But no matter how hard she tried, she couldn't get the forest of her life to blur as she attempted to focus on the work in front of her. Her grandmother's house, with its sloping floors and sagging porch that clung to the mountainside with the same grit Granny possessed, remained fixed in her mind.

Granny hadn't had much to her name, but she always had her stories. Tess's favorite had been about the trip she'd taken to Gulf Shores as a child. Granny had vowed to take her someday, and Tess had loved her for it, even knowing her grandmother had been too old, too frail, and too poor to take anyone anywhere.

When circumstances forced Tess off the mountain that raised her, she'd made a beeline for the coast depicted on that tiny, faded magnet.

But as fate, or God, or whoever deserved the credit would have it, Tess never made it to Gulf Shores.

Tess pushed back from her desk, groaning. The past was just too close to the surface today.

She exited the workshop and took the long, graveled path that wound through the woods to the cabin where her best friend and business partner lived.

She knocked on the front door, and the home health nurse let her in.

"Hello, Margery. Is Amos up for visitors?"

The woman smiled. "I'd say so. He just finished up lunch, and you'd think the food was full of vinegar for as snarky as he's feeling."

Tess laughed as she walked down the hallway. She was more than a little proud that the business venture she and Amos had started fifteen years ago not only paid the bills but also made sure the man who'd given her a purpose for her life had the care he needed in the home he loved.

"Amos?" she called out right before she stepped into the living room, knowing the exact scene she'd witness—Amos in his favorite recliner, hooked up to oxygen while he watched television.

He clicked it off, banishing the melodramatic image from the screen as she entered. She bit the corners of her cheeks to keep from letting him know she'd caught him watching his soaps.

"What did ya bring for me?" he rasped.

"Nothing today."

The man's face fell a fraction, and she wished she'd thought to grab one of the watches on the shelf and come up with a question or two to ask him. His health had forced him to become homebound for the past few years. And as hard as she'd tried to tempt him back to the workshop now that he was out of the woods, he insisted it was for the best if he stayed put.

One of the few points in life they didn't agree on.

"I just needed to clear my head and thought I'd come aggravate you a minute or two."

"Happy birthday." He wriggled his silver caterpillar eyebrows.

She sputtered. "It's not my birthday." That had been last week. Not that anyone knew that.

"Maybe not. But seeing as you won't tell me your birthday, I always count the day we met. Eighteen years now, isn't it?"

"I guess," she said as if his assertion was of no consequence. But it was disconcerting, realizing she'd lived half her life in Fairhope. It was almost enough time to make the first part of her life seem like a story she'd been told by someone else.

"Why'd you do it?" She picked up the folded newspaper occupying the neighboring recliner and sat.

"Why'd I pick up a ragamuffin girl wandering down the road who refused to tell me a thing about who she was or where she came from?" He scoffed. "I've given you the same exact answer every single time you've asked."

She grinned at the elderly man. "I've got a rotten memory. Tell me again."

He shook his head and pursed his lips in mock annoyance. "Cause God told me to. No other reason than that. Plain and simple, Tess Holcomb."

She wasn't sure what she thought about the idea of a God up in heaven caring about the likes of her. But believing in Amos? That was second nature.

That day, when she confessed she'd run out of money and had nowhere to go, he took her to his sister Candy's souvenir shop with the vacant apartment over top. In the span of a few hours she gained a roof over her head and a job. It'd been so simple to sidle into a new identity.

"How's that great-niece of mine working out?" Amos's question jolted her back to the present.

"Becky always has fresh ideas." Tess inwardly cringed and then spat out a question that had been simmering under the surface since he recommended hiring the girl. "You think we should take her on as a partner?" It was well within his rights to make the decision. He was the majority holder in Timeless Restoration and the sole owner on all official documentation. And though Becky was impulsive, she knew marketing.

He let out a bark of a laugh. "Have you lost your senses? The girl is smart as a whip, but she's young yet. Who knows if she'll stick around after she's earned that MBA she's chasing." He gave her a sly grin. "She still launching half-cooked ideas without asking?"

Tess nodded. "Yep. But it's hard to be mad. Every single one of them has brought in more revenue, but I'm pretty sure she's the cause of the gray hair I found on my head last week."

Amos crossed his arms over his chest. "I know you prefer people to feel like they work with you instead of for you, but it's okay to stand your ground when it counts. Timeless is your baby. Your dream. Say no to her every now and then. They'll all respect you more for it."

She nodded. "I hear you."

They spent another half hour talking shop. When she headed back to work, she wasn't certain she'd be able to concentrate any better than she had earlier. But at least she felt a little more like the person she'd become since landing in Fairhope.

She reentered Timeless through the barn's back door and headed for her office. Before she reached it, an unfamiliar masculine laugh echoed through the space, pulling her up short.

The workshop floor was usually a place of quiet camaraderie that flowed with a gentle rhythm—quiet conversations and the sound of tools. Each artist's project required the utmost concentration. Field trips and apprentice visits were meticulously scheduled to avoid unplanned disruptions. This noise did not belong.

She passed her office in the back, walking quiet as a cat and headed for the open area partitioned with toolboxes and tables where the other craftspeople worked. Mingling with the unfamiliar male voice was Adreonna's and Becky's laughter and gleeful responses. Tess paused when she turned the corner.

A man with an athletic build stood with his back to her, hands shoved in his jean pockets, hip casually leaned against a workbench. Whoever it was behaved far too at ease for an uninvited guest.

Amos said she needed to be firm with her boundaries. She stood tall and stepped forward, clearing her throat.

"Can I help y—" The question died on her lips as the man turned his mega-watt smile on her. It felt as if her heart flopped straight out of her chest and withered on the concrete floor.

His smile morphed into something wistful and apologetic. "Hey, Tink."

She tried to catch her breath, but all the oxygen had fled the room. Unlike the mystery box, she could not pretend away this specter from her past.

He took a step forward, and she took one back.

A dance she'd perfected eighteen years ago when Elliot Sullivan ruined her life.

Or saved it.

She'd never been quite sure.

Acknowledgments

Huge thanks to the entire Revell team. It has been such a joy partnering with you all to bring my stories to readers. Kelsey and Robin, can you believe this is our fifth book together? Your editorial voices will forever live in my mind as I write. I have learned so much from each of you!

To my agent, Tamela Hancock Murray, I am so thankful for your guidance and encouragement.

To the birding group that collided with my young family in the woods many years ago, I might not know a single one of your names, but you inspired this book. You drew us in with your excitement and wonder about birds as you took the time to point out rare species to my then bouncing and wildly energetic toddlers.

River, my German shorthaired pointer, you were the sole inspiration for Piper. Now the world knows the sweet and dramatic handful you are. Our family can always count on you for a daily dose of laughter. Maybe one day you'll come back when we call. I've never seen any creature that loves running as much as you do.

To my parents, Jeff and Paula, and my second parents, Kenny and Lisa, thank you for your enthusiasm for my books. I'm pretty sure that at least half the copies I've sold are because you've told people about them. The other half are likely because of Caleb's efforts!

Caleb, Ellie, Levi, you all are my daily encouragement team and enthusiastic fan club. You're also the people I count on to remind me that it's time to step out of the fictional world and live in the real one. I couldn't be prouder of the people you are growing to be.

To my husband, Justin, thank you for always cheering me on. You've supported this dream of mine from day one. Thanks for giving me the space to discover who God created me to be.

Jesus, my Savior and faithful friend, thank You for the birds. An exhausted new mother with a baby who almost never slept spent hours staring out the window into the backyard, watching the birds as she held a little boy who only found comfort when she was standing and swaying. You gave her arms to comfort the boy, and You brought cardinals, sparrows, goldfinches, buntings, chickadees, nuthatches, swallows, and hawks to her backyard to comfort her as she learned to navigate this strange new season of life.

Amanda Cox is the two-time Christy Book of the Year award–winning author of *The Edge of Belonging*, *The Secret Keepers of Old Depot Grocery*, *He Should Have Told the Bees*, and *Between the Sound and Sea*. She holds a bachelor's degree in Bible and theology and a master's degree in professional counseling, but her first love is communicating through story. Her studies and her interactions with hurting families over a decade have allowed her to create multidimensional characters that connect emotionally with readers. She lives in Chattanooga, Tennessee, with her husband and their three children. Learn more at AmandaCoxWrites.com.

MEET AMANDA

FOLLOW ALONG AT
AmandaCoxWrites.com
and sign up for Amanda's newsletter to stay
up to date on exclusive news, upcoming
releases, and more!

Be the first to hear about new books from Revell!

Stay up to date with our authors and books by signing up for our newsletters at

RevellBooks.com/SignUp

FOLLOW US ON SOCIAL MEDIA

   @RevellFiction

Dear Reader,

Thank you for selecting a Revell novel! We're so happy to be part of your reading life through this work. Our mission here at Revell is to publish stories that reach the heart. Through friendship, romance, suspense, or a travel back in time, we bring stories that will entertain, inspire, and encourage you. We believe in the power of stories to change our lives and are grateful for the privilege of sharing these stories with you.

We believe in building lasting relationships with readers, and we'd love to get to know you better. If you have any feedback, questions, or just want to chat about your experience reading this book, please email us directly at publisher@revellbooks.com. Your insights are incredibly important to us, and it would be our pleasure to hear how we can better serve you.

We look forward to hearing from you and having the chance to enhance your experience with Revell Books.

The Publishing Team at Revell Books
A Division of Baker Publishing Group
publisher@revellbooks.com

Revell